Songs of Spring

A Novel

Naomi Wark

ISBN -13:978-1734432923
Library of Congress Control Number: 2022904970
Dragonfly Press
Camano Island WA
naomiwarkauthor.com

Songs of Spring is a work of fiction. Major historical events are portrayed to best of the author's ability. The characters are fictitious and are not intended to represent actual living persons.

The spring came suddenly, bursting

upon the world as a child bursts into

a room, with a laugh and a shout and

hands full of flowers.

Henry Wadsworth Longfellow

Acknowledgments

Poet John Donne said, "No man is an island." Though I write in solitude, I have not written this book alone. I was first inspired to write this story after discovering old diaries, and hand-scrawled notes left behind by a family member. Numerous scenes for *Songs of Spring* were based upon entries made in these early diaries, including the Alaska Yukon Exposition in 1909, the 1918 pandemic, and college life at the State Normal School in Ellensburg, Washington. Thank you to the late author of these diaries.

An old African proverbs states, "Oran a azu nwa" which means, "it takes a village to raise a child." My village consists of numerous individuals to whom I owe a debt of gratitude. After a book club discussion of my debut novel, *Wildflowers in Winter*, members sparked the idea of writing another book using the same main character. Thank you to these readers for encouraging me to write this prequel novel. Thank you to my fellow authors in the Sno-Isle Writer's Group for their critiquing skills that helped me improve my craft. Thank you to every person I turned to for specific input on medical scenes, birthing scenes, historical events, and general impressions. My most sincere appreciation goes to my husband. Throughout the countless hours of writing, he always believed in me, read my work, and offered invaluable input.

Contents

Prologue

Named after the Duwamish and Suquamish Indian chief, Seattle lies on a strip of land between Puget Sound and Lake Washington. Two mountain ranges lie beyond. The Olympics dominate the western part of the state, and in the east, the Cascade Mountain Range stretches to California. The unparalleled beauty of the water and the mountains, along with the mild climate, the forests of one-to-two-thousand-year-old trees nearly four hundred feet tall, made an attractive settlement for the Coast Salish peoples. The Suquamish and Duwamish tribes lived in the region for thousands of years before Europeans or white settlers arrived. They continue to live here today. By the time white settlers reached Puget Sound, there were as many as seventeen villages settled by the Duwamish tribe.

In 1851, the families of Arthur and David Denny, Carson Boren, William Bell, and Henry Yesler settled at Elliott Bay among stands of old-growth forest. Yesler's sawmill soon became the largest industry in the fast-growing town. The names of these families and others who followed still live on in the streets of downtown Seattle named in their honor. From this handful of families, the population of Seattle swelled to nearly 81,000 by 1900, and by the mid-1920s, the population of Seattle approached 320,000. It is during this period of extreme growth that *Songs of Spring* transpired. Though inspired by diaries left by a beloved family member, *Songs of Spring* is an imagining of the lives of Edna and her older sister, Pearl, and how society and the events of the first few decades of the twentieth century shaped their lives.

Chapter One

1902 – First Day of Spring

Anguished cries carried into Pearl's bedroom. Alarmed, she sat up from the small flour-sack mattress stuffed with batting. She looked around, confused because her bed lay empty with its covers tossed in a heap at the foot of the bed. Adrenaline pulsed through her body. She tensed as she recalled her mother's condition and her aunt's arrival the previous afternoon. Another cry from her mother, and Pearl flung the quilt off. Her pulse quickened as she snatched her robe and slippers and hurried to the kitchen where the usual aroma of bread fresh from the oven, was absent. Aunt Marie stood hunched over a cast iron pot of water on the wood stove that sent up a veil of steam fogging the nearby window. The warm humid air, filled Pearl's lungs and beads of sweat formed on her forehead. She wiped them away with her sleeve.

"Where's Mama?"

Without turning, Aunt Marie jerked her head in the direction of the bedroom. "Your mother is in labor. Her cramps are severe, more than is typical with a second birth." Aunt Marie went to the sink and pumped water into a glass. "I'm preparing for the delivery."

"The baby's coming? Now?"

Aunt Marie turned. Dark circles under her eyes revealed her lack of sleep. "It won't be long."

"Where's Papa? Why isn't he here?"

"He left for the logging camp. Childbirth is no place for menfolk." Her aunt handed Pearl the water glass. "Go on—take this to your mother."

1

Pearl hurried to her mother's room as water sloshed over the top of the glass. She knocked on the heavy wood door before she pushed it open. "Mama." Pearl edged inside. Stagnant air, heavy with sweat, assaulted her. "Auntie says the baby's coming."

Her mother's face strained in agony. She extended her hand and forced a smile. "That's right. The baby is letting me know in no uncertain terms. Today is the day."

Pearl shuddered at the sight of her mother's distress. She crept to her mother's side and held the cool water with a shaking hand. "Are you okay?"

Lifting her head and shoulders off the stack of down-filled pillows, her mother grimaced. She took the glass and emptied it in long deep gulps while Pearl supported her head. Handing the glass back to Pearl, her mother sank back onto her bed with a thin smile. "I know after ten years as an only child you haven't been looking forward to being a big sister, but you don't have to worry. Having another baby won't prevent us from loving you as much."

Pearl had thought often during the past seven months about the impending birth and how the baby would disrupt her happy life. She would no longer be the center of her mother and father's attention. Their "little gem," as Papa often called her. It was only a matter of time before she would be helping care for her new brother or sister. "Why do you want another baby after losing so many?"

Even with her face lined with worry, Mother's eyes twinkled. "Someday, you'll understand."

Pearl didn't understand. How could she? She only understood when the baby outgrew the bassinet, she'd find a crib in her room next to her bed. Another concession with which she'd have to live. "What about high school? You and Papa promised I could move away after eighth grade. Now you won't be able to afford it and I'll have to stay here and help take care of the baby so you can keep up with your sewing."

Her mother stroked Pearl's uncombed brown locks. "Is that what you're worried about?" Wincing she bit her lower lip and smiled weakly. "You don't need to worry. We will make sure you get to go to high school. I promise."

Aunt Marie dashed in holding the pot of water, steam floating around her, with clean towels and bedding draped over her arms.

At the sight of her aunt's intense gaze, Pearl stepped aside. "Is Mama going to be all right?"

With a damp cloth, her aunt dabbed at her younger sister's face. "Your mother will be fine. I've birthed six babies this year, and it's only March. Since becoming a midwife ten years ago when Eugene started school, I've ushered over two hundred babies into this world."

Pearl's breathing slowed. Although her face was white as the bed linens, her mother tried to reassure her with quivering words. "I'll be fine, honey. I'm in good hands. Your aunt's a fine midwife. She'll take care of the baby and me. Today is the beginning of spring. It's a lovely day to welcome the miracle of new life into the world. Our new little gem."

There it was. The baby wasn't even born, and he or she already had stolen the nickname Pearl thought was reserved for her alone. Pearl watched her mother wiggle and writhe, moaning from the pain. How could something that caused her mother so much agony be a miracle? "May I stay home from school? I want to be here when the baby comes." With the birth so near, and her mother suffering, Pearl knew it would be impossible to focus on her studies.

Without looking at Pearl, Aunt Marie barked, "A birthing room is no place for a girl of ten."

"Please, Mama, I can fetch things for Auntie."

Her mother held a hand up to silence any further protests from her sister. She nodded. "It's okay, but do as your aunt instructs."

Without warning, her mother flinched and cried out. Marie blew out her breath. "I suppose you could be useful."

Pearl clenched her fist. Pushed aside, even before the baby arrived. Why couldn't her parents be happy with one child? With her? She skulked from the room. Behind the closed door, the commotion came louder and more frightening with each cry. Time seemed to drag while her mother's yelps of pain quickened and grew in intensity. With each outburst, Pearl winced and covered her ears, paralyzed with fear. Her mother's pain was beyond normal birthing pain. Her aunt had said as much. Pearl's brain buzzed with memories of promised babies that never came. Grown-up words not intended for her ears. Words like *miscarriage*. A minute later, her mother's moan, like the bleat of a calf, sent a shudder down Pearl's spine. She ran back and saw her mother grasping her knees, her face contorted in pain. The expression on her aunt's face made Pearl's blood run cold.

"What's wrong?"

Her aunt remained focused on the delivery but couldn't disguise the fear in her voice. "The baby's coming. It's breech. The bottom is coming first instead of the baby's head. I'm afraid the umbilical cord might be wrapped around the baby's neck."

Pearl saw panic in her aunt's eyes. Pearl's breath became labored, and a bitter taste rose in her throat. Her heart pounded. "Is this baby going to die like the others?"

Her aunt glared at Pearl. Pearl instantly regretted her question as her aunt's fear reflected in her mother's eyes. Guilt stabbed her along with the realization the baby her mother had longed for, for so long, the baby whom Pearl hadn't yet met and even resented, might die even before taking its first breath. A knot tugged at her heart, the ache overwhelming. Pearl straightened. "What do you need me to do?"

"Grab the forceps from my birthing satchel on the chair. It looks like large tongs. Then encourage your mother to keep pushing."

Pearl's legs buckled under her like a rag doll. Her stomach turned upside down, the feeling her mother called green about the gills. She craved a glass of sweet, creamy milk to coat the sourness in her throat. The sight of her mother's face dripping with sweat forced her to push her worry aside. Pearl grabbed the instrument and gave it to her aunt, then took a washcloth and wiped her mother's forehead.

"Abbey, I need you to push." Aunt Marie's hands moved to her sister's abdomen. "I'm going to feel for the position of the baby.

Her mother's words came faint, almost inaudible. "I don't know if I can."

Pearl gripped her mother's hand and pleaded, "Please, Mama, you have to do what Auntie says." When her mother leaned in, Pearl supported her shoulders and lower back and urged her on.

Aunt Marie bent over her sister.

Pearl watched her aunt's hand disappear inside her mother; the unsettling image forced her to shut her eyes.

"The baby's not getting any oxygen. I can't seem to reach the umbilical cord." Marie's voice rose. "We're losing her."

Pearl's eyes shot open and fixed on the blood seeping onto the sheets underneath her mother. Who? she wondered. Who were they losing? Did it matter? Losing either her mother or the baby would destroy her. Too frightened to move or look away, Pearl watched her aunt's quick movements. With a final kneading of the taut belly, her aunt reinserted her hand into the birth canal. "I'm going to try to maneuver the baby into position."

Afraid to move, Pearl didn't take her eyes off her aunt.

"One more time, Abbey. One more time. You can do it."

Pearl's mother leaned into her bent knees and with a sudden burst of energy emitted a long wail. Marie's hands moved with care and skill from years of practice. She sighed and eased the baby out. Her face tight. Her eyes narrow and focused. She held her breath as the baby's buttocks and folded legs emerged. Then the upper torso slid into her arms. She cradled the small milky-coated body, keeping its tiny arms close to its sides. Tense, she extended her arms and palms as the baby's head appeared, blue, silent, and unmoving, with the umbilical cord wrapped around the infant's neck. For a moment, all sound, even breathing, ceased. Then in a swift movement, Aunt Marie slipped the cord off the baby's neck and straightened it to allow the lifesaving oxygen to reach the infant.

Pearl glanced at her aunt. She prayed for her mother to live. She prayed for God to give her aunt the wisdom to save the baby. And she prayed for forgiveness for her selfishness. *Please, God, don't let the baby die.*

Turning the blue-faced infant over, Marie placed a short sharp pat across its bottom. Pearl held her breath. The baby coughed, sputtered, and finally began to wail. The cry grew louder with each breath, and each breath brought more color to the baby's face. Pearl felt her muscles relax as the veil of fear lifted and a surge of relief brightened the room.

After she clamped off, cut, and tied the umbilical cord, Aunt Marie's face relaxed. "It's a girl." Aunt Marie placed the newborn onto a clean sheet, wiped her with a damp cloth, swaddled her in a blanket, and laid her on her mother's chest. Her forehead wet, her hair a matted mess, Pearl's mother wore a weary but satisfied smile as she cradled the babe against her bare breast. Pearl felt her cheeks redden, but she didn't turn away.

Marie wiped her forehead with her sleeve, brought her hand to her chest, and relaxed. Pearl stared at her aunt, awed by her knowledge and ability to handle such a stressful situation. She wondered if she would ever have the strength to cope under such pressure.

Her mother took Pearl's hand and drew her close. "Say hello to your baby sister, Edna Marie."

As Pearl bent in to kiss her sister on the forehead, Marie's frightened whisper, pulled her back.

"Dear, God." Marie's hands flew to her gaping mouth.

Pearl's eyes followed her aunt's gaze. Blood gushed from between her mother's legs.

"Your mother is hemorrhaging."

Pearl didn't know the word but recognized the grave situation.

"Take the baby." She threw back the rank-smelling sheet and kneaded Abbey's still swollen belly like she was kneading bread. Marie turned to Pearl. "Does your mother's hand feel cold? That's a warning her blood pressure is dropping from loss of blood."

Pearl lifted the baby to her shoulder and reached for her mother's hand. "She's shaking, but it's still warm." Pearl shuddered as her aunt continued to knead Mama's belly. Pearl noticed her breathing mimicked her mother's uneven short puffs.

After several long minutes, Marie blew out a long shallow breath. "She's going to be okay. The placenta is out."

Pearl let go of her mother's hand and rocked Edna. She pondered the anguish and pain her mother had suffered to give birth to Edna. She wondered why any woman would want to have children.

Aunt Marie took Edna from Pearl's arms and cooed to the wrinkled infant.

The sound reminded Pearl of the mourning doves that nested in the cedar trees along the edge of the field.

"I'll stay until your mother has regained her strength. She needs her rest, and Edna will sleep a lot too. The birth has taken a lot of energy from both of them."

Drained, Pearl darted outside to the back porch. She gulped in crisp air filled with the lingering scent of wildflowers in sharp contrast to the stale rank air of the bedroom. A familiar fluty song drew Pearl's attention. She searched the branches of the apple tree for the songster. Overhead, a speckled brown bird, its eyes ringed in white, sat atop a bulky nest of twigs, moss, and grass, likely protecting several eggs. The thrush continued its spring song. Outside, everything was alive. Like the flowers, her sister began as a tiny seed planted nine months earlier in her mother's womb. Today, after so much expectation, a new life entered the world like the blossoms of spring. Pearl raced to the meadow as fast as her slippers and bathrobe allowed. She knew the perfect birthday gift for her new sister. Sunlight warmed her face as she plucked spindly stalks of purple loosestrife and pink fireweed dancing amid the wild daisies in the tall grasses. She waved away the bees as she gathered daisies before adding orange poppies that shown brightly next to the pastel palette of the other wildflowers.

She raced back to the house, took a Mason jar from the oak Hoosier cabinet next to the stove, and filled it with water. She hadn't asked for a baby sister, but the events of the previous hours had changed her. She pledged she would always be there for Edna, no matter what.

Chapter Two

1906 – Farewell

Edna stood on her tiptoes and gazed over the railing of the pier at the sleek white boat taking her big sister away. Pearl had said she'd never leave her, but as she pointed to the boat, her eyes watered as she studied the large block letters painted in black on the hull near the front. Though she knew most of her ABCs, she didn't know the word the letters spelled. She named the familiar letters. "*A, L,O,N*. I don't know the rest. What does it say Mama?"

"It spells, *Athlon*. That's the name of the steamship." Her mother squatted next to Edna. "Gracious, not even five years old yet, and you know so many letters."

Edna raised her chin to the salt-laced air. "Pearl schooled me."

The engines of the steamship roared to life. A spray of water spewed behind the boat in spits and splatters. Seagulls fought over scraps on the dock, then startled by the roar of the ship's engine, they lifted into the air and circled the boat. White steam billowed from the large black stack, sending a cloud into the otherwise clear-blue, late-summer sky. The rolling waves reflected the afternoon sunlight. Edna pointed to the water. "Look, Mama. There are stars on the water."

Men in overalls moved in a quick, practiced ritual along the dock from pillar to pillar, freeing big heavy ropes from the metal cleats and tossing them to the workers onboard. No longer tied to the pier, the boat slid smoothly away as if on a sheet of ice. The horn blared. Edna jumped at the loud shrill blast. She put her hands over her ears. Though she couldn't see Pearl, Edna waved in the direction of the departing vessel. She knew somewhere in the crowd gathered on the upper deck of the steamboat her big sister stood, waving back.

Edna continued to watch the departing ship sail away, at first slowly, then as it pulled from its moorage, the boat gathered speed. She fought back her tears and sniffled. "When is Pearl coming back?"

Mother smiled, though her lips quivered too. "She'll be home before Christmas."

"That's too long." Sadness swept over Edna like the waves of the giant ocean that took her sister from her. She still had Mama and Papa, but it wasn't the same. Pearl always read her stories, taught her songs, and colored with her, and each night when Pearl turned out the kerosene light, she'd whisper, "Don't worry, I'll always be here for you." Pearl had lied. She had left her.

Clearing his throat, Papa grumbled through his whiskers. "No point in standing around any longer. Might as well get home and get about our chores before the entire day is wasted." Without any sign of emotion or waiting for a response, he spun around and marched away from the dock.

Mama reached for Edna's hand. "Come along. We don't want to keep your father waiting."

Not wanting to leave, Edna planted her feet and clung to the railing. Leaving meant accepting her sister was gone. Mama stiffened and reached for Edna's hand.

"No. I don't want to. I want to watch the boat."

Mother put her hands on her hips and narrowed her eyes. "That's quite enough, young lady. It's time to go."

Edna wrinkled her brow but released her grip on the cold railing. Mama's long brown skirt brushed along the wooden planks as she stepped with long strides following her father. Edna scurried along beside her mother toward the livery stable. Her eyes downcast and burning, Edna chewed her lip to keep from crying. Papa hated it when she cried. Most of the time, Mama tolerated it. Sometimes she even understood and comforted Edna. Only Pearl never scolded her. Pearl hugged her and soothed her whenever she felt mad or frustrated. How could she live without Pearl?

As they neared the stable, Edna hurried to catch up before Papa or Mama could scold her. She sniffled and swiped her eyes with her sleeve, then climbed into the back of the buggy beside her mother. Edna gathered her wool coat tighter around her. "Why did Pearl leave, Mama?"

Her mother shook her head. "You know why. We've talked about this. Your sister has completed her primary years of education. Port Orchard is a small town, and there's no secondary school here. Pearl is going to Seattle to live with your Aunt Marie and Uncle Leland. She'll go to high school there. No more questions."

Edna wrapped her hands in her skirt. She wished she could hide her feelings so easily. Last night Pearl told Edna being an only child would be fun. "You'll have Mama and Papa all to yourself." Edna wasn't too sure. For her entire life, she only knew about sharing her days, her nights, and her room with her sister. Right now, the only person in the world Edna wanted and needed had gone away to a place Edna didn't even know.

At a crack of the whip, their mare, Nellie, trotted toward their home. Edna reached across the buggy's rear seat and grabbed the doll Pearl had given her the prior evening. She brought the muslin rag doll to her chest and embraced it. "You're the only friend I have now, Miss Molly."

When Nellie stopped in front of their house, Mama helped Edna down from the buggy. She shooed her up the walkway with a kind insistence. "Nap time."

Edna padded to her bedroom. It looked different, nearly bare without Pearl's belongings. Without Pearl's clothes hanging on the rod, the small single closet had room to spare. Pearl's first crochet project, a granny-square afghan knitted with pink, purple, and white yarn, still covered the spread, a hopeful sign of Pearl's eventual return. Though a pillow lay atop the bed, the pillowcase Pearl had embroidered was gone. Edna plopped onto her bed and curled up with Miss Molly, her new companion, her new best friend, but Miss Molly would never replace her sister. She looked at her thumb but resisted the comfort she'd long ago outgrown.

Mama came in. She stroked Edna's cheek, kissed her on the forehead, then smiled and reached for the flour-sack doll. "Did Pearl tell you I made Molly a long time ago when Pearl was even younger than you?"

"Uh-huh." Edna ran her fingers over Miss Molly's faded face, with blue button eyes, an embroidered nose, and red lips turned up into a permanent smile.

"I like her hair." Edna combed her fingers through the strands of brown yarn stitched atop Molly's fabric head and parted into two ponytails. Though well-loved with her worn, smudged yellow and orange dress, Molly was special and Edna hugged the doll close.

"I'm glad you like her. Pearl loved her as much as you do. Now go to sleep. You'll feel better when you wake."

No nap, no matter how long, would make her feel better. An aloneness neither her mother, nor Miss Molly, could fill overwhelmed her. Her eyes tired, Edna let her head droop to her chest. She pulled her legs in tight, hugged her doll, and dozed off.

The sweet aroma of baking bread drifted into Edna's room, and her mouth watered. Each week her mama baked two loaves of fresh bread on big bricks inside the cast-iron stove. Edna gathered Molly in her arms and trudged out to the front room. Papa sat in his green-velvet wing chair with the Port Orchard newspaper folded over and tight in his grip. His pinched lips closed around his pipe, which seemed to grow right out from his beard and mustache. He raised his eyes from the paper and smiled behind the cloud of smoke that instantly reminded Edna of the curling smoke from the departing *Athlon*. Edna frowned, but Papa had returned to reading his newspaper. She plodded into the kitchen for the glass of milk she got each day after her nap.

Mama poured a half glass. "Just a little milk today; we're almost out, and the milkman isn't coming again until Thursday."

Today a special treat of warm bread served with homemade currant jelly sat on the table. Edna remembered trudging behind Pearl across the field to the bushes bordering the property and picking the ripe tart berries with Pearl. She remembered eating so many berries that day she got a tummy ache. After finishing her bread and milk, Edna pulled her footstool over near the stove. "Can I help?"

Mama held out a wooden spoon, and Edna placed Molly on a nearby chair. Edna grabbed the long-handled spoon and stared into the pot filled with squash, potatoes, and chunks of beef. "Mmm. I like the dumplings."

"Remember, it's hot." Mama watched hawk-like, holding Edna's hand in hers to assist with the stirring.

As steam escaped the bubbly pot, the scent of her mother's garden herbs tickled Edna's nose. When she thought Mother wasn't looking, she lifted the spoon to her mouth for a taste. Mother narrowed her eyes but smiled. "How does it taste?"

"Good, but I don't like the turnips. Only Pearl likes turnips. I wish she were here."

Her mother's glance of disapproval warned Edna. She jumped off the stool and ran to her bedroom. She snatched the afghan from Pearl's bed and clawed at it. She tugged at the colored yarn, stretching it out of shape.

"What are you doing?" Mother stood in the doorway, with her hands folded across her chest.

Edna dropped the blanket and began to sob.

Her mother shook her head, but instead of hollering, she squatted down and held Edna tighter. "I'm sorry, but you had better get used to being alone."

Edna bit her lip. She may have to get used to being alone, but she didn't have to be happy about it.

Chapter Three

1906 – Onboard the Athlon

From the top deck of the *Athlon,* Pearl waved to her family on shore, but within minutes, Sinclair Inlet faded to a mere speck. A speck. That's how big Pearl felt as the steamer sliced through the vastness of Puget Sound. Unlike the steamer, she had no sense of direction, no definite course for her future besides the lofty goal of becoming the first person in her family to graduate from high school. The last time she'd been onboard the *Athlon* was two years earlier when she had attended her cousin Charlotte's wedding. Now she was moving into Charlotte's empty room to attend Seattle High. The rippling waves lapped at the hull and blew mist into the breeze. Pearl licked the salty spray from her lips. She recalled her teacher, Miss Ambrose, asking her about her plans for the future before the eighth-grade exam. "I hope you are going to be able to continue your education."

Pearl shrugged. "My parents want me to continue my studies, but I'm afraid it would be selfish. My sister's only four, and Mother's busy with sewing jobs and keeping up the farm. Papa works on Vashon and only comes home once or twice a month. Even when he's home, he needs my help with chores."

From the creases on Miss Ambrose's forehead, Pearl guessed her teacher had heard similar tales from other students many times before. The teacher placed her hands upon Pearl's shoulders and gazed at her. "It's often hard on families, but you owe it to yourself to further your education if you are able. It's unfortunate these days few children over the age of fourteen continue in their studies, especially young girls." Miss Ambrose shook her head without

13

attempting to hide her dismay. "You're a smart young woman. Think about it."

Standing on the bow and gazing out over the water as white foam churned cold and threatening beneath the hull like drifts of snow, Pearl wondered if she'd made the right decision. Pearl shivered as she remembered a sister ship of the Mosquito Fleet, the *Clallam*, sank two years earlier, resulting in the drowning deaths of more than fifty souls. The thought of the passengers leaving home, never to return, cast a sinking feeling over her. What if something happened to her in the strange, vast city? Engulfed in indecision and uncertainty, Pearl shuddered with the same anxiety she'd felt last spring talking with Miss Ambrose. Pearl gripped the side rail so tightly her fingers turned blue and stiffened.

Though she'd loved being an only child, after her sister's birth, Pearl had delighted in having someone with whom she could share her days. She had looked forward to sharing their dreams throughout their lives. Now, moving away and leaving Edna behind, Pearl knew Edna would feel abandoned. She closed her eyes, wishing she could forget her promise to always be there for Edna. Pearl felt alone, adrift on the vast ocean, clouded in the unknown and her spirits were as damp as her hair from the saltwater spray as she made her way inside to sit for the remainder of the one-hour crossing.

The steamer was nearly at capacity, but a man about the same age as her father, with a clean-shaven face and a kind smile, scooted across the varnished mahogany bench to make room for her. He nodded. "Please, miss, have a seat."

Tendering a smile, Pearl set her luggage down. She smoothed the navy blue twill skirt Mother had made especially for this occasion and slid onto the seat next to the gentleman. She shifted uneasily and though she was not cold, she clutched her arms to her chest, and rubbed them.

"Traveling alone?" The stranger eyed the two pieces of baggage at her feet.

Uncomfortable, Pearl pulled the suitcases closer and glanced around at the numerous passengers lining the many benches. She suppressed her nervousness. "Yes, sir."

"Is it your first time to the big city?"

"No. I've been several times. My aunt and uncle live in Seattle. I'm going to live with them while I attend high school."

The man's head bobbed with obvious pleasure. "I believe that is wise. I imagine these modern times will require much more education than in my day. I consider myself lucky. My parents were hardly well to do, but I managed to become the first in my family, not only to go to high school but also to attend university. My name's Lucien. Doctor Lucien Chapman."

"I'm Pearl Mooney. Pleased to meet you, Doctor Chapman." Pearl took in the stranger's dark suit and the top hat sitting on his lap, along with the black leather bag at his feet. "Do you like being a doctor?"

"It's hard work. Long days, but it is extremely gratifying healing another's ailments and possibly even saving a life."

Pearl nodded. "Do you know Dr. Wilkes in Port Orchard?"

"No. I'm sorry, I don't. I work in Seattle. I'm on my way back home. I take the steamer once a week to visit the navy yard in Bremerton and help the naval doctor there with his needs."

Pearl sat enthralled by the accomplished man who put her at ease. "My mother's a seamstress. She knows several navy wives."

"A seamstress is a fine profession. Do you know what course of study you wish to pursue?"

Having never considered her future, other than not wishing to become a seamstress like her mother, Pearl blurted out the first thing that popped into her mind. "My aunt is a midwife. She delivered my younger sister. She's assisted with lots of deliveries. Maybe I could be a midwife."

Doctor Chapman nodded, appearing impressed by her words. "That's a mighty fine path, but even these days, especially in the cities, midwives are growing out of favor. I believe in time you'll see most women going to a hospital to deliver their babies. Have you given any thought to a career in nursing? It's a growing field."

Intrigued by his suggestion, Pearl arched her brows. She'd never even considered such a thing. Port Orchard had only one regular doctor, and though a woman worked at the office, she strictly handled menial office tasks. "Do I need to go to the university if I want to be a nurse?"

"Ah." Doctor Chapman rubbed his chin. "Not at this time. Most nurses don't even have their high school diplomas. Heck, when I became a doctor near twenty years ago, most doctors didn't attend any university or medical school. Most don't have medical degrees today, but I expect it won't be long until it's required. The field of medical arts is growing and changing rapidly. Some states now have nursing licensing laws. Can't say I'm up to date on the latest, but I can assure you your high school education will pay off."

A flash of inspiration struck her. Pearl chewed on her lip and peered out the window. Overhead arced a bright shiny sky. Dr. Chapman's words and her memory of Edna's birth sparked a thought. Perhaps she would study to become a nurse. The *Athlon* gently turned. Looking through the expansive windows toward the distant south, the majestic icon of Washington State's landscape, Mount. Rainier, ascended like a noble ruler peering down on the city. Then the shoreline came into view, reaching out to the water with welcoming arms. Looking beyond Colman Dock, Pearl spied what she guessed was the towering Alaska building. Papa told her it stretched over two hundred feet into the sky and was the tallest building in Seattle. A group of seagulls, keeping pace with the boat, flew alongside, welcoming her to her new life. Now, with the skyline of Seattle within view, a last-minute tremble of fear gripped her.

"You'll be fine."

Pearl glanced back at Dr. Chapman.

"I'm sure you feel the pressure of making not only your parents proud, but also your teacher and the town."

Pearl nodded. He'd plucked the words right from her head.

"It's okay to be a bit fearful, but remember: despite the uncertainty of your future, the vastness of your opportunities is endless, but it is up to you to write your own story, sing your own unique song."

Beyond the window, the sound stretched endlessly. Pearl swallowed. Dr. Chapman was right. Her whole future stretched out before her, no matter how uncertain. As the *Athlon* jockeyed into its place at the dock in Elliot Bay, Pearl's optimism soared as tall as the clock tower of the Colman terminal building. She thanked Dr. Chapman, lifted her luggage along with a boost of self-confidence, and started down the plank to find Uncle Leland. For a moment, her confidence wavered. What if she reached the bottom and no one was there to meet her?

On the shore, tall stacks from port-side businesses spit dark sooty smoke into the otherwise clear sky. Papa had warned her of the large-scale work knocking down hills and moving dirt to level the city and make it easier to navigate with a horse a buggy. Pearl glanced ahead to the steep hillside where her aunt and uncle lived. Massive mounds of dirt arose like misplaced crumbling forts amid the modern brick castle-looking buildings that reached toward the sky. Crosses atop steeples marked the churches on the surrounding hills. Gulls screeched overhead, diving toward the disembarking passengers, hoping for tossed tidbits.

Above the voices, all speaking as if they were in a constant state of urgency, a man's voice arose from the hubbub of disembarking passengers. "Pearl Mooney!" His hand shot into the air with a grand waving motion.

The knot in Pearl's stomach released. She returned the wave. Stepping out from the crowd, Pearl looked back across the water to the mass of land on the other side—back to where her journey began a mere hour earlier. Yet here in Seattle, with its skyline with towers jutting into the sky, Pearl felt a world away. She picked up her pace and headed toward her uncle.

Uncle Leland wove through the disembarking passengers. He relieved Pearl of her heavy bags. "How was the trip?"

Pearl's stomach still reeled and rolled from the voyage. "Fine, thank you."

"The buggy's nearby. You'll be settled in your new room soon. I'm sure your aunt has dinner prepared. You are hungry, I hope."

Seated up front, Pearl gazed upon the steep hills and the tall brick buildings so different from where she grew up. Everything and every sound seemed heightened, more alive. People walked with hurried steps. Even the horses and buggies moved with a quickened tempo, with an air of purpose. After a short ride, the buggy slowed.

"Here we are." Her uncle nodded as the horse turned and trotted down a gravel lane toward a modest brick house with the carriage house alongside. "Welcome to your new home."

Within the past three hours, Pearl had left her childhood home and traveled across Puget Sound to arrive at her new home. She had

17

a sudden urge to hug her mother, but her mother wasn't here. Her insecurity awoke. Time would tell if she would sink or swim.

Chapter Four

1906 – New Beginning

A commotion of clomping hooves and voices outside the bedroom window woke Pearl the following day. Light from a post outside illuminated an unfamiliar white stand of drawers and a small bedside table. Pearl shifted in the strange bed. As the haze of sleep lifted, she remembered she'd exchanged the peacefulness of her childhood home for the fast-paced city life in the Broadway Hill area of Seattle.

A rap on the bedroom door startled Pearl. She sat and pulled her covers to her neck.

The door creaked open. "Are you awake?"

In the dim light of the late summer morning, Pearl blinked. For a moment, she saw her mother in her aunt's smiling face that hadn't aged in the past few years. Though five years older than her mother, her aunt's auburn hair, piled atop her head, made her appear younger. Instead of the plain, floor-length, gingham, house dresses her mother wore most days, Aunt Marie wore a white lacy blouse with poufy sleeves and a slim, fitted burgundy skirt. The tailored fit showed off her trim figure, even at over forty and after birthing two children.

"Did you sleep okay?" Aunt Marie asked.

Still uncomfortable in her new surroundings, Pearl returned the smile. "Yes, thank you."

"You'll find cloths for washing in the washroom. Take your time, then come down to breakfast. We want to show you the city before you begin your classes tomorrow." A whisper of perfume lingered as her aunt shut the door behind her.

Pearl thought about her earlier visits to Seattle. A city that signified progress, so unlike Port Orchard. A city where buildings appeared to grow taller with each visit and where the latest appliances and modes of transportation were beacons lighting the way for the rest of the state.

Delighted to have an indoor washroom instead of a drafty outhouse, Pearl grabbed her grooming supplies and nearly skipped down the short hallway. Light reflected from the single light bulb on the wall. She couldn't wait to soak in the white claw-foot tub, a luxury she'd never experienced. The ease of tugging on the chain to empty the wall-mounted overhead tank on the wood-seat commode was a far better experience than the cold outdoor privy back home, merely a pit with a wooden lid on hinges to reduce unpleasant odors. Even the faucet was an improvement over pumping water every time you used the sink. Opening her tin of Dr. Graves tooth powder, she brushed her teeth then dabbed on some Mum deodorant. Returning to the bedroom, Pearl slipped out of her nightgown and into her drawers, chemise, and corset. She tugged on her stockings and fastened her elastic garters, then pulled on a pink cotton sailor dress, the only fancy dress she owned. With her ankle-high brown boots laced, she was ready to face the new day, ready to change, ready to grow, like the city that surrounded her.

The aromas of breakfast greeted her in the kitchen, where instead of the black coal-burning stove, a modern-looking, white cast-iron cook stove warmed the room.

Uncle Leland sat at the table. He looked up from his newspaper. "How's your room?"

"Fine, thank you. It's so kind of you to open your home to me. I'm sure I'll be comfortable."

Turning from the stove, Aunt Marie placed a platter of hot flapjacks on the pink-and-blue floral tablecloth. She nodded for Pearl to take a seat in front of the waiting plate of sausage and eggs. "We're happy to have you. The room has been empty since Charlotte married and moved out nearly two years ago. We're so proud of you for continuing your education."

Pulling out the chair next to her uncle, Pearl speared a couple of flapjacks, then drizzled hot maple syrup over the top. Her stomach gurgled as the syrup soaked into them. She moved her fried egg and

20

sausage away from the oozing syrup. Famished, she gulped several bites before the sound of footsteps drew her attention.

Her cousin Eugene strode into the kitchen. "Good morning." He pulled out a chair next to Pearl.

Pearl stammered an awkward greeting. Other than at Charlotte's wedding, she hadn't seen much of her cousin over the past five years since he'd moved to Washington from Wisconsin. With the expanse of the blue-black water separating their homes, the two families only got together once or twice a year. Two years older than Pearl at sixteen, Gene looked a lot like his father with his chiseled features.

He struggled to squeeze his long legs under the table without bumping into Pearl. "Are you looking forward to high school?"

Pearl scooted her chair over to give Gene more room. She wrinkled her face. "Yes, but I'm a bit nervous about attending such a large school."

"I'm sure Seattle High is going to be a lot different from your old school."

"Yeah. The school in Port Orchard has only two rooms. Most of the time, there are fewer than one hundred students total for all grades. Mama says it's the only high school in Seattle. I bet it's big."

"It's big, all right. Holds fifteen hundred students. I don't think we have that many kids yet, but it's probably twice as many kids as when it opened four years ago. There were less than a thousand kids when I started school there."

Already worried if her small-town school had adequately prepared her for secondary school, Pearl felt a new worry leap into her brain. She'd never considered the additional adjustment of struggling to fit in among so many other students. Her stomach fluttered at the thought of a school so big it held over a thousand students. Her mother always called her case of nerves "butterflies" in her stomach, only to Pearl, it didn't feel like butterflies; it felt more like bats. Big bats. And the thought terrified her. Reminded how Aunt Marie encouraged her mother to take deep breaths to calm her, Pearl inhaled in a feeble attempt to slow the beating of her heart. "You're a junior, aren't you, Gene?"

"Yeah. I graduate next year, though I'm planning on attending the University of Washington after graduation. Maybe go into medicine."

21

Pearl swallowed a bite. "I met a doctor on the steamer yesterday, Doctor Chapman. He told me most of the doctors these days have to attend university."

"I know. I expect to have four more years of formal education. I'm glad we have an outstanding four-year institution so close at the University of Washington. I'll be able to live at home and focus on my education instead of working to pay for room and board."

Aunt Marie took a seat. "No sense fretting about that today. Today is a day for showing Pearl the sights."

Uncle Leland smacked his lips. "As soon as everyone is finished eating, we can go." He pushed away from the table.

Pearl wolfed down her remaining bites and carried her plate to the sink. She grabbed the bar of soap and a dishcloth. Marie joined her with a towel in hand. The routine of washing dishes helped make Pearl feel at home. Dishes back on the shelves, her aunt thanked her and went to her bedroom.

Lured into the parlor by fast-paced vaudeville music, Pearl found her uncle in a brown leather chair, smoking a pipe. The woodsy aroma reminded Pearl of her father. An ache of loneliness gripped her, despite the cheery melody that resounded from a big, gold, cone-shaped funnel sitting atop a carved oak sideboard.

With wide eyes, Pearl walked over to the music machine. She read the metal plate affixed to the device, identifying it as a Graphophone.

"You ever seen one of those?" Uncle Leland pushed himself off the chair to join her. Pearl stared at the rotating cylinder.

"No. How does it work?"

Her uncle cranked the machine. "I buy different moulded [1]cylinders like this. This one is music by Arthur Collins. When the cylinder rotates, the recorded music plays."

Amazed by the invention, Pearl shook her head. She couldn't wait to see the other surprising inventions there were in the city.

When her aunt came in and proclaimed it was time to go, Uncle Leland removed the cylinder from the music player. "We can listen to more later. I'll put on Billy Murray when we get back."

---

[1] Accurate spelling of the time.

Pearl grinned. "Is he the man who sings 'Yankee Doodle Boy'?"

"Yep, that's him. Got a whole bunch of his songs. I think you'll enjoy his music." He led the way to the door. "Time to get going."

Thrilled, she followed her uncle out the door. "I want to see as much of Seattle as possible."

In the city, besides walking, the streetcar would be her primary mode for getting around. Though her uncle owned a buggy, their home's proximity to the city, and the widespread and inexpensive streetcar routes, made the streetcar and trolley a more efficient mode of transportation. With an eager skip to her steps, Pearl caught up with Aunt Marie, who was far more pleasant than she'd been when she was Mama's midwife. Gene shuffled along behind them until his mother turned and instructed him to quit lollygagging.

"I'm coming." Gene quickened his pace. "But I get to show Pearl around."

Less than ten minutes later, a bell rang. The red and white trolley rolled to a stop. Uncle Leland deposited nickels into the fare box for each of them, and they all climbed aboard Streetcar #8 of the Seattle Electric Railway Company. Other passengers on the long wood bench scooted closer together, and the streetcar purred and continued its trek up Pine Street until it reached 15th Avenue East. Pearl sat wide-eyed as she stared out the window. The houses grew larger with each passing block. After only minutes, immense white wood houses and red-brick mansions surrounded by masonry walls, lined the streets. "These houses are bigger than the stores and shops back home."

When the trolley jerked to a stop, Uncle Leland pointed to the lush green lawn decorated with tall deciduous and evergreen trees. "This is Volunteer Park. It's one of Seattle's largest parks. They moved a cemetery to build it. It was named in honor of the local city folk who volunteered in the Spanish-American War."

Pearl stared at the beautiful urban park, far surpassing any park in her sleepy town. Families gathered with picnic baskets on blankets spread underneath the shade of the trees, their leaves tinged with red and gold. Couples walked hand in hand on the long winding cement walkways underneath long-ago planted evergreens. She wondered if someday she too might walk along the same walkway with someone special. Several passengers stood and headed for the door. Excited to explore the spacious park, Pearl rose along with the others.

Uncle Leland, who remained in his seat, shook his head. "We'll have plenty of time to visit here again during your stay."

The streetcar lunged and lurched ahead. Pearl grabbed at an overhead railing to maintain her balance before she plopped back on her seat. Uncle Leland pointed out the window in the direction opposite the boundary to the park. "This is Lake View Cemetery where the city moved the bodies previously buried on the property of Volunteer Park, back in 1887."

Pearl took in the expansive low-cut lawn dotted with neat rows of marble headstones and granite monuments that memorialized the dearly departed, standing solemn and serene against the backdrop of the water and the snowcapped Olympic mountains. Though some headstones sat high above the lush lawn, they stood dwarfed by the tall evergreens and deciduous trees planted to enhance the beauty of this final resting place.

Uncle Leland slid into the seat next to Pearl. "Almost all the city's founding fathers are buried here with the adjacent plots open for their descendants."

For the first time, Pearl thought about her mortality and the mortality of her parents. She wondered if they'd be buried together in Port Orchard and, when the time came, if she'd have a resting place next to them or next to her own husband and family.

The overhead lines directed the streetcar along its route down First Hill toward the city center. Her uncle tapped her on the shoulder, drawing Pearl's attention out the window to the gigantic hillsides. "At one time, these hills were covered with the tallest trees on earth and were even steeper than they are today. Around ten years ago, the city started shaving off the high parts of the bluffs to make it easier to traverse the steep hills. They used the dirt to fill in the low areas, including the waterfront where your boat docked."

Pearl stared at the dug-away hills. Solitary buildings and houses sat perched atop mounds of dirt, looking like eagles sitting on nests in barren trees. "Sounds like a lot of work."

"Officials thought the only way the city would ever grow was to make the terrain less hilly. I hear work's gonna be going on for quite a while yet."

As far as she could see, massive hillsides of mud with houses positioned precariously on stilts, rose above the new lower elevation. Images from her schoolbooks popped into her brain. "It reminds me of the massive pyramids of Egypt rising above the desert sand."

The motorman stopped the streetcar. Outside the window, a street sign read "Yesler Street." The driver looked back at the remaining passengers and called out, "Pioneer Square. Heart of the Business District. Streetcar terminus."

Her aunt and uncle, along with Gene, rose to disembark. Eager to stretch her legs, Pearl followed them down the steps. A line of people stood waiting to board the car to travel in the opposite direction. Two cylindrical columns flanked the massive archway entrance to the block-long and six-story-high brick Pioneer Building, and across the wide two-lane street stood the equally impressive Seattle Hotel. Horses whinnied as they led carts and passengers along the brick road, passing streetcars as they clicked and clomped along. Men in high-buttoned waistcoats, pressed slacks, hats, and walking sticks, some with leather satchels, all stern faced, walked with purpose into tall brick office buildings or hotels that lined the bustling sidewalk. Women, equally dressed, sporting hats the size of serving platters decorated with ribbon and silk flowers, strolled in a more relaxed pace in pairs or crowds, out for lunch or a day of shopping at leisure.

Pearl decided that when she finished school, she would find a well-paying job, like nursing, and she'd dress to the nines like these women.

An overhead sign on the small outdoor kiosk across the street caught Pearl's eye. "Root beer 5 cents." Her mouth watered. Papa had given her five dollars for spending money for her first three months. She fingered the coins in her coat pocket.

Uncle Leland marched over and winked. "Don't imagine you like root beer?"

While she waited for her refreshing drink, Pearl gazed along the street. White-globed, iron streetlamps stood on both sides of the walkways, resembling elegant sentries, and a newsboy stood on the corner hawking papers. With his white shirt sleeves pushed up to his elbows, he waved a newspaper in the air. "Extra! Extra! The New York Highlanders win sixth consecutive game."

"What do you think?"

Pearl saw her aunt watching her. "I wish it were nighttime, so I could see the lights illuminating the streets. Port Orchard doesn't have electric lines yet. Mama can't wait to have lights, and she's squirreling away money to buy an electrical stove."

"Yes. Seattle is the envy of the state. We've had electricity for several years, and I do appreciate the luxury, and in time, your mother will too."

Uncle Leland and Gene returned with brown glass bottles of Hires Root Beer. She gulped the icy, frothy beverage, the spicy sarsaparilla awakening her taste buds. "Thanks. This tastes great. I hardly ever get a soda at home."

Looking away from the streetcar station, Pearl spotted a tall totem pole. Her gaze took in the full height of the pole that appeared to be about five stories high.

"Do you want to see it?" Gene motioned with his head toward the towering wooden pillar. "Tlingit Indians from Alaska made it." Gene turned his head to peer at his parents. He lowered his voice as if he were about to share a deep dark secret. "Several Seattle businessmen were visiting an Alaskan village. They thought the village was abandoned, so they chopped the pole down, rolled it to the beach, loaded it in their ship, and brought it here." Gene chuckled. "Turned out the tribe was only away at their fishing camp and were none too happy to return and find their totem pole missing."

They hurried across the street ahead of her aunt and uncle. Pearl ran her hand over the smooth carved wood and studied the features of the carved birds, and perhaps a wolf and a bear. Blue, red, black, and white paint highlighted their eyes, mouths, and beaks.

"It's pretty impressive, isn't it? It's over a hundred years old." Uncle Leland scratched his chin as he stared at the pole.

"Sure, but isn't it wrong to keep a stolen totem pole?"

Her uncle cast a sideways scowl at his son. "Seattle made financial reparation to the tribe, so the debt is settled."

Pearl dipped her head and considered the circumstances. "I guess." She examined the striking totem from a century ago, looking out of place against a modern city of brick and stone.

"Come on." Gene nudged her and headed away from the water.

Four blocks later, Uncle Leland stopped walking. "This is King Street Station. It opened only four months ago."

Awed, Pearl stared up at the clocktower until her neck hurt. Seattle was so vastly different from Port Orchard with all its progress and modern conveniences. "That's the biggest clock I've ever seen."

"The station serves the Great Northern Railway and the Northern Pacific Railway." Gene pointed to the red brick tower looming over them. "There are clocks on all four sides of the tower. Each one faces a major city and shows that city's local time. The clocktower is the tallest building in the city. Even taller than the Alaska building. I read it was modeled after the bell tower of Saint Mark's Basilica in Venice, Italy."

"May we go inside, please?"

"I haven't seen it myself." Uncle Leland grinned and headed for the large double glass doors on the west side of the building. Inside the main entrance, dozens of travelers carrying briefcases and suitcases strode with a sense of purpose over the polished cement floor inlaid with white and black mosaic tiles. Pearl followed her uncle past rows of high-backed double-sided wooden benches in the massive waiting room facing the boarding platform. She stared at the opulent detailed design.

"This is called the 'Compass Room'." Her uncle pointed to the floor. "And that's known as a compass rose."

Pearl turned in a circle. The center was laid out in a design similar to a compass. Light reflected off the marble wainscoting that lined the lower portion of the walls. A young child hopped across the streams of light that shimmered across the floor. A multi-globed bronze chandelier hung suspended above the compass rose from an elaborate plaster disc resembling a rose.

Following his niece's gaze, Leland continued, "I read in the *Post-Intelligencer* that the ceiling was designed after a famous palace in Florence, Italy." Leland laughed. "It's probably the closest I'll ever get to seeing Italy."

Triple-globe bronze wall sconces circled the perimeter, illuminating a band of inlaid green iridescent glass tile on the walls. Daylight streamed into the L-shaped station from circular windows trimmed with white plaster designs high above them. Two shrill, sharp whistles pierced their conversation.

"That means a train is leaving." Gene tipped his head in the direction of the train tracks and took off. "Come on. Let's go see the train."

Recently arrived passengers bustled by, anxious to get to their appointments or to baggage claim. Feeling like a fish swimming against the stream, Pearl hurried after Gene and reached the boarding platform in time to hear the big brass bells *clang, clang, clang* as the engine hissed and gray steam billowed from the stack. The large black wheels began to roll with a *chuff, chuff, chuff, chuff* coming faster and faster as the iron beast roared to life.

Excited by all the new sights, Pearl only felt the gnawing in her stomach when her uncle suggested getting lunch along the waterfront. She had to walk faster than usual to keep up with her cousin as well as her aunt and uncle. They retraced their steps back to Pioneer Square and turned down First Avenue heading north. The sound of loud chants coming from several blocks away drew Pearl's attention. She stopped walking, along with other Sunday strollers, and gazed down the street. A throng of women carrying signs and banners marched toward them. "What's going on?"

Aunt Marie flashed a knowing grin. "It's a march of the suffragettes."

Pearl stood mesmerized by the sheer number marching in their direction. As the crowd grew nearer, Pearl made out more men among the group of women. "Is that about giving women the right to vote?"

"That's right." Aunt Marie's face brightened. "Women could vote in Washington from 1883 to1888 until the Territorial Supreme Court revoked their rights. I remember voting for President Grover Cleveland the year he lost to President Harrison."

"May we go see them?" Pearl glanced at her uncle for his approval.

"Your aunt is involved with the movement; she'd be marching alongside these fine ladies today if we weren't entertaining you."

At the intersection of First and Madison, the family stepped back and waited for the suffragettes to pass. The women in front of the group carried a long banner with large letters. *It's a Matter of Justice.* Pearl had never given any thought to women's right to vote. Only one day in this new city and Pearl already felt a spark of inspiration to make something of her life. She remembered Doctor Chapman's words. Her opportunities were endless. An ember ignited. "Will you bring me to the next march?"

Her aunt put her arm around Pearl and squeezed. "I'd love to. Since Charlotte doesn't live nearby, it will be nice to have you join me."

After a quick stroll along the waterfront, they gathered on the bank along the shore. Her aunt pulled out slices of fresh bread and cheese, which they ate as they looked out across Elliott Bay.

Uncle Leland pointed to a large island in the distance. "That's Bainbridge Island. If you look south of the island, that's the Kitsap Peninsula and Port Orchard."

Pearl stared at the mass of land—her hometown. It didn't seem far away, but she knew this new city would shape her future.

Uncle Leland tugged at his pocket watch and announced the day was getting late. "I think we've seen enough for one day."

Though she longed to see more of the city, especially Wallin and Nordstrom on Fourth and Pike, which all the girls back home talked about, Pearl saw Gene follow his father without a word. Out of respect, she trailed behind. She had nine more months to explore her exciting new city and to prove to herself and her parents she was worthy of their sacrifice.

Chapter Five

1906 – Life Without Pearl

Entering the kitchen, Edna stared at the floor, her chin buried in her chest, her forehead crinkled, and her lower lip protruded. Edna plopped onto a wooden kitchen chair and seated Molly on the chair next to her.

Her mother put Edna's breakfast of scrambled eggs and a glass of milk on the table. "You remind me of an apple-head doll." Her mother imitated Edna's pouting face. "I don't want to hear any more about Pearl leaving. We talked about this. Your sister must continue her schooling so she can have more opportunities than I did. When you're the same age, you will move away too."

Edna banged the spoon on the table. "Why? Pearl knows how to read and how to cipher numbers." "I need her. Doesn't she love me anymore?"

Mama hugged her. "Pearl will always love you, even if she is not here. You'll learn to play by yourself, like your sister did when she was your age. She didn't have anyone to play with, and she managed fine. You'll get used to it."

Edna narrowed her eyes. It wasn't fair. She was only four. She would be alone with Mama for two more years, then she would spend all day in school and make friends. Friends who would not move away and leave her alone.

After breakfast, Mama flung a shovel of coal into the stove before heading out for the daily chores. Edna tagged along behind Mama.

"Soo-Ee, soo-Ee." Mother slopped the pail of table scraps into the old washtub for the stinky swine. Edna wrinkled her nose as the pigs lumbered over and slurped, then gobbled the potato peelings, chicken fat, and other leftovers. Her mother carried the empty bucket to the water pump and filled it with water half a dozen times before nodding toward the henhouse. The chickens lifted their heads from their search for bugs and worms among the assorted weeds, salal, and Oregon grape growing around the coop. Though the hens ran free and for the most part ate bugs and grass, sometimes they got corn or table scraps. "Can I feed the chickens today, Mama?"

Mama reached deep into her apron pocket and pulled out a handful of cracked corn.

"Goody." Edna skipped over to the excited birds. "Here chick, chick, chick." The skittery birds surrounded her in a noisy, frantic dance as she flung the kernels to the ground. The clucking intensified as the dozen salt-and-pepper-speckled and butterscotch-colored pullets gobbled their treat. Edna wiped the dust from the corn onto her dress. With the hens busy pecking at their food, Edna picked up the basket outside the entrance to the coop. She ran to the nesting boxes, pushed aside some straw, and found two eggs. She set them in the basket, careful not to let them break.

"Good job." Mama always watched Edna collect eggs from the lower roost for a bit before she collected the eggs from the higher row of wooden boxes.

Next, they were off to the barn. Edna stood back while Mama heaved the heavy wooden barn doors open. Nellie always welcomed them with a snort and a neigh. Edna climbed onto an overturned milking pail. Mother dipped into one of her pockets and passed a carrot to her.

"Here you go." Edna reached up high and stroked Nellie's nuzzle before extending the carrot to the mare. The horse lifted her chin in appreciation and gobbled the carrot in two bites before turning her attention to the alfalfa her mother tossed into the stall.

With the pitchfork back in place, and the egg basket on her arm, Mama pivoted toward the barn door. "Time to gather vegetables from the garden."

Edna grabbed the produce basket by the barn door. Minutes later, the basket was so heavy with green peas, tomatoes, peppers, and onions she could no longer carry it. She handed it to her mother, who tucked a couple fresh carrots and beets into her deep apron pockets.

31

"That's plenty for today." Mother brushed off her hands smudged with alfalfa and soil and headed back to the house.

Edna followed Mama to the pump to wash up before lunch. Since Pearl left, midday meals were small—a slice of bread with jam, canned fruit, and a glass of milk. Though tired after lunch from the busy morning, Edna fought back her yawns. "I don't want to take a nap. I'm a big girl now."

"Big girl or not, you still need a nap. Maybe next year, you'll be old enough to go without a nap. Run along now. I have sewing to do."

Gathering her beloved and only companion, Edna dragged her feet on the way to her room and found a book Pearl used to read to her. She lay back on her pillow, sitting Molly by her side. "Do you want me to read to you, Molly?" Edna flipped open the blue cloth-covered storybook with black lettering and pretended to read aloud about Goldilocks. Edna liked the story of the bold little girl who marched into an unfamiliar house where she made herself at home sitting in three chairs and eating three bowls of porridge at the kitchen table. "...the last bowl was just right." Edna fell asleep with the book in her hands.

After her nap, Edna found her mother humming as she swung back and forth in the old bentwood wicker rocker, a ball of gray yarn at her feet. Her wood knitting needles clicked as she wrapped yarn around them, forming quick even stitches from her years of practice slipping the wool around the needles while the other end slid through her fingers. Not bothering to look up, she asked Edna if she had a pleasant nap, then took a sip of tea from her blue-and-white china cup on the small oval table next to the chair.

Though Mother seemed content in the quiet stillness, Edna missed her sister reading to her or playing the piano and teaching her new songs. Sometimes Pearl wrote in a small journal. After writing, she sometimes read parts from it to Edna before she tucked the red book in the back of the closet on the shelf Edna couldn't reach. Edna looked out the window to an empty swing Papa hung from the old, gnarled apple tree in the yard. "I wish Pearl could push me on the swing."

"You're old enough to swing by yourself."

Edna pouted. Swinging alone wasn't any fun.

"You're going to have to get used to doing things by yourself. Do you want to watch me make this scarf for Daddy? When I'm done, I can make one for you. Would you like that?"

Nestled all comfy on the green sofa, Edna stuck out her lip. "I don't need a scarf."

Not missing a stitch, her mother sighed and slipped her yarn from one needle to the next, paying no heed to Edna.

Edna crossed her arms and sat defiantly. After a few minutes of silence, her mother set aside her yarn and half-knit scarf.

"Come and sit next to me. You can help me sew."

Edna hesitated and made a face before she plucked her blanket and Miss Molly from the sofa and climbed onto the stool next to her mother's chair. "Why can't you play with me?"

Mother heaved a frustrated sigh. "Maybe later. I have a dress to finish and some alterations to complete. The navy wives are keeping me busy."

Edna didn't care if the ladies in town or the navy wives had new dresses. Bored, she stuck her thumb in her mouth. The sucking soothed her.

Her mother frowned. "You haven't sucked your thumb since you were two. You should be thankful I have the work, especially from the wives of the shipyard workers. We can use the money."

Over the next several weeks, Edna spent many hours sitting on the brown footstool beside her mother's Singer sewing machine. Mother pumped her foot on the treadle and eased fabric through it while the machine hummed. Mama promised someday, when Edna was older, she would teach her to sew.

"I can sew now. I can make clothes for Molly." Edna snatched a strip of fabric with green and blue flowers on it. She ran the soft, smooth fabric across her cheek and smiled. "Molly likes this cloth." Edna folded the fabric and wrapped it around the doll.

Mother smiled. "We can make a dress for your doll when I'm done with my work."

Tired of watching her mother sew, Edna huffed. "You're never done with your work."

Mother looked at Edna with a resigned smile and pushed aside the dress she was sewing. She pulled out several folded pieces of cloth.

She held a long yellow measuring tape from Edna's head to her toes. "My how you're growing. Soon you'll be as high as the wheat in the field."

Edna giggled. "When I'm big like Pearl, I'll move away too."

"Let's see." Mother held samples of fabric out for Edna to see. "It's about time for a new dress. Which of these do you like best?"

Edna furrowed her brow as she examined her choices. The first piece looked like something her mother might wear, with blue and white stripes and bold rose-colored flowers. She stroked each of them and held them to her cheek. Finally, she pointed to the tiny flowers on a field of green.

Mother gave her a scrap of fabric along with a pair of small blunt-tipped scissors and showed her how to hold them. "You can make a dress for Molly while I work on yours."

Edna placed her chubby fingers into the small round holes. She cut two openings for the doll's arms to slide through and a hole for her doll's head. Next, Mother threaded a needle. She showed Edna how to run the needle through the fabric and pull the thread to gather it along the top along the neck. Slipping the new dress onto her doll, Edna beamed. "See, Mama. I can sew like you."

Mama nodded. "Perhaps someday you'll become a dressmaker like me."

Edna wrinkled her nose, hopped off her stool, and skipped to the oak Hoosier. Filled with all of Mama's cooking tools, the bottom drawer also held Edna's slate and white chalk. Edna struggled to yank the drawer open.

Mama looked up from her Singer and watched Edna tug at the long wood drawer that sometimes got stuck. "Do you need help?"

"I can do it myself," Edna replied firmly and yanked at the drawer, almost losing her balance and falling on her bottom in the process. She grabbed the slate and placed Molly next to her in the adjacent chair. Pearl loved drawing and coloring. She had handed Edna her first crayon as soon as she could hold a spoon. Gripping the chalk, Edna drew circles, squares, and triangles, trying hard to shape them into animals. Edna bit down on her lip, erasing, when necessary, with a small piece of sponge. The chalk scratched across the slate as she printed her name at the bottom in large letters exactly as Pearl taught her. Edna flinched at the sharp squeaky noise, then brushed the white dust from her dress with her hands, leaving them white and gritty. She favored coloring with the box of eight Crayola crayons, a birthday gift when she turned four. She knew all eight colors in the box: red, orange, yellow, green, blue, violet, brown, and black. She glanced at the simple chalk outlines on the black slate. "Please, Mama, may I use the crayons and my coloring book? I can color a picture for Pearl. I promise I'll be careful and won't break any of them."

Mama reached high into the highest cupboard, where she stored her best teacups and saucers. She handed Edna the small golden-yellow-and-dark-green box.

Edna traced her finger over the number five on the box. "These crayons costed five cents." She fished out her only coloring book and sat at the table. With a wide grin, she flipped through several scribbled pages of black, lined drawings, stopping on a picture of farm animals. Pearl always insisted Edna color the animals correctly, so Edna selected the brown waxy color to fill in the horse and yellow for the duck. When she got to the pig, she wrinkled her face. "Oink, oink, pigs are pink. I don't have a pink crayon." She grabbed an orange crayon. Her face tight with concentration, she filled in the animals. Pleased with her effort, Edna plucked out the black crayon and printed her name on the top of the page in large block letters as Pearl told her the children did in school. Returning the crayons to the box, Edna ran to her mother and thrust the page in front of her. "Look, Mama, see the animals I colored for Pearl."

Her mother stooped down and tousled Edna's long curly hair. "You did a fine job. Pearl will like how you colored the animals. How about we go into town and take it to the post office and mail it to Pearl?"

Chapter Six

1906 – High School

Monday morning, Pearl hurried down the hall, anxious for the first day of school. Gene sat hunched over a stack of griddle cakes twice as high as what Pearl and Edna together might eat.

Aunt Marie placed a plate in front of Pearl. "Gene will make sure you get to your classroom and show you around and introduce you to some of his friends during the lunch hour." Aunt Marie hummed as she cracked an egg into a pan. "Do you want a fried egg, Gene?"

"No time. It's getting late." Gene raised his chin toward the door. "Eat fast. We need to get going. Classes start at eight thirty, and we need at least fifteen minutes to walk to school."

Pearl nodded as Gene pushed back his chair and unfolded himself from the seat. She shoveled in her last two bites and gulped her milk. She blew out her breath and straightened. "I'm ready." She hoped her words sounded more confident than her queasy stomach indicated.

Gene called a quick goodbye to his mother and headed for the door. Following on Gene's heels, Pearl stopped short. She ran back to her room and grabbed the new slate Papa bought her for her big day. By the time she reached the stoop, she had to sprint to catch up with her cousin, now half a block down the sidewalk. Closely built houses with an occasional business lined both sides of the street, a sharp contrast to the wheat fields and pastures she passed on the way to school back home. As they turned the corner, the street sign read, "Broadway." The narrow road became a wide expanse, busy with horses and buggies, streetcars, and cable cars.

36

"C'mon, Pearl, we don't have all day."

Though Gene's voice hinted of teasing as much as impatience, Pearl shook off her wandering thoughts and scurried to join her cousin. Her empty lard pail, now filled with her lunch, bumped against her leg as she ran. They walked in focused silence the last few blocks, and after a half mile or so, Gene stopped.

"This is it."

Pearl gazed upon the four-story stone structure; its upper floor lined with high arching windows. In the corner of the school lot, an American flag waved from a pole a story taller than the school. She shook her head at the sight of the grandiose building. "I could never imagine a school this big. It looks like a castle."

"It should." Gene grinned. "It was modeled after the Petit Palais, built for a huge exposition in Paris, France, back in nineteen hundred."

"It's beautiful."

A sudden surge of students appeared and rushed toward the large wooden doors. Gene grabbed Pearl's arm and hurried her along. "We have to hurry, or we'll be late."

With a renewed sense of excitement, Pearl threw her shoulders back. Regardless of the building's overwhelming size and the large number of students, her confidence ballooned.

The marble floor gleamed, reflecting the illuminated bulbs overhead. Passing the open doors lining both sides of the hallway, Pearl peeked inside a room where neat rows of desks, many filled with eager boys and girls sat awaiting the start of the new school year. Pearl passed a large glass case with half a dozen trophies and photographs of both boys and girls in sports attire, posing proudly after their successes in football and basketball.

"That's last year's basketball team." Gene pointed to one of the taller boys standing in the back row. "That's me, right there."

Pearl leaned in to make out the small grainy figure from the photograph posted along the back of the case next to an orange pennant with large black letters spelling out "TIGERS," the team's name. On one side hung what appeared to be a girl's uniform, black baggy shorts, and an orange shirt with a black sailor tie and trim. "Do girls have a basketball team too?" Pearl's face brightened at the prospect so unlike her small-town school.

Gene bobbed his head. "The basketball team is fairly new, but if you're not interested in basketball, there are a lot of different clubs to join, including a mandolin club and the debate team. The school has a reputation for its varied curriculum."

On the opposite side of the trophy case was a boy's football uniform, with the same black and orange motif duplicated in the trousers and shirt and the name of the team mascot on the left chest.

"Wow." The opportunities available to her in this new city were unlike anything she had imagined. Though she had a lot to learn, Pearl was ready for the change, ready to forge her own path in life.

Chapter Seven

1906 – Christmas Holiday

As Christmas approached, Mother climbed to the attic and pulled out boxes of ornaments along with the porcelain angel for the top of the tree. Each day closer to Christmas meant one day closer to seeing Pearl. One morning, the sound of the eggbeater, clinking bowls, and banging cookie sheets, replaced the hum of Mother's sewing machine. Edna peeked into the kitchen, warmed with pleasing scents floating in the air. She scampered to her mother's side, her tummy anticipating the treats. "What are you making?"

"We have to churn butter before we can bake any cookies."

Edna furrowed her brow. She didn't much care for the taste of butter. But she liked to watch the sweet, thick, white cream that settled atop the milk as in transformed into butter, and most of all she loved the cookies made from the firm yellowy spread.

"The milkman has delivered today's milk along with extra cream. Do you want to help me fetch it?"

Edna followed her mother to the front porch, where she lifted the lid of the wood milk box and removed the wet gunny sacks used to keep the milk cool. She picked up a small glass bottle of cream from the crate and handed it to Edna. "Careful. Don't drop it." Next, she hoisted two heavy glass bottles out and returned to the kitchen. She poured the rich cream from the top of the milk bottles into a wooden drum sitting on the floor. "We must let the cream set a few hours to ripen. Then we can begin." Mother wiped her hands on her apron. "Run along and dress for the day. You can play until it's time to make the butter."

Two hours later, Mother stuck a long-handled wood spoon into the cream in the churn. She nodded with approval as she withdrew the spoon for Edna to see. "See how the cream is nice and thick?" She emptied the contents of Edna's smaller bottle into the churn. Then she placed the lid with its attached plunger, which looked like a long mop handle, on top. Mama gripped the handle and vigorously plunged the pole with the funny disc at the bottom, up and down, turning it as she worked. "Do you want to help?"

Edna climbed onto her stool and made a face. "I don't like butter."

"I know, but we need butter for the cookies, and I know you like cookies." Mama placed Edna's small hand over the handle. Together they lifted the plunger to the top before pushing it down. "After we make the butter, you can help me bake the cookies."

Within minutes, Edna's arm ached. And her hands hurt from Mother's hands over hers for so long. "I'm tired." Edna pulled away and rubbed her arms for a moment.

The cream slowly turned thick and thicker. Eventually, it separated into small balls of pale-yellow butter and thin cloudy buttermilk. At last, Mother declared it was ready. "Fetch me the cheesecloth and lay it over the bowl on the table."

Edna scampered to the counter and snatched the white airy cloth. She smoothed it over the rim of a large glass bowl on the table. Mother dumped the cream, now a solid but milky blob, onto the fabric. She lifted the cloth over the bowl and squeezed. A cloudy white liquid oozed from the cloth and dripped into the bowl.

Mother took the lump of firm light-yellow spread remaining in the cheesecloth. She held it under the faucet and pumped water over it to rinse the now solid mass of butter. "Now, for the easy part." Mother pressed the fresh butter into a wooden hinged box. "This is the mold to shape the butter into a cube for easy measuring. We're almost ready to begin baking." Mother walked to the kitchen sink, held one hand under the faucet as she pumped, and scrubbed the remnants of the thickened cream down the sink. She returned to the bowl of white liquid and poured a small bit into a glass. She handed the glass to Edna. "This is buttermilk or whey. It's what I use to make my buttermilk biscuits." Mother swirled the bowl before she poured the rest of the thin white liquid into the empty cream bottle and returned the buttermilk to the milk box on the front porch to keep it cool.

Edna sipped the buttermilk with a frown and swiped her mouth with her sleeve. "Yuck. It's sour." She pushed the glass away. "Can we make the cookies now?"

Mother sighed with a hint of a smile and pulled a brown hardcover book from the top shelf of her Hoosier. She plopped the book on the table and sat next to Edna. "What do you think we should make? I have my *Fannie Farmer* cookbook right here." Edna ran her fingers over the gold lettering and scrolling but couldn't read the names without any pictures to help. Mother thumbed through the pages of the big book then she stopped and jabbed her finger on a recipe. "Today, we are making Burrebrede like my mother used to make when I was your age."

Edna faltered as she repeated the odd-sounding word.

"Don't worry. You'll like them. They're Scottish shortbread." Mama dug into the drawer and fished out her measuring spoons. She placed the small spice jars on the counter. "Cinnamon, sugar, allspice, ginger, and cardamom." The spices tickled Edna's nostrils as her mother measured them and put half in a bigger bowl. She measured the softened butter and added it. Next, Mama measured out flour from the big steel bin underneath the Hoosier. She stirred the stiff dough with a wooden spoon and pressed it into a square cooking pan. Holding the bowl with the remaining spices, Mother handed Edna a spoon. "Would you like to sprinkle this on top?"

With great care, Edna spooned the rust-colored spices over the top of the shortbread dough. When she finished, she smiled, pleased with her contribution.

Mother returned the smile and slid the pan into the hot oven. "Remember, the cookstove is hot."

Licking the batter from the spoon, Edna batted her lashes at her mother.

"Yes, when they're done, you can have one before we store the rest in tins."

Edna rubbed her tummy. She hurried to get Molly, then sat by the oven and waited.

♪ ♪ ♪

Snowflakes danced on Edna's bedroom walls from the streams of light teasing through the patterns in the white lace curtains. Outside, big billowy flakes floated down for the third straight day, covering everything with a blanket of white. Edna ran into the kitchen in a panic. "Will Pearl make it home if it's snowing?"

"Of course, she will. The snow won't prevent the ship or stop your father and Nellie from going to town. Now run along and play. I've work to do."

Edna skipped off to entertain herself. In two days, Pearl would be home, and they would build a snowman. Throughout the day, Mother stoked the stove with dry wood to keep them warm through the long cold night. As bedtime approached, the wind howled and groaned. Eerie rattling sounds and creepy moans pierced the thin panes of glass, sending a shudder along Edna's back. Outside limbs cracked and thudded to the ground. She flung her arms around her mother for comfort.

"It's only the wind," Mama reassured her with a loving embrace. A moment later, without warning, the front door flung open. The door banged as it slammed against the wall. Mother flinched. With only one kerosene lamp lit, the room was cloaked in darkness, but a shadowy figure appeared in the doorway. Taken aback, Mother grabbed the old cornstalk broom by the stove and edged toward the front room. Edna cowered in the fabric of her mother's long dress Mother lunged toward the intruder with the broom lifted high overhead. "Get out!"

The man brought his hands to his head. At the same time, he cried out, "Stop, Abbey. It's me, George."

Her mother stopped and froze like the icicles hanging from the roof. She brought her hands to her mouth. Mother's tone softened. "My gracious. George?" She lowered the broom. A twinkle replaced the fear in her mother's eyes. The broom thudded to the floor. She rushed into the arms of the bulkily dressed lumberjack. "George. You startled me. I wasn't expecting you until tomorrow morning. I thought you were a stranger breaking in. What on earth?" She pulled away and studied him before bringing the back of her hand to his forehead. "You're pale and sweaty, burning with fever." Mother eased the heavy wool coat off Papa's shoulders and put her arm around him and coaxed him to the sofa.

Edna took the coat from her mother and watched with fear and confusion as her father dropped onto the cushioned seat.

"I'll be fine. I just need a hearty dinner and a hot bath. Got the chills. Been cold and snowy at the camp this week. Dropped below freezing some nights, and the water basin froze over. Boss said I wasn't much use to him anyway, might as well go home. So, here I am."

Mother disappeared to the bedroom and returned with the duvet from their bed. She wrapped the down-filled throw around her husband. "Rest. You can bathe after dinner. I'll make you a cup of tea."

Papa managed a tired smile and winked at his daughter. Edna knew he always preferred a hard cider when he came home, but he nodded as Mama rushed to the kitchen. Edna cuddled next to him and touched his red cheek. His sweaty skin warmed her even through the scratchy whiskers, "I'm glad you're home. I missed you." Despite the chill and the wind beating on the house, Edna would sleep soundly with her Papa home and Pearl coming the next day.

The next morning the smell of freshly brewed coffee tickled Edna's nose. Mama didn't drink coffee, so Edna knew her father was feeling better. She ran to the kitchen.

Her father sat at the table, sipping from his favorite mug. "I'm guessing you want to go with me to pick up Pearl?"

Edna cocked her head. "I thought you were sick."

Mama placed a plate of toast and eggs in front of Edna. "I can't convince him to stay in bed another day. Insists he's going into town to meet Pearl, so we're all going."

Edna's eyes sparkled like the light dancing off the delicate strands of tinsel she helped Mama hang so carefully on the boughs of the tree in the corner of their sitting room. Tomorrow was Christmas Day. The whole family would be together again. After four long months of waiting to see her sister, Pearl would be home for two weeks. Edna gobbled her breakfast and rushed to dress for the joyous reunion.

Mama pulled open the oven and withdrew a metal box filled with hot stones.

The door thumped open. Papa pulled out a handkerchief from the pocket of his bibbed overalls and wiped the sweat from his brow. "Nellie's bridled. You womenfolk ready?"

Mama studied him and again put her hand on his forehead. "Are you sure you're well enough to go to town?"

Papa waved Mama off with a gloved hand. "I'm fine." He sniffed and swiped his perspiration with his jacket sleeve.

Mother shook her head in surrender and grabbed the coats. Outside, Nellie, pranced in place, ready to go. Mama placed the metal box on the floor in the back and climbed in beside Edna. "This will keep us warm during the long ride."

Father flicked the reins, and Nellie trotted along the snow-covered road. Edna shivered and shrank into her coat, running her feet over the heated stones. At last, the waterfront and the Southworth Ferry dock came into view. Gazing east across the dark, murky water, Edna watched as the white pointy hull of the vessel chugged, chugged, closer and closer. She bounced in her seat. Excitement tingled down her spine. "I see it. I see the boat."

From the black pipe, steam spit high into the winter wind before vanishing into the low looming gray clouds. Father pulled the buggy next to the livery stable and climbed down to settle with the livery owner. When he returned, Mama stepped down and lifted Edna to the ground. The man led Nellie away to the barn to be fed and watered before the ride back. In her eagerness, Mama hurried ahead. Edna took her father's hand and followed her mother toward the wharf. By the time the family reached the pier, the steamship had docked. Deckhands leaped from the deck and skillfully tied the boat to the pylons. Edna peered over the metal railing and watched the passengers as they stepped off the boat onto the wooden gangway. Mama stood silent, hands over her mouth. Papa looked deep in concentration as he scoured the ever-growing crowd of people scurrying off the boat and up the planks to those awaiting their arrival.

The last time Edna was at the dock, she'd come to say goodbye to her sister. Today the *Athlon* had returned her sister home. "Is that her?" Edna squealed and pointed toward the disembarking travelers.

A slender figure with a gray coat and purple tam lifted her arm and waved. Her voice carried above the commotion from others gathered on the dock. "Papa, Mama, Edna!"

Edna waved her arms in the air. "I see her. Pearl's here." Edna started off in a run.

Her mother reached out to stop her. "Hold on. She'll be here soon enough."

The moment Pearl stepped off the gangway, she rushed to her family. Dropping her case, she flung herself into her sister's waiting arms.

A hint of a smile escaped from behind her Papa's dark bushy beard. He took Pearl's lone suitcase. "How was the crossing?"

"Not too rough, Papa. I've missed you and Mother so much."

Mother kissed Pearl on the cheek. "It's been quiet without you. The piano has sat silent since you left. I trust you'll play a Christmas tune or two for us this evening."

Edna studied her sister. She looked different. Older. Edna hoped she wasn't too old to color or read to her or to sing songs together. Being next to Pearl warmed Edna. She wouldn't need the lap blanket on the way home or the hot stones. Edna reached deep into her coat pocket and held out a cookie.

"What's this?" Pearl's eyes sparkled at the sight of the round sugar-coated delight. "One of Mother's snickerdoodles?"

Edna brought her index finger to her lips and glanced at her mother. She swallowed a giggle and kept her voice low. "I saved it from last night."

Father strode to the livery while the women waited. As soon as Nellie trotted up, the mare greeted Pearl with a whinny, and in response, Pearl pushed the horse's forelock from its face before she climbed into the buggy next to Edna. "I can't wait to see the Christmas tree and eat Mama's goodies."

"Mama made mincemeat pie with raisins and beef and suet." Edna made a face, and they both giggled.

Less than an hour later, Nellie stopped in front of the house. Pearl gazed out across their small farm and frost-covered barren field where wheat and corn grew in the spring. "It's so quiet and peaceful here compared to Seattle."

The women climbed from the buggy, and Pearl collected her bag. She reached over and scooped a clump of snow, then tossed it. "Tomorrow, we can make a snowman."

Edna jumped up and down. "I've been waiting for you to make a snowman."

While Papa led Nellie to the barn, Edna followed Pearl inside. The tree dominated the corner of the front room where the sideboard had been pushed aside to make room. Pearl gazed at the fresh gingerbread men and the shimmery tinsel. "It's beautiful." She caressed the ornaments hand-painted with bright red poinsettias, Santa Claus, and holly, that hung from small hooks on the fir scented boughs as if it were the first time, she had seen them. "These stars Mama made from colored beads are still my favorite." Pearl inhaled. She grabbed her suitcase and headed to the bedroom. "I've missed home so much."

"Do you have your own room at Auntie's, like I do? Edna climbed onto her bed. She sat cross-legged and watched Pearl unpack her things.

"Yes. It's nice, and they have indoor plumbing, and the bathroom is right down the hall from my bedroom. No more outhouse and no walking outside into the cold late at night and no pages from Sears and Roebuck."

Edna's eyes narrowed in a questioning look. She pulled a face of disgust. "What do you use?"

Pearl laughed. "Toilet paper. Soft white sheets, which we flush away down the drain into a sewer."

"Really? Do you think someday we'll have an indoor toilet?"

"Of course. Many of the homes in the city already have indoor toilets and washbasins. Uncle Leland says it won't be long before every house in America has indoor plumbing."

With the entire family gathered around the dinner table for the first time in months, Edna beamed, captivated by her sister's stories about the enormous school, which held ten times more students than the small schoolhouse in town, and about living in the city with all its modern buildings and inventions.

"There are electric light poles along the main streets and even in some of the neighborhoods. Uncle Leland says they're getting electricity in their home soon."

46

Edna wasn't sure how electricity worked, but from her mother's wide eyes and her father's raised brows, she knew it was important.

Her mother whispered. "Can you imagine? One light bulb and the whole room will be bright. George, have you heard of when we'll be getting electricity in Port Orchard?"

Father scratched his chin through his beard. "The guys at the Grange figure it's a way off. Reckon this town has a bit more growing to do before Kitsap County has the tax base needed to install all the electrical poles and run all those miles of electrical lines."

Her father gazed at Pearl while rubbing his chin. "I've read about the kinetoscope or motion pictures Mr. Edison is inventing. You got any of those moving pictures yet in Seattle?"

Pearl shook her head. "Not yet, lots of theater houses for silent films and vaudeville acts, though."

Her mother brought her hand to her mouth in shock. "Vaudeville? How scandalous."

"Don't worry, Mother. Nothing like you're thinking. No burlesque or anything so racy. Though I haven't been yet, the shows at the Olympic Theatre contain acrobats and singers and lots of animal acts."

"What kind of animal acts?"

"All sorts. I saw a poster with a dog jumping rope and a monkey on roller skates. Even miniature ponies."

A slight chuckle emerged from her father's buried smile. "I'll be. Now that would be something worth paying to see. A monkey on roller skates."

Pearl grabbed her father's arm. "Promise you'll come and visit sometime. I'm sure Auntie and Uncle would take all of us to the theater for a show."

"Please, Papa. May we?" Edna's head bobbed as if on a spring. "Pleeease."

Her father raised his hands, palms up, in defeat. "We'll see. Maybe when Pearl returns to school we can all go to town and attend a vaudeville act."

Mother shook her head looking unconvinced. She finished her bite and nodded with resigned enthusiasm. "I suppose we could go sometime. Marie is always after me to come for a visit." She looked at Pearl. "You haven't told us how your studies are going."

Pearl's eyes brightened. "I love the city. School is difficult, but I'm doing well. I'll receive my grades right after the break."

Mama smiled. "Have you given any thought to what you want to do with your life?"

Pushing her plate aside, Pearl leaned forward. "I met a doctor on the *Athlon*. He said I should think about continuing my education and attending the university so I can become a nurse."

"The university?" Papa scratched his beard. "I don't know. Sounds expensive. I'm not sure how we will manage that."

Mama waved off his worry. "That's a lofty goal, but there's plenty of time to plan for the future."

"Gene's going to the University of Washington. He wants to be a doctor. Doctor Chapman said the medical field is going to be important in the future. He said these days girls can be anything. Even a doctor."

"Can you imagine, George? We could have a doctor and a nurse in the family."

♪ ♪ ♪

When morning came, Edna bounced up. "Are you awake? It's Christmas Day."

Pearl stirred and mumbled. "I am now." They climbed from their beds, grabbed their slippers and robes, and dashed out to the front room. With the heavy, dark drapes pulled back, daylight reflected off the delicate blown-glass orbs hanging from the boughs of the tree.

"Santa's been here." Edna clapped her hands as she stared at the boxes wrapped in brightly colored green and red papers covered with holiday designs. Fallen fir needles lay sprinkled over the wood-planked floor and scattered packages were adorned with sprigs of holly or brightly tied raffia ribbons or satin ribbons leftover from Mother's sewing projects. Edna's gaze focused on a square box, the most decorated gift of all. She started to reach for it but thought better of it when she saw Papa, who was seated in his chair, dip his chin to his chest and peer over the tip of his pipe.

"When can we open our presents?"

Mother floated into the room dressed in a fitted deep-crimson dress of patterned brocade. "You know that we attend services at the Methodist church on Christmas morning to celebrate the birth of the Christ child." She peeked over her spectacles. "You girls run along and get dressed. Papa, it's almost time to get Nellie ready."

Papa sighed, tapped his pipe empty, and headed for the door.

♪ ♪ ♪

Edna and Pearl made a beeline for the door as soon as Nellie came to a halt. Her mother called out to them. "Wait until everyone is inside. I don't want to see any gifts opened until your father and I are seated."

Edna and Pearl threw their coats on the coat tree and sat in front of the tree. Mother fueled the wood stove and handed out cups of homemade eggnog, including one for Papa, which Edna knew had brandy added to it. Once Father was seated and nodded his approval, Mother handed her the square box. Edna tore at the paper decorated with sprigs of holly.

"What is it?" Pearl leaned closer to peek.

Edna freed the unwrapped gift and placed it on her lap. She took hold of the handle and lifted the top off a woven basket. Inside, the basket was lined with the same cotton print as one of her pinafore aprons. With a grin she showed off a small pair of scissors, a red pincushion shaped like a tomato, and several spools of thread. Edna fumbled inside the basket for a moment, then with a thimble on her pointer finger, she held it out for all to see. "Look, my very own sewing basket. Now I can sew clothes for Molly."

"There's another present." Papa pointed toward the back of the tree.

Hidden behind the lowest boughs, a box wrapped in shimmery white paper and adorned with a big fancy bow looked to Edna like a store-bought present. She studied the script letters on the tag and sounded them out. She squealed, "It's from Santa Claus." Edna grabbed the box and shook it.

"Open it." Pearl pleaded.

Freeing the box of its paper, Edna placed it on the floor and pried open the folded top. She plunged her hand inside and withdrew the

49

soft cuddly gift. "It's a stuffed bear." Edna clutched the golden-colored bear to her chest.

Papa beamed. "I hope you like it. It's called a teddy bear, named after our president, Theodore Roosevelt."

"I love it! Thank you."

Mama urged Pearl to gather her gifts.

Looking under the tree, Pearl found two gifts with small tags bearing her name. "I'm sorry I didn't have a chance to make anything for any of you." She picked up the boxes and slid back next to Edna.

Mama scooted closer. "Don't worry. Papa and I know you are busy with your studies. Completing your education is the most important thing for you to do right now."

Pearl unwrapped her first gift and held up a new composition book. Unwrapping her second gift, Pearl squealed.

Papa leaned in and rested his hands on his knees. "Those are Joseph Gillott pens from England; best dip pens and nibs made. Ordered them special for you." He looked down his pipe. "I trust you'll put them to good use."

Pearl's voice shook as she rushed to her father's side and gave his shoulders a quick hug. "Thank you, Mama, and Papa. I promise. I won't let you down."

Chapter Eight

1907 – Luna Park

Onboard the *Athlon* returning to Seattle for her second year of school, Pearl stood on the deck as she had the previous September. No longer the insecure fourteen-year-old, today as she waved goodbye to her family, she stood tall, eager to start school again. Her tough first year behind her, Pearl now had new confidence and friends who shared her dream of something more than marriage and a family. She suspected many of her new friends would have exciting summertime adventures to share with her while all she did all summer was chores and help Mama mend clothes. Her most exciting adventure of the summer was a visit to the new Athletic Club which had opened recently in town but didn't even have a swimming pool.

Pearl drew her shawl around her and looked back one last time in the direction of home. Nearly dusk, the sky glowed peach and pink, muted by the cloud of steam from the large smokestack.

"Nice night." An older gentleman tipped his hat to her as he passed, his cane tapping on the teak deck. As the steamer approached downtown Seattle, passengers spilled onto the bow, their hushed *oohs* and *aahs* filling the air. A small crowd stood pointing toward the shore. Pearl turned her gaze to follow theirs across Elliot Bay to the southeast. As spectacular as the sunset was, she was unprepared for the sight onshore. Like sparkling diamonds against the tawny dusk of night, spires and towers stood aglow, draped with strings of lights. A display of twinkling decorations unlike anything Pearl had ever seen lit the night and reflected off the dark waters of the bay. "Wow. What is that?"

A fellow passenger pointing off in the direction of the display responded. "You don't know? That's Luna Park, the biggest amusement park in Seattle."

Pearl remembered the articles in the daily *Post-Intelligencer* last May about the new park opening soon on Alki Point.

"They say Luna Park rivals Coney Island in New York with lots of new-fangled thrill rides and a boardwalk."

She nodded. "I read about it last spring when I was in Seattle. The paper wrote it was going to be the biggest attraction to hit Seattle since the flurry of the Klondike gold rush."

Spying her luggage, the gentleman nodded. "Looks like you're staying in the city?"

"Yes, I'm staying with my aunt and uncle while I attend my second year at Seattle High."

The passenger nodded his approval. "You need to ask your kin to take you if they can."

Pearl knew Gene was excited to go. She guessed he had urged his parents to let him go with his friends shortly after it opened in late June. She hoped she would have the opportunity to experience all the thrills promised in the paper's photographs and articles.

Unable to take her eyes off the distant wonderland, Pearl nodded. "I hope I can go soon."

"Well, miss, I hope so too. I'm sure you'll have lots of fun. There's plenty to keep you busy, lots of food and rides. You can see the roller coaster from here." He pointed out in the direction of the park. "They also have a water slide and the biggest natatorium you've ever seen."

Pearl raised her hand to shield her eyes from the reflection of the setting sun on the rippling waves and stared at the pier that stretched out over the water. The figure eight of the roller coaster, illuminated with lights, appeared in the distance. Its track climbed skyward, beckoning both those on land and those on the sea to experience all the park offered. The ship made a sharp turn, and the lights of Luna Park disappeared behind her. The familiar Colman Dock came into view. The boat glided smoothly into its slip. Pearl bade goodbye to her fellow traveler, got in line to disembark, and soon spied her cousin waving at the end of the dock.

Gene ran toward her. "Let me take your suitcase."

A few steps later, Uncle Leland joined. "Welcome back. How was the trip?"

Not wishing to sound nervy, Pearl bit her lip. She remembered her mother's rules on etiquette and held back her desire to see Luna Park. "It was fine. Thank you, Uncle." She handed her other suitcase to her uncle but couldn't resist turning her head to stare off in the direction of the park.

Gene tipped his head and narrowed his eyes as he watched her. "You saw it, didn't you? I can tell. Your eyes are as big as the nightlights on the promenade. You saw the lights of Luna Park from the boat."

Unable to hide her excitement, Pearl stopped walking. "Is it as big as it seemed from the boat?' She glanced back and forth between her uncle and her cousin. "Have you been?"

Gene's grin gave away his answer. "It's the biggest amusement park I've ever seen. Twelve acres. I went opening day with three of my friends, but my parents said when you got here, we'd all go again."

"Do you mean it, Uncle?" Pearl nearly jumped out of her boots.

"Of course. Hopefully, the crowds have died down with summer over and the opening weeks behind us. We can go later this month when I have a Saturday off."

♪ ♪ ♪

Two days later, eager to see her friends again, Pearl rushed out the door ahead of Gene. Dozens of students gathered outside the school doors talking about their summer break, with almost everyone talking about the amazing park. She felt she must be the only one in the school who hadn't visited Luna Park since opening day on June twenty-seventh. Maybe the only one in the whole Seattle school district.

A month after Pearl arrived, Uncle Leland announced they would spend the following Saturday at Luna Park. Saturday morning, Pearl sprang out of bed and dressed in her Napoleon-blue day skirt. Mother had sewn a large ruffle across the bottom of the loosely pleated skirt, mainly to increase the length to make up for the two inches Pearl had grown over the summer. Pearl smoothed her ruffled white cotton blouse with balloon sleeves. She admired her reflection in the mirror, confident that she appeared mature, with the addition of the sash completing the de rigueur of the times.

Aunt Marie poked her head into the room. "I've got towels, but don't forget your swimsuit. I am looking forward to a dip in the warm salt water."

Pearl rummaged through her drawer, thankful for the foresight to bring swimwear. She dashed to the front room. Her aunt stood posed by the door, wearing a fitted waistcoat and a wide-brimmed green hat swathed in tulle, with a forest green-feather curling from the side.

Uncle Leland, with his hands on his hips, nodded. "It appears everyone is ready." He opened the door, and the family paraded out for the short stroll to the trolley stop at Terrace and Broadway. Less than fifteen minutes later, the family stood with others, near Second and Cherry underneath the "LUNA PARK" sign. Moments later, trolley number thirty-five pulled to a stop in front of them. An advertisement reading "At Luna Park Today." was affixed to the streetcar's cowcatcher. Eager and impatient, Pearl squirmed on the uncomfortable wooden seat. She looked out the streetcar window as it traveled along Spokane Street and across the bay's tide flats before it rattled to a stop at the gate to Luna Park.

Scores of riders stepped off the trolley to be greeted by the cheerful chirping of the calliope pipes from the carousel inside the park. Holding firmly to the bag carrying her funds and swim attire, Pearl felt her eyes widen at the sight of the rides and amusements spread from one end of the pier to the other. She pushed close to her relatives as the hordes of men, women, and families, all dressed in their Sunday best, moved like a school of darting fish toward the white cone-shaped double entrance with lavish trim and a large cutout heart atop the scrolled letters spelling out *LUNA PARK*. Pearl's heartbeat quickened, and her mouth watered at the scent of the hearty ten-cent roast beef sandwiches all her friends insisted she try, along with the sweet sugary confections of cotton candy and ice cream she'd splurge on. She opened her pocketbook and fingered her funds for the day.

Uncle Leland stepped ahead to the ticket taker, who stood beneath a row of flags and banners. "Admission for four." He paid the ten-cent admission for each of them, even though Pearl insisted she had adequate money. "I'll cover your admission. You can pay for any rides or amusements."

Pearl thanked him and entered the park. On the left, a broad sign with bold letters announced "The Canals of Venice." In the background, music echoing from a tall bandstand was almost drowned out by the clanging cars rolling over the roller-coaster tracks; the bells, buzzers, and bellowing coming from the busy midway; and the carnival barkers loudly hawking their wares.

Gene fixed his eyes on his father. "Please, Dad, may Pearl and I go on our own? We can meet later at the natatorium and have lunch together."

Aunt Marie pursed her lips. "Tsk. It's a shame there's still such a crowd."

"Please, Aunt Marie, we'll stay together." Pearl brought her hands together in a prayerful plea.

"It's all right with me." Pearl's uncle raised his hand to shoo the two off. "Be in front of the natatorium precisely at noon."

Aunt Marie huffed. "I insist we eat before we go swimming. I don't want to go to the pool until we're done with everything else we want to do." She surveyed the sight. "As I remember, there are tables near the café. We shall meet there, have lunch, and after sufficient time, we can go to the swimming hall before we return home."

Pearl clapped her hands. She thanked her aunt and uncle as Gene tugged on her arm to follow him. She shot a glance around the entire amusement area from one ride to the next with signs identifying them including, "The Cave of Mystery" and the "Giant Whirl," along with a giant swing.

"First—" Gene pulled her away and headed left— "we are going down the "Shoot the Chutes." It's the most fun."

Several dozen people of all ages stood in line, animated and eager for their turn to board the boat and race down the two-hundred-foot-long wood-framed track.

The ride attendant directed Gene and Pearl forward. "Next."

Pearl held out her ticket to the young man. He cocked his head and studied her for a moment while taking the red ticket from her. "You go to Seattle High, don't you?"

"Uh-huh." Her heart fluttered. "My name's Pearl."

The young man's dark eyes sparkled as he gazed directly into her eyes. "I'm Stanley. I've seen you around campus." He nodded toward the waiting gondola, then helped them into their seats. Four other riders were already seated. "Have a fun ride," he said.

As the car jerked ahead, Pearl thought she heard Stanley call out something at the last moment. In a flash the car bolted down the track. Pearl's heart leaped to her throat as she heard the screams from the riders. The entire ride lasted only a matter of seconds before the boat flew off the track, momentarily traveled airborne, and splashed into a large pool. Pearl and Gene roared with laughter as a refreshing spray of water splashed across them and the other riders.

Gene stepped off the ride. "Well? What did you think?"

With her chest pounding a bit quicker than usual, Pearl gasped through her heavy breathing, "It was fun. Can we go again?"

Gene hesitated with a dubious smile. "Are you sure it's only because of the ride?" He raised his eyebrows and flashed a goofy grin.

Pearl's face flushed. She turned away. The fluttering in her chest slowed, but Gene had guessed right. As thrilling as the ride had been, she wanted even more was another chance to see Stanley. She had to know if the final look he gave her was a wink.

Two hours later, the duo found a free table near the concessions. Tired, hungry, and thirsty, Pearl was ready for a break. She surveyed the food concessions and located the Summer Garden Restaurant advertising roast-beef sandwiches for a dime. Pearl knew she had burned through at least a dollar, including buying a photo postcard to send home. The photo showed their heads atop a line-drawing of a man and woman's body on a slide. The lettering read, Shooting the Chutes at Luna Park. Pearl quickly decided no matter how much she had to sacrifice for the rest of the school quarter, she would remember this day forever, and she would splurge on fairy floss before the day was over.

When her aunt and uncle met up with them, everyone agreed upon the roast-beef sandwiches. Uncle Leland went to purchase them along with sodas and iced tea. After eating, Marie reminded them it was wise to wait before swimming, so no one got stomach cramps. Among the many exhibits, a large sign hung across the entrance to a small building. "Infant Electrobator, Admission Free." Intrigued, Pearl asked if they could go inside. A small crowd gathered around an enclosed metal box with glass doors. Pearl stood on her toes to peer around the taller visitors and was shocked to see a newborn baby inside, tightly wrapped in blankets and asleep. "What is that?"

Aunt Marie put her arm around her niece, "It's another name for an incubator. It is used to keep premature babies warm until they grow stronger."

Pearl pointed to the small, enclosed structure. "I wish I could open the door and hold the baby. Wouldn't that be better than leaving the baby in a box?"

Her aunt smiled. "It sounds like you love babies as much as I do. Have you thought about becoming a midwife? I remember how much help you were when I delivered your sister."

Watching the helpless baby, Pearl recalled her sister's birth and the scare of the breech delivery. Her thoughts about becoming a nurse intensified. She shook her head. "Maybe, but I've been thinking of becoming a nurse. I think I would make a good nurse."

"That's a lofty goal. I'm proud of you. I'm sure you'll make a fine nurse someday."

Pearl whispered goodbye to the infant and Gene directed all of them to the end of the pier. "This is where the daredevil acts take place." A sandwich board heralded the show of the day, "Slide for Life." The signage proclaimed a man would slide down a seven-hundred-foot cable, hanging by his teeth.

"That's impossible. It would rip his teeth out." Pearl stared at the high tower. The stuntman, barely visible, stood at the edge of the platform, peering down at the gathering crowd.

Uncle Leland chuckled. "He doesn't really hang by his teeth. He bites down on a leather bit with a small pulley attached. The pully is clipped to the cable."

Pearl shook her head as she stared up as high as a skyscraper. "That still sounds dangerous to me."

An announcer on a megaphone directed all eyes upward. The crowd stood, mouths agape. Every woman and child held their hands over their mouths in a united gasp. Pearl held her breath, certain the performer would drop to the unprotected ground below. But several long seconds later, the crowd burst into loud cheers and wild applause as he landed on his feet at the end of the rope only twenty feet or so from where they were standing.

Pearl applauded until her hands stung. She couldn't wait to tell her parents and Edna about her day.

"Well," Aunt Marie stammered as she held her right hand across her chest. "That was about as much excitement as I can take. It's getting late. Is everyone ready for a refreshing saltwater dip?"

The previous year Pearl had gone with several of her classmates from Seattle High to the indoor saltwater pool at Alki Point, but Pearl was unprepared for the vastness of this new building. Inside, three pools greeted guests; two huge saltwater pools fed directly by Elliott Bay and one freshwater pool. Overhead, a second-floor gallery circled the pools for easy viewing by spectators.

"Hurry and change into your swimsuit, Pearl." Gene pointed out the women's and girls' changing rooms as he and his father veered the opposite way to their appropriate dressing rooms.

Marie headed into the changing room, and Pearl rushed after her. Within minutes she found herself splashing in the largest swimming tank in the Northwest.

♪ ♪ ♪

Even though practically everyone in the school had previously visited the park, Pearl couldn't wait to tell her classmates about her experience. She wondered if Gene had told his mother about Stanley. Since her aunt hadn't broached the subject during breakfast, Pearl breathed easier with her romantic thoughts still private.

Giddy with the memory of Stanley's smile, Pearl couldn't stop thinking about the first boy who had caught her eye. Knowing he attended Seattle High made it difficult for her to concentrate throughout the day. During mathematics, she drew a disapproving scowl from her teacher and an embarrassing sharp verbal warning to get her head out of the clouds. In six months, she'd turn fifteen. Would her mother and father allow her to date? At every opportunity between classes, she glanced down the hall. While she ate her lunch, her mind wandered from the conversation with her friends as she scanned the spacious dining room, hoping for a chance to see him.

"Who are you looking for?" Maeve eyed her with a sly smile.

Pearl wanted to tell her best friend about Stanley, but the chance encounter was short. Maybe he extended the same smile to all the patrons as simply part of his job. Pearl's insides whirled and swirled like cream in a butter churn. The grins on the faces of her friends informed Pearl they suspected something was up.

Too self-conscious to let on, Pearl played coy. "No one. Just looking around." No boy had ever expressed interest in her before, and in grammar school, she'd never been interested in anyone. But with only four boys in her graduating class, all friends from the first grade, there was little likelihood of anything more than friendship. Her friends shrugged off Pearl's response and returned to their lunches. For the first time in her life, Pearl considered her appearance and wondered if she was attractive enough to draw the attention of a boy. Glancing at her friends, Pearl felt a twinge of envy over Maeve's latest new outfit and her porcelain complexion and perfect nose. Pearl ran her fingers through her blonde hair; thick and curly, it was the one feature she felt confident drew the jealousy of others.

By the time the final bell rang, Pearl had convinced herself the young man's smile meant nothing. Disheartened, she shuffled her way across the dirt ball field, kicking up dust. She was upset over wasting the day thinking about the meaningless encounter. At the sound of her name called from behind her, Pearl's heart somersaulted.

"Wait up, Pearl."

Pearl chewed on her lip. She recognized the familiar voice and hesitated before she turned around coming almost face to face with Stanley, mere feet away. "Hello." Pearl held her enthusiasm, trying to not come across as eager and easy.

Stanley shifted his weight and glanced at his feet as he drew zigzags in the dirt with his shoe. "Hi. I was wondering..."

Pearl refrained from smiling, but a warm flush spread across her cheeks as she waited for the awkward young man to finish talking.

Stanley took a deep breath, looked into Pearl's eyes, and continued, "I-I w-was wondering"— his tone was shifting from high to low like an out of pitch piano—"if you would like to go to the nickelodeon with me?" He blushed at the sound of his cracking voice. "Unless you have a boyfriend."

"A boyfriend?" She brought her hand to her mouth to muffle her giggle. "No. That was my cousin with me."

Stanley's head jerked upward; his eyes animated. "The Crystal Theatre downtown on Second Avenue has vaudeville on Saturday evenings. Do you think your parents will let you go?" His nerves showed as he shifted his weight back and forth again.

"Vaudeville? I don't know. I'm not sure what that is."

"Oh." Stanley flushed a bit. "It's nothing inappropriate. Live theater, mostly comedy at the Crystal Theatre."

"I, uh, would like to go with you. I live with my aunt and uncle right now while I attend school. I'll have to ask them."

"Do they live nearby? I can walk you home so you can ask."

From behind her, someone called her name. She turned around to see Gene approaching. Pearl noticed her cousin's wrinkled forehead as he sized Stanley up.

Sensing Gene's concern, Stanley greeted Gene with an outstretched hand. "Stanley Rosenberg. I'm a junior here at Seattle High. I met you at Luna Park on the Chute the Shoots."

Accepting the greeting, Gene nodded. "I remember. I'm Pearl's cousin, Gene. What are you two talking about?"

Uncertain whether to be angry at Gene's nosiness or pleased by the chivalrous act of a big brother, Pearl pushed her resentment aside. She stiffened and clutched her books to her chest. "Stanley has asked me to go to the nickelodeon with him. Do you think it will be okay?"

Gene studied Stanley with greater intensity before he rubbed his chin and bobbed his head. "I suppose, but my parents will want to meet you first."

♪ ♪ ♪

The next evening Pearl paced around the house with her stomach turning topsy-turvy until her aunt accused her of wearing out the rug and suggested she sit down and relax. Her mouth dry, Pearl second-guessed her decision to allow Stanley to come calling. She'd never been alone with a young man, and she had no idea what to expect at her first vaudeville show. A sudden urge to flee overcame her.

"I thought your young man was coming at six o'clock?" Uncle Leland glanced at the grandfather clock in the parlor as the brass pendulum bonged the first of six chimes. "He's late."

Aunt Marie frowned at her spouse. She glanced over at Pearl. "Never mind him. I'm sure your young man will be here shortly."

A minute later, a firm knock at the door signaled Stanley's arrival. Uncle Leland held up his finger and went to answer the door. As instructed, Pearl stayed seated on the sofa in the front room along with her aunt. Pearl heard the voices but couldn't make out the conversation. Finally, Stanley ambled into the room. He introduced himself to Aunt Marie before he turned and acknowledged his date. Pearl looked to her aunt for permission before she disappeared to fetch her coat. She handed her wrap to Stanley, who assisted her in putting it on before leading her to the door.

"Be sure to have her home by nine o'clock." Uncle Leland's tone left no room for negotiation.

Stanley stiffened in military-like posture, his words clipped and formal. "Yes, sir."

Pearl hid her disappointment. Nine o'clock sounded a bit early. She wondered if they'd have to leave before the final curtain. It didn't matter. Pearl was over the clouds with giddiness and grinned the entire way to the trolley stop.

♪ ♪ ♪

Walking down Second Avenue toward Pioneer Square to catch the trolley after the theater, Pearl's mind was in the clouds. Life in Seattle was exciting and invigorating compared to life in Port Orchard. Light posts along Second Avenue illuminated Pioneer Square where Pearl spied the familiar totem pole. She grabbed Stanley's hand and hurried toward it. "My aunt and uncle brought me here when I first arrived in Seattle." Noticing men walking east toward colorful signs with lights overhead, Pearl started off in their direction. "Is there another theater over there?" She tipped her head to a boisterous crowd loitering outside a building where several women had gathered and shimmied up next to some men.

Stanley spun Pearl around. "I hear that's the seedy part of town. The ladies from church are always trying to save the souls of these people." He pulled her back toward Second Avenue.

Pearl looked back over her shoulder to see a woman running her hand through a man's hair before taking his hand and disappearing into one of the brick buildings. "Save their souls from what?"

Stanley shook his head, "It's called the Tenderloin District."

Puzzled, Pearl cocked her head. "What's does that mean?"

Her date's eyes darted up and down the street. He cupped his hand to his mouth. "This is where the brothels are. Despite the best efforts of the Christian women's groups, Seattle is almost as famous for its brothels as its rain. Your aunt and uncle would frown upon us going that way." He grasped Pearl's hand. "Come on; we need to go. I see the trolley coming."

Chapter Nine

1908 – Conflict

Since her first date with Stanley, Pearl had struggled to keep her focus on her studies. She wondered briefly if she should have transferred to the new high school in Bremerton to be closer to her parents and Edna, but the daily commute would limit her study time and the modest stipend paid to her aunt and uncle was far less than room and board would be living in Bremerton. Pearl continually had to remind herself of her obligation to complete her education. Miss Ambrose's words replayed in her head. She owed it to herself as well as her parents and even her aunt and uncle who had opened their home to her. Though she ached to see her parents and her sister again after so many months away, as summer approached, Pearl's mind wandered to lazy summer days lying underneath the trees in Volunteer Park or holding hands with Stanley as they strolled along the downtown waterfront. When he begged her to stay a few extra weeks after the end of the school year before returning home, the temptation tugged at her.

During the last week of classes, Aunt Marie pulled Pearl aside. "I need to talk with you."

Her aunt's pursed lips and tight face sent a shudder bulleting down Pearl's spine. Her chest tightened. She fell into a chair across from her aunt while Marie unfolded two lavender sheets of paper and pushed them across the table. Pearl recognized the stationery.

"I've received a letter from your mother. Your father is quite ill. Suffering long bouts of pneumonia."

Through a parched throat, Pearl's words came in a whisper. "Is he going to be okay?"

"He's not been to work for the past week, and the doctor's ordered him to bed rest." Avoiding Pearl's gaze, Aunt Marie brushed away crumbs from the table. Her voice softened. "With the ever-growing fear of tuberculosis...." Aunt Marie looked away as her words faded.

"Tuberculosis?" Scarcely able to speak, Pearl swallowed.

Her aunt shook her head, then reached out and grasped Pearl's hand. "Even the doctor can't be certain it's TB. But your father's lost weight and has been feeling unwell for some time. He has a fever and is tired all the time. If it clears up soon, it means it was only influenza."

Pearl's nasal passages burned; her body crumpled. She closed her eyes and buried her face in her hands. In the darkness, her mind dismissed her earlier imaginings of days spent with Stanley. Of walks, picnics, and tender displays of affection. Mama and Papa needed her. Edna needed her. And her family was more important than anything else.

The next day Pearl waited for Stanley at the bottom of the school steps. Clouds glided past in the calm blue overhead, shifting shapes with the subtle changes of the wind. Next week Pearl would attend Gene's graduation, and in the fall, he would start his classes at the University of Washington with plans to study medicine. Next year, Stanley would graduate and face his future. Soon, it would be her turn. It seemed only months ago she'd stepped onto the *Athlon*, a scared schoolgirl; nearly two years later, she had matured. Her hopes and dreams were more defined, almost tangible enough for her to reach out and touch them. Like the clouds, the direction of her life, too, could be altered by circumstances. She worried about her father. What if he was unable to return to work? Would she have to give up school and her dreams, and get a job to help support the family?

She looked at the sky again. The small puffy cotton-ball clouds had merged into one whopping billowy pile of batting. She hoped someday, like the clouds, all the fragments of her dreams could merge. How could she pursue her education, have a career and still be a mother, if her father couldn't work? What would the family do for income? She wanted to have it all. She hugged herself, comforted by the thought any goals would come in small achievements.

Stanley's voice jolted Pearl from her daydream. "Have you given any more thought to staying here for a couple extra weeks?"

She forced a smile and blinked away the dreamy thoughts of their summer together. "I can't. My father is sick. I've got to return to help my family."

♪ ♪ ♪

The day after school was out, Pearl hugged Gene goodbye. She wished him well with his summer job.

Gene raised his chin and puffed his chest. "I'm fortunate to have found a position working in a medical lab, even if it is cleaning and washing beakers. It will familiarize me with the medical equipment and assist with my tuition in the fall." He shuffled and shifted a bit before leaning in with a hug. "Send your parents, especially your father, my best wishes." He grabbed her bags. "I'll get these for you."

With a handkerchief, Marie dabbed her cheeks. "Goodbye, dear. I'm sure things will work out and we'll see you in the fall. Wish your father a speedy recovery."

"I will." Pearl turned to her cousin. "Will you still be here when I return?"

"Of course. There's no use paying for a boarding house when we live close to the university."

Pearl followed Gene out the door.

As the buggy lurched forward, Pearl cocked her head at a voice calling her name. She looked back at the house to the empty porch.

"Wait up, Pearl." This time the voice came clear.

Uncle Leland drew the reins in. Pearl turned to see Stanley rushing alongside.

Stanley dropped his head. With his hands on his thighs, he heaved deep breaths. "I had to come to say goodbye."

Uncle Leland nodded. Pearl climbed down. Stanley stood, hands in pockets until Pearl leaned in and gave him a quick hug. She hopped back onto the buggy, and she was on her way home again.

Chapter Ten

1908 – First Day of School

Her mother's touch made Edna stir under the covers.

"Wake up, dear. You don't want to be late for your first day of school."

Her eyes fluttered for only an instant before Edna's face brightened to match the rays of sunshine playing peekaboo through the curtains. She'd waited for this day since she was a little girl watching Pearl march out the door each morning. She sat up and looked across the room. "Pearl, are you awake?"

Pearl grumbled and stretched in the next bed.

"Wake up, Pearl. Today's my first day of school." After spending her summer with Pearl, picking berries, going on walks, and spending hours by her father's bedside practicing her phonics, today, she would make friends her own age. With the excitement of a Christmas morning, Edna jumped from her bed.

Her mother had laid out her clothes and leaned down to tousle Edna's hair. "Get dressed and come to breakfast. Don't dillydally. You have a long walk ahead of you." She cast a glance at Pearl as she turned to leave. "Are you coming?"

Pearl swung her legs to the side of the bed. "Yes, I'm coming. I'll walk Edna to school."

Edna's forehead and brows wrinkled. "I'm a big girl. I don't need you to walk me, Pearl. I know the way."

"I know. You're a big girl, but in a few days, I'm leaving again for school and won't be back until Christmas break."

"Okay." Edna conceded with a shrug. Seeing her clothes on her bed, she snatched the navy-blue cotton dress with a white lace collar and ribbon at the waist and hugged it to her. "Look, Pearl. Mama made me a new dress." She tugged on a pair of black woolen stockings, pulled the dress over her head, and laced her boots. She turned her back to Pearl, who buttoned the dress. A sliver of insecurity poked at her. "Do you think I can take Miss Molly to school? She'll be lonely without me."

"I don't know if it's okay or not." Pearl squatted and spoke barely above a whisper. "But I'll tell you a secret. I took Miss Molly on my first day." She grinned. "I'm not sure if teachers allow such things these days."

Edna wrinkled her nose and chewed on her lower lip. She looked at Molly, squeezed her to her chest, and placed her on the bed. "I'm sorry, Molly. I have to go to school alone."

When she walked into the kitchen, her mother led her to the table. She placed a firm hand on Edna's shoulder. Edna frowned in anticipation of the upcoming ritual. Edna jerked with each drag of the comb through her long thick curls. Her scalp hurt with each set of tangles the silver comb snared. "I wish my hair wasn't so long."

Mother sectioned off Edna's hair. Edna winced as a barrette with a bow affixed, snapped into place. Mother handed her a small silver mirror. "You're lucky to have such beautiful hair. Do you want me to braid it?"

Edna gazed into the mirror. "Not today." She shook her head, satisfied as she turned her head side to side and admired the bright blue bow.

Mother glanced at the clock on the mantle and called to Pearl. "You girls better hurry and eat your breakfast. It's getting late."

Eager to start her school day, Edna gobbled her soft-boiled egg and her bowl of cream of wheat with honey. Mother waited by the door with Edna's coat in hand.

Edna slid into her outerwear and beamed. "I'm ready."

Her mother sighed as she bent over to hug Edna. "Run along now. Don't forget your slate and your lunch pail."

Edna dashed over to the table by the coat tree. She snatched her lunch pail and the slate, no longer a toy for drawing pictures. Today the slate would be used to cipher her numbers and practice her letters. Pearl rushed by, grabbing her coat as she passed. "Goodbye, Mother. I'll be back soon."

Edna bit her lip and looked back toward her bedroom. Mama squatted down and kissed her on the forehead, then Edna turned and strode out the door.

On the way to school, Edna recited her alphabet and showed Pearl how well she could count.

Pearl wrapped her arm around Edna's shoulder. "I bet you're going to be the smartest person in first grade."

With each step, mud oozed from the dirt path after the night drizzle. As she neared town, other children darted out from merging paths and nearby houses, wearing their best smiles and their best clothes.

"Hello." Edna greeted each one as they came into view. A few of the younger children waved and returned her greeting. Others, mostly older boys, ignored her and brushed past at a quick pace. Two miles later, they reached the bottom of Sydney Hill. Sweaty and with aching lungs, Edna stopped to catch her breath as she gazed at the two-story white schoolhouse. A neat row of orange and yellow flowers lined the gravel path leading to the flagpole, welcoming the students to the new year.

The massive brass bell clanged, and Edna covered her ears. A moment of fear flooded her. What if the teacher was mean? What if the other children didn't like her? She stared at the bell tower rising high above the roof and threw her arms around her sister. "I'm glad you walked with me. I wish you could stay."

"You'll be fine. You're going to love it."

Edna clutched her slate closer to her. "Are you sure?"

"I'm sure." Pearl patted Edna on the shoulder. "Go on, gather with the others at the flagpole to recite the pledge to the flag. I'll see you after school."

Another quick hug and Edna raced to where the rest of the students gathered. Edna gazed at the flag. She didn't remember how many stars were on the flag and quickly counted four rows of eight stars and two rows of seven. One more star than the flag had when Pearl started school. Edna stood along with her classmates looking lost.

A stern-faced matron stood underneath the pole. "Quiet down. We will gather here each morning for the pledge before going into the schoolhouse." She placed her right hand across her chest. "Repeat each line after me. I expect you to memorize the pledge by the end of the week."

Following along Edna recited. "I pledge allegiance to my flag...²" Edna stood erect, her shoulders back, her chest out. Along with her class, she dutifully recited each line of the Pledge of Allegiance.

After the pledge, the matron clanged a triangle and in silence, the students turned and marched up the steps. Inside, the children stood hesitantly by each of the two classroom doors, one for the first two grades and the other for grades three and four. The upper grades were taught in the two classrooms upstairs. Edna glanced at the sign on the door. *First and Second Grade.* Her classroom. She skipped inside, eager to start her formal learning. She focused on the woman who stood at the front of the room. She was younger than Pearl's teacher, Miss Ambrose, and unlike the woman at the flag she wore a smile.

"First grade?" The young teacher pointed to the side wall. "Find a hook and place your lunch pail on the shelf, then find an empty seat in one of the first rows."

Pearl had told Edna that she would be seated in the front row with the other abecedarians. Edna couldn't say the word correctly, but Pearl told her it meant the first-year students and those who had recently learned their ABCs. A young fair-skinned girl scooted over in one of the double seats, and Edna slid next to her. For the first time, she was in her own classroom, not Pearl's classroom or at home where she pretended to be a teacher and her dolls and teddy bear were students. Butterflies fluttered inside her tummy. She knew her ABCs and how to count, but what did she know about playing with other children? What would she say to these other children? Maybe she wasn't ready for school after all. Edna wished she had Miss Molly with her for support.

In the front of the room, an oak desk held several apples and stacks of books in neat rows. Behind the desk, a long gray slate board hung from the wall. Above the slate board, large letters painted in red demonstrated how to print the alphabet in upper and lowercase letters.

---

² The original wording of the Pledge of Allegiance inaugurated in 1892.

A large black stove roared to life along the far wall, its heat dispelling the chill of the early morning.

Edna glanced at her seatmate with strawberry-blond hair who stared at her hands folded in her lap. The girl across the aisle rubbed her arms. Edna ran her hand across the rough-planked table in front of her.

The teacher thumped the desk with her hand. "Attention, please. Take your seats and quiet down."

Everyone quieted, straightened, and all heads faced the front of the classroom.

"Good morning, children. This classroom is for the first and second grade only. If you are above that level, please leave and find the appropriate classroom for your grade level."

A couple students giggled when a red-faced, gangly boy pushed off his chair and scurried out the door.

Clearing her throat, their teacher began again. "I am your teacher for this year. You are always to address me by my surname, Miss Finney." Turning to the blackboard, she picked up a piece of chalk. The chalk screeched with each large printed letter. Placing the chalk back on the shelf, the teacher spun around. "Now, children, what do you say?"

Without hesitating, the class responded in unison, "Good morning, Miss Finney."

Edna guessed her young teacher wasn't much older than Pearl, though her dark hair wrapped in a tight bun atop her head gave her the appearance of looking older. Her high-collared white blouse with long fitted sleeves and floor-length navy skirt looked more like something Edna's mother might wear than an outfit for a young woman Pearl's age.

Miss Finney held up a small wooden stick. "I do not like to use this for punishment, but I will if I have to." With that, she banged the stick on her desk with a sharp movement. The *thwack* brought uncontrolled spasms of fear, particularly among those seated in the front row. Edna shuddered in her seat as she imagined the sting from the stick. Miss Finney marched over to the black stove placed midway along the exterior wall of the room. She raised the handle and yanked open the door. Inside, lightning-bug sparks of orange danced above the flames. Slivers of dark gray smoke snaked out the open door, sending a sooty odor of burning wood into the room. Miss Finney grabbed a scoop from along the back wall. She dipped into the coal bucket next to the stove and showed the large black hunks to the students. "If the stick is not effective, or if you continue to misbehave, you will be breaking chunks of coal instead of taking your recess." The schoolteacher turned; her voice softened. "Please stand and say present when I call your name."

Edna sat at attention with her hands folded atop the desk. She listened to each name. One by one, her classmates stood while the teacher checked off their names on a list. The girl with strawberry blond hair was Inez Fletcher, and Art, tall with dark wavy hair, sat in the back row. Susy and Berta sat along the front row. When Edna heard her name, she bounced off her chair and recited "present" as instructed. After all the students were checked off, Miss Finney handed a book to each first grader. Edna ran her hand over the gray cloth-covered book decorated with black trees and examined the letters indicating the book's title, *The Arnold Primer.* She flipped through the pages, eager to begin. "How do you do? What is your name? My name is Dan." She thumbed ahead, her fingers tingling, anticipating all the joy of learning to read an entire book on her own.

"Please close the books and pay attention to me."

Lost in the pages of her book, Edna didn't hear the instruction. A sharp whack on her desk jolted her back. Miss Finney leaned over Edna; her face was so taut, Edna wondered if her bun was pulled too tight. Another flick of wood against the planked desk made Edna's heart race, and sweat formed on her forehead. Though Pearl had warned her about the stick, seeing it and hearing it rap against the table mere inches from her made her feel glued to the bench.

With an abrupt motion, Miss Finney slammed Edna's book shut. "Edna Mooney. Are you paying attention?"

The weight of the book as it closed, pinched the tips of Edna's fingers. Her hands shook. She stuttered, her eyes pleading for sympathy. "I'm sorry, Miss Finney." Not wishing to fall into disfavor with her teacher the first day, Edna straightened and faced her teacher's glaring eyes. "I promise to pay attention."

The basics of reciting and printing the alphabet, printing her name in block letters, and writing the numbers from one through ten provided no challenge for Edna. Watching the teacher in control of the entire class, Edna knew right away she wanted to be a teacher when she grew up.

When at last, the big hand on the large wall clock met with the little hand, the entire class stood and gathered their lunch buckets. "You will have one hour for eating and your recess time." She grabbed a small brass bell, and with a flick of her wrist, the bell reverberated throughout the cozy room. "When you hear this bell, it is your signal recess is over. You are to march in an orderly and silent manner back to class."

The door creaked open. An older boy from the upper-grade class poked his head inside. "Follow me. There is to be no talking. No running. Stay in line." The assigned proctor led the students down the hall to the stairway. Instructed to walk in rows of two students, Edna imagined a parade of horses clomping side by side, pulling a carriage. She stifled her giggle, remembering the earlier threat. Any loud noise or running would result in a loss of privileges, like recess, or even worse, a smack across the knuckles with the ferule ruler.

In silence, the children marched into a large basement room and sat at tables within their age groups. Minutes later, the older children joined them and took their places around the remaining tables. Lunch pails clunked open, and in a matter of seconds, all mouths were busy munching biscuits spread with jam or honey or sometimes a sausage patty or a fried-egg sandwich. Edna climbed onto the long bench next to three other girls her age, including Inez Fletcher. Unwrapping the cloth napkin inside her bucket, Edna turned to Inez. "I've got a corn muffin with honey, an apple from our tree, and..." Edna fumbled to the bottom of the pail and found something wrapped in a small dishcloth. Unwrapping it, she held it out for Inez to see. "I have a snickerdoodle." Inez smiled, revealing two missing teeth as she dug into her bucket. She withdrew her sandwich and waved it in front of the others.

"What kind is it?" Edna leaned in for a closer look.

Inez placed it on the table. "I have an egg and sausage on a biscuit. Mother made a special lunch for my first day."

Edna shrugged and looked down at her muffin, not as content with her simple lunch.

"I don't mind sharing." Inez held the biscuit out. "You can even have the first bite."

Edna wrinkled her face as she considered the offer. She looked down at her snickerdoodle and broke it down the middle. She pushed half over to Inez, accepted the biscuit, and took a bite.

The proctor strode between the tables nodding his approval for their good behavior. When most of the children were finished eating, the proctor instructed them to form a line again. Edna lined up with Inez and the others from her table. They followed the older boy in silence outside to the playground that stretched to the end of the school property. Edna took in all the outdoor activities. A half-dozen swings hung from a sturdy steel beam, far better than the lone tire swing hanging from her apple tree at home. Three teeter-totters ran next to the swings, and nearby, two hopscotch boards painted onto a small strip of black surface like the paved roads in the city drew the younger girls.

Each child spied their favorite activity, and they scattered pell-mell, like thrown seed across the field. Though hopscotch was primarily a girl's game, Edna knew from the times she went to school with Pearl when she was only four, that boys sometimes were seen hopping on one foot along the hopscotch squares. Today, the boys gathered balls from a wooden bin or raced for the teeter-totter. Edna clapped her hands, delighted by the attention from several girls who clamored for her to join them. "C'mon, we need someone on the teeter-totter." Inez ran up to her, holding out a skipping rope. "Do you want to skip rope with me?"

Edna waved them off. "I want to watch the boys play marbles." She darted to one corner of the playfield. She stood on the sidelines, chewing her lip while Art and other boys lined up their shots and flicked the steelies and aggies toward the center of the circle trying to knock the other player's marble out of the ring. Edna liked the concentration and skill required. Pearl told her sometimes the boys played for keeps even though it was frowned upon. She watched Art cheer when he made a successful play.

Edna stepped forward. "Can I play?"

The boys all stopped and gawked at her. "Girls can't play marbles."

"Why not?"

One of the older boys shrugged. "Dunno. It's just the way it is." He ignored Edna and resumed his play.

At the bee-like sting of rejection Edna stomped her foot. "That's not true. My sister is in high school, and she told me girls can do anything they want." She turned and ran across the playfield. Someday, she told herself, she would step forward, despite what boys said. She would take on the boys in marbles, and she would show them she was as good as any boy. And she would win.

Chapter Eleven

1908 – Visiting Pearl

The week before Thanksgiving, Edna brightened from Mother's surprise. "How would you like to go to Seattle and see Pearl this weekend? Your aunt is expecting us. We'll spend Saturday night, and in the morning, we'll go to the market on Pike Place before we catch the steamboat home."

Edna clapped. "I can't wait until school is over so Pearl can move back home."

Her mother squatted and clasped Edna's shoulders, "Pearl still has two more years of school. She may not move back home. Your sister's nearly a woman now."

Edna looked down at the floor.

"I know you miss her. Papa and I do too. But you're in school now, too, and it won't be long before you're so busy with friends you won't even think about Pearl."

Edna shook her head. She would never forget her sister. "Is Papa coming too?"

"No. Papa has to stay and catch up with the chores."

Edna sighed. She was going to see Pearl, and that was all that mattered.

The next morning Edna woke to the rooster's crowing. Shivering from the morning chill, Edna dressed in a hurry. She tugged at her wool stockings, then slipped into her long-sleeved poplin dress. After cramming her cold toes into her boots, she laced them and fetched her wool scarf and muff from the closet to help keep her warm on the ride across the sound. Her mouth watered from the smell of maple drifting down the hall, summoning her to breakfast more urgently than her mother's words.

Mother rushed around, wiping her hands on her apron before removing it and tossing it on a chair. "Hurry up. Papa's got Nellie ready. We want to catch the ten o'clock steamer."

♪ ♪ ♪

On schedule, the horn tooted its final boarding call. Edna covered her ears. She stood on her tiptoes and craned her neck. This time, instead of waving from the dock, Edna was aboard the steamship. Papa wasn't one to stay behind and see them off, but Edna waved all the same to the strangers on land as they watched their friends and loved ones sail away. She stood with her chin raised. She wondered if those on the dock were envious like she'd envied Pearl every time Pearl had sailed away, leaving her behind with her emptiness and her yearning. Frustrated by her inability to see over the top railing, she stepped onto the lowest rung of the guardrail and pulled herself up. She peered down at the dark, choppy water and shuddered.

A moment later, Mother yanked her off the railing with a stern look. "Be careful. The water is freezing, especially this time of year. You won't last long if you fall in."

Crossing her arms, Edna squinted. "I want to see better."

Her mother hoisted her to her hip with an *oomph*. "You're getting heavy."

Hearing one more long blare of the horn, Edna waved her hand in wild, exaggerated movements. The *Athlon* chugged away from land for its one-hour crossing to Seattle. With a big exhale, her mother plopped Edna back to the bleached gray deck. The boat slid farther and farther from the dock. Stretching as far as she could see, and wearing a cap of white foam, the murky black sea gurgled like soapsuds in Mother's washtub. Shivering, Edna drew her coat tighter. "Is Pearl going to meet us at the dock?"

"No. We're going to take an electric trolley from the dock to your aunt's house."

Taking her gaze from the hypnotic waters, Edna looked at her mother. "What's a trolley?"

"A trolley is similar to a carriage, but it's pulled along wires by electricity instead of horses."

Edna tipped her head. "How can a carriage move without horses?"

Mama pulled her wrap a little tighter and turned her face from the buffeting wind. "You'll see."

Edna hopped up and down, unable to contain her excitement.

"Let's go inside. Your nose and cheeks are turning pink."

"Please, Mama, I want to watch the seagulls longer." She returned her focus to the water. The occasional gull squawked as it soared on the gusty winds alongside the boat. Edna clutched her hands together tight inside her cozy muff. She giggled when salty spray blew across the bow and splattered across her face. Wiping her cheeks with her furry muff, she grimaced at the taste of salt on her lips.

As the ferry neared the dock, black, goose-size seabirds stood perched on wood pilings with their wings extended like scarecrows guarding a cornfield.

Mother reached for Edna's hand. "Come along. We need to return to the departure deck to disembark."

Wishing to watch the large vessel as it pulled into the dock, Edna resisted as long as possible, finally giving in before Mama got angry. They crowded together with dozens of other passengers as the boat struck the pilings and shimmied into place at the Colman dock. A rush of bodies surged down the walkway to the terminal building and out onto the streets. Edna's hand hurt from Mother squeezing it so tight. She wanted to pull herself free from her mother's grip, but the sight of the large crowd pushing past in quick steps encouraged her to hang on for fear of getting lost. She skipped alongside to keep pace with her mother's long strides until safely away from the rush of people arriving and departing the busy waterway.

When her mother slowed, Edna caught her breath. Mother relaxed her grip. "The trolley stand should be nearby."

Edna's eyes widened as she took in the confusion of the narrow streets where horses with buggies plodded alongside long metal buses with narrow wires attached to lines running overhead reaching toward the sky. She pointed down the street. "Is that a trolley?"

"That's a trolley. Come on, we need to walk to one of the trolley stops." Mother hurried down the sidewalk with Edna on her heels.

At the corner of Second and Yesler, Mother stopped and sat on a bench underneath a sign that read, "Trolley Stop." Only minutes later, a clinking and clanking on the rail tracks announced the arrival of the Seattle Electric Railway. Edna clapped her hands as she climbed aboard the black and red streetcar. Behind her, Mama plunked her coins into the wood fare box, and seconds later, the trolley lurched forward. Edna pressed her nose to the window as the trolley passed tall brick stores and businesses lining the downtown streets. In the distance, the snow-topped mountain her mother called Mount Rainier, appeared to sit above the clouds as if perched on a throne. Within a few blocks, the trolley turned and lumbered up a long hill. When they reached the top, the conductor called out, "Broadway and James."

"That's our stop." Mother stood and tugged the cord hanging along the side of the car. A tinny clink signaled the conductor, and the trolley rolled to a stop.

Edna followed her mother down the aisle and outside. Everything from the wide paved streets to the row of different-color houses standing side by side like crayons nestled inside a box looked so unlike Port Orchard.

"Come along. It's only three blocks to her house." Minutes later, Mama stopped in front of a modest two-story house. Edna didn't remember her aunt's house from when she was three. It wasn't far different from their own house, but the white paint was brighter, newer looking. Wood steps led to the covered porch flanked by columns partially nestled in the glossy green ivy climbing the columns all the way to the porch overhang. Edna ran up the walkway as fast as she was able to run. Before she reached the steps, the door swung open, and Aunt Marie stepped out, arms outstretched.

"I'm so glad you came to visit."

Remembering her manners, Edna returned the greeting as she peered around her aunt and spied Pearl waiting inside.

"Go ahead. Pearl's anxious to see you too."

Edna darted up the stairs and into her sister's arms.

Chapter Twelve

1908 – Pearl's Beau

Pearl held her sister in a long embrace before letting go and holding her at arm's length. "I can't believe how tall you are. You've grown even in the past two months."

With her hands on her hips, Edna grinned, showing off two missing teeth. "My teacher, Miss Finney, told me I was tall for my age, and she told me I'm smart too. I told her you schooled me at home."

Pearl recalled her resentment and her immaturity the day Edna was born. She also recalled the promise she'd made to her aunt that day. The promise she would always look after Edna. She realized she'd played a role in helping shape her sister's life. A warmth spread over her. So far, she'd succeeded in setting a good example, and she couldn't imagine her life without her sister. Edna would forever be a part of her life, no matter what the future held for each of them.

Pearl took Edna's overnight bag as her mother and aunt stepped inside. Then she led them up the stairs to her room. "Mama, you get the bed, and Edna and I will sleep on the floor." Pearl lifted Edna's bag to the bed, then faced her mother. "Aunt Marie told me she wrote to you about Stanley. Is that why you're here?"

Her mother's eyebrows arched, but Pearl couldn't read her mother's emotions as she spoke. "I want to meet the young man who is courting you."

Aunt Marie called from the front room. "Come down for tea and cookies when you are done freshening up."

Mother shooed Edna downstairs. "Run along. Tell your aunt we'll be right down."

A nervous energy ran down Pearl's legs, and she shifted her weight and looked down at her trembling hands. "I guess you have some questions you want to ask me about Stanley?"

Her mother tried her best to look unconcerned as she laid out her garments on the bed. "I had no idea you were so serious about him."

Pearl stammered. "We're not serious. He is a year older, and I wasn't sure he still wanted to be friends this year."

Her mother's concerned gaze bore right through Pearl as she imagined the newly popular X-ray machines did. "Hmmm. Your aunt tells me you see him most weekends, and he walks you home after your basketball games on Friday nights. Sounds serious to me."

An awkward silence shrouded the conversation while Pearl found the strength to look her mother in the eye. "Don't worry, Mama, we're not..." Pearl turned toward the door wiping her sweaty palms on her dress, unsure what else she could say.

A few minutes later, Mother planted herself in an armchair across from Pearl. She ran her hand over the burgundy velvet cushion.

Aunt Marie nodded. "Before you ask, yes, it's one of the chairs from Mama and Papa's old house. They asked if I wanted it. I hope you don't mind they didn't ask you."

"Not at all. It looks better here than it would in my house." Abbey pushed her glasses up the bridge of her nose and fixed her gaze on Pearl.

Wishing she could avoid the conversation; Pearl grabbed a gingerbread cookie from the plate and took a quick bite, and took her time chewing.

Aunt Marie got right to the point. "As I discussed in my most recent letter to your mother, I have invited Stanley to join us for dinner this evening. Since you are spending so much time with him, your mother should meet the young man who has taken a shine to her daughter."

Edna cocked her head and grinned at Pearl. "Is Stanley your boyfriend?"

Pearl groaned. She nudged Edna with her elbow. This was one of those times Pearl wished she were an only child again. "Yes. I guess he is."

Edna bounced on the seat. "Pearl's got a boyfriend."

Mother's narrow gaze put a quick stop to the teasing. Though she was far from choosing a mate for life, at sixteen, Pearl secretly longed for a more intimate relationship. So far, their attempts at making out proved a bit awkward, not at all sensual. A quiver of warmth stirred inside and spread over her body and cheeks with her thoughts of romance. She couldn't squelch the feeling everyone around her saw it in her flushed face. She tried not to think about the night behind the bleachers after one of her games.

"Tell me about Stanley. Do you know what his plans are for the future?"

Pearl shifted uncomfortably. Her pulse raced. Manners dictated she did not argue with her elders, but her exasperation bubbled over. She shook her head, desperate to stop the interrogation. "All I know is, he has a brother, and his uncle builds furniture. You can ask him anything else you want to know when he gets here."

Pearl stuttered an apology, but her mother looked as if she'd sipped sour milk. She turned to Marie. "I'll take that tea now."

At six o'clock sharp, Pearl jumped at the sound of a knock at the door. Uncle Leland answered the door while Pearl sat with her mother and Edna on the sofa. Mother paged through the latest issue of *Good Housekeeping*, trying her best to appear disinterested though Pearl couldn't help but notice her foot tapping the floor. Edna giggled as she held Miss Molly, pursed her lips, and made kissing sounds. Pearl shot a cold stare at her sister, who bit her lip and looked away.

Earlier, Pearl had warned Stanley to be on his best behavior and not broach the subject of his Jewish ancestry or make any attempt at humor, which Pearl was sure would be read as a smart-aleck response. She relaxed when he walked into the room dressed in a brown suit with a three-button jacket over a white shirt. He immediately removed his hat and tipped his head to acknowledge Pearl's mother and sister. "Pleased to meet you, Mrs. Mooney." He bowed toward Edna, who sat with a grin as wide as her face. "Pleased to meet you, too, Edna. Pearl's told me so much about you."

Stanley found a vacant chair, facing his jury. "Thank you for inviting me. I look forward to getting to know you, as I'm sure you want to get to know me."

Mother nodded her approval.

The clenching in Pearl's stomach relaxed. Thus far, he had won over her mother, and the evening looked promising.

Chapter Thirteen

1908 – Market at Pike Place

In the morning, Edna hugged Pearl goodbye. "I like your friend. He's nice. Mama likes him too." Clinging tight to her sister, Edna tried not to cry. Even now, Pearl's absence weighed heavy, like the massive anchor she'd seen on the *Athlon*. Watching Pearl talk with Stanley, Edna feared losing her big sister. What if Pearl stayed in Seattle and began her own life? A life without Pearl. When would she see her again?

"We have a trolley to catch." Mother's command pulled Edna from her sister's comforting embrace.

Edna sniffled, released her hug, snatched her overnight satchel, and kept pace alongside her mother to the trolley stop. Once onboard the trolley, Edna peered out the window and took in the sites so different from Port Orchard, from the houses to the people walking along paved sidewalks lined with tall light posts. Though it was daylight and the lights were out, Edna had seen the lit posts from the window last night. Edna wondered when they, too, would have electric lights in their home. Small grassy parks appeared every few blocks, and rows of stately houses as big as mansions lined both sides of the roadways busy with horses and even a few automobiles. As the trolley rolled down the steep hill, Puget Sound appeared in the distance behind the buildings that towered high into the sky, taller than she'd ever seen.

At the bottom of the hill, the trolley turned onto one of the main streets. Edna gazed in amazement at the window display of dozens of shoes in Wallin & Nordstrom on Second Avenue and Pike Street next to the MacDougall and Southwick Company. Edna remembered Inez telling her she and her mother sometimes came to the city and shopped in these department stores. Edna had seen Inez's store-bought dresses. She wished she could go inside to peek, maybe feel the shimmery fabric, but she didn't ask. She didn't want to sound envious of Inez. Instead, she ran her hand over her handmade dress, knowing how much time her mother spent sewing it. She gaped at the four-story, brick building with the enormous sign on top, "Bon Marche." She immediately tugged at her mother's coat. "Look, Mama. That's where Aunt Marie bought my birthday dress. I recognize the letters from the box the dress came in." The trolley jerked to a stop. Edna looked at her mother with wide eyes, hoping this was their stop. She wanted to look at the elegant dresses in the window of the Bon Marche. The dresses like the ones worn by princesses in her fairy tale books. When the trolley started again, Edna looked over her shoulder, back at the fancy store. Someday she would come back and buy a dress and be a real live princess.

At last, Mother tugged the cord once more and stood to get off. "Be sure to look both ways down the street before you cross. There's more traffic here than at home." At the sound of an odd honking sound, *ooga, ooga*, like a loud, annoying goose, Mother grabbed Edna's hand and pulled her closer. Edna gazed in awe as the shiny black vehicle moved along the road so close, she could easily reach out to touch the tiny lights that hung from its sides. She giggled as a horse and buggy driver refused to yield to the new gas-powered buggy.

"I've never seen an automobile. It's so pretty."

"Mr. Henry Ford calls that a Model T. Your father says one day every family in the country will own an automobile instead of using horse-drawn carriages."

"Even us?"

"Yes, even us."

Edna's gaze followed the automobile as it bumped along the cobblestone road, drawing stares and waves from everyone it passed. Edna waved after the car even though it was too late for the car's driver to see her. Ahead, a big white sign with red letters announced they had arrived at the public market on Pike Street. Today the market was crowded with people shopping from wagons filled with apples, berries, and vegetables, while horses pulling carriages pranced along

84

the cobblestones dodging buyers and modern-day automobiles. The aroma of fruits and flowers fought with the barnyard smell of horses. A fluty wavering sound of wooden pipes sent Edna dashing in the direction of the music. An organ grinder stood on the sidewalk, cranking the handle of a small street organ, while a small black and white monkey wearing a black cap danced on his shoulder and held out its tin cup. Women smiled, and men tipped their hats and flicked coins into the cup held by the furry creature as they passed. Edna skipped in circles to his tune until her mother handed her a coin. She studied the bright shiny penny, one of the new ones, with a picture of President Abraham Lincoln instead of an Indian wearing a headdress. She ran over to the organ grinder and plopped the penny in the cup.

Mother took her hand and led her to the produce stand. "Come, we still have our shopping to do." She looked over the blueberries, cauliflower, and eggplant, all delivered by local farmers early in the morning while those who worked in the downtown businesses still slept. She stopped and sniffed the cantaloupe, still loaded on the back of a wagon. Selecting one, she paid the farmer and placed it in an oversize shopping bag. Wanting to trot or move about, the horses shook and whinnied their protest at being tied to the hitching post.

As they strolled past the street vendors, Edna licked her lips at the sight of the deep-purple plums piled in bins. "Please, Mama, may we buy some plums?"

"I guess we can get a few."

Edna plucked a firm plum from the basket and took a bite. Sweet sticky juice dripped down her chin. Mother laughed, then pulled a handkerchief from her purse and wiped it away. She handed the man a few coins.

Strolling along, Mama gazed upon the rich purple blackberries, her father's favorite. He preferred them on Mama's hot steamy shortcakes smothered with freshly whipped cream. She marveled aloud at how the farmers' vines still produced berries this late in the year. She counted her money. "Our canned fruit and berries will have to do until summer comes and we can pick more wild berries on our own." Mother passed by the apples without a glance. They had apple trees still heavy with Rome and bright Red Delicious apples. Next, they strolled over to the fish. Edna scrunched her face and plugged her nose. She didn't much care for fish, though she knew Father loved any of the numerous kinds of fish and shellfish fresh from Puget Sound. Mother inspected a silver fish laid out on blocks of ice. The scales glistened in the light, making it shimmer like the fabric of the fancy dresses in the department store windows. Edna watched the men dressed in black pants and jackets with high rubber boots gather fish from wooden crates loaded in a wagon and place them on ice to restock the bins.

Mother stared at the display. "What kind of salmon is this?"

A tall, burly guy with an unshaved ruddy face tossed another fish onto the ice. "Coho, otherwise known as Silver. Caught this morning right off the coast between Seattle and Bremerton. Doesn't get any fresher than this." Mother shook her head. "It won't keep for my long journey."

"No worries. I can pack it so it will keep several hours."

Mama sighed. "Papa's home now; he'll love the surprise. I'll take a small fish."

The fisherman wrapped a small block of ice in a piece of burlap, then wrapped everything in several sheets of newspaper. "This should do."

The sharp, almost burned aroma of ground beans overpowered the air at the last stop. Mother selected a pound of the fresh ground beans for Father and strolled over to the assortment of tea leaves. Edna bent over the wood bins and sniffed the delicate scent of orange tea leaves and the cinnamon's strong spicy scent that stung her nostrils. Her mother took her time selecting a small bag of green tea leaves before she glanced around for a final look. A display of jars caught her eye. "This clover honey will be perfect with my tea and biscuits. That's enough for today. I'm afraid I've more than spent my week's budgeted funds. We should probably get going. We still need to catch the trolley to the ferry."

As they walked away from the market toward the trolley station, a solemn, sorrowful song echoed in the distance. Edna tipped her head and strained to hear the sad voices. "What's that?"

"Come along." Mama prompted as she turned a corner, nudging Edna along. "We're almost there."

At the corner, Edna looked toward the singing, now joined by a loud clanging. Men with big heavy hammers hoisted them high and clanked them down against the wooden walkway they were building.

Edna stopped walking and studied the scruffy-looking men wearing white and black outfits with heavy shackles and chains wrapped around their ankles. "Who are they? Why are they chained together?"

Her mother heaved a heavy sigh. She stopped and bent over Edna. "They're prisoners, bad men who have done bad things. They are chained so they can't escape while they are working to fix the sidewalks."

Edna looked at her mother. "What kind of bad things?"

"It doesn't matter." Her mother's tone sounded sharp; impatient, she grabbed Edna's hand and hurried toward the clanging of the approaching trolley.

Chapter Fourteen

1909 – Daydreams

With her mother's approval of Stanley, Pearl worried less about their relationship and increasing affection. By the end of her junior year, Pearl found herself daydreaming about a future with him. She worried how their feelings might change during the coming year in his absence. And then, there was college. Would Stanley wait while she continued her education another two years beyond high school?

Seated on the wood bleachers next to Stanley's parents and his brother, Pearl looked over the packed auditorium of proud parents, family members, and guests attending the graduation ceremony of the nearly three-hundred graduates from Seattle High class of 1909. The atmosphere was so different from her eighth-grade ceremony with only a dozen graduates. The band leader stood and lifted his baton. Black-uniformed band members followed in concert and raised their clarinets, flutes, and trumpets to their lips. While the band played its bellowing notes, the graduates started down the aisle to what had become the most popular graduation march, "Pomp and Circumstance."

"There he is." Stanley's younger brother Simon jumped off his seat and pointed out to the sea of black-robed students wearing mortarboards. "Do you see him?"

Self-conscious around Stanley's family, whom she'd met only once before the graduation. Pearl contained her enthusiasm. She nodded and stared in the direction Simon pointed. After the principal and the valedictorian addressed the crowd, the principal took the podium and started calling out last names alphabetically. When the school principal reached names beginning with the letter, *R*, a row of students stood and paraded to the front to await the announcement of their names. Pearl sat on the edge of her seat and watched as Stanley Rosenberg marched across the stage to accept his diploma. She imagined herself on this same stage a year from now with her proud parents and Edna watching along with her aunt and uncle. Noticing the pride in Stanley's parent's eyes, Pearl imagined her mother and father beaming as they applauded her accomplishment, and she imagined her own satisfaction over her achievement. Stanley returned to his seat among his fellow graduates. Pearl's optimism rose. With three-years of school behind her, she was confident she would sail through her senior year. She could already imagine her life at the University of Washington as the first girl in the family to attend college.

Watching the graduates reminded Pearl of her aunt's words from the previous evening and a dull ache gripped her heart.

"Maybe it's for the best if you break up. He's the first boy you've dated, and you certainly don't need the distraction in your final year. Especially if you are planning on attending the university after high school."

The thoughts saddened Pearl. She'd protested. "Stanley's not a distraction. He supports my desire to become a nurse. I'm still in the top ten percent of my class. Besides, in two weeks I'll be going home for the summer, and Stanley's moving to Kirkland to apprentice for his uncle building furniture. It's a respectable skill, and Stanley will be able to make a comfortable living. We'll hardly see each other during my final year."

Pearl pushed the conversation to the back of her mind. When the last of the graduates disappeared through the doors, parents and family members followed along into the cafeteria decorated with crinkly orange and black paper streamers for light refreshments and congratulations. Her stomach flip-flopped. She wondered what would happen to their relationship after the night's festivities.

By the time Pearl spotted Stanley across the room, he had returned the rented gown and stood dressed in the same loose-fitting, brown three-button suit he'd worn the night he met Pearl's mother. Stanley grinned from ear to ear as fellow students surrounded him with handshakes and slaps on the back. She caught his eye, and he left his friends to join her and his family.

A microphone crackled and reverberated with a shrill noise, drawing all eyes and ears to the front of the room. Mr. Booker, the school principal, took the wood stage. "Tonight, is your night, but we will not tolerate any unacceptable behavior. So, enjoy the punch and cake, and find yourselves a dance partner."

The music of Ada Jones and Billy Murray skipped across the Graphophone as Pearl melted into Stanley's arms under the watchful eyes of parents and school chaperones. Stanley's family reminded him to pay heed to Pearl's eleven o'clock curfew and waved goodbye.

Stanley promised to get her home in time. Minutes later, Stanley nuzzled her neck with a soft kiss. A tingle tickled her spine and warmed her from within. "I'm getting bored with the dance." He looked around at the decreasing crowd. "How about we duck out?"

"Where will we go?"

"You'll see. Trust me."

Chapter Fifteen

1909 – Home Again

B ack home after her third year of high school, Pearl welcomed the old routine. She tended to Nellie, fed the pigs and hens, and strolled along the rows of sweet peas, carrots, and potatoes, plucking enough each day for the evening meal. Edna clung to Pearl, showing off her new reading skills or begging to be pushed on the swing. Entertaining her sister kept Pearl's mind off her absent beau and free from the shroud of guilt hanging over her from the events of graduation night.

After morning chores, Edna tugged on Pearl's arm and led her to the kitchen. "C'mon, Pearl. Let's color." She opened the lower doors of the Hoosier and took out her coloring book and crayons. She tore a page from the book and thrust it toward Pearl.

Pearl stared at the outlined drawing of children playing. A gloom fell over her. She missed the city with its theaters and the women's marches, but she missed Stanley most of all. She was worried about what the next year held as she continued to live in Seattle while he apprenticed over an hour northeast of the city, in the town of Kirkland.

"You're not coloring?" Edna pointed to the half-completed page. "What's wrong, Pearl? Aren't you glad to be home?"

"Of course, I am. I just miss my friends from school."

Edna batted her eyes. "You mean your boyfriend, Stanley?"

Pearl ignored Edna's teasing and reached across the table for a crayon. "There's no place I'd rather be than here with you and Mother and Father. This is home." Out of the blue, words from one of her favorite books, *The Wonderful Wizard of Oz,* popped into her head.

"There's no place like home." Port Orchard was home and comforted Pearl like an old worn sweater. But deep down, unease gnawed at her like pesky moths eating away at her trouble-free life.

For days, Pearl's appetite wavered, but the feeling always passed. Tonight, her stomach gurgled, and her mouth watered from the rich aroma of the breaded pork chops and the potatoes she'd dug earlier in the day, baked with a white sauce until they turned golden brown. As she passed the bowl of freshly picked peas to her father, she noticed his face had taken on a sallow, sunken appearance. "Are you feeling okay, Papa? Maybe it's time to find work somewhere other than the logging camp."

Her father jerked his head up. "Is this what they're teaching you in that big fancy school? To question your father? You don't need to worry about me. The camp cook, Mary Alice, does a fine job making sure we're well fed."

"I'm sorry, Papa, but you need more than good food to stay healthy. You told me how the cabins are falling apart. How are they going to hold up when winter comes? No wonder you've been feeling so poorly."

Pearl watched her father and wondered if she'd pushed the topic too far. The wrinkles in his forehead relaxed before he spoke again.

He shook his head. "I hear enough of that talk from the doctor. You haven't spoken about that chap you've been seeing? What's his name? Stanley?"

Her father's unexpected words stopped Pearl midbite. She resisted the urge to make eye contact. Did he suspect something was up? Her face warmed. Could her father see deep into her soul and discover her secret, the secret she prayed she would never have to reveal?

"Have the two of you gone your separate ways since he's completed his schooling?"

Her jaw clenched. "No. I'm sure he'll write to me once he's settled in his new job."

Papa stroked his beard. "Your mother says he's learning to build furniture. Sounds to me like the young man is smart. Hope he's smart enough not to jump into marriage."

Pearl shot an uneasy look at her mother, but her mother appeared unfazed.

Edna dropped her fork. A few peas bounced from her utensil and rolled on the table. "Is Pearl getting married?"

Pearl gasped. She wanted to shrink away. "No, honey. Not for a while anyway. I still have another year of education. I might not even see Stanley next year."

Her mother reached across and patted Pearl's hand. "We think Stanley is a fine young man, but we want to make sure you finish your education before you get too serious."

"Don't worry. I'm not. I promise I'm going to finish my schooling." As if her stomach detected the hesitancy in her voice, it flipped and tumbled to match her stumbling words.

"That's good." Papa's face relaxed a bit as he cut another bite of the roast. "Still thinking of becoming a nurse?"

Pearl squelched the uneasy feeling in her stomach and straightened her back. "I might not come home next summer. Aunt Marie thinks I'd make a fine activist. She even took me to a couple marches for women's rights."

Papa's face scrunched like he'd eaten a rotten egg. "Like Susan Anthony? How can you make a living protesting in the streets?"

"I wouldn't march for a living. I'd march because I want to make a difference for women's rights. Pearl watched her father's reaction before she continued. "Lots of young women my age are becoming involved." Unexpectedly, excitement replaced her discomfort. The thrill she'd felt during the marches downtown returned. "Aunt Marie told me women in Washington had the right to vote last century. She said she even voted in 1884 for Grover Cleveland."

A sparkle flashed in her mother's eyes. "I remember how proud Marie was that day. She never told me who she voted for."

"Well, Mama, maybe this time around, you'll get the chance. One of the state representatives is trying to get a bill on the ballot this November."

Her mother's face now reflected her own enthusiasm. "Do you think it will pass?"

Pearl nodded. "Aunt Marie and the ladies from the march are all confident. Can you imagine? In three years, you might be able to vote for the first time for the twenty-eighth president."

Her father cocked his head.

Pearl tensed, uncertain about her father's views about such things, especially working at the lumber camp where most men had less than her eleven years of education.

"I guess progress can be good. No reason women shouldn't have the same rights as men these days and even have a career."

"I agree. That's another reason I want to study nursing. Aunt Marie says it won't be long before women are going to the hospital to give birth instead of having babies at home with a midwife like you did."

"Nonsense." Her mother looked puzzled. "Women have been giving birth at home since the beginning of time. Even Doc Wilkes never went to no university, and he's done right fine by this town."

"Times are changing, Mama. Lots of women are attending university these days and getting not only undergraduate degrees but graduate degrees in subjects like chemistry and math. Auntie says there's no reason why I can't do the same. I can go to the University of Washington."

Her father shook his head with such force Pearl thought he'd strain his neck. "How do you propose we pay for such lofty dreams?" He pushed his plate away. "Not sure how much harder you expect me to work. We're already tightening our belts to provide for your living stipend."

No longer hungry, Pearl pushed her food around on her plate and lowered her voice. "Aunt Marie says I could stay on with her and Uncle. I plan on getting a part-time job to pay for tuition and pay something toward my room and board. Auntie says I can probably get a job with the Women's Suffrage Association, maybe answer the phones and mail flyers to encourage other women to get involved in women's rights."

Mother took her napkin and blotted her lips. "There's plenty of time to talk about the university. Eat up. I have an apple pie sitting on the windowsill to cool."

Alone in her room after dinner, Pearl's thoughts turned to Stanley. Impatient to receive a letter, reassurance he still thought of her, Pearl worried about the distance separating them. She wondered if the saying "out of sight, out of mind," rang true. Even if their relationship survived the summer, what would come of it when the school year started again?

Songs of Spring

♪ ♪ ♪

Only a few weeks after she arrived home, Pearl woke in a cold sweat despite the warmth of the day. She clutched her bed covers to her chin. Her head ached, and her stomach's meager contents growled and rebelled. She jumped out of bed and tried to remember the last time she was on the rag. Pearl swallowed. For the first time since the onset of menses, her cycle was late.

Each day her fear grew without any hint of her period. She couldn't ignore nor hide her circumstances much longer. When her mother looked at her sideways and questioned her lack of appetite, Pearl explained she was adjusting to the well water after becoming accustomed to city water from giant water towers fed by the Cedar River. She doubted her mother believed her story and knew her deceit wouldn't last much longer. One morning, the churning in her stomach swelled and moved into her throat. She swallowed the bitter taste of sour milk. She rolled to her side, drew her legs to her chest, and took in several deep breaths until her stomach settled and the rising acid subsided. The small bedside alarm rattled like a raspy relentless crow. Pearl swung her legs to the side of the bed and sat up.

"Are you okay?" Edna clambered out of bed. "Do you want me to fetch Mama?"

Pearl shook her head and barked at her sister sharper than intended. "No. I'm fine. I don't need Mama." Noticing Edna's confusion and concern, Pearl took her hand and softened her tone. "I'm fine. I sat up too quickly, that's all. It's nothing to worry about."

Pearl flinched with the knock at the door.

Mother poked her head inside. "Are you girls awake?"

Pearl's swift overly enthusiastic response, "Yes, we're up," brought a suspicious glower from her mother.

Mother tipped her head in concern and sat on the edge of Pearl's bed. "Are you feeling okay? You look pale." Mother motioned with her head toward Edna. "Go wash up and pour yourself a bowl of cornflakes. I'll be right out." After Edna shuffled from the room, Mother turned her focus to Pearl. Pearl couldn't help wondering if her mother picked up on the faint odor of her nausea.

95

Mother placed the back of her hand on Pearl's forehead. "I hope you're not coming down with the flu that's going around." She patted Pearl's hand. "I'll get water on the stove for ginger tea."

Relieved her mother thought it was the flu, Pearl sank back to the pillow. Her head spun, a dizzying whirl, like the spinning wax cylinders of the Graphophone, matching the turmoil in her stomach. She remembered her mother's morning sickness during the early months she carried Edna nearly eight years ago. It wouldn't last long, she could hide her nausea for that long, but other indications of her possible condition would undoubtedly appear.

Edna returned to the room with her bangs wet from washing her face. She plodded to her sister's side. "Aren't you feeling well?" Edna stood over Pearl with a wrinkled brow and her pouting lip. "You're not as fun as you used to be before you went away."

"I'm sorry, Edna. I promise. I'm going to be fine. I have a lot on my mind."

"What? It's summer break."

Pearl shook her head. "Grown-up stuff. Go get ready; I'll be right behind you." Pearl pushed herself to dress. She rushed to the outhouse with an unaccustomed urgency. Adjusting to the discomfort and the crudeness of the catalog pages after enjoying the comfort of an indoor privy exacerbated Pearl's unhappiness over her situation.

Back inside, she prayed the grumbling in her stomach would subside so she could enjoy Mama's homemade bread.

"How are you feeling?" A crease of worry wrinkled her mother's forehead as she placed the cup of tea and a slice of toasted bread in front of her daughter. "This should help."

Pearl sipped the hot ginger tea. Between sips, she nibbled her toast. With each bite, she paused to ensure the food agreed with her. "I'm better. I'm sure it's nothing to worry about." She took another sip of the soothing tea, which settled her stomach almost immediately. "After breakfast, I'll go help Papa with the chores."

Breathing in the fresh summer air stifled the last of Pearl's discomfort. She looked around the yard and saw her father exiting the barn. "Nice to see you up and around. The chores are done, except for the hens."

Edna exited the hen house, skipping toward her. "I collected the eggs." Edna beamed as she held out the basket with a half dozen eggs. "You can help me feed the hens."

Pearl followed Edna to the chicken coop. She looked around, hoping to invent another task once she fed the chickens. Anything to stay out of the house and avoid her mother while she invented answers for yet to be asked questions. The hen house needed painting, but she dismissed the idea. It meant a trip to town and money for paint. She would have to keep busy with outdoor play and maybe a walk to town with Edna to buy a soda.

At the dinner table, keenly aware of her mother watching her, Pearl ate with unhurried bites.

"I thought you liked meatloaf." Mother's words drew all eyes to Pearl.

Pearl breathed deeply and stammered. "I do, but I'm not hungry."

Her mother's raised eyebrows alerted Pearl her fibs were wearing thin. "Are you sure you are all right? You've hardly eaten since you've come home."

Her stomach growled. Uncertain if she could keep any food down, Pearl scooped a forkful of bland mashed potatoes.

"Leave the girl alone, Abbey. She's probably got a lot on her mind. You're not worried about your grades, are you?"

Pearl studied her father's face. He was smiling, not frowning. "No. I'm confident I passed."

Edna cocked her head. "I can't wait until you finish school and move back home."

Gripped by emotion, Pearl's words faltered. She shook her head. "I don't think I'm going to move back home. I want to stay in Seattle."

Pearl's father straightened in his seat. "Your sister says she's going to be a nurse. She's going to continue her studies after high school and make us all proud."

Out of the corner of her eye, Pearl noticed her mother beaming. Whatever reluctance her father held onto the previous night had vanished and was now replaced with his stubborn determination to prove his daughter would do something with her life.

"Your mother and I respect the discipline you have shown in your studies." Father punctuated his statement with a narrow gaze. "I know you won't disappoint us."

Pearl swallowed hard. A lot of discipline lay ahead. A discipline she knew she had already failed. Her parents had sacrificed so she could attend high school. They were willing to continue their sacrifice so she could continue to improve her path in life. She couldn't let them down, but an intense unease continued to swell inside her. Even as she was allowing her father his dream, a dream that only a week earlier she professed to possess, she worried she would be unable to fulfill it. She worried her illness was something more than the flu. Something that would last another eight months or so.

Edna put down her fork and asked to be excused. Papa seemed to read Mama's eyes and pushed away from the table, leaving Pearl alone with her mother.

Her mother reached for Pearl's hands. Her voice carried a directness that indicated she wasn't going to settle for any more stories. "Is there anything you want to tell me?" Her mother slid a chair closer to Pearl. "I'm your mother. Don't you think I know when something's wrong? You were always excited to talk about Stanley in your letters home. But since you've come home, you haven't even mentioned him. Are you two having troubles?"

Pearl wouldn't, she couldn't, confess her loose morals and permanently damage the relationship with her mother until she was certain. She blurted out her preplanned explanation. "Stanley told me he loves me. I'm simply confused right now."

Her mother got up and Pearl followed. Mama pulled her into a tight embrace. "I love you too. Know whatever you need, I'm here."

As Pearl hugged her mother, she held onto the prayer that she wouldn't have to put her mother's love to the test.

Chapter Sixteen

1909 – Foreboding

Pearl stood in the meadow of prairie grass dotted with daisies and purple bellflowers, orange poppies, and wild lavender asters. Invigorated, she reached for a tiny daisy and plucked the petals one by one. "He loves me. He loves me not." She quit before the outcome could become apparent. It wasn't that she trusted the flower's fortune-telling ability, but she thought it better to not tempt fate either. She closed her eyes and imagined Stanley alongside her. She'd only been home for a few weeks, but she ached for his touch, especially today as she stood alone, her queasy stomach rebelling even with the meager food it held.

Sitting on a large rock at the edge of their farm, her once favorite getaway spot, she lowered her head between her legs. "Breathe deep," she told herself before she heaved. Pearl wiped her mouth with her sleeve and took a deep breath. She quickly turned away from the vile pool that stank and made her gag. Waves of memories whirled in her head. She replayed the night, only weeks ago—the night she knew even then could change the course of her life. She wanted to shove the memory back into the furthest recess of her mind, to forget about the night. Instead, the memories arose like the bile in her throat. She looked around the meadow to ensure Edna hadn't come out to search for her. Relieved by her solitude, Pearl crossed her arms over her chest and hugged herself with firm pressure, wincing at the undeniable tenderness in her breasts. She bit her lip, and blinked away the tears.

Pearl stared along the gravel lane leading away from the family home. The home she had left three years earlier to fulfill her dream.

Now she feared her dream would be derailed. If only she could relive the last evening she and Stanley had spent together. The promise of marriage had started it all. She now wondered if it had only been a scheme, an attempt on his part to compel her to give in to his desire. Pearl squeezed her eyes shut. Recall flashed like frames from a silent movie.

Her daydream began with Stanley's graduation ceremony the last week of May.

"We won't see each other all summer. You're going home, and I'll be going to Kirkland to begin my apprenticeship."

Pearl couldn't suppress the momentary smile, remembering how proud she was of her handsome beau, tall and thin with wavy dark hair. She did love him, and the position he'd been offered in Kirkland to work with his uncle at Rosenberg's Furniture was a wonderful opportunity for Stanley and for their future together. The apprenticeship would provide him with a secure job and enough income to allow them to marry someday and live comfortably. She remembered Stanley's words. The words that began a series of events that brought her to this meadow today, scared and uncertain of the future they spoke of that night. From the huge boulder of granite, Pearl looked out to the vastness of the meadow and remembered graduation night when they snuck out early from the dance and stopped at Volunteer Park on the way back to her aunt's house.

Stanley pulled her close underneath a stand of evergreens, shielded from the street, quiet at the late hour. "We need to make this a night to remember."

Pearl recalled how her breath caught in her throat as he slid his hand down the front of her dress and inside her camisole. He cupped her breast. She remembered the warmth that stirred inside her, unlike anything she'd felt before. She squirmed and closed her eyes tight, reliving the moment of intense surrender. She panted a subconscious moan. She froze, then opened her eyes and shot a gaze around. She was afraid somehow someone could read her impure thoughts.

"It will be okay; I promise." Stanley sounded so wise and comforting that night. "You do trust me, don't you?"

His promise echoed as she recalled the experience which only excited her more and fanned the intense fire burning within her. A blast of guilt shrouded her. What had she done? Would her mother see in her face how she'd allowed Stanley to unbutton her bodice? How he slipped his hand inside underneath her corset while she looked down to see her breasts exposed and watched while Stanley explored her body. And then...Pearl closed her eyes tighter, an attempt to quash the memory. She'd felt the dampness from the grass when he had lowered her to the ground behind the stand of trees in the far corner of the park. As she did that night, Pearl now stiffened her memory so sharp, she once more melted and felt warm inside the private, most personal part of her.

Stanley dismissed her concern. "No one will see us. We're all alone. Just you and me." Then he was on top of her.

Even now, weeks later, she could smell the musty grass and feel the unfamiliar arousal that followed. Pearl brought her hands to her mouth and jumped off the rock. As it neared sunset, a chill teased the summer air and goose-bumps speckled her arm, but a hot flush crossed her face, a flush of lust, a flush of shame. The remaining contents of her stomach once more shifted and shuffled toward her throat. The few minutes of weakness, her willingness to wholly give herself to Stanley, no longer a sweet memory, now a bitter taste in her mouth.

She shouted to the empty meadow. "No, it cannot be! You promised it would be okay, Stanley." Her plans for the summer had folded like the poppies in the field as night descended. She started in the direction of the house and saw only darkness. Her chest heaved with despair; then, in the dark, a sliver of light poked through the window.

♪ ♪ ♪

Over the following two weeks, Pearl often prayed to a God she barely knew. A God she'd learned about during periodic Bible classes when her mother had attended Sunday services years ago. "Please, I promise not to be with a man again until I'm married. Please, God, I can't be with child." When her time of the month came and went for the second time, with no sign of her menses, and the morning sickness lingered, Pearl yielded to her condition. Time to face the consequences. For weeks, each night as she lay in bed, she imagined her mother's pained expression, tight lips, and eyes filled with disappointment instead of hope. She'd wait until late in the evening after dinner to break the news to her parents so she wouldn't have to face their glaring looks of disapproval throughout the day.

At the dinner table, Pearl's heart thumped so hard in her chest she glanced around, convinced everyone heard the pounding too. The intensity in her mother's eyes and her silence hinted she suspected something was wrong. As soon as Edna finished her potatoes, Mother excused her. "It's a pleasant evening. Clear your plate, Edna, then run along and play outside." Without further warning, Mother stiffened in her seat, pushed her plate aside, and chided Pearl. "Your father and I demand to know what's gotten into you since you've been home. You've simply not been yourself."

Panicked, Pearl's entire body trembled. Too afraid to make eye contact with her father, she managed to stutter. "May we go into the sitting room, please?"

Pearl dragged herself to the front room and waited until her parents were seated. Her eyes stung. She couldn't look at them. Instead, her eyes darted around the room in paranoid fear. She sank into the Victorian Eastlake chair across from her parents, a wedding gift to them from her paternal grandmother, Rose. She wondered for a moment what kind of wedding and what kind of gifts she and Stanley might have received, if only…

"Well? We're waiting." Her mother's sharp words came with a firm tap of her foot on the throw rug.

Pearl swallowed and looked into her mother's eyes. Her confession spilled out with bursts of sobs. "I think I'm with child."

Time stood still for Pearl. Though her parents didn't speak, their eyes spoke plenty. Pearl allowed herself a moment to think everything would be okay. Her parents would understand. After all, they married young. They, too, had no doubt made mistakes in their lives.

Her moment of optimism vanished, interrupted by her father's biting tone. "With child." He stood with such abruptness the sofa shook as he pushed himself up.

Pearl's gaze jerked to her father. His eyes flared with anger. A fit of anger she'd never witnessed before. The floor shook as he stomped over to her. He loomed over her, asserting his place of authority. "You're having a baby? How did you let this happen? Did your young man, Stanley, force himself on you? Tell me the truth."

The way her father spit his words, especially Stanley's name, enraged Pearl even as the pit of shame into which she'd fallen deepened. As shameful as lying with Stanley out of wedlock and carrying his child was, the thought that her father could believe she'd been violated in such a way was even more distressing. She sprang to her feet and faced her father. Her posture stiffened with her resolve to match his crossed arms and glaring eyes. "You want to know? I'll tell you. Stanley Rosenberg didn't force himself on me."

For several heartbeats, Pearl's words hung in the air, heavy as a rain-filled cloud ready to trigger a storm. Finally, her mother's glare, like a bolt of lightning, bore into Pearl. Her mother's voice cracked through her hands, cupped over her mouth, stifling her gasp. "You gave yourself to him, freely? Why?"

Pearl swallowed, moistening her parched throat. "Yes, Mother. I love Stanley and he loves me." All her secrets were out. Except for the final one. The one she and Stanley spoke of that night. The night that changed everything. With a determined voice, she glowered at her parents. "Stanley wants to get married. He has graduated and has a good job. I want to marry him, then we can keep the baby."

Her father shook his head. "That's out of the question. What do you know about love? And what kind of name is Rosenberg? Where are his people from?"

Risking further fury, Pearl glared. "His parents immigrated from Sweden. I know as much about love as you and Mama did when you married at sixteen."

Her mother bolted to her feet, clutching her head. "That's enough, young lady. Temper your attitude.

"I am of legal age. You and Father can't tell me what I can and can't do."

Her father raised his hand. For a moment, Pearl shuddered, fearful he might strike her. "Does he even know about the baby?"

Pearl cast her eyes down as she shook her head. "Not yet. I wanted to wait until I was certain."

"What about your education? Your mother and I scrimped and sacrificed so you could live in the city and attend high school. What about your plans to become a nurse and do something with your life? You realize getting married and raising a child changes everything?"

Her father was right. She had plans for herself, as her parents had had plans for her. But that was before. Before Stanley. Before she'd missed her monthly cycle. Twice. Her secrets were now exposed. Barren, like a tree in the deep of winter, Pearl couldn't stop the tears. "I'm so sorry, Mama and Papa. I didn't mean to let you down."

Her mother dropped her chin, clutching her head as she shook it. "I can't believe you acted so irresponsibly. You're supposed to be a model for your sister. You were supposed to finish high school, maybe go to university."

Her father stomped to the door. "I will not allow your condition to bring shame to our family. You know you cannot continue to live here. You will need to move away until the baby arrives." The door slammed behind him.

Pearl's head throbbed. She wished she could make her parents feel better. She didn't want to leave home, she needed their support, but deep down she knew what her parents would insist upon. Seconds later, the front door creaked open. Pearl and her mother turned. Edna stood in the doorway, her eyes wide with fear and confusion. "Mama. What's wrong?"

Mama shooed Edna to her room to get ready for bed. Pearl wanted to follow Edna to their room and bury her head in her pillow. She wanted to fall asleep and wake in the morning to find it was all a bad dream. Instead, her mother sat, her shoulders slumped, her face tight, suddenly appearing older than minutes earlier. Pearl went to her and squeezed her shoulders.

Her mother glared as she delivered her final message. "Your sister is too young. She must not ever learn about this"

Pearl put the tea kettle on the stove, then excused herself. Edna lay on her bed, her back to the door. Pearl wanted to explain to her sister the reason for her parent's outburst but didn't dare speak of it after her mother's warning. Pearl bent down and kissed Edna on the cheek and whispered. "Everything is going to be all right. Go to sleep now. Tomorrow will be brighter." Pearl wished she could believe her own words. Mother was right. Pearl had failed to set a good example for Edna as she promised. Unable to wait any longer to inform Stanley, she pulled out a sheet of paper and the fountain pen Papa bought her for Christmas. She fished under her mattress and retrieved the two letters he'd written to which she'd not responded. She sat on her bed and reread his words. No longer able to hide from the truth, Pearl's hand trembled as she wrote.

July 27, 1909
Dear Stanley,
It is with mixed emotions I write to you. I am sorry I have not responded to your letters sooner. Since returning home, my days have been plagued with uncertainty and physical discomfort. I fear for the news I must share with you now and hope my news does not influence your intention to marry me. After two months of doubt, I am now certain I am with child. Your child. I am certain my parents wish me to place the child for adoption and I'm afraid they will send me away. This is not my wish. If you still love me and wish to marry, please make arrangements with the courthouse in Seattle at the earliest possible date and send word. I have enough money to take the steamer to town and catch a trolley to the courthouse where we can meet. In the meantime, I will continue to try and obtain my parents' blessing.
With loving regard,
Pearl Mooney

Tomorrow she'd walk to town to buy a postage stamp and post the letter.

The bang of the door before dawn, Monday, released a bit of Pearl's tension. Father would be gone for the next two weeks, and she hoped his anger would lessen with the crack and falling of each tree.

With her father gone, her mother, though still sullen, was empathetic. She fretted over Pearl's health and offered advice on coping with her condition. At the end of the week, her mother handed Pearl a letter. "I wrote to your aunt about your situation. I don't need to tell you she was both shocked and hurt by your actions while living under her roof."

Pearl curbed her anger. If she were to survive these next few months, she would have to bury her feelings a lot. "I'm sorry."

"Being the Christian woman she is, Marie has offered you an honorable option to being sent away. Your cousin, Charlotte, has been unable to conceive. You can return to live with Marie as part of her family as you have for the past three years, and she will ensure the best care for you. She will be there to assist in the infant's delivery. When the baby comes, Charlotte and David will raise the child as their own. Your baby will remain in the family, and you'll always know how the baby is faring."

Pearl buried her face in her hands. "No." She shook her head in defiance. "You can't expect me to watch my baby being raised by someone else. Every time I saw Charlotte with my child...I don't think I could stand the heartache."

Her mother patted her hand. She tried to sound concerned, but her tone expressed a mandate. "You need to consider the alternative. You can't go out in public, especially in a small town like this, without being shunned by everyone in town. Every tongue will cluck. You can't sit at home for the next six months. If you don't move in with Aunt Marie and agree to have Charlotte and David raise the baby, I'll have no other choice other than to send you to a home for unwed mothers and other girls of unsavory character."

Like water through a ruptured dike, Pearl's emotions gushed. This couldn't possibly be happening to her. She wouldn't let it. She yanked her hand from her mother's tender hold. "Why won't you approve of my marriage? You've met Stanley. You told me was a fine young man."

"I'm sure he is, but you cannot finish your education if you're married and burdened with the responsibility of a child. I've done okay, but I've always wondered how different things would be if I had more than a sixth-grade education. After the baby is born and placed for adoption to a good home, you can return home. We will send you off at the end of summer to coincide with the beginning of the school year. No one outside this family will need to know of your condition. And your sister is too young to be told. Do you understand?"

"It's not fair. It isn't yours or Father's decision to make." Pearl fought the urge to push more. If she pushed too far, she'd be out on her own, and not even Aunt Marie could help her then. "I remember the day Edna was born. I resented having to share you with another baby."

"I know."

"But when everything turned scary, and I thought Edna might die, I saw how you looked at Edna." Pearl's lips quivered. "I understood how you could love someone you hadn't yet met. I saw the pain in your eyes with the thought of losing her. I know the seed growing inside me is only the size of a pea, but I already feel love for this baby. The same kind of love you felt for Edna, even before you saw her." Pearl raised her hands in prayer. Her tone pleading. "Please don't make me give my baby away."

Chapter Seventeen

1909 – Reality

As mid-August approached, Pearl's stomach relaxed. The churning and somersaulting from the morning sickness eased. A calm acceptance replaced the tightness in her chest and the hazy uncertainty of her future.

Though her mother clung to misgivings of marriage and refused to listen to Pearl's desire to keep the baby, each day she held her evening embrace a little longer, a little tighter. Her words came softer and with more warmth.

"You're my oldest daughter. I've always had such high expectations. Our desire has always been for you to finish twelve years of education and take a job before settling down and raising a family."

One afternoon, a gentle knock on her bedroom door drew Pearl from her melancholy. Her face brightened at the sight of two dresses draped over her mother's outstretched arms. "These will help to hide your growing belly. Now you can live at home a bit longer until your condition can no longer be concealed."

Pearl held up the dresses. The first one, a navy and white cotton voile print with a billowy skirt, and generous fabric gathered at the waist. The second dress was light pink with a high neck crisscrossed with lace at the empire waist. Pearl's throat tightened as her eyes welled. "They're perfect. Thank you, Mother."

Her mother stepped out. "I'll make sure Edna leaves you alone so you can try them on."

Pearl sat on her bed and ran her hand over the soft feminine fabric that she could easily envision on a party dress. Under normal circumstances, being with child brought happiness and good wishes.

But not for her. Not on this day. Mother had shown her acceptance with this peace offering, and Pearl was determined to feel joy. Pearl ran her hand over her belly as she undressed. Her condition hit a new level of reality. She stared hard into the mirror. A lump formed in her throat. She swallowed. In only a matter of weeks, her condition would be obvious to the busybodies in town. She squinted and tried to imagine her belly as extended as a beach ball. Her porcelain skin permanently marked by purple and red scars like those she'd seen on her mother. "I can't do this." She slumped onto her bed. She still had her dreams. She still believed in her endless opportunities. Having a baby meant surrendering herself to another. A helpless infant. She was too young, and she was too selfish. Her parents were right. She would finish her education first. There would be plenty of time for a baby after she became a nurse.

♪ ♪ ♪

The following days moved in painful slow motion as she awaited news from Stanley. Each day Pearl rushed to greet Mr. Schmidt when he arrived with the mail.

After the third day, Mr. Schmidt shook his head. "Must be something important. Sorry, missy, only have communications for your father today. Perhaps tomorrow."

Pearl sank to the stoop. Her future, filled with hope three months ago, now looked gloomy and fraught with worry. From the day of Edna's birth, Pearl had imagined herself as a mother. She recalled not only her mother's elation but the atmosphere of joy surrounding her sister's birth. She remembered how her mother beamed when all the ladies extended congratulatory wishes of good health whenever they passed on the street in town. Now, in contrast, Pearl's untimely condition filled her mother's eyes with disappointment and humiliation. The rare times Pearl accompanied her mother to town, the women on the streets passed by without a second glance, though Pearl's unease left her heart racing and her palms sweating. If any passersby had detected even a hint of scandal, their wagging tongues would ripple like waves throughout the small town, leaving her parents the target of vicious gossip. Pearl imagined the busybody hens would wish hell and damnation upon her for bringing embarrassment upon her family and by extension to the small community.

When her father returned home at the end of the week, he ignored her. Pearl guessed he wished her invisible or at least gone. Gone from his sight, gone from his mind, so he could ignore the uncomfortable situation of her being with child.

Pearl felt shame. Shame like the Gustoff children felt in elementary school. A shame they wore like their ill-fitting, frayed clothing. Shame that segregated them from the others in school as they played apart from their classmates. Unlike the Gustoff children, born into poverty, Pearl had created her own shame, the kind of shame that comes without pity or charitable acts from even the kindest and most Christian neighbors and friends.

Pearl had witnessed her mother's kindness and charity. Though her own family wasn't wealthy, Pearl and Edna were comfortable, and they never did without food or clothing, especially with her mother's skill as a seamstress. They always wore clean, well-fitting clothes in good repair. As the oldest of seven, Gunter Gustoff, the same age as Pearl, dropped out of school at the end of sixth grade to go to work at a Lake Kapowsin logging camp down south between Tacoma and Mount Rainier. Pearl had been with her mother in town when Mrs. Gustoff came for dry goods and her mother asked about the family.

"My Gunter sends home forty dollars almost every month." Mrs. Gustoff's tired face wore a broad smile as she lifted a bolt of fabric from her basket and placed a hand on her bulging belly. "I can't tell you how much that helps. Haven't had a new dress since God knows when, but my condition requires it. Not sure when I'll find the time with all the young uns but it better be soon." She sighed through a good-natured smile.

Pearl remembered watching with pride as her mother took Mrs. Gustoff's hand. "You bring that fabric by my place when you can. Bring along a pattern and I'll make it for you." Pearl saw the lines of unease on Mrs. Gustoff's brow. Her mother quickly patted Mrs. Gustoff's hand. "Not to worry. No charge for a neighbor."

Mrs. Gustoff clutched Pearl's mother's hand and held on for several long seconds. "Bless you. Bless you, Mrs. Mooney. You are a kind and nonjudgmental woman."

Walking home, her mother sighed as she shook her head. "Sometimes, life's circumstances are beyond one's control. Poor Mrs. Gustoff. Not her fault her husband is uneducated and unable to provide for his own."

With the last of the dinner dishes in the sink, Papa shooed Edna off to bed, his narrowed eyes warning her he would accept no talking back. Alone with her parents, Pearl shuddered. Her father's sharp words silenced her before she could tell them about her doubts. "Your mother and I have made a decision."

Pearl shrank into her chair and stared at the floor.

"It's obvious you can't return to your Aunt Marie's to continue your schooling. And your mother informs me you're unwilling to accept your aunt's kind offer."

Pearl lifted her head and locked eyes with her father. Her entire body tensed and tightened, forming a knot in her stomach.

"We can't have you seen in public as long as you are unwed and in a motherly way."

Without so much as a blink, her father's hard eyes reinforced his orders. "You will return to Seattle early in September before your condition is apparent. Your mother has found a place for you to live until the baby arrives. You will be able to pursue your studies there."

Pearl looked at her mother, expecting a small amount of sympathy, some expression of condolence, some kind, nonjudgmental words of acceptance like the ones she'd extended to Mrs. Gustoff. Pearl yearned for any indication her mother's decision was relaxing, but she maintained a wary posture. Pearl's doubts vanished. "What about the baby? I want to keep him." Not daring to look at her father, Pearl's lips quivered, and the pit of her stomach roiled like butter in a churn. She looked into her mother's eyes, hoping to find a measure of comfort.

"You can't be serious." Her father's harshness made Pearl shudder.

"We've sacrificed too much for your education. There will be plenty of time to have another child later when you're married."

111

Ignoring him, Pearl sought a morsel of sympathy, a grain of understanding. "Fine. I want to get married. Stanley's a good, kind man. He loves me and will be able to provide for me. Isn't that what you want for me?"

Her mother brought her hand to her forehead. Sadness and defeat showed in her eyes.

Pearl caressed her barely protruding belly. "Any day now, I'll hear from Stanley. I told him I want to marry him and keep the baby." Her chest heaved with the weight of uncertainty. What if Stanley didn't answer? What if Stanley agreed with her parents?

Her father shook his head. "No matter. Your mother and I feel it would be best for both you and the baby to place the baby with a family that is prepared to raise a child. You're not wed, and even if you do get married, everyone will know the child is illegitimate. You don't want your child growing up burdened by that stigma."

"I don't care about that. This isn't the dark ages. I may not have many rights, but right now, I have the right to keep my baby."

Her mother, unable to remain silent any longer, shook her head. "That is out of the question. Marie told me a friend of Charlotte's found herself in a family way, out of wedlock. Her parents sent her to a refuge for fallen girls called the Florence Crittenton Home. You have shown us that you are weak and in need of direction. You are fortunate to have such a home that will house and care for you while allowing you to continue your education. When it's time, they will place the baby in a proper home. As long as you are under our roof and we are supporting you, you will do as you are told."

The decision had been made. Pearl's opinion ignored. Pearl surrendered. "Okay, I'll go away to the Florence Crittenton Home and give my baby up for adoption."

Feeling hopeless and helpless, Pearl sulked. Days passed without word from Stanley. She wondered if Stanley had revealed their secret to his parents and if they had received the news with less objection, less judgment, than her parents. A knock at the door caught her attention. She opened it to see Mr. Schmidt waving a letter in his hand. "Is this what you've been waiting for?"

Pearl grabbed the letter from Stanley along with several other pieces of mail. She tossed the rest onto the kitchen table. Her heart pounded with the fierceness of a war drum as she slogged to her room. As she stared at the plain white envelope posted from Kirkland, Washington, her hands trembled. What if Stanley spurned her and rejected any notion of taking responsibility? What if he had moved on and agreed with her parents it was for the best to put the child up for adoption? Her heart raced. She held her breath and slipped her finger under the flap. *This is it. This letter holds the key to my future.* She unfolded the single-page letter.

August 08, 1909
My Dearest Pearl,
I hope this letter reaches you before you are required to move away. I was relieved to finally receive correspondence from you after so many weeks with no word as to your well-being. I will not pretend to be thrilled by this unexpected news. It has taken me several days to process my response. My apprenticeship is going well, and my uncle has guaranteed me a position of stable employment and an adequate income. I have confided in my uncle, Frederick, who has proven to be a support to me. My parents are less enthusiastic about the situation. My parents have agreed not to stand in my way if I wish to marry. I would be honored to take you as my wife if your parents are in agreement. My uncle will stand in as a witness, but two witnesses will be required, and a license must be obtained in advance of the ceremony. Please forward your new address so we may keep in touch. If your new residence allows, I should like to call you there so we may discuss our plans further. As to the child you are carrying, if your parents decide our marriage adds legitimacy, and if you desire to keep the baby, I shall do everything within my power to support you both. I vow you will not face this alone.
Yours truly,
Stanley Rosenberg

Chapter Eighteen

1909 – Sent Away

By the end of August, Edna watched as her mother grew increasingly short-tempered, her pinched face as sour as vinegar. Whenever her father was home, he avoided everyone, spending his days outside or in the barn, seldom sitting in his chair with his newspaper and his pipe.

Edna's tummy hurt every day, but she was reluctant to tell her mother. Instead, she chewed on peppermint leaves from the garden to soothe the churning inside. She didn't understand why her parents were so angry with Pearl. At night, Edna tossed and turned in bed while harsh whispers from across the hall invaded her sleep like phantoms. Sometimes, Pearl lay across from her sobbing into her pillow or dashed outside in the middle of the night to use the privy.

Most days, Pearl had little desire to talk or play with Edna, preferring long walks away from the house. Edna didn't want to upset her mother or sister, but she needed to know why her life was so upside down. Shooed from the house one morning, bored with Molly and her swing, Edna spied Pearl strolling across the field. She trailed behind and found Pearl perched atop a rock so big Edna could not climb up.

"Go away," Pearl told her. "I want to be alone."

"What's wrong, Pearl? How come no one will tell me anything?"

Pearl brought her hands up, covering her eyes. "You're too young to understand."

"I'm seven years old. I'm not a baby." Edna thought about the raised voices, followed by whispers. "Is Mama having another baby? Is that what you don't want me to know?"

Pearl shook her head, but her gaze softened.

"No, Mama's not having a baby."

"But I heard her telling Papa about the baby."

Pearl cast her eyes downward. She mumbled, swung her legs around, and turned her back to Edna. "Go back home, please."

Stunned by her sister's sharp words and angry tone, Edna's lips quivered. Though Pearl had always been sympathetic to Edna's crying, she would not let Pearl see her cry today. Edna turned and ran back to the house with tears running down her cheeks.

Alone on the porch, after dinner, Edna heard booming voices that shook the windowpanes. When the shouting stopped, footsteps stamped nearer. Edna jumped from the swing and hid on the far side of the milk box as the front door banged opened. Her father stomped down the steps hollering over his shoulder, "Don't wait up for me."

Edna held her breath. She hoped the pounding in her chest didn't reveal her presence. She crouched lower behind the wooden box and watched her father disappear into the barn. The wide heavy doors slammed with such force Nellie neighed her disapproval.

A queasiness gripped her. She understood Pearl's desire to be alone. Edna raced down the steps like a fawn on gangly legs. When she reached the outcropping of rocks, she clawed at Pearl's rock in a feeble attempt to hoist herself up. She settled for a smaller perch and stared toward her home. Then she buried her face in her hands, sick with worry. Why did Papa say Pearl needed to go away? How could she survive without her sister?

Edna didn't know how long she sat. Her mother's call from across the field broke the silence. The sky had grown dark. Goose bumps covered her arms.

"Edna. Where are you?"

Unwilling to surrender her solitude to the angry exchanges at home, Edna ignored her mother until her mother's tone became pleading and frantic. "Please, Edna, come home."

Knowing she couldn't stay away forever, Edna exhaled her frustration and jumped down. "I'm over here." She waved her arms and dashed toward the house, uncertain what lay ahead.

Mother stood with her arms crossed across her chest as Edna crept up the stairs. "Where have you been, young lady?" Not awaiting a response, she ordered Edna to her room. "Run along. It's time for bed."

Edna bit her tongue and sulked. She wished she'd remained on her rock, a far better place to be than being holed up in her room with nowhere to go when the screaming started again. Edna wished her family had a Graphophone so she could turn the sound up loud enough to drown out the angry booming confrontation that came from the front room and even her closed bedroom door couldn't mute. Not bothering to wash, she slipped into her nightgown and hunkered under the covers hoping to drown out the tension that threatened her family.

Hearing footsteps in the hall, Edna turned her back to the door, yanked the covers over her head, and pretended to be asleep. The door creaked open. A figure moved across the room toward the empty bed. From the sliver of moonlight splintering through the curtains, Pearl's silhouette appeared. Edna stopped holding her breath and peeked out from the covers to see Pearl pulling a trunk out from underneath her bed. Edna threw back the covers and sat up. "Sissy, what's wrong? What are you doing?"

Pearl turned with a jerk and wiped a sleeve against her cheek. She glanced toward the door and shook her head. "Nothing's wrong. Go back to sleep."

"But I heard you crying and Papa yelling." Edna straightened. "He said you have to give it away. What is he talking about?"

Pearl sat on the foot of Edna's bed. She stroked Edna's long curls. "You'll understand someday. I have to leave for a while, but I promise I'll be back as soon as I can."

In a panic, Edna cried out to her sister. "Where are you going?"

Pearl silently raised her index finger to her lips to quiet Edna. "We can't talk about that now."

Unable to control the emotions bottled up for so long, Edna released her frustration. Her persistent cries brought her mother rushing into the room. Pearl turned away and continued to search through the metal trunk.

Edna tensed. She wanted to crawl under the covers, but Mother had seen her.

"What did you tell your sister?" Mother scowled and shook her finger at Pearl. "Now look what you've done. You've upset the last innocent person in this house." Mother frowned, gathered Edna into her arms, and smothered her in a giant hug.

Barely able to breathe, Edna pushed away from her mother's embrace. "Pearl hasn't done anything to make me cry. I heard you, and I heard Papa yelling. You're making her leave. Please, don't make her go away."

Mother shot a glance at Pearl, then noticed the open trunk on the floor. "What do you think you're doing?"

"I'm packing. It's what you want, isn't it?" Pearl's narrowed eyes glared.

"No, dear, this is not what I wanted. None of this is what I wanted. Go to bed. We will talk about it in the morning."

After Mother disappeared, Pearl slipped into her nightie.

Edna sniffled. "You're leaving, aren't you?

Pearl sat on Edna's bed. "Yes, but you'll never be alone; you'll always have Mama and Papa. And I love you, and I'll be thinking of you even if I can't be here with you. Now, shhh, go to sleep. I'll hold you." Pearl lay next to Edna. "Do you know where I hide my diary?"

Edna raised her brows and offered a slight nod.

Pearl kissed Edna on the forehead and wrapped her arms around Edna until she drifted off to sleep.

♪ ♪ ♪

The next morning, Pearl's bed was empty. A sinking feeling swallowed her. Panicked, she ran to the kitchen where her mother and Pearl sat in silence. Mother sipped from the brown mug she always filled with cold coffee sweetened with fresh cream and sugar. Pearl nibbled bird-size bites of hot mush. She noticed her father's coat missing from the old oak hall tree in the screened porch even though he'd only been home for one night. "Where's Father. Has he gone back to the camp?"

Mother sat stone faced, not responding. Edna cast a sideways glance at her sister, who looked up for only an instant and offered a silent, quick nod.

Edna pulled out a chair at the table and climbed onto the seat. Mother got up in a daze. She walked to the stove and returned with a bowl of hot porridge, placing it in front of Edna.

"Mama? What's wrong?"

Her mother spun around. "Your sister is returning to school today. You need to say goodbye to her. It will be a while before you see her again."

Edna stopped eating midbite. "Will she be home for Christmas?"

"Not this year. Enough of the questions. This is not your concern. Mrs. Fletcher is coming by around nine o'clock to pick you up. You will spend the day with the Fletchers' while I take Pearl to Seattle. Mr. Fletcher will return you after dinner. I should be home by then."

Edna finished her porridge then stomped into the living room. As always, Mama's sewing table stood piled with fabric. She recognized the remnants from the two new dresses Mama made for Pearl. She stole a glance back to the kitchen where Mother stood over the cookstove. Edna snuck over to the sewing table and saw a Butterick pattern buried underneath the fabric remnants. She looked at the drawing of the women on the envelope. What did it mean? Edna thought about Pearl's mood changes and her queasy stomach over the past two months. She remembered Inez saying her mother was sick before Inez's sister was born. If her mother wasn't having a baby...? As quickly as the question popped into her head, she knew why her parents were sending Pearl away.

♪ ♪ ♪

Throughout the day, her sister's tearful goodbye from the morning resounded in her head like a haunting wind on a stormy night she found it difficult to think about anything but Pearl. When Mrs. Fletcher dropped her by the house after dinner, the house stood dark. No light shone from the windows, and no hints of food cooking on the stove escaped from the kitchen chimney. Biting hard on her lip, Edna turned the doorknob and stepped inside. The chill in the quiet house informed Edna the stove had not been stoked all day. She rushed to her bedroom, holding onto a sliver of hope. Throwing the door open, Edna froze. The open closet revealed a bare space where

Pearl's clothes once hung and the shelf that once held Pearl's clothes, lay empty.

"Goodbye, Pearl," she whispered to the lonely room where she'd cried herself to sleep less than twenty-four hours earlier. She stomped her feet. The floorboards creaked and groaned. She sank onto her bed as her knees buckled. How could her parents make Pearl go away? They knew how much Pearl meant to her. Pearl was gone. This time for good.

Remembering Pearl's words from the previous night, Edna ran to the closet. Pearl's muff hung from a hanger. Edna reached up high and felt inside Pearl's secret hiding place. The red cloth-covered diary was gone, but Edna found something else. She withdrew a folded note, straightened it on her lap, and read the short goodbye.

> Dear Edna,
> I knew you would find this. I had to leave, but it's for the best. I don't know when I shall see you again, but I promise to write to you when I can. I am sorry I brought shame to the family. My thoughts are with you, even if we can't be together.
> Pearl

Crumpling the note, she threw herself on her bed. She cried until she felt drained. With Pearl gone, the weeks of whispers and secrets, the hollering, and Mother's icy behavior would cease, but Edna's sister, her confidant, was gone, and Edna didn't know when she would see her again.

A loud whinny startled Edna. She sniffled and grabbed a handkerchief from the side table and dried her eyes. She hurried to the kitchen.

Her mother stopped inside. Her eyes wide with surprise. "I hoped to be home before you got here." She placed her pocketbook and her parcels on the counter. "Are you all right? It looks like you've been crying."

Unable to hold back her frustration any longer, Edna bawled, "You made her leave."

Her mother's shoulders slumped. "We had to."

"Why?" Edna shouted louder than she intended. "Is it because Pearl is having a baby?"

Her mother's eyes narrowed and pierced Edna with a sharpness she'd never seen. "What did Pearl tell you?"

"Nothing. I heard you and Papa talking. You said it would be best for the baby, and I saw the patterns on the sewing table."

Her mother crumpled and collapsed onto a chair. "Come here. We didn't want you to know. You're so young." She pulled Edna in close. "Your sister is not married. Her being with child is not considered acceptable. It's best for everyone for her to have the baby in a place where no one knows her. After the baby is born, a married couple will adopt the baby and raise the child as their own."

Edna pulled away from her mother. "I don't understand."

"You will in time. Let's not talk about this anymore right now. Go read in your room until dinner is ready."

Edna squinted her eyes and stomped off.

Chapter Nineteen

1909 – Florence Crittenton Home

Disgraced and embarrassed, Pearl stood glassy-eyed. Her cheeks flamed as red as the austere brick facade of the two-story Florence Crittenton Home that loomed mere yards in front of her. "Please, Mama, don't leave me here."

Though Dunlap was only a short distance due east of Port Orchard, as a bird flies, with Puget Sound separating the two towns, the route took several hours, including a steamer crossing and a trip on the train.

Pearl's mother ignored her daughter's pleas and spoke her first words since the train station in Seattle. "We've discussed this. This is the only place near Seattle where no one will judge you. This home was established for girls in your condition. The home has a fine reputation, and we're lucky to have such a hospitable environment. It will be a haven for you until the baby arrives. Come along now. The headmistress is expecting us."

Her mother's biting tone felt like a slap. Pearl's cheeks burned at the thought that her mother had lost all respect for her. Pearl's fingers tingled. She wiggled them to restore the flow of blood to the bright pink digits that had gripped her suitcase too tightly and for too long. Slow and uncertain, she plodded behind her mother, her heart pounding with increasing intensity with each step closer to her new home. Her mother threw back her shoulders as she yanked open the heavy door. Inside, the wooden plank flooring wore a shine of varnish.

Her mother stood somber, pocketbook clutched to her chest, and looked up and down the sterile hall, then led the way. Pearl dutifully followed her. In the otherwise silent cavernous hall, their steps echoed in staccato taps like drumsticks striking against cymbals. Pearl peeked through the small windows on the closed doors along the way. Girls sat at desks with their attention focused on teachers in the front of the room writing their lessons on the chalkboard.

In front of the last door on the right, Mother stopped walking. Pearl's heart beat in quick time like the Sousa march she had practiced over and over again on the piano. She read the black lettered sign outside the door. "Anna Dugas Barrett, Director." Mother knocked with a nervous almost inaudible knock. Pearl cringed, imagining the shame her proud mother felt forced into this uncomfortable situation.

The headmistress called through the closed door. "Come in."

Mother urged Pearl into the room ahead of her. Miss Barrett sat straight-backed; her hands crossed. She directed them to chairs opposite hers which was behind a massive oak desk piled with folders and forms.

Placing her lone piece of luggage on the floor, Pearl sank into the chair next to her mother. She studied the woman with gray-streaked hair pulled back in a tight bun. Miss Barrett's high collar and stern face made her look a decade older than Pearl's mother. Her dark eyes looked at Pearl with a no-nonsense, business glare that straightaway sent a shudder of fear through Pearl.

She paused before pushing her spectacles higher on the bridge of her nose. "You must be Pearl Mooney."

Pearl nodded before looking at her hands folded in her lap. She wished she could hide the shame creeping in.

"I'm Abbey Mooney." Her mother tapped Pearl on the shoulder in warning to straighten up and show proper decorum.

Anna Barrett nodded to Mrs. Mooney, then turned her full attention to Pearl. "I'm sure you have a lot of questions, Pearl. I'll be happy to answer them." Anna Barrett cleared her throat awaiting a response.

Pearl looked at the director, shocked that Miss Barrett was concerned about her. She finally spoke. "Are all of the girls here in a family way?"

"Many are." She leaned forward. She unfolded her hands and brought them to her chest. "Some of the girls are here due to an unstable home life in which their parents are not always able to care for them. Others are homeless, and otherwise in danger of going to the bad side."

Pearl shifted in discomfort. Did the director consider Pearl's condition, her decision to engage in illicit behavior, depraved and shameful? Was Pearl one of the girls who had fallen to the bad side? She fidgeted with her clammy hands.

With her full attention focused on Pearl, Anna Barrett spoke in measured words. "You are fortunate to have parents who, under the circumstances, want only the best for you. Some of the girls here are from the streets; they've sold themselves for the pleasure of men."

Pearl's eyes widened, stunned girls of her age were drawn into such a seedy profession. She couldn't imagine growing up in a home not filled with love or being forced to earn money as a whore. Pearl had witnessed the goings-on in the downtown red-light district, known as the Tenderloin District, when she went to the theater with Stanley two years earlier. She remembered how he told her gentlemen were known to bring their business associates to dine and enjoy fine spirits in the company of some of Seattle's most beautiful and cultured women living in brothels managed by Madame Lou. Pearl cast a tender glance at her mother.

"The Florence Crittenton Home will be a safe and nurturing home to you during your time here. The staff is here to offer you hope and help."

Framed awards and certificates decorated the walls of the small, neat office. The largest photo was of a dark-haired man with a gray mustache. Underneath, it read, "Charles Nelson Crittenton, Founder" Next to his photo, was another photo taken in eighteen-ninety-five, Cofounder, General Superintendent of National Florence Crittenton Mission, Dr. Kate Waller Barrett. Pearl's eyes widened—a female doctor. She thought about her meeting Dr. Chapman and how he motivated her to pursue a career in the medical field.

Filled with regret, Pearl turned and studied the woman across from her. "Is that you? Are you a real doctor?"

Anna Barrett chuckled. "No. I'm Anna Barrett. Kate Barrett is my aunt. She cofounded the Crittenton Homes. Her dedication to the mission inspired me to get involved. I assisted in opening this location, the sixty-fifth Crittenton Home to open in the nation. Kate is an amazingly accomplished woman. Yes, she's a real doctor, as was her grandfather before her.''

Taken aback, Pearl straightened and looked more intently on the director. "I didn't know women could become doctors. Doesn't she have a family?"

The director nodded. "Kate was married for sixteen years and had five children when she got her medical degree in Georgia. There were few women in medicine in those days. I imagine it hasn't changed much.''

Pearl wrinkled her face. "If she's a real doctor, why does she work for a place like this instead of in an office with patients?"

The headmistress leaned in, hands folded in front of her, and offered a warm smile. "Doctor Barrett is a deeply religious woman, married to a reverend. She's a highly respected woman who has spoken all over these United States.

Curious, Pearl looked back at the photograph. "What does she talk about?"

"That is quite a story." Anna Barrett appeared eager to share. "Wherever she wishes to open a new home for the downcast women, she tells the same story to inspire the local community to support her cause. When her first child, Robert, was an infant, a young girl with a baby came to the rectory where they lived on a snowy night in December. Kate realized the young girl had no one. Moved by the woman's plight, Kate and her husband cared for her. Kate's father, a southern gentleman, considered girls who conceived out of wedlock as soiled. She was taught from a young age that fallen women were a disgrace to their families and to society.''

An unsettling reaction, shame mixed with remorse, shrouded Pearl. She found it difficult to look at the woman who sat five feet in front of her, but there was a sparkle, a warmth and compassion, in Anna Barrett's eyes that held Pearl's attention. "I don't understand. If she considers girls like me a disgrace, why did she help found this place?"

The director squeezed her eyes closed for a moment as if she were trying to pull the story from somewhere deep in her mind. "I asked her about her experience with the young girl at the rectory. I still remember her words."

Even Mother was at the edge of her seat as Anna Barrett continued. "She told me about the time she met the young woman." Anna Barrett's eyes seemed to look past Pearl into the past before she continued. "At that time, she entered into a covenant with God that so long as she lived, her voice would always be lifted on behalf of these outcasts and her hand would always be held out to aid the fallen and wayward girls."

Overwhelmed by the compassion of the reverend and his wife to the young mother, Pearl felt a weight lifted from her chest. She straightened and wiped her clammy hands on her dress. Even with five children and a husband, Kate Barrett pursued a lofty goal. She became a doctor. She overcame so much to help young women like Pearl, who had stumbled and made mistakes. Pearl swallowed the lump in her throat. She fixed her gaze on the director, wondering if Anna Barrett possessed the same compassion as Kate Barrett. Pearl asked the only question that mattered to her. "Will I be allowed to keep my baby?" Feeling her mother's burning stare, Pearl refused to make eye contact and refused to acknowledge her opposition to the idea.

Her mother's sharp words informed Pearl she'd spoken out of turn. "Pearl, we've had this conversation."

Miss Barrett glanced at Pearl's mother before she continued. "There will be many factors to consider before a decision is made. Please understand, our policy is to strive to keep the mother and child together. Our goal is to reform our girls. We require all students to take parenting classes during their entire stay. We see motherhood as a means of reform. Think of this home as a training ground to help you become a responsible mother. We will ensure you have adequate medical care and keep you safe from the scorn of society while allowing you to complete your courses in higher learning. Except in extreme circumstances, Crittenton policy opposes the separation of mother and child for adoption, we believe children should be kept out of institutions."

Hearing these words of hope, Pearl felt a newfound confidence wash over her. Knowing her mother would disapprove, Pearl blurted out her news. "But I'm going to marry the baby's father."

Her mother's gasp drew Miss Barrett's attention. "One should not enter into the institution of marriage simply because a child is on the way, but if that is what you and your beau decide and you have the support of your families, the staff here will support you. You have time. Until then, I encourage you to keep an open mind. We can work with you as to your length of stay." The director opened a file on her desk and thumbed through the papers. "I see you are due in around mid-February. We will be keeping close tabs on your progress during your time here. Now, would you like to see the facility?"

♪ ♪ ♪

Pearl and her mother followed Miss Barrett down the hall to the classrooms. "You will be expected to maintain a full course of study to correspond with your assigned grade. I understand this will be your fourth year."

"Yes, ma'am."

Miss Barrett stopped outside a room. Peering in the glass of the door, Pearl observed two rows of young women, hands folded on the desks.

"This is the class you will be joining. These young women will graduate at the end of the term."

"What if they deliver their babies before the term ends?"

Miss Barrett reached for the door handle. "Of course, that is often the case, but most of our young women are encouraged to stay for up to six months after the baby's birth to nurse their young ones and ensure their readiness and maturity. We believe that to be in the best interest of the child and the mother. This stay is adequate in most cases to allow a full docket of classes for students to meet the requirements of the public-school program."

Miss Barrett turned the knob and pushed open the door.

All eyes turned and looked at the three women when they stepped inside. The teacher acknowledged the director of the school with a curt nod then rapped on the desk with her hand to draw the girls' attention again. The classroom was full. Pearl imagined the dozen or so young girls all had dreams. Dreams that were drifting away like rudderless ships after a storm. She wondered if her own dream of becoming a nurse would slip away too. After a few minutes, Anna Barrett swept her arm to motion them back out the door.

Out in the hall, Miss Barrett continued to point out the various rooms along the way. "In addition to a classroom for each of the four grade levels, we have two maternity wards, a dining room, and a social hall."

Mother nodded with each room she passed, obviously pleased by the surroundings. "How many girls reside here?"

"We are able to house fifty and are almost always at maximum capacity. You are fortunate there was a room available. I'll take you upstairs to where all the dorm rooms are."

After lugging her suitcase around all day, the march up two flights of stairs drained the last of Pearl's energy. She wondered if she would continue to tire more easily as the months wore on. Her mother's energy was endless when she was carrying Edna.

"Here we are." Miss Barrett stopped and knocked on a door, waiting for only a moment before entering the room. "This will be your home for the next year."

Hearing the words brought a sense of permanence and stung like a yellow jacket. Pearl stepped inside. The sun shining in gave a homey warmth to the tidy room. Two single beds lined one wall and a third bed stood against the opposite wall, with each cloaked in a colorful quilt.

Miss Barrett pointed to the lone bed. "That bed will be yours. There should be an empty drawer in the bureau for your clothes as well as closet space."

Pearl looked around and spied the single bureau. A vase of daisies and wildflowers sat on top. The memory of picking flowers after Edna was born brought happy anticipation followed by panic. A tremor of cold sweat swept over her. How would she face this birth without her mother or her aunt by her side? Her words trembled. "It's very comfortable."

Anna Barrett nodded in response. "Yes, we strive to make the rooms cheery and comfortable. All the rooms are furnished by different church and civic organizations. The Methodists, the Elks, and the Masons have all donated to us, so the furnishings vary from room to room. The kindhearted church ladies even made quilts for each bed. We want your time here to feel as much as possible like home instead of an institution. Classes should be out soon. I'll leave you to unpack and settle in. It won't be long before your roommates return. I'll be back at that time to make the introductions." She turned and left Pearl alone with her mother.

"It's nicer than I expected, don't you think?" Pearl's mother's face relaxed. "I hope you believe me; we're not doing this to punish you."

Not certain she believed her mother, Pearl breezed over to the window and peered out. "I know." Outside, in contrast to the busy city streets of Seattle an hour away, the small town of Dunlap was almost sleepy. A large manicured grassy area surrounded the home with flower beds of roses and other cheery blossoms dotting the grounds. From a large, gnarled tree hung a swing like the one Papa had made for Edna. Pearl remembered her home, and her eyes misted.

"Are you okay?"

Pearl flung herself into her mother's arms. As her mother gripped her in a tight embrace, a storm of pent-up emotions found release. "I can't do this alone, Mother. Please don't leave me."

Her mother held on for several seconds, finally pulling back, she looked Pearl square in the eyes. "You are strong. You will survive. If you need anything, call your aunt. She'll come by and visit if it's allowed." Her mother kissed her on the forehead, then without another word, she turned and was gone.

When the door closed, Pearl collapsed onto the bed. She buried her face in her hands. An unfamiliar queasiness washed over her. Not morning sickness. For the first time in her life, Pearl was alone, abandoned, and isolated from anyone and everyone who had ever cared about her. She ached for someone to hold. She ached for her mother to return; she ached for Edna; she even ached for Papa. Most of all, she envisioned her prince charming riding in and taking her away from all of this. She sat in silence too miserable to move.

She wasn't sure how long ago her mother had walked out, but without warning, cheery voices came from the hall, and the door was flung open.

♪ ♪ ♪

For the next three months, Pearl followed a routine far more regimented than her routine at Seattle High. Though the classes at Florence Crittenton were smaller and more disciplined, her days played out much the same as they had her three previous years, with classes from eight thirty to four and a midday break for lunch. Pearl found the environment of the all-girl school where every student had much at stake, more focused. Spurred by Kate Barrett's achievements, Pearl vowed to learn as much as possible during her time there. Her dreams of becoming a nurse might not be realistic right now, and her endless opportunities might be limited, but Pearl was determined to reach for the stars. If Dr. Barrett could achieve all her dreams— marriage, a family, and a career—why couldn't she? The thought gave her a purpose.

Thrilled to be taking a course in physical science that would include a section on chemistry, Pearl had to first sit through the unit on astronomy. Though she had never given thought to the formation of the galaxy or observing the planets, her interest was piqued when her teacher, Miss Mathewson, told the girls their unborn babies might be among those who witnessed a rare astronomical event. Pearl listened with interest along with the rest of the class.

"How many of you have heard of Halley's Comet?" No hands went up, and Miss Mathewson continued. "Halley's is the only known short-period comet that is visible to the naked eye from Earth appearing on a regular schedule, and the only naked-eye comet that might appear twice in a human lifetime." Miss Mathewson paused and surveyed the students. "Halley's comet passes by the earth only every seventy-six years or so. For most of us, we will see it once in our lives if we are lucky. Since the comet is expected to next appear in mid-May of 1910, your babies will all be in a unique situation. If they're lucky, some of your children may still be alive when the comet next visits in 1986."

Pearl quickly ciphered. By 1986, she'd be ninety-four, much older than anyone on either side of her family. Still, she held onto a sliver of hope that at eighty-four, Edna would still be alive. She imagined her child and Edna staring up into the night sky and together watching the miraculous comet cross the sky. But she knew it was only a daydream since her child would never know his birth family.

Chapter Twenty

1909 – Alaska-Yukon-Pacific Exposition

A dark cloud seemed to move in when Pearl moved out. Instead of seeming relieved, Papa grew increasingly quiet and moody. He no longer tousled Edna's hair or called her his little gem. Edna wondered if he would ever get over Pearl's indiscretion and the shame she brought to the family. Then early in September, Papa sprang from his chair with a rap at the door. For the first time since Pearl went away, her father's face brightened. She couldn't recall seeing her father so excited in a while. As he swung the door open, he called out, "He's here."

Mama scurried into the front room. Untying her apron strings as she rushed to the door, she tossed her apron on the side table. She brought her hands to her cheeks. "Robert, so nice to see you again." She grabbed him by the arm and pulled him inside. "Come in, please. Take a load off."

Edna studied the man with curiosity, even though Mama had warned her more than once about her curiosity and how curiosity killed the cat. He was dressed all fancy, not in flannel shirts and heavy denim dungarees. Edna had only seen such formal attire on men at church or in town on Sundays when the townsfolk strolled the streets and men talked about work and women gossiped about the latest scandals. The stranger was taller than her father, and his presence loomed even larger with the height of his top hat. He must be a man of importance.

"Edna, this is Mr. Barth, an old family friend. He's visiting all the way from Wisconsin. Can you say hello?"

Edna bobbed her head in greeting. "Hello, Mister Barth."

Mr. Barth squatted to Edna's eye level. He extended his hand. "Pleased to meet you, Edna. How are you this fine evening?"

She offered her hand and grinned, showing off her last missing tooth, as she grabbed Mr. Barth's hand. "I'm fine, thank you, sir."

With a hearty chuckle straight from his belly, Mr. Barth straightened and tugged on his vest. "Good. Good."

Father led Mr. Barth into the front room. Mr. Barth handed his knee-length brown tweed overcoat and tall hat to Edna's mother and settled into the blue velvet settee. When a shrill whistle from the tea kettle drew her mother's attention, she called to Edna and disappeared back into the kitchen. Mother placed several cookies on a flowered porcelain plate. The whistle of the copper tea kettle faded. Mama poured herself a cup of hot water then put it on a tray along with two cups of coffee and the cream and sugar bowls and headed to the living room.

Edna returned to their guest and presented the plate of cookies. "Would you care for a cookie? They're my favorite— snickerdoodles."

Though Mr. Barth was tall and husky, with reddish-brown hair, his size no longer startled Edna. He smiled underneath the bushy red mustache. Thanking her, he took two cookies and a napkin. He opened the cloth napkin across his lap as Edna's mother and lady friends did.

Mr. Barth took a bite, then cocked his head. "Don't you have an older daughter? Pearl, isn't it? Is she here?"

Edna's jaw dropped. She stopped in her tracks and stared at her father, waiting to see how he would explain her sister's absence.

Papa rubbed his chin before responding. "No, she's living in Seattle now, going to school, her final year."

Father raised his brows encouraging Edna to continue serving as her mother emerged with the coffee. She offered her father a cookie. After taking a single snickerdoodle, he set the plate on the table and nodded permission to Edna. She took a cookie and hurried to the Eastlake chair in the corner of the room, away from the adult conversation but still within hearing range.

Mr. Barth took a sip before speaking. "I'm sure you are proud of her. I'm glad you received my post. I'm here on business as I stated, but what a perfectly wonderful reason to visit old friends, eh? And see a few of the sights of Seattle at the same time. How fortuitous that the Alaska-Yukon-Pacific Exhibition is going on during my stay."

Edna perked up. Several classmates had boasted that they had gone to Seattle during their summer break to see the sights of what they called a world's fair. The first held in Seattle. Edna jumped off the chair and scooted it a bit closer to the conversation.

"Word is, this fair you're hosting is beyond anything offered at the World Fair in Philadelphia or even Portland, Oregon in 1905, but the beauty of your mountain alone was well worth the trip. It certainly surpasses any of the hills we have in Wisconsin."

Father took a gulp of what he called his daily boost. "It's a beautiful piece of the country here. Wait 'til you see the campus of the university, the site of the exposition. The main pavilion was built so visitors can see Mount Rainier from the grounds when they first enter." Father reached for a folded copy of the *Port Orchard Independent* on the coffee table. "Been keeping this here article since I received your post. The paper's got some great photographs of opening day." He tapped his index finger on the newspaper before handing it to his guest.

Mr. Barth skimmed it for a moment before speaking. "Says here, President Taft himself sent the signal that officially opened the Exposition, all the way from his desk at the White House."

Mama leaned in; her face crumpled in confusion. "How is that possible?"

Their guest continued to read aloud. "The gold telegraph key was studded with gold nuggets taken from the first mine opened in the Klondike."

Straightening in his chair, Father nodded. "That's right, Abbey. A single spark traveled across the lines all the way to Seattle. As soon as they received the spark at the Expo site, they struck a gong, unfurled a bunch of flags, and topped it all off with a twenty-one-gun salute. Yessiree, wish I'd been there. Bet that was a sight to see. Horns, whistles, and confetti, along with eighty-thousand people the first day alone. I imagine it left quite a mess for those street sweepers."

Though her cookie was long gone, Edna sat quietly, hanging on every word from this odd man with a strange accent. Eyeing the plate of cookies, she craved another but didn't want to draw attention to herself since no one had shooed her from the room yet. Unable to hold back, she blurted out, "My friend Inez said they had fireworks."

Flashing a smile, Mr. Barth rubbed his chin. "My business associate from Washington visited last week. He told me it was the biggest fireworks show ever in the state, and dear friends, I'd be honored if the two of you and your daughter joined me as my guests at the fair."

No longer interested in cookies, Edna stared at Mr. Barth.

He cocked his head and flashed a grin in Edna's direction. "Would you like to go to the biggest fair this state has ever seen, young lady?"

Eyes as big around as the snickerdoodles, Edna looked from her mother to her father. "May we, Papa? Please."

Her father rubbed his beard like he did whenever he was considering something. "Sorry, Bob, I'm not a businessman like you. Got to return to work come Monday."

"Well, that settles it. We're all going to the world's fair tomorrow."

♪ ♪ ♪

Edna bounded out of bed early and rushed to the kitchen. Mr. Barth sat at the kitchen table with steam rising from his coffee cup. He looked up when she appeared. "Are you excited for the day?"

Edna took a chair next to him and nodded furiously. "I sure am, Mr. Barth."

"My given name's Robert, but you can call me Uncle Buddy instead of Mr. Barth. Your parents are feeding the animals. As soon as they're done, we'll get going."

Two hours later, Uncle Buddy tossed a small train case along with a black leather bag onto the carriage floorboard. He assisted Edna and her mother aboard the buggy, then climbed up and took a seat up front next to Papa.

Spying the overnight bag, Edna raised her brows. "Are you leaving?"

"I'm here on business representing the Union Pacific Railroad. I'm fortunate to have enjoyed a night of hospitality from your folks, but when I leave the fair tonight, the railroad is putting me up at the brand-new Hotel Sorrento while I conduct business."

Papa bobbed his head. "I hear the Sorrento's a first-class place; supposed to have amazing views of Elliott Bay."

The whip cracked, and Nellie whinnied and galloped away. At eleven o'clock, the *Athlon* pulled into its slip at the Colman Dock. Scores of women and men dressed to the nines spilled down the gangplank from the steamer.

Edna looked down at her pretty pinafore with blue flowers embroidered on the eyelet lace and her finest black, ankle-high shoes that took a long time to lace but made her feel grown-up and grinned. The entire crowd dashed toward the yellow trolleys that ran along the waterfront. It looked to Edna as if all the passengers were headed to the fair that people said was "the world's most beautiful fair." With a firm grip on each other's hand, Edna and her mother followed Uncle Buddy and Papa as they threaded their way through the crowd toward the street.

Her mother's grip tightened. "I've never seen such a crowd in my entire life. Hold on tight. We don't want to become separated."

Papa put his arm around Mama's shoulders and guided her away from the scurrying throngs to the streetcar stand where trolleys with placards reading, "Alaska-Yukon Exposition," lined up in a long row. Onboard, Edna found a seat near the window. Mama picked up a copy of the *Seattle Times* someone had left on the seat and sat next to Edna. Offering the last empty seat to a woman, Uncle Buddy and her father stood, each with a firm grip on a pole for support. With her nose against the glass, Edna took in every sight she passed, especially the huge brick stores of Frederick and Nelson and Wallin and Nordstrom. Though Inez and her mother sometimes shopped in the city, Mama never bought from these city stores. Sometimes, she ordered a pair of shoes or bloomers and corsets from the Sears and Roebuck catalog.

Mama read the paper, then turned to Uncle Buddy. "Says here half a million people visited the fair the first week alone."

"Wouldn't be surprised. It made the news even on the East Coast. It is, after all, called a world's fair."

In a matter of minutes, the trolley jerked to a stop. From the moment Edna stepped off the streetcar, she was mesmerized. Sunlight shone golden off the snowcapped peak of Mount Rainier, looming in the distance as if positioned there intentionally to impress the visitors from out of town. Men in dark suits or waistcoats and tall top hats or bowlers paraded with their best walking sticks, heads held high. Women in their Sunday-best gowns—sashes and long draped skirts or tailored dresses—with large bonnets adorned with flowers or colorful feathers, strolled toward the University of Washington campus. Music soared above the crowd from yet unseen sights. The chattering of thousands of visitors melded like a gaggle of geese.

"We're here." Uncle Buddy swept his hand toward the most magnificent buildings Edna had ever seen. "What do you think?"

"Gracious." Mama held her hand over her open mouth. "I never could have imagined such a spectacle."

Following the pathway and the direction of most of the fairgoers, Edna walked between her new friend, Uncle Buddy, and her mother. The line for admission stretched over a block, but it pushed forward quickly. Father reached for his wallet, but Uncle Buddy waved off the offer. He pulled out two one-dollar bills for the three adult tickets and one child's fare. The ticket seller handed him a quarter in change. Uncle Buddy handed it to Edna with a wink.

Following the surge of people moving toward the main entrance, Papa pointed out the enormous silk rectangles attached to tall poles and waving in the wind. "These flags represent the many countries that have exhibits here."

"Wow." Edna tipped her head to see flags in colors more plentiful than those in her box of crayons. She didn't know which countries they represented, and she couldn't imagine counting them all.

Uncle Buddy handed their tickets to the uniformed ticket takers, and they were inside. Edna stared unblinking and wide-eyed at the sight of an enormous circular basin with a sign that read, "Geyser Basin." In the middle, a fountain shot water high into the sky before it splashed into the pool below. Curved buildings flanked each side. Uncle Buddy swept his arm in a grand gesture across the courtyard and surrounding structures. "This is called the Arctic Circle and the Cascade Waterfall."

"What's that?" Edna's eyes widened at the sight of the waterfall that appeared to gush from the ground at the entrance to an enormous, white-domed building.

"That's the Alaska Monument and the US Government building, the largest building on the entire grounds. When it gets dark, they'll light up each of the six waterfalls with different colored lights. It should be quite a sight."

Edna's father studied his old friend. "How do you know so much about our fair?"

Uncle Buddy reached into the inside pocket of his jacket and pulled out a crumpled booklet. "Some of my business associates visited last month. They told me all about it and gave me this guidebook." Buddy strode with quick steps toward the Alaska Building. Edna scurried along past hundreds of people seated around the edge of the fountain. The wind caught spray off the fountain, tickling her face with a mist. She spun in a circle to take in the sheer size and wonder of it all. In the distance, behind the building-lined boulevards, lay a lush green lawn as far-stretching as the meadow behind her house.

"It's so beautiful." Edna gazed in awe at the tens of thousands of flowers that bordered the blanket of green with a kaleidoscope of color in neat fragrant plantings.

After spinning in a circle Edna resumed her grip on Mama's hand and quickened her steps to keep pace with the long-legged Uncle Buddy. Inside, Alaskan native artifacts filled the building.

Mama stopped in front of an exhibit, "Gold Camps of Alaska." "Remember what I told you about your grandfather's gold claim?"

Edna recalled the letters her mother had read to her. She'd even seen the small nuggets Grandfather Mooney found when he first went north. But now, everywhere Edna looked, her eyes fell upon gold. Gold bricks, gold nuggets, gold jewelry. Beyond all the gold stood an igloo and two dogs. Edna pulled free from her mother's grip and ran to the huskies.

Two Eskimos from Siberia and Alaska, wearing buttonless shirts of animal hide and bulky boots of fur, grinned, exposing their short teeth. "These dogs are part of a dog-sledding team."

A man hawking souvenirs called out. Edna turned to see him holding out a small doll. She ran to the souvenir stand. The man stroked the doll's fur coat and showed Edna the white fur boots. The doll was so different from her other dolls at home.

"What about you, little lady? Would you like an Eskimo doll?

"May I get one, please?" She turned to Mama and pleaded.

Mother shook her head. "Not today."

Edna held out her quarter. "But I have money."

Despite Mama's resistance, Uncle Buddy stepped forward with a few coins. "Please, let me. Your little girl should have a souvenir to remember this day."

The California exhibit looked and smelled like a giant produce market with tables spread with fruits and nuts. Edna turned a corner and stopped in her tracks. A life-size elephant stood on a large wooden base.

Uncle Buddy chuckled. "See that? The entire elephant is made from walnuts."

Farther along stood a full-size cow made from almonds and a bear made from raisins. Though her feet were getting tired, Edna trudged along, sure she would never see such amazing sights as these ever again in her life. It seemed the sights and sounds of the entire world stretched before her.

Beating drums up ahead drew Edna's attention. She tugged at her mother's hand. She slipped past a fellow with a funny flat hat pulling a small two-wheeled cart with two people aboard. Edna squeezed among the adults blocking the exhibit from her view and stood on tiptoes to peek over the bamboo fencing that separated the display from the onlookers. Then she stared into a hut with a tall straw roof at a group of dark-skinned stubby men, naked except for loincloths, like pictures she had seen of American Indians. They had darker skin than the Indians and wore small hats resembling baskets atop their short black hair. Zigzagged lines ran across their chests and covered their arms. Edna stood with her eyes wide and her mouth open as she watched the men chant in low guttural sounds, stomping their feet and dancing with animated jerky movements while they beat on tom-tom drums made from animal skins. Mesmerized, Edna danced along with them. Beside them, another group of women and men crouched around a campfire. Edna blushed at the sight of the women, naked from the waist up, who poked at the embers with sticks, their eyes distant, emotionless. Mother found her way through the crowd and reclaimed Edna's hand with a sharp warning to stay close.

"Look, Mama. Who are they?"

"The sign says they're Igorrotes."

Behind the fence, straw and mud structures dotted the grounds. Edna edged closer to the sign affixed to the fence. The sign beckoned visitors to see for themselves the primitive wild people. "They're wearing hardly any clothes, and even the men are wearing necklaces." Edna giggled.

Her mother glared and explained about the strange culture. "This is a savage tribe from the Philippines. They still eat dogs and people."

Her father's firm hand gripped her shoulder and prompted her away. "That's just a sensationalized exhibit intended to shock you. Come on. There are a lot more suitable things to see."

Strolling past exhibits on agriculture and machinery, Papa fixed his gaze on an enormous log in the forestry building. "The building is built from unhewed timber logs." He motioned Edna closer. "Look at this." He stood with his arms crossed as he read about the prized exhibit that stood in front of the building. "One-thousand-year-old log, sixteen feet in diameter. Even I've never seen anything this massive in all my years of bucking and loading logs."

Uncle Buddy led the way past a railroad, a miniature volcano, and a pyramid-shaped exhibit for Egypt. He stepped aside to let a suited gentleman extend the legs of a tripod before he snapped a photograph of the Asian buildings with beautiful sloping roofs that Mother informed her were Chinese temples.

At the familiar fluty sound of calliope music, Edna looked around. Spying the revolving horses in the distance, she tugged on her mother's sweater. "May I, please, Mama?" Edna pointed toward the carousel and held up her quarter. "I still have my money."

Papa nodded his approval, and Edna skipped the whole way to the amusement rides along a brick walkway wearing splotches of melted ice cream, spilled soda, and numerous fair confections. A sign to the entrance marked "Pay Streak" and beyond that, lay a city block of exciting, inviting, magical rides and delicious and delightful sumptuous treats. A fairy tale come true. Children waited in long queues for the rides with amusing and thrilling names, like "Foolish

House" and "Tickler." Scents of buttery popcorn and spun sugary fluff of pink Fairy Floss rose above the heavy grease suspended in the air from burgers on the grill.

A call came from behind the concession stands. "Buy your raffle ticket. Only twenty-five cents."

Uncle Buddy motioned with his head in another direction. "Abbey, you, and Edna can check out the weekly raffle. Every week is something new—bushels of apples, baskets of nuts. Last week's prize was a milk cow. You never know what the prize is for the week. George and I are going to see the manned flying machine. We'll meet you at the carousel in a while."

Edna took her mother's hand and headed off to see the raffle prize.

A gray-haired woman selling tickets smiled as she gripped a roll of tickets. "Get your tickets here, only two-bits. Win a beautiful, healthy baby boy."

Edna's eyes bulged. Surely, she'd heard wrong. Is this what Mama meant when she said Pearl had to give her baby away? Edna stared at her mother, who looked as shocked as Edna at the sight of the woman collecting coins from interested spectators and handing them red raffle tickets.

"The child is only one month old. Step forward and see for yourself what a handsome lad he is."

Unable to hide her shock, Edna tugged at her mother's sleeve. "Mama? Is this what is going to happen to Pearl's baby?"

Her mother's gaze jerked from Edna to the middle-aged woman in a white uniform and a white hat. "No. Of course not. Pearl's baby will be delivered in a facility with good standing and will be placed for adoption to a proper home."

Edna read the sandwich board advertising the raffle and bearing a poster of the chubby-cheeked baby and "Washington Children's Home Society." "This place says it's a children's home. What if the place where Pearl is staying sells her baby? How do you know her baby won't be given away like a cow?"

"What?" Her mother studied the sign and the woman who was selling tickets for a chance to win a baby. "Come along. We need to go."

Edna looked over her shoulder as Mother led her away and toward the carousel. Her head whirled with unanswered questions.

After the sun went down, the air turned chilly. Under the dark cloudless sky, lights came on from every corner of the fairground, illuminating the displays and inviting people to linger and to see more sights. Fireworks soared across the sky over Elliot Bay, fanning out in bursts of red, white, blue, and gold. All Edna could think about was the baby boy who was being raffled off. What would become of Pearl's baby? Would the innocent child be snatched away from Pearl and vanish as quickly as the flashes of light streaking through the sky?

Chapter Twenty-One

1909 – Acceptance

L ess than three months after she arrived at Florence Crittenton, Pearl was sitting in class when a rap on the classroom door drew her classmates' gaze to the back of the room. Miss Barrett strolled in and motioned to Miss Crawford. The teacher's skirt swooshed as she hurried down the center aisle past Pearl and her classmates. Whispers emanated from the more audacious girls. Pearl watched her teacher, who was involved in deep conversation. Miss Barrett's presence during the middle of class certainly meant news of significance. When Miss Crawford closed the door, all heads jerked toward the front of the room. With the room eerily silent, Pearl jumped when Miss Crawford placed her hand on Pearl's shoulder. The teacher leaned in with a low but firm voice. "Pearl Mooney, please gather your books and go with Miss Barrett."

Fearful of what terrible offense she might have committed, Pearl winced, wishing she could sink into her chair. *What could be serious enough to call me from class?* Her hands shook as she stacked her tablet and textbooks. A pencil rolled off the desk onto the floor. A few girls giggled, but upon seeing Miss Crawford's narrowed eyes bearing down on them, they stifled their chuckles. Pearl got up, avoiding her classmates' questioning eyes, and made haste to the door. Her footsteps sounding on the floor kept time with her pounding heart. By the time she closed the door behind her, her cheeks flushed, her palms felt sweaty, and her palpitations had quickened.

Out in the hall, Kate Barrett stood emotionless, offering no clue for her interruption of class. Stoic and firm, she instructed Pearl to follow her. Without questioning, Pearl obeyed, like a prisoner led to the gallows. She wondered if the headmistress heard the gurgles from her unsettled and knotted stomach.

Dr. Barrett opened the door to her office.

Pearl stopped short at the sight of her mother sitting at Dr. Barrett's desk, her hands folded atop the hat on her lap. Her unannounced visit and solemn face panicked Pearl. "Is Daddy okay?"

"Your father's fine. I came to see and talk with you. It's of an urgent matter which couldn't wait for the postal service."

Dr. Barrett sat at her desk. "Your mother and I have discussed your progress here. She's made a proposition that she'll share with you." Pearl tipped her head in confusion. "What is it?"

Miss Barrett tried to hide a slim smile. "I think you two will be more comfortable discussing things in private in the day room. Take your time. You can return to class whenever you're ready."

Pearl's mother got up and put on her hat. She smiled at Miss Barrett, nodded, collected her handbag from the floor, and headed for the door.

Once they reached the day room, the comfort of the white Victorian sofa, gilded with gold, did little to ease the awkwardness of the moment. Convinced her mother's unexpected arrival brought unsettling news, Pearl extended her hands in a questioning posture. She stared long and hard into her mother's blue eyes for a hint of the reason for her surprise visit. "What is it, Mama? Why have you come?

"Your father and I have agreed to support your decision to marry Stanley upon your graduation." She took Pearl's hands and gazed into her daughter's eyes. "Dr. Barrett wrote to us and informed us you are well ahead of the other girls regarding your studies and your involvement in parenting classes. If you continue to work hard, she will oversee the graduation examination after the birth of the baby. She's confident you will succeed and earn your high school diploma ahead of schedule."

Her mother's enthusiasm relieved the knots inside her stomach, and Pearl breathed easier.

142

"Once you've delivered the baby and have earned your diploma, you will be able to procure a solid position in the workplace, and you may leave here and get married. Your father has written to Stanley's uncle. He has assured us you will have a room to live in as long as Stanley is in his employ. It's settled then. You have our blessing."

"Thank you, Mother, but what about the baby?"

"Since you will be moving to Kirkland, surrounded by strangers, no one will ever need to know you were with child."

The news of her parents blessing her marriage thrilled Pearl, but it wasn't enough. Pearl pulled her hands away. "I don't understand." She shook her head with a firm, exaggerated movement. "I appreciate your and Father's blessing. It means a lot to me to have your support. I want to marry Stanley, but I'm going to keep the baby, our baby."

Pearl's mother shook her head. "Think about what you're saying. Your father worked so hard for nearly twenty years to give you and your sister the best life possible. He's smarter than most people realize, but in our day, education wasn't for the common man or certainly not for young girls. Your father and I only attended formal schooling for six years. You had the opportunity to go to high school. If you have a child, you will never be able to fully apply the education you worked so hard to obtain."

"If I have a child?" Pearl sprang to her feet and placed her hands on her belly. "I'm having a child, Mother. The only decision is who will raise the baby." Pearl heard the quivering in her voice as her eyes misted. She fought back the emotion rising inside her, a wave ready to crash upon the shore and wash her dreams away like footprints in the sand. "I remember when Edna was born. How scared we were of losing her. Do you remember? If you'd lost Edna, I know you would have been devasted. That's how I feel about my baby. I love my baby and want to raise it. You can't give my cherished baby to a stranger. No one could possibly love my baby as much as Stanley and I will."

A fog of silence hovered over them as mother and daughter sat absorbed in the gravity of the moment. Pearl could almost see her mother thinking as her eyes seemed to search back in time. Nearly a minute passed before her mother reached deep into her pocketbook and withdrew a white handkerchief. She shook her head and wiped her forehead. Then, as if it were a flag of surrender, she lowered the

143

cotton hankie and heaved a surrendering sigh. "I can't have your baby given away like a cow."

Pearl raised her brow, shocked by the sudden concession. "What does that mean?"

"It's something Edna said." Her mother took a breath and took Pearl's hand in hers. "It doesn't matter. I know you will make a fine mother, and I know you will love this baby like you love and care for your sister. You're right. No one else will love the baby as you and Stanley will."

Pearl wiped her eyes with the back of her hand. "Are you saying I can keep my baby?"

"Miss Barrett will be thrilled to hear the news. She's assured me you have demonstrated the essential qualities of good character necessary for child-raising." She stuffed the handkerchief back into her purse. "We have work to get done in short order if you are to be legally wed in time for the baby's birth to be recorded as legitimate.

Pearl closed her fingers in a prayerful pose. "Thank you, Mother, but what about Papa? What will he say?"

After a long-resigned sigh, her mother continued. "Your father's still upset. He needs time. We agree getting married will help eliminate the stain of your indiscretion. Parents never stop loving their children. Family always stands by family. It doesn't matter what you've done."

Moved by her mother's words, Pearl melted into her mother's embrace. She reached deep into a pocket in her skirt and withdrew a folded sheet of paper. "Here." She handed it to her mother. "Will you come and be a witness?" Pearl waited and watched as her mother unfolded the letter Stanley wrote to her after he'd learned the news of Pearl's situation.

A slow smile came to her mother's face as she read the short letter. "It sounds like Stanley is eager to make an honest woman out of you. I will meet you at the courthouse when you have agreed upon a date. After the date is arranged, I will meet with Dr. Barrett and make the necessary preparations for you to leave here."

"Since I will not be delivering the baby here, will you ask Aunt Marie to come and assist with the delivery?"

"I'm sure she'll be delighted." Mother bent and picked up a paper bag she'd put on the floor. She withdrew a garment and held it out at arm's length to reveal a white lace dress. "I wanted you to have this and wear it for your wedding after the baby came."

Stunned, Pearl took a moment to comprehend what her mother was holding. "That was your wedding dress. I recognize it from the photo on the mantle."

Her mother nodded with pleasure. "Your grandmother made this dress for me when I became engaged to your father. My marriage, though at times difficult, has been filled with many good times. Maybe passing this dress on to you will bring you the strength to face the challenges as well as the joyful times."

Moved by her mother's thoughtfulness, Pearl held back her emotions with her hands in a prayerful pose before she took the dress and held it in front of her. She stroked the satin and lace bodice embellished with dozens of pearl beads. "Thank you, but I don't think it will fit in my condition." She raised her eyes and smiled to lighten the mood.

"I'm a dressmaker, remember? Since it appears we'll be having a wedding soon I'll make the necessary alterations to the waist and raise the hem to make the style less formal. She wrinkled her face and fumbled with the pearl beads.

"I'll remove these embellishments since"—her mother paused and rubbed her chin— "since your wedding won't be in a church and we don't want to draw attention to your blossoming figure."

"How long do you think until it's ready?"

"Not long. I brought my measuring tape so we can take some quick measurements. I'll get to work on it right away."

Chapter Twenty-Two

1909 – Married

Pearl hugged her mother goodbye at the bottom of the stairs to the Crittenton Home. Her gaze followed her mother's quick steps down the street until she disappeared around the corner. Pearl wanted to run after her and thank her once more for her blessing, but her mother had a trolley to catch, and Pearl had to deal with the many tasks at hand. Overcome by the shocking news, Pearl stood immobile. A slight smile crossed her face as the events of the afternoon sank in. She rubbed her bare arms, covered with goose bumps from the fall chill, then made her way up the stairs and back inside. Despite her growing abdomen, now late in her second trimester, the weight she bore somehow seemed lighter. Pearl walked as fast as she could to Kate Barrett's office. She knocked on the closed door, waited for a response, and approached the desk. "Please, Dr. Barrett, may I use the phone?"

Maintaining a steady gaze, Dr. Barrett planted her elbows on the desk, crossed her fingers in contemplation, and rested her chin on her hands. "The phone is to be used only for the most pressing occasions." She paused. "I trust your call is of an urgent nature?"

Pearl nodded, then stammered. "Yes."

The headmistress's dark eyes softened. A smile crossed her lips.

"I need to set a date to apply for a marriage license."

"I understand your desire to marry after your child's birth and the adoption, but there's plenty of time for that. The baby isn't due until February, as I recall." Miss Barrett's voice took on a hopeful

146

tone. "Is there a change of plans of which I have not been made aware?" She motioned for Pearl to take a seat.

Pearl plunked onto the chair. Barely pausing to take a breath, her conversation with her mother spilled out.

Miss Barrett's eyes danced with delight. "Well, that does appear to be urgent, doesn't it? Are you sure your beau wishes to begin married life with a child? "

"We know it isn't ideal, but Stanley is earning an adequate income. Mama told me you're willing to administer my exam early. I'm sure I'll pass. We have the support of not only our parents but Stanley's uncle who will provide us housing for only a small stipend while Stanley works at the furniture store."

Miss Barrett drummed her fingers on the desk, grinned, then reached for the earpiece from the black candlestick phone. "Does your beau have access to a telephone?"

"He lives in Kirkland. His uncle's business doesn't have a telephone yet, but the Gibson Hotel takes messages for the residents of the town. He knows the owners. They'll get word to Stanley to call here." Pearl stopped to catch her breath. "It is okay for him to call me here, isn't it?" Pearl's hands trembled in her lap as Miss Barrett took a long moment to consider the request.

"Of course, he can call here, but to protect your reputation and our school, only leave the number which he should call. Do not indicate from where you are calling."

By the time Pearl left word for Stanley to call her, it was late in the day, and Pearl's last class, Botany, was underway. Pearl tried to disguise her joy when she walked into the classroom, but as all heads turned, eyes wide and filled with questions, Pearl couldn't keep the happiness from her eyes and the smile from her face. It seemed cruel to boast of her good news, but she wouldn't lie to the other less-fortunate girls who had no beau and those who would be giving their babies up for adoption. Perhaps her news would offer them a sliver of hope.

The moment the class bell rang, everyone jumped to their feet and spilled into the hallway. With half a dozen girls surrounding her and prodding her with inquiries, Pearl felt as popular as the glamorous stage and film actress, Mary Pickford, who was the same age as Pearl. Surrendering to their bombardment of questions, Pearl blurted out her news. "I'm getting married."

The girls in various stages in their pregnancy, and with eyes filled with hope, asked in unison, "And the baby?"

Unable to hide her joy, Pearl patted her stomach and nodded. "I'm going to keep my baby." Tears ran down her face and glistened on the cheeks of a few of the other prospective mothers.

The week after her mother's visit, Stanley drove to the Crittenton Home in his uncle's car and picked up Pearl for the forty-minute drive to the King County Courthouse on a typical mid-November day in Seattle. Rain splashed on the sidewalk, wetting their shoes, and dripping down their coats as they dashed toward the grand white-stone building on Seventh and Alder. Even the damp weather could not hinder their enthusiasm as Pearl and Stanley nearly skipped to the main entrance to file their application of marriage and begin their three-day waiting period before marrying.

A week later, her mother placed Pearl's belongings from her stay at the Crittenton Home into a suitcase. Stanley carried it out and strapped it to the rear of his uncle's ruby-red Rambler. Pearl said her goodbyes to her fellow dormitory companions and wished them well. Miss Barrett wore a satisfied look of pride as she waved goodbye, and Pearl climbed into the front seat next to her betrothed.

Though her mother approved of Pearl's marriage, she still looked at Stanley with the eyes of a wary cat. Pearl hoped the skepticism would pass once the stress of the wedding and baby was behind them. Settled in the back seat, her mother asked Stanley if he knew where he was headed.

"Yes, ma'am. I remember the way to your sister's home on Broadway Hill. Pearl told me you would be spending the night there tonight."

Her mother huffed, but Pearl maintained her gaze ahead, reminding herself to remain composed. She took solace in knowing this was her last night as a single woman.

The following morning, Pearl slipped into her mother's old wedding dress, now altered to fit Pearl's budding figure. Mother helped her pin her hair in a loose bun atop her head. Pearl gazed into the full-length mirror in Charlotte's bedroom, the room she'd called home for the previous three years. The room where she would have lived this school year while she completed her last year at the newly renamed Broadway High, if she had been responsible instead of giving in to temptation. After dreaming for so many years about her future and what lay ahead, her future had arrived. Instead of moving on to the University of Washington to complete her nursing studies as she'd dreamed since meeting Dr. Chapman, raising a family was in her future. But she felt no loss as she cradled her growing belly and felt a small kick, a nudge of impatience from the unborn child. The image in the mirror of a beautiful bride reflected her fantasies. Relief swathed her, fitting her like the smooth, satiny gown that disguised the reason for the rushed matrimonial ceremony.

"It fits like a dream." Her mother's reflection appeared in the glass. Despite the smile on her mother's face, Pearl sensed her mother's eyes hid disappointment. Her mother removed her glasses and wiped her eyes. She sat on the edge of the bed and patted the pale-yellow spread. "Come. Sit down for a minute."

Pearl arched her brows. She held her breath, panicked by what her mother might say in these last few minutes. Did her mother have second thoughts? Pearl lifted the hem of the gown and edged to the bed.

Mother opened the silver handbag she held in her lap and withdrew a box. Pearl gazed at the rectangular box, about two inches wide and eight inches long, wrapped with several strands of raffia tied into a bow.

"I wanted to give you something special for a wedding gift, but you know money is tight."

Pearl glanced at the long narrow box her mother held. She recognized it. "You've done enough already." Her mother dabbed at her glistening eyes with a blue floral hankie.

A quick knock at the door drew their attention. Aunt Marie poked her head inside. "Are you about ready? We should be leaving soon."

Pearl lifted the top off the box. She gasped at the sight of the gift, moved by her mother's kindness, and recognizing the significance of her gesture. "You're giving this to me?"

Mother nodded. "You told me how much you liked this necklace when I wore it for Charlotte's wedding. I haven't worn it since."

"Your mother gave you this when you got married. Are you sure you want to give it to me?" Pearl gazed at the single strand of natural pearls. She recalled the story her mother told her five years earlier. Veiled in disgrace, Pearl fingered the luminous spheres. The strand was radiant, the way she should have felt on her wedding day. Instead, a quivering cold swept over her. The color drained from her cheeks. Unable to look her mother in the eyes, Pearl swallowed the lump in her throat. "I can't wear this."

Mama patted her hand. "Why not?"

"You told me Christians adopted pearls as a symbol of purity and innocence. That makes them a perfect gift for a new bride." Pearl hung her head. "I'm no longer pure and innocent." She brought her hands to her face, to hide her shame and shield herself from her mother's judgmental glare.

Instead, soft eyes filled with love looked back. "It's okay; that's merely an old legend. Don't take it to heart."

Pearl shot off the bed, dropping the necklace to the bed covers. "It's not. I saw how excited you were when Charlotte got married. I saw how you looked when Charlotte and David exchanged vows. You wanted me to have a real wedding, in a church, with family and friends in attendance so you could stand proud next to me in your finest dress and wear this necklace again. I wanted a church wedding too. I imagined Papa walking me down the aisle and Edna as a bridesmaid. Instead, I'm having a quickie wedding in a courthouse. I'm sorry."

A long silence followed. Pearl's chest tightened. She worried about the stress on the unborn child and cradled her belly.

Rising, her mother picked up the pearl necklace from the covers and stood behind her daughter. She put her hands upon Pearl's shoulders. "Maybe your situation is not what we planned or wanted for you, but I still want you to wear this and keep it. I named you Pearl for a reason. Pearls have a simple beauty. Whatever mistakes you've made, you will always be my precious Pearl." She fastened the strand around Pearl's neck. "Maybe you'll have a daughter. Someday you can pass these on to her. I plan on being here for her wedding to see your daughter wearing it."

A loud banging on the door spun Pearl around. "We're coming."

Hurried to the door by Uncle Leland, everyone made their way down the walk to the waiting vehicle.

"There's no way you can take the trolley in a wedding gown. Your aunt and I will be taking you to town." Uncle Leland stood resolute. Within minutes, the car was parked less than a block from the prominent sandstone and brick Victorian courthouse. He pulled the pocket watch from his vest. "One thirty-five. Plenty of time to meet the judge in his chambers at two o'clock."

Pearl smoothed her dress as she stepped out of the automobile behind her mother. They followed the sidewalk to the courthouse. From the bottom of the steps, Pearl grinned at the sight of Stanley waiting on the stairway landing. He paced back and forth next to a middle-aged gent, certainly Uncle Frederick. Even from a distance, Pearl saw the optimism in his eyes that erased any doubt she'd had about Stanley's intentions.

Stanley introduced his uncle to everyone, and the wedding party made their way to the third floor. At precisely two, the door from the chamber opened, and Judge Gilliam strode in carrying a burgundy-colored book. His long generous sleeves swooshed against his black robe. Judge Gilliam greeted them without unnecessary attention focused on Pearl's apparent maternal state. With the utmost decorum, all business, he noted the time on his pocket watch and offered a brief congratulations before taking his place in front of a formal mahogany desk. He rubbed his long white beard. "You only need two witnesses, but I see you brought a few."

Without ceremony, without elegant bouquets lining the aisle, without the pageantry of maids of honor in prom-like dresses, and without the bridal chorus playing in the background, the judge stood before the young couple. "Are you ready to begin?"

Uncle Frederick and Pearl's mother stepped forward while Aunt Marie and Uncle Leland took their places on the first of several wooden pews. Though Pearl managed to look straight ahead at the judge, she couldn't help but envision her dreams whirling away. A tornado, swallowing shattered hopes of a large wedding, a fulfilling career, and a few more years as a single young woman free to experience life.

Stanley leaned in and took hold of her hand. "Are you okay?"

Pearl blinked her insecurity away, inhaled, forced a smile, and nodded. She'd learned there is always a calm after the storm and dreams were ever-changing, shifting and transforming. Today the course of her life shifted in a new direction, one she would have to face with a new determination, with new optimism. She took Stanley's hand and repeated the words after the judge. The entire ceremony lasted less time than the effort to dress or drive to the courthouse. By two-fifteen, Judge Gilliam pronounced the words that made the unborn child legitimate. "I now pronounce you man and wife." Self-conscious with the audience, Pearl glanced at her mother and saw for the first time in many months, she wore a genuine smile. Pearl leaned in and placed a quick soft kiss on Stanley's lips. The first kiss since she'd left Seattle for Port Orchard. Minutes later, they stood at Judge Gilliam's enormous oak desk. Mother and Uncle Frederick signed their names on the lines for the witnesses, then Stanley put his signature on the line for the groom before handing the pen to Pearl. For the first time, Pearl penned her new legal name, Pearl Anna Mooney Rosenberg.

Chapter Twenty-Three

1910 – Firstborn

In mid-February, only three months after her marriage, contractions gripped Pearl's taut abdomen which now bore numerous purple stretch marks.

"They're a badge of honor," Aunt Marie told her when she arrived to help Pearl prepare for the birth. With the date of her indiscretion fixed, it was easy to anticipate the approximate arrival and avoid last-minute preparations. Pearl rubbed her belly to ease the discomfort of the sharp pains now coming about ten minutes apart.

"It's time for you to take to the bed. Remove your corset and everything else except your drawers and chemise."

Pearl pursed her lips and winced through the pain. "Thank you for being here to help me through this."

"I'm glad to do this for you. Maybe someday you'll be the one helping other women deliver their babies." Her aunt turned away. "I'll let Stanley know the time is near."

Pearl sat on the edge of the bed and slipped out of her dress. She looked around the cozy apartment over the furniture store that Stanley and his uncle had labored long hours to prepare. Someday she and Stanley would have their own home. For now, the small space with its refinished table and chairs and reupholstered living-room pieces was a blessing to behold. Pearl marveled over how the room that once held surplus unfinished furniture had been transformed into such a comfortable home with only a coat of fresh paint on its walls and the rough-hewn oak-plank floor sanded and varnished.

The increasing frequency of stabbing pain ratcheted up Pearl's anticipation. She breathed through the intensity before she collapsed onto her bed and drew the covers up. When Aunt Marie reappeared, Pearl's breathing calmed. "Do you think you could teach me to be a midwife, Aunt Marie?"

Aunt Marie took Pearl's hand. "I'd like that, but I hear it won't be long before women start going to the hospital to deliver their babies."

"That's what Dr. Chapman said. But there are plenty of small towns like Kirkland, around Puget Sound that aren't big enough for hospitals. They will still need midwives for many years."

"That's a conversation for later." Marie moved with haste, motioning for Pearl to help lay out a heavy blanket and layers of clean towels over the bedsheets. "Time to lie down again."

Heavy swift footsteps clomped up the stairs, and Stanley appeared in the doorway as another spasm struck.

With her hands on her hips, Aunt Marie looked at Stanley. "It's time. The baby's coming."

Stanley's voice cracked. "What should I do?"

Aunt Marie took him by the arm. "I'll take care of Pearl. You may check the kettle on the stove and fetch it if it's boiling." Aunt Marie plopped a stack of clean white towels on the foot of the bed, then fluffed the pillows underneath Pearl's neck. "I'm going to wash my hands so I'll be ready."

Each contraction reminded Pearl of the day when, as a ten-year-old, she'd helped her aunt deliver Edna. She'd long forgotten her early resentment of the new baby and having to share in her parent's affections. Now, eight years later, her emotions bounced like a rubber ball between apprehension and excitement as she mentally readied herself for birthing her own child. Determined to have the strength her mother demonstrated during Edna's birth, Pearl concentrated on the work ahead.

The bedroom door creaked open. Pearl relaxed at the sight of Stanley carrying a kettle of water. "Are you doing okay?"

Though a stabbing sensation pierced her side and shooting pains ran down her back, Pearl managed to say, "I'm craving a pickle."

"You know the old saying, a sure sign you're having a boy." Marie winked with a smile.

Pearl's insides clenched. She let out a stifled cry. Marie shooed Stanley from the room. "This is no place for you now. Run along and tend to your work. I'll let you know when the baby's here."

Terrified, Pearl's voice raised in alarm. "What if something goes wrong? What if the baby is breech like Edna was? I'm scared."

"Don't worry. I checked with Frederick. There's a doctor in town. I'll send your husband to fetch him if necessary." Marie folded the blanket over partway and placed both hands on Pearl's stomach. She pushed on Pearl's abdomen to check the position of the baby. She patted Pearl's shoulder. "The baby will present headfirst."

Pearl took another breath. The contractions came sharper, faster, more severe. She stifled her cries the best she could.

"You're doing fine." Marie pulled the covers back over Pearl. "Your labor is progressing exactly as it should."

Pearl glanced at the plain gold band on her left-hand ring finger. She took comfort in knowing her baby would enter the world legitimate. Though it would happen in a bare-bones apartment over a furniture store, this baby would not be born in shame.

Four hours later, Marie checked her again and nodded. "It's time." She took Pearl's hand and squeezed it tight. "Are you ready?"

Her shoulders and lower back supported by her aunt, Pearl leaned in and gripped her knees and pushed.

After several minutes of exertion, with Pearl's energy depleted, Marie gave another instruction. "Pearl, I need you to push again. This is it."

From deep inside, Pearl drew her last bit of energy. She let out a howl., then remembering her sister emerging with the umbilical cord around her neck, Pearl held her breath. Still, with fear, she stared hard into her aunt's eyes. "Is my baby okay?"

A soft pat on the baby's backside brought a healthy wail. Exhausted, Pearl dropped back onto the bed.

Marie placed the baby, still connected to the cord, and covered with his protective waxy white coat, on Pearl's chest. "It's a boy."

For the second time in her eighteen years, Pearl faced a life altering experience. When Edna was born, Pearl was told it was up to her to be an example to Edna. Now she wondered what Edna would think about her when she got older and realized the gravity of what Pearl had done. She flicked aside the sting of guilt. Today, she bore her most important role yet, as a new mother with lifelong responsibilities and as a lifelong example to her son. She would not let her child down as she had let her mother and Edna down.

Pearl gazed upon her newborn son, his skin pink and wrinkled, covered with tiny white spots. His breathing came in trembling, whisper-like puffs, like petals of a delicate flower quivering in the soft breeze. Her shaky breath calmed. A comforting sensation swathed Pearl, soothing her like a mohair sweater. In that instant, Pearl understood the meaning of love. She understood the feeling her mother tried so hard to relay when she delivered Edna, and she understood all the sacrifices her mother made for her daughters. She brought her son to her breast and gazed upon him. She realized whatever goals in life she still wished to pursue, her life now had purpose and meaning.

♪ ♪ ♪

Minutes later, Stanley stood in the doorway. He hesitated before entering and approaching Pearl's bedside. His hands shook as he put his hand on Pearl's shoulder and squeezed it. "Are you all right?"

"I'm tired. But I'm fine."

Stanley gawked at the sight of his fair-skinned son. "I was so worried about you and the baby."

Marie put her arm around Stanley's shoulder. "Pearl and the baby are both fine. You don't need to worry."

"He has your nose." Stanley's eyes sparkled. "Have you settled on his first name yet?"

Pearl rocked the infant as she spoke. "I like the name Victor. It means conqueror, or victorious, which is how I feel right now. We've conquered so much, and we're together with a healthy son."

"Victor Frederick Rosenberg." Stanley nodded. "It's a fine strong name."

"He's asleep, and I'm tired." Pearl extended her arms to hand the baby to her husband. "Time for Victor to adjust to his own bed."

Stanley stood immobile. Petrified by insecurity, he hesitated before he reached his shaky arms out.

Aunt Marie stepped in and transferred Victor into his father's arms. "Don't be scared. He won't break."

Stanley's eyes glistened. "I never told you—Uncle Frederick was married about twenty years ago. Both his wife and infant daughter died during childbirth. I never knew until I began working with him. He bent down and kissed Pearl on her forehead. "I'm so thankful you both are safe."

With Victor safely in his arms, Stanley carried him to the makeshift cradle, a blanket-lined wooden drawer pulled out from an old dresser that needed refinishing before it would be sold and fetch a handsome twenty dollars. "This will work for a month or so. I'll have a real bed ready for him before he outgrows the dresser drawer."

Chapter Twenty-Four

1910 – Aunt Edna

A knock upon the front door sent mother scurrying to answer. Edna peered into the living room and saw the postman hand her mother the mail before he reached into a satchel and withdrew a postcard size sheet and handed it to her mother.

"Mr. Pritchard asked me to deliver this telegram that came across the wire yesterday."

Mother ignored the mail and stared at the telegram. She clutched it close to her bosom and thanked the postman.

"What is it, Mama? Is everything okay?"

Her mother's eyes glistened. "Come and sit down."

Edna bit her lip and shuffled to sit next to her mother at the kitchen table

"Pearl had her baby. A boy. His name is Victor."

Edna saw the Western Union Telegram still in her mother's hands. "Can I see it?" Edna read the short typed-out message. *Victor Frederick Rosenberg. Born, February 12 1910. Mother and baby healthy.* Edna shook her head. "I don't understand."

Her mother wrung her hands. "I guess you're old enough. I should have told you right away. Your sister got married shortly before Thanksgiving. It was a civil ceremony in front of a justice of the peace."

"Why couldn't she wait until I was there?"

"Being in a family way, she couldn't wait. She wanted to keep the baby, and the only way was for her to get married as soon as possible."

Edna stared at the slip of paper. "Does that mean Pearl is never coming home again?" Edna wondered if, by some miracle, her mother would have another baby so she wouldn't grow up alone. Edna cast a sideways glance at her mother's tight face and tired eyes. No. Her mother was too old, nearly forty. Edna was alone, like Pearl had been at the same age. Then it struck her. "Am I an aunt?"

Mother drew Edna close. "You will always be Victor's Aunt Edna.

Edna clapped her hands. "When can we go see the baby?"

"He's still too young for visitors. Maybe next month we can take the train to Kirkland."

Edna clasped her hands in a pleading pose. "Papa too?"

Her mother shook her head. "We'll see."

Edna chewed her lower lip. "I'm going to draw a picture for Victor." She dumped her worn crayons onto the table and fetched a sheet of clean butcher wrap. She rested her chin in her hands before drawing three figures of different heights, made a face, crumbled her drawing, and dropped it to the floor.

"What's wrong? Why did you do that?" Mother walked over and unfolded the crumpled ball.

"It's not special. I want to make something special for Victor."

Her mother sat next to her. "How would you like to learn to knit?"

"Can I make Victor a sweater?"

Mama chuckled. "You're old enough to learn to knit. But knitting a sweater might be a bit difficult." Her mother fished around inside her yarn satchel. "How about we start with a pair of booties." Withdrawing two skeins of yarn, Mother held them out for Edna to choose.

Edna puckered her brow before conceding. "Okay." She brightened, stroked the yarn, and selected a skein. "I think Victor will like blue better. Besides, it's the softest."

"Blue it is." Mother dropped the pale-yellow yarn back into its place and withdrew a pair of wood knitting needles. "These should do nicely."

Edna watched while her mother demonstrated how to hold the needles and cast on a short row of stitches. She cocked her head paying close attention as Mama explained each step.

"Insert the needle, wrap the yarn, then twist and dip the needle to push the completed stitch off."

It looked easy enough. Mother snuggled next to Edna as she took the knitting needles, and with a bit of awkward fumbling, attempted the moves. She pouted at her inability to duplicate her mother's motions on her first attempt.

"Don't worry." Mother reached across and helped Edna maneuver the yarn around the needles for a few stitches.

Edna pursed her lips, bit her tongue, and tried again. "Yarn and needle in the left hand. Insert needle here." Edna squinted with each deliberate step. "Wrap, hold it, pass it through, and slip it off." Edna exhaled and grinned. "I did it. I know how to knit." Edna chewed on her lip through the entire first row.

"It's a start." Mother patted Edna on the shoulder. "After you've completed nine more rows, let me know. I'll show you the next step."

A half hour later, Edna tired of holding the yarn and needles. She slid off the sofa and carried her task to show her mother, busy in the kitchen. "I have ten rows."

Mother counted the rows. "Perfect."

Edna raced back to the sofa. Her mother joined her and took the needles from Edna. Edna concentrated so hard her head hurt. She focused on how her mother dropped stitches, decreasing the width. A narrow blue rectangle took on a new shape. "Okay, ready for you to knit twenty more rows."

Edna picked up the small odd-shaped bootie, and before long, the form of the project shifted. "It looks like a letter T."

"Indeed, it does." Mother took the bootie from Edna and quickly cast off the stitches. She folded the finished project. "You can thread a needle now and sew the pieces together at the toe.

Edna scurried to fetch her sewing kit. She threaded a needle and put her thimble on her finger. Within minutes she held out the finished booty. She was impatient to make the mate, but Mother insisted she spend time reading and ready herself for bed. "You can finish the other booty tomorrow." When you're done, we'll wrap them and take them to town for mailing."

Edna frowned. She wished she could to see her nephew in person.

Chapter Twenty-Five

1910 – Halley's Comet

Though motherhood kept Pearl busy and fulfilled, by April, she yearned for something to occupy her mind in the absence of school.

Uncle Frederick thumbed through the orders for furniture piled on his desk. "I could use help with the paperwork. Business is booming. Kirkland is more than ten times larger than when I opened shop five years ago. I can't keep up with the invoicing and ordering of the goods."

Pearl jumped at the opportunity to apply what she had learned in her mathematics classes and help repay Uncle Frederick for his kindness while still staying home to care for Victor. "I promise, I'll do a good job for you."

"Peter Kirk sure knew what he was doing when he selected this location right on Lake Washington. I'm sure this city will continue to grow."

Pearl picked up several orders from the desk and glanced at them. "I'm willing to learn anything you want to show me."

"I can show you the ropes right away. Can't pay you, but I can take something off the rent."

Every day while Victor napped in a bassinet by her side, Pearl placed orders for supplies and sent off invoices to customers. Each day she made the short walk to downtown Kirkland, pushing Victor in his pram while she delivered bills to customers, stopped by the post office, and bought the paper for Uncle Frederick to read each evening. By now, headlines in the Seattle Post-Intelligencer announced the long-awaited arrival of Halley's comet, expected to be seen by the naked eye in mid-April for the first time in seventy-five years.

Months earlier, when she had first learned about the comet, Pearl had only dreamed of seeing the comet with her child. Now, within a matter of weeks, she would hold Victor and gaze up to the heavens to witness the once-in-a-lifetime event. Pearl stopped walking and skimmed the paper. The reporter wrote about the last time the comet appeared in 1835 noting that it could be plainly seen after sunset every day for perhaps a month. A story caught her eye, and Pearl refolded the paper to read it more easily.

Pearl hurried the rest of the way home as fast as the wheels on the buggy allowed. Out of breath, she burst through the door and called to Stanley.

Stanley wiped sawdust from his hands onto his overalls as he rushed to the door. "What's wrong?"

"When the comet appears next month, a poisonous gas in the tail will snuff out all life on the planet."

Stanley looked at Pearl as if she'd lost her mind. "What are you talking about?"

She thrust the paper in front of him. "Look." She jabbed at the frightening headline that roared like a raucous crow. **"Is there poisonous gas in the tail of the Comet?"**

Taking the paper, Stanley read aloud. "Early in February, Yerkes Observatory in Wisconsin announced they'd used a new scientific process to discover a poisonous gas, cyanide, in the tail of Halley's comet." He skimmed the remainder of the article before he looked at Pearl. "It seems scientists and astronomers hold conflicting views on what this means."

"What's all the commotion in here?" Pearl's frantic voice had drawn Frederick from the warehouse. He took the paper from his nephew and read it. He chuckled as he placed the paper onto the table. "You can't trust everything you read, even if it is in print." Shaking his head, he patted Pearl on the hand. "Superstitions about the comet go all the way back to the medieval times. Sometimes reporters like to sensationalize the news to sell more papers."

"How can you be so sure this isn't real?"

"I guess you're going to have to trust that long after the comet is gone, we'll all still be here. There are a lot of other astronomers who think this theory is bunk. Mr. Halley believes humans have seen the comet since the year 1531, and no one has died because of it. Now, put the mail on the desk, and don't give another thought to this story."

♪ ♪ ♪

From mid-April, when Pearl first stood outside the furniture store and stared with amazement at the glowing orb 140 million miles above the earth, she secretly feared the French astronomer's prediction. Too embarrassed to tell Stanley, each night she gazed into the sky, and with each passing day, she breathed easier. Thinking of the end of civilization sent a cold tremor over her. She rubbed her arms to warm herself.

On April 21, the newspapers all proclaimed Mark Twain's death, corresponding to the day after the comet reached its nearest point to the earth. The article noted that Mark Twain was born November 30, 1835, only two weeks after Halley's comet last appeared. Twain himself predicted he would go out with the comet's next appearance. His prediction now true, Pearl's worry increased over the Frenchman's proclamation that by mid-May when Earth passed through the tail of the comet, all life on earth would cease. Pearl remembered reading *The Adventures of Tom Sawyer, The Adventures of Huckleberry Finn,* and *The Prince and the Pauper.* She remembered quotes in the newspaper from the accomplished humorist, including one that particularly stayed with her. "The two most important days in your life are the day you were born and the day you find out why."

"It's going to be all right. I promise." Stanley wrapped his strong arms around her.

Comforted by Stanley's confidence, the tightness in her chest loosened. Each night she stared into the sky and held her breath. The now-fading comet traveled farther and farther away from Earth. Soon, Halley's comet was gone from sight for another seventy-six years. Not only had her life not ended, with her husband and her son by her side, she realized her life was only beginning. Pearl stared down at Victor, swaddled and warm, oblivious to the wonder that sped across the sky. She might never have the chance to become the nurse she hoped to be. Maybe protecting her son was enough. She relaxed into Stanley's embrace, content in believing she had a purpose, here with her family. "It was silly to think the world would end. I hope Victor is lucky enough to see it again in his old age."

Chapter Twenty-Six

1912 – The Titanic

The week after Easter, Edna stood with her classmates, their hands across their hearts, focused on the crisp new American flag, now with forty-eight stars honoring the newly named states of New Mexico and Arizona. The classroom door creaked open, interrupting their recital of the Pledge of Allegiance. Edna turned and saw Martin edging in, his shoulders drooped, anticipating his scolding.

Intolerant of tardiness, Miss Davis pounded her hand on her desk and demanded all eyes return their focus to the front of the class. "And what is your excuse for tardiness today, Martin?"

Scrunching his flushed face, Martin stammered. "I'm sorry. My newspapers were delivered late this morning. They had to hold the press for the latest news to come in across the wire." Martin's eyes drifted up toward Miss Davis's glare. "I was instructed to sell every paper 'cause everyone would want to read the latest news."

The entire class knew Martin's family relied on his meager earnings from selling the local newspaper downtown each morning, and Edna squirmed, embarrassed for her classmate.

Miss Davis crossed her arms and tapped her foot "And what exactly was so pressing in the news today?"

Martin slid out of his coat and put his lunch bucket along the shelf. When he turned back around, Edna saw his puffy red eyes. He gripped the morning edition of the *Port Orchard Independent* and unrolled it to show the headline to Miss Davis and read aloud. "The ocean liner *Titanic* sank yesterday; 1,500 souls drowned."

"Gracious." Miss Davis crossed herself like Inez's family did when saying grace before their evening meal. She bowed her head for a moment before returning her gaze to Martin. "What happened?"

"Paper reports it hit an iceberg."

Edna recalled what her father read in the newspaper the previous week when the ship left for its maiden voyage. He boasted it was the grandest and largest passenger vessel in the world and how he dreamed of someday having the chance to sail on something so spectacular.

Miss Davis rubbed her forehead and motioned for Martin to be seated.

He stuffed the newspaper under his arm, swiped his nose with the back of his hand, and slid into his seat.

As Miss Davis called for attention, Edna wondered how something so enormous could slip beneath the surface of the water and take so many lives. She'd heard about a few accidents involving steamers on Puget Sound that ran aground or even sank, like the *Multnomah* had only a few months earlier. Sometimes people even drowned as a result, but she'd never heard of so many people dying at one time. She thought about the times she'd crossed the sound on the *Athlon* and the *Inland Flyer*. She wondered if there were children aboard the *Titanic* and if they were safe or maybe some were among the dead. She shivered at the thought.

♪ ♪ ♪

For the first time in her life, the thought of death plagued her with restless sleep. Images of the specter illustrated in her Charles Dickens' book haunted her dreams. She worried about Pearl and Victor crossing the sound when they came to visit, and she worried about her father boarding the *Athlon* to go to Seattle. What if the boat sank? Would her family perish in the water like the passengers on the *Titanic*?

"No point in fretting over unfounded worries," Mama scolded when Edna mentioned her worries. "The waters of the sound are lots safer than the Atlantic Ocean. Besides, there are no icebergs on the sound."

Just as the worries of the Titanic faded, Edna arrived home from school one day to find her mother sitting at the kitchen table clutching a postcard. "What's wrong, Mama?"

"Your dad's father, your grandfather Henry, died last week. I'm afraid your father will take the news of his passing quite hard."

Edna had never met her grandfather or her grandmother. They lived in Wisconsin and had neither the means nor the inclination to travel across the United States to visit. Though her grandfather's death had little impact on her, she imagined the loss she would feel if her father died.

"I'm certain your father will want to attend the burial and assist his mother with her affairs."

Edna frowned. "Will he be gone long?"

"At least a week, probably more. Caledonia, Wisconsin, is two thousand miles away. That's nearly three days each way by train. The fare alone is going to be a hardship. I'll be working long hours taking in extra sewing jobs to earn extra money. I'm going to need a lot of help from you."

"I can help you with your sewing jobs, Mama. I can assist with alterations and simple darning tasks." Edna remembered her first sewing project the previous year, in fourth grade. After sitting and watching her mother for so many years, sewing an apron proved to be an easy task for Edna. She'd even embroidered her initials on the corner of the apron in hopes of earning a higher mark on the project. She remembered how surprised she was when Miss Matheson, her domestic science teacher, held a competition at the completion of the class.

"Every student will vote for who they think sewed the best apron."

Even now, a year later, Edna burned with resentment as she recalled voting for her friend Berta's apron. When Berta won the competition by one vote, Edna was furious and didn't speak to Berta for over a week.

When her father returned home Friday evening, Edna flung herself into his arms and hugged him as tight as she could. Three days later, Edna and her mother piled into the buggy to see her father off.

At the steamboat terminal, her parents hugged. Then her father waved to her, turned, and strode away. The engines fired up and spit water. Steam spewed from the stack. On the top deck, passengers waved to those on the shore. A photo from the newspaper of the waving crowd on the top deck of the *Titanic* as it departed Southampton and headed for New York flashed into her head. She shuddered at the image. A chill washed over her. She ran toward the gangplank after her father. "Don't go. What if something happens and the boat sinks or the train tips over?"

Her father stopped and turned around. He set his bags down and sighed but wrapped his arms around her. "I'll be fine. Be a big girl and help your mother." Edna grabbed his coat to prevent him from walking away. Her father huffed and bent lower to kiss her forehead, then turned and continued toward the blaring horn of the *Athlon* that would ferry him to Seattle to catch the Northern Pacific. Edna buried her face behind her hands so Papa couldn't see her tears flowing.

Her mother drew her close and whispered. "Don't worry. He'll be back safely."

♪ ♪ ♪

Ten long days later, her mother prepared a roast beef with Franconia potatoes marinated in the beef juices and Papa's favorite ginger cake. Edna busied herself with chores to make the house sparkle for her father's return. She boiled the linens early in the day. While they hung on the line, Edna swept the floor. As the dinner hour neared, Nellie's whinny brought Edna to the window. She ran outside and threw her arms around her father. Then she drew back. His dark, solemn eyes now looked sunken into his pale, worn face though his cheeks looked flushed as if he'd applied rouge like the church ladies wore on Sundays. His legs quivered like a gangly calf as he walked up the walkway to the door. Mother jumped from the buggy and helped him inside to their bedroom, where he collapsed onto their bed. Once sturdy and filled with endless energy, her father was suddenly frail, and Edna worried.

"What's the matter, Daddy?"

Her father closed his eyes. "Just tired, nothing for you to fret over."

Edna draped an orange-and-yellow crocheted afghan over him. "I'll make you a cup of tea, Papa." When the kettle whistled, Edna filled a cup. Her hands shook as she moved with haste to the bedroom. Papa welcomed the hot drink, gripping the cup in his trembling hands. He forced a smile and patted her hand but couldn't hide the pained look on his face. To avoid upsetting her father, Edna didn't cry.

Mother came in a few minutes later and adjusted his pillow. "You're burning up. I'm calling Doctor Wilkes."

Edna stood, unable to move or speak. Her father hated doctors and hated even more spending hard-earned money on them.

"Don't need the doctor. I just need a good night's sleep in my own bed. Didn't sleep much on the train.

"What about food? Did you eat anything?"

Her father patted his stomach. "I had me a mighty fine meal. Cost a pretty penny, but I figured it was a one-time thing. Gotta say, for a buck-fifty, had an oyster cocktail, some clam bouillon, mutton, fancy mashed potatoes, brussels sprouts, and a fancy dessert they called a torte."

"Do you think you can eat something?"

Papa shrugged. "Better try if I'm going to report to work tomorrow."

Mother stood firm, her hands on her hips. "You're in no condition to report to work tomorrow, George. You need to rest a while."

"You know I can't. Kingsbury will lay me off if I miss any more days. Lots of younger fellas ready and willing to work for the pay I'm getting at the logging camp. Plenty of people willing to jump into my position."

Her mother shook her head and walked away. When she returned, she held out a plate of potatoes and beef cut into bite-size pieces like she used to do when Edna was younger. "Let me help you." She lifted a spoon of potatoes to his lips.

Papa struggled to speak, but he had a difficult time catching his breath through his frog-like croak. He slapped at Mama's hand. "I don't need you to feed me. I'm not helpless."

169

"No, you're not. But you're sick." Her mother placed the back of her hand on Daddy's forehead, then she shook her head and crossed her arms over her chest. "You're going to kill yourself, you old fool. Eat now." She shooed Edna out, before she got up, and followed Edna out the door.

For the next two days, Father lay in bed. Despite the honey and licorice-root tea Mama coaxed into him, his constant cough brought an edge of panic to both. On the second day, her mother pleaded, "You need to see the doctor."

Her father barked back. "Ain't got money for such nonsense. Besides, it's just a cold."

"We'll find the money. I'm not going to have you die in this bed."

Terrified by the word, a cold panic gripped Edna. Papa had returned from his long trip safely. He couldn't die here at home in his own bed. His frail body, pale as the bed linen, was now drenched with sweat, which beaded on his forehead. She grabbed a wet cloth and wiped her father's brow.

Her mother stood over him, her arms crossed over her chest. "The symptoms don't appear to be simply a cold. Your heart is beating unsteadily, and you're still burning with fever. I'm worried." Her mother's raised voice sounded sharper, with a firmness Edna had not heard since the late-night squabbles with Pearl. "If your symptoms worsen, you won't be able to work. Then what will happen to us?" She untied her apron, flung it onto the bedside chair, and stomped toward the door. "I'm going into town to fetch the doctor. I need you to stay here with your father and watch over him. Do you understand?"

A wave of panic swept over Edna at the thought of being left alone with her father. She trembled as her mother grabbed her coat. On the verge of tears, Edna called after her. "I don't know what to do."

"Keep his fever down with plenty of water and the cool cloth." Her mother called over her shoulder as she rushed out. The door banged behind her.

Alone in the house with her sick father, Edna wished Pearl was here. Pearl would know what to do. Edna wanted to run to her room and get Molly, but she resisted. She was ten now. "Be strong, Edna. You need to be strong."

♪ ♪ ♪

The sound of horses trotting up the drive woke Edna from where she had fallen asleep in the chair next to her father's bed. As her lids fluttered open, she noticed her father's crooked smile.

His rough, scratchy voice frightened her. "Hope you had a nice nap."

Edna squeezed his shoulder as the front door flung open. Her mother called out before she led Dr. Wilkes into the room.

"How's the patient doing?"

Edna shrugged. "Papa's okay, I suppose."

Standing over Papa, Dr. Wilkes turned to her mother. "I need to examine him alone."

Blinking sleep from her eyes, Edna shuffled from the room.

"Run along and climb into bed." Mama tipped her head toward Edna's bedroom.

"Please, Mama, let me wait until the doctor is finished."

While the doctor tended to her father, Edna tapped her foot and rocked with nervous energy. After what seemed hours, the doctor entered the room. With a grim face, he sat and spoke to Mother. "A healthy person has a body temperature of around ninety-eight. Your husband has a fever, upwards of one-hundred-two. I consider that quite serious."

"Can you help him?" Mama's eyes were wide with fear. Edna shuddered and wiped her eyes with the back of her hand.

"I recommend cool baths, and I'll give you a small bag of willow bark for tea. He should drink as many liquids as possible. Any form of alcohol is not advisable."

Mother thanked Dr. Wilkes, fetched his coat, and followed him to the door. The doctor stopped and turned around. "Your husband is weak. I'm concerned about his fever and his dry cough. Praise be, I don't think he has the consumption. He told me he recently returned from a long train trip back east. I suspect he likely has the influenza. Lots of that going around, especially in close quarters. He's got many of the symptoms, including the flushed face." He shook his head as he slipped into his coat, then grabbed his medicine bag. "You need to watch him closely. Keep me abreast if he doesn't improve."

Edna looked at her mother, whose body seemed to melt into itself with relief as she thanked the doctor. Doctor Wilkes put a hand on her shoulder. "Keep an eye on him." He shook his head with his eyes narrow and focused. "He could take a turn for the worse. If you notice any confusion or if he has trouble breathing, let me know. For now, I suggest bed rest for at least a week, along with plenty of fluids, and limit your exposure and your daughter's exposure as much as possible. He may be contagious."

Chapter Twenty-Seven

1913 – The Move

Victor smiled as he sat on the floor stacking blocks of leftover wood Stanley had sanded down. Pearl looked around the four-hundred-square foot space she called home. Her conveniences were equal to those in her family home in Port Orchard with several upgrades, including a water closet and a kitchen area with a modern icebox and even a gas range. Uncle Frederick's kindness allowed them to live on Stanley's modest earnings and put aside money to buy their own place someday.

Still, the confined quarters and the routine left Pearl feeling trapped and questioning her accomplishments in the past twenty-one years. She remembered marching with the women in downtown Seattle. Women had fought for and won the right to vote in this state. But last November, she'd not been old enough yet to cast her vote. Instead, she sat home while Stanley and Uncle Frederick and even her mother and aunt went to the local school or the Elks club to cast their votes for the Democratic candidate for president, Woodrow Wilson.

Her dream of attending the university had faded with the passing of the past three years, but her desire to do something more still crept into her fantasies at night and lingered during the quiet hours of the day. Her life was good, but it was far from the lofty imaginings of the day she crossed the sound and met Dr. Chapman. Today, as a familiar discomforting feeling washed over her, she sensed another detour ahead. She fetched a glass of water and nibbled on some saltine crackers hoping to squelch the churning in her stomach. Over the past week, her appetite had diminished. She watched her son stack his blocks. First three high, then four high before they tumbled. She watched Victor pinch-faced, persevere and try again. This time the stack reached five high before it wobbled and fell. She stiffened her posture and shoved aside her feeling of insignificance. She needed to follow her son's lead and keep striving for a loftier goal.

A yelp from the workshop downstairs jolted Pearl to attention.

"Pearl? Are you there? I need help. Hurry!"

Pearl scooped up Victor and dashed down the stairs and into the workshop. Uncle Frederick hunched over, with a blood-stained rag wrapped around his left hand. Checking the area for nails and wood splinters, she kicked aside some scrap wood and set Victor on the floor. Instructing him to stay seated, she looked at Uncle Frederick. "What happened?"

"I was pairing out dovetails, and the chisel slipped. I've cut my thumb and hand."

The blood-stained woodworking tool lay on the ground. She clutched her forehead in her hands and tried to remember the first-aid lessons learned during her parenting class at the Florence Crittenton School. Blood oozed through the cloth. Pearl shook her head, the cloth wasn't clean, but she knew she shouldn't remove it. "Is it deep?'

Fredrick looked at his hand, his face turned pale. "Yes, I had to pull the chisel out. I'm sure it took off half my thumb."

Pearl helped Uncle Frederick to the floor where he rested his head against the wall. "When is Stanley due back from the deliveries?"

Uncle Frederick shook his head. "Not for hours."

"Lift your arm. Keep the hand higher than the heart."

She took hold of Frederick's hand. It was turning cold. She remembered what her Aunt Marie uttered when Edna was born and her mother was hemorrhaging. Uncle Frederick's blood pressure was dropping. "Are you feeling okay?" She gazed into Frederick's eyes.

Pearl swept Victor into her arms. "I'm going to call the doctor."

Uncle Frederick stared at her in silence through his dilated pupils. Pearl ran all the way to the Gibson Hotel. She instructed them to dial Doctor George Davis. "He's on extension Black 392. Tell him to hurry. My uncle has lost a lot of blood. He's in the back of

Rosenberg's Furniture Store, in the workshop. The door is unlocked." Pearl dashed back to the furniture store.

By the time Stanley returned from his deliveries, Pearl had helped Frederick to his room where he was asleep with thirteen stitches in his hand and on two fingers. Stanley pulled Pearl close as they lay in bed. "I spoke to the doctor to thank him. He said your quick thinking saved a lot of blood and maybe the use of my uncle's hand." Stanley seemed to read Pearl's mind. "Do you ever regret getting married and not becoming a nurse?"

Pearl held her breath. She didn't want to confess her desire. She had other things on her mind and now wasn't the time. "I love the life we have, but sometimes I can't help wondering if there is something more for me, for us. I know I can never become a nurse but I want to learn midwifery. I'm sure my aunt will teach me what she knows."

Stanley sat up with such abruptness, Pearl startled, afraid she'd upset him.

Stanley's smile eased her trepidation. "I've been thinking I need a change too. We need our own place, and I'm ready to venture forth on my own. What do you think about moving?"

Her heart thumped wildly. She leaned in to hug Stanley, but her tender breasts made her pull back. She held her breath as Stanley's eyes raised in concern. She looked down at her belly and sighed. "Your timing is perfect. I'm afraid we're about to outgrow this space."

Stanley cocked his head and stared at Pearl. "Are you with child again?"

Pearl held her breath. "I hope you're pleased. Victor is already three, and he's so bright. I know he'll adjust well to having a sibling. It was hard on me being an only child for ten years before Edna was born. I hate to have Victor grow up without brothers or sisters closer to his age."

Stanley pulled her close and kissed her with a passion she didn't expect.

"You can open a furniture store north of Kirkland near the new shingle mill. You have a solid reputation and plenty of customers, especially with the town growing."

"Though there's plenty of business to sustain two stores, it wouldn't be right. It's the perfect time for us to make a move and for me to establish a reputation for myself somewhere else, away from Kirkland."

"What about your uncle? Will he be okay without your help?"

"Don't worry, the doctor believes he'll regain most of the use of his left hand in a month or two. He's fine. He'll bring on another apprentice to help."

"But we're settled here. We've met so many people. We have the ferries on Lake Washington, even a new automobile ferry. It's finally easier to commute to Seattle to see family."

"I know. I want to stay close enough to visit our families, but I don't want to move back to the city. It's grown to over three-hundred-thousand people, and I've come to prefer the smaller towns. Besides, I don't imagine there's room for an independent craftsman to compete with the large department stores with all their fine Eastlake and Victorian furniture shipped from the East Coast."

"Your customers know your quality and fine detail work is as good as the pricey pieces the department stores are selling."

"We're not likely to find such affordable rent of only twelve dollars a month, including utilities, anywhere around here. I've read land is cheap east of Lake Washington along the newly expanded railroad line. New communities are popping up everywhere as the electric interurban route expands, and more steamers are traveling from the city across Lake Washington." Stanley's eyebrows raised, hopeful, and questioning. "What do you think?"

Pearl thought about the day she'd left home and faced the unknown. Moving away to a new town where they knew no one was scary, but she'd overcome so much and was stronger for it. She recalled Dr. Chapman's words. "The vastness of your opportunities is endless." She flashed a smile. "I think it's a wonderful idea."

For the next few weeks, Pearl poured over the *Kirkland Reporter,* reading about the ever-expanding settlements springing up around Puget Sound due to the ferries and growing number of automobiles. It appeared particularly young families were pushing north of Seattle and Lake Union and East of Lake Washington to where timber was plentiful and logging continued to thrive as the railroad lines extended farther and farther east, providing a means to transport logs. Every evening when Victor was asleep, Pearl and Stanley studied maps and real estate advertisements. They plotted their course east to

Redmond, then due south along Lake Sammamish to Issaquah. When the weekend came, they grabbed their coats, bundled Victor in his winter bunting, and climbed into Uncle Frederick's Model T Touring car. Though it was mid-March, the twenty-mile drive in the open car would be cold and would take several hours. Stanley ran his hand over the shiny blue paint and beamed as he jumped behind the wheel, grinning ear to ear at his rare opportunity to drive. Stanley turned the key, and the engine rattled to life. "If I were a betting man, I'd expect someday the town of Issaquah will become a booming town like Kirkland. If we get a business up and running, we'll benefit from the growth of the town."

As they traversed paved roads leading to gravel and eventually dirt, Victor laughed and grinned, his eyes as wide with wonder as Pearl's. Along the shore of Lake Sammamish, they passed old cedar-plank houses, reminders of the town's original residents, the Snoqualmie Indians. Newer homes sprouted along the lake, where logging continued to thrive in the still verdant virgin forest. When Stanley spotted a sign indicating they'd entered the town of Adelaide, he pulled the car off the road and got out. Newly erected buildings lined both sides of the narrow lane, including a lumber factory on the north end and, farther down the road, a store, a hotel, a blacksmith shop, a tool house, a foreman family home, and bunkhouses for fifty men. "This is the town Uncle Frederick told us about." He looked east up to the hills and pointed to a gully carved deep into the forest. "That's what they call a skid road. Men fell the trees, and oxen haul them to the gulley where they travel downhill to the lake before they're milled or shipped down to Frisco. What do you think, Pearl?"

"It's pretty, and there's plenty of timber. Do you suppose there's indoor plumbing this far from the city?"

"Probably not, but it will come in time. It took a while for Port Orchard to get electricity, but the city eventually grew large enough. You didn't have an indoor bathroom growing up. You'll get used to it again."

Pearl's heart beat a little faster. For the first time in her life, she was embarking on a path that would lead her to a home of her own. She gripped Victor's hand and inhaled the earthy cedar and fir trees standing tall and sturdy like lookouts greeting all who passed through.

177

"We're almost to Issaquah." Stanley climbed behind the wheel once more, and Pearl and Victor piled in. "We'll follow the lake south, then take a break."

The short drive along the lake with the cool spring breeze blowing through the open-topped automobile invigorated Pearl. Heading south, she saw a stream of smoke sending curls and columns into the sky.

Pearl pointed out a dark, tall domed-shaped building. "What is that?"

Stanley peered toward the growing cloud of smoke as he motored along the lake. "Looks like a sawmill." As they neared the building, they entered a town called Monohon. A boarding house and small cabins dotted the hillside across from the lake before the mill came into sight. "This is the Allen and Nelson Sawmill. If we find land not far from here, I'll have a convenient mill to provide me with finished wood.

By the time Stanley parked the car in front of the town hall in the small town of Issaquah, Pearl's stomach gnawed with hunger. They crossed the street to a grassy area and spread out a blanket.

"This is a fine town. Seems to have everything we need. I wonder how it got its unusual name?" Pearl opened the picnic basket and set out fried cornmeal pone, cheese, and rice pudding with raisins.

"Frederick told me the town was originally named Squawk, an Indian name meaning the sound of birds. I guess there were lots of waterfowl that squawked in the nearby creeks."

Pearl remembered Aunt Marie telling her Seattle was named after Chief Sealth, the chief of the Duwamish Indian tribe. From Puyallup, south of Seattle, to Spokane in the eastern part of the state, cities, mountains, and rivers were named after various Indian tribes who inhabited the state long before white settlers came. Their culture was still evident in artwork, weavings, even the totem pole in Pioneer Square. As Pearl and Stanley collected the remains from their picnic lunch, Victor scampered across the grass and plucked tiny white flowers, which he carried back. "Look, Mama, for you."

After eating and strolling downtown Issaquah, the family returned to the car and headed east. "Won't be long now, a few miles away on mostly easy roads." Less than twenty minutes later, Stanley spied a FOR SALE sign along the roadway. A red arrow directed them. He turned the car onto a dirt road where they bumped and bounced along in silence for several minutes before Stanley hit the brakes in front of a white sign posted along the Raging River. "This is it. This is the place we read about in the advertisement. The town is named Preston." Pearl nearly leaped from the car before it rolled to a stop. "Oh, Stanley, it's perfect. And it's close to Issaquah."

Stanley turned off the ignition. "There's supposedly a shingle mill around here somewhere too." They climbed out and gazed around the forested plot. "The advertisement says forty acres. The asking price is fifty-dollars." Stanley scratched his bare chin. It reminded Pearl of her father scratching his beard whenever he was deep in thought. Victor scampered away, collecting stones and stuffing them deep into his pockets. "Sounds like a fair price," Stanley rubbed his chin. "We have over seven-hundred dollars saved thanks to Uncle Frederick. It's going to be a lot of work and of course, take a lot of money to clear a spot for the house, and without city water, we'll require a well." Stanley turned in a circle. "This place is farther out than I thought. Closest town of any size is Issaquah. Didn't pass any electric poles for several miles. What do you think about living without electricity? We can use coal for cooking the same as you had in Port Orchard, and I can build a fireplace for heat."

Pearl closed her eyes and considered the question. "What about plumbing? Would I still have an indoor bathroom?"

Stanley thought again as he ran his hand over his chin. "As long as we can dig a shallow well and install a manual pump, we can have a modern bathroom. You'll have to pump the water instead of simply turning on the faucet like with the city water you're used to."

Pearl tipped her head to the sounds of the forested land. She wrapped her arms across her chest. "It's so peaceful. You can hear the gurgling of the river from here. Just think, all this would be our backyard. As long as I have an indoor commode, a built-in bathtub, and running water, I'll be okay. How long do you think it will be before the power company brings power this far?"

"Hard to say, it might be several years."

Back at their home in Kirkland, Pearl and Stanley calculated the costs to improve the land and build a home. Stanley arranged for contractors to inspect the land for feasibility and for a well. Pearl studied the designs of houses from a borrowed Sears Roebuck and

Company catalog titled *Book of Modern Homes and Building Plans*. She marked pages of house plans suitable for their growing family and still be within their budget.

"I found the perfect home. Sears promises that a buyer with only rudimentary skills can assemble a kit home in ninety days." She stabbed her finger at the drawing identified as "Modern Home No. 167." "It's only $753.00, for all the materials, and the whole house, including the labor, cement, and brick can be built for $1573.00. And it has an indoor bathroom, but plumbing, electrical wiring, and heating are not included."

Stanley's tired eyes brightened. "Well, that price sounds promising. Of course, we won't need a kit house, we have our own timber, but it gives me an idea what to expect." He studied the catalog. "I like the layout. I can draw up the plans and have a draftsman look at them. We can save on labor if my brother, Simon, helps with the construction." Stanley studied the catalog, which boasted cheap, accessible, and quality housing. "The corner turret reminds me of the stately homes in Seattle." Stanley patted Pearl's belly. "With a little luck and a lot of help, we can move in before the new arrival."

Thirty days later, with the land feasibility completed to their satisfaction, Stanley and Pearl took seats opposite a stout man in a black three-piece suit perched behind a large oak desk at Issaquah Bank.

He greeted them and invited them to sit. "As I understand, you will be paying cash for the land but wish to borrow to improve the property and build a house."

"That's right. When I spoke to someone here earlier, I was told with the records of my current earnings, I am eligible to borrow up to thirteen-hundred dollars."

The banker reviewed his copy of the loan agreement. "You are correct, Mr. Rosenberg." He handed a pen to Stanley and tapped the bottom of the form. "That amount is right here. Your signature goes on the bottom line."

Pearl held Victor, who struggled to run free, while Stanley read and reread the fine print over several pages, then looked at her. "It's the right thing." Stanley tapped the pen on the desk before nodding and scrawling his name on the line.

The banker stood, tugged at his vest, and checked his pocket watch. "Congratulations. You are now customers of Issaquah Bank."

♪ ♪ ♪

The dream of owning their own home now within reach, Pearl's stomach knotted at the thought of the immense task ahead. "The baby will be here in less than six months. Have you spoken with Simon yet?"

"He'll be out of school for the summer in a few weeks. He's willing to come and help me throughout the summer." Stanley rubbed his forehead before running his hands through his hair. "I can't finish the house without him, and it's a lot to ask of him to help all summer when he can get a paying job elsewhere." Stanley raised his brows. "I'll need to reimburse him in some way."

"I understand. Pay him what you think is fair. It will still be cheaper than hiring out."

Stanley exhaled and nodded. "Don't worry. I ciphered the figures for the well and the water lines. We may have to wait a while for electricity to reach us, but with the new slope coal mines bringing more miners, I don't imagine it will be long before the population swells enough for the county to bring in electricity. I can make money selling the logs to the mill, so I'm confident we can keep within the budget."

With Stanley's brother agreeable to help, and workers scheduled to cut trees and dig the well, Stanley quit his job at the furniture store to assist with the clearing and begin framing the house.

After two weeks apart from Stanley, Pearl packed a picnic basket and an extra set of clothes, and hopped into the car with Uncle Frederick for the long drive to Issaquah. Dark circles of fatigue furrowed beneath Stanley's eyes as he took the basket of bread, cheese, fruit, and drinking water.

"How's the boarding house in Monohon?"

Stanley and Simon shrugged. "It'll do fine until we get the house framed and the well and plumbing in. Then we can start sleeping here."

Separated from Stanley for weeks at a time, Pearl remembered her childhood and her own father's absence from her life. She wondered how her mother had managed household and farm chores with two children. Without Stanley to help at the furniture store, Uncle Frederick relied even more on Pearl to fulfill the task of bookkeeping and maintain adequate supplies, as well as greet customers. She collapsed in bed each night, often allowing Victor to fall asleep next to her. She ached for her husband's touch, and as her condition progressed without him around, she felt the same loneliness she'd felt when she carried Victor and he was absent.

Within four months, and with Stanley and Simon working seven days a week, their home had many modern conveniences, including an indoor bathroom with a commode, bathtub, and sink. For now, they would use kerosene lights, and for the most part, heat the home with a wood stove from the endless supply of logs available to them. And someday soon, they would have electricity.

Summer brought visitors flocking to spend the day on Lake Sammamish. The region had grown in popularity for tourists since the Lake Shore & Eastern Railroad Company completed a track along the eastern shore bringing more business to the Allen and Nelson lumber mill, now the anchor of Monohon. Worried about finances after months with no income, Stanley found temporary employment on the south shore of the lake, managing rental cottages and renting rowboats to tourists. Each night he returned home tired and weathered from being in the sun all day. Still, he pushed himself, hanging cabinets and finishing the details for their spacious home until at last, mere weeks before the arrival of their second child, Stanley announced the house was done.

Chapter Twenty-Eight

1915 – Visiting Pearl

Pearl paced on the planked walkway at the Issaquah Depot, waiting for the Northern Pacific Railroad to arrive, eager to see her family and at last show them her home. One-year-old Henry squirmed in her arms like an anxious cat wishing he could run around the white barn-size building, so different from the King Street Station where her mother and sister's train trip originated.

Victor stomped his foot and whined. "When are Grandmother and Auntie Edna going to get here? I'm tired of waiting."

She tousled five-year-old Victor's hair, the same way her father had tousled hers twenty years earlier. "The train should be here soon." Pearl gazed down the track as far as she could see. Much like her own life, the track had a clear beginning, though she didn't know where it ended; she knew only that it extended far into the distance.

Stanley joined her and followed her gaze. "What are you looking at?"

Pearl pressed her lips together and contemplated the twist of fate that separated her from her parents and sister throughout her high school years and continued today. "Edna's going to graduate next year and my parents will most likely move to Seattle, and now we have moved farther away again."

"Do you miss Seattle?"

"I loved the city. I miss the bustle of the outdoor market on Pike Street and the marches with my aunt, and I miss the parks."

As if reading her mind, Stanley drew her close. His breath on her ear excited her. "I remember lying on the grass at Volunteer Park and holding a special young girl."

A tickle of desire embarrassed her, making her pulse race.

A tug at her sleeve drew her back. Victor pointed to the crowd. "Is everyone here waiting for Grandmother and Auntie?"

Pearl glanced at the dozen or so people waiting for arrivals or standing outside on the platform. "No, they're waiting for someone they know who's arriving on the same train. Or they're waiting to board the train to travel east to Ellensburg or Spokane."

In the distance, a long shrill whistle announced the train's arrival. Victor jumped up and down. "I see it! I see the train!" He pulled on his mother's arm. "They're here."

Grabbing her son's hand, she led him in a hasty retreat away from the track. The sleek black and orange beast roared closer and closer. Victor covered his ears as Henry snuggled deeper into Pearl's chest. With a giant hissing sound, the locomotive screeched to a stop in front of the eager crowd on the platform. A crisply dressed uniformed man appeared in the open door, extended the steps, and stepped aside. Men, women, and children stepped off the train peering at the waiting onlookers for their special someone to greet them.

Unable to contain her delight, Pearl jumped and waved when Edna and her mother appeared at the top of the steps. She called to them, and her words rose above the din, drawing glances. She rushed to her sister. "I've missed you so much." Pearl reached out to hug Edna.

Victor held back for a few seconds, then rushed into his grandmother's arms. She took a step back and brought her hand to her mouth. "Goodness, you're such a big boy."

Victor lisped through two missing front teeth. "I'm going to be tall like Papa when I get older."

Pearl handed Henry to her sister. "I'll trade you." She passed her toddler to Edna in exchange for the lighter-weight overnight bag.

Stanley reached for her mother's baggage. "I hope the ride wasn't too long."

Her mother shook her head. "Two and a half hours from the city, not counting crossing the sound yesterday. But it's worth the time to finally see you and your family again."

Pearl kissed her mother on the cheek. "You're looking well."

Mother took her daughter's hand. "I feel well." She stroked Henry's dark curls.

Pearl beamed. "He's got his father's hair. Can you believe he's almost two?"

Stanley pivoted and headed away from the station. "Let's get you to our house. You're probably ready for a proper rest."

At the street, he strapped the bags to the rear fender of a dark-green Model T, while Mother and Edna piled into the back seat with Henry. Victor climbed in after them. The key turned, the push button engaged, and the Ford rumbled and bumped along.

Pearl's mother ran her hand over the diamond-tufted cushioned seat. "Your father assured me we can buy a car as soon as we save enough money. After reading an advertisement in the *Ladies' Home Journal* about the new Ford, I convinced him to let me learn how to drive. The ad stated it's the ideal car for a woman to drive. Simple to operate and nothing to puzzle at or be confused by."

Pearl glanced over her shoulder with a broad smile. "Driving is great fun. But it's not as fun to drive on the dirt and gravel roads as on the paved streets."

"I can't wait to see the house you built. Is it far?"

Pearl looked toward the back seat. "It's about seven miles, but the roads aren't paved for the last few miles. We'd like to show you our furniture store first. It's only a short distance from here, right downtown on Front Street, and then we can drive along Lake Sammamish. It's beautiful."

Minutes later, Stanley parked in front of the store. Edna stared up at the sign. *Rosenberg's Furniture Store.* "Isn't Rosenburg's the name of your uncle's store?"

"Yes. We decided using the family name would eventually garner a reputation for both my uncle and me. The stores are far enough from each other we're not in competition."

After a brief tour, everyone piled back into the car, and Stanley headed northwest. The small stores and sidewalk businesses disappeared, replaced by a forest of towering cedar and pine trees.

Pearl's mother closed her eyes and inhaled. "I wish Seattle smelled as fresh and woodsy."

When the lake came into view, Pearl pointed. "That's Lake Sammamish. It's named for the Indians who once lived in this whole region."

Her mother shook her head. "It's so peaceful here. It's beautiful the way the sun reflects off the water, like a mirror."

Mama and Edna gazed at the lake, to the logs piled high on the shore. A steam-fitted crane loomed over the lake like a Seattle skyscraper. "What's that?"

"It's called a derrick. It's used to lift the largest logs."

Her mother looked off to the distance, past the mill. A steamboat chugged away. "Where does the steamer go?"

"The *May Blossom*, travels north to the end of the lake, then up the Sammamish River heading northwest to Bothell and to the north end of Lake Washington."

Pearl pointed in the direction of the steamer's route. "That's the Allen and Nelson Mill Company, where we buy most of the wood Stanley uses to build his furniture."

Stanley turned away from the lake, then retraced his route back to Issaquah before he headed east on Sunset Highway for several miles. Eventually, the road shifted to a gravel and dirt road. Victor bounced on the seat. "There's my schoolhouse when I start school." He pointed out the window. "See, Auntie Edna?"

Edna turned her gaze to follow Victor's pointing finger. "It doesn't look too different from the two-room schoolhouse your mother and I attended at your age."

Victor beamed. "Mama says you're going to be a teacher. Can you be my teacher?"

Edna shrugged. "It's going to be a few years yet. We'll have to see."

Pearl shook her head. "If you thought Port Orchard was small, there are only about four-hundred-fifty residents in Preston and only about fifty students at the school. But it's growing every year. By the time you earn your teaching certificate in seven years, it might even be a pretty good-sized town. There's still plenty of logging in the whole region. There's also a small one-room school in Monohon, which is growing in part due to the mill and the only canvas boat and canoe manufacturing company in the state."

The car turned onto a narrow dirt road hidden by tall cedar and fir trees. It bumped along over rough patches and several potholes. A half mile later, the car rolled to a stop. Stanley smiled and turned off the ignition. "We're here."

Pearl watched with pride as her mother's face brightened. "It's beautiful. It's the biggest log house I've ever seen."

"It's nearly thirteen hundred square feet. Three bedrooms."

"Three? My goodness. Is there another baby on the way?"

Stanley cocked his head and glanced at Pearl. "Not yet, but maybe in time. I've got your bags. I'm sure Pearl is eager to show you the house."

Chapter Twenty-Nine

1916 – End of Grammar School

The night before Edna's eighth-grade exam, her mind whirled with worries over what a failed exam meant. She admired her mother's talents but couldn't imagine sewing dresses or making hats for a living. Her entire life she'd dreamed of becoming a teacher. Failing the test meant an end to her dreams and to the expectations her parents had for her. She couldn't let them down as Pearl had. She had to complete not only high school, but college as well. The need to compensate where Pearl failed nibbled away at her.

At six thirty, her alarm clanged reawakening her worries. She got dressed and braided her hair before wrapping and pinning the braids around her head.

Mother poked her head into Edna's bedroom. "Are you ready for your big day?"

Looking in the mirror over her bureau, Edna ran her hand over the pink taffeta and the ivory cotton lace insets in the bodice of her dress. The latest in fashion that didn't require wearing a tight-fitting corset. "I'm ready." She gave a nod of approval to her reflection, then strode to the kitchen.

Edna pulled up a chair, then speared two hot cakes from the platter and placed them alongside a sausage and over-easy egg.

Her mother sipped on a cup of green tea sweetened with fresh cream and honey. "I'm sure you'll pass with flying colors."

"I've always been proficient with writing and spelling. It should be easy to obtain the eighty percent required to pass the grammar section." She stopped and took a few bites from the maple-syrup-coated buttermilk hot cakes. Her head pounded. She rubbed her temples. "I'm worried about the United States history and civics sections. I've been studying extra hard, but the classes aren't as interesting, so the material is more difficult for me."

Her mother smiled. "You'll be fine."

The reassurance helped ease the tension tying her stomach in knots.

"It's important for young women these days to further their education. I know you don't want to dedicate your life to sewing, though I am proud to say it has served this family well."

By the time she reached the school, the clanging of the final bell sent her dashing toward the door and down the stairs to the basement lunchroom for the important exam. A gray-suited man from the state educational authority stood at the front of the room and peered over his wire-rimmed glasses. He waited until each student found a seat at tables for eight, spread out to minimize the inclination for students to share their work or otherwise cheat. Atop each table lay sixteen sharpened number-two yellow pencils.

The exam proctor pounded on a large wood desk to gain their attention. "This exam is administered throughout the state of Washington. Grading is uniform, so there is no chance of favoritism. All students are required to pass the sections in what you've come to know as the three R's, as well as pass several more complicated subjects such as physiology."

The eagle-eyed proctor peered over his spectacles as he completed the instructions, then stared at the large wall clock. "I realize one student is still absent, but everyone was informed of the penalty for tardiness. Any late-comers will have an automatic deduction in points."

At the stroke of nine, the proctor marched to the door the second Martin zipped in, nearly careening into the proctor. The proctor straightened his glasses, then glared at the latecomer before shutting the door with an exaggerated bang, signaling the test was about to be handed out. Edna gulped in a big breath. She cast a quick grin at Martin, who wiped his brow with his sleeve and winked back as he slid into an empty seat. A somber wake-like silence fell over the room. All sets of eyes fixed straight ahead.

The proctor marched down the center aisle and handed out the test booklets while proffering the instructions. "Please keep your eyes on your own work. You are not to turn your papers over until instructed to do so. At the beginning of each section, I will instruct you regarding the time allowed. When I call time, all pencils are to be placed in front of you immediately. Any questions?"

Butterflies took flight in Edna's stomach.

The proctor watched the clock until the second hand ticked to the twelve. He made a note of the time, then pointing toward the students with his fountain pen, he gave the order. "You may begin."

Edna flipped the booklet over, whispered a silent prayer, then turned to the first page. The first section was English grammar. Her confidence soared as she flew through the first pages. An hour and a half into the exam, her hand hurt from gripping the pencil too tightly. She set it down and listened to the instructions for the civics section. She opened and closed her right fist, releasing the stiffness in her joints as she glanced around with glazed-over eyes at her classmates.

The proctor's unemotional words came from the front of the room. "You may turn the page."

Edna set her jaw and flipped another page. She snapped her fingers, drawing a glance from one of the boys seated closest to her. Her breathing relaxed as her studying paid off and the facts reviewed in recent days popped into her mind. She grabbed her pencil and began.

After three hours of deep concentration to recall words, rules, facts, and figures, Edna's eyes burned from the concentration. She put her pencil down and blinked a few times. She looked at the clock. Nearly seven minutes remained until the proctor called time. She flipped back two pages and reviewed her work. Confident in her answers, she closed the test booklet and folded her hands over her work.

"Time. Put your pencils down. Beginning with the first row. Bring your booklets to the front of the room and put them on this desk. You are to proceed in silence until you have left the room."

After placing her test on the proctor's desk, Edna hurried out of the building. She sat on the steps to wait for Inez.

Instead, Martin came over. She could see sweat beading his forehead. "How do you think you did on the test?"

"Okay, I guess. I hope I passed."

Martin looked down at his feet, shifting his weight as he stuttered. "Do you know how to dance?"

Shocked, Edna considered his out-of-the-blue question. "Of course. All proper young women know how to dance. I took a course in ballroom dancing only last year."

"Will you go with me to the eighth-grade dance?" He stopped and lowered his voice. "Unless you're already going with someone else."

Edna had noticed that on occasions during the year Martin had looked at her with a goofy grin, but she never imagined he had any interest in her. She thought about how much she enjoyed his easygoing manner and her stomach flip-flopped. "Of course, I'll go with you."

Before Edna knew what happened, he'd leaned in and planted a kiss on her cheek. She blushed and brought her hands to her face. "Oh my."

♪ ♪ ♪

Edna tried to push aside her worries about the results of her exam. Her mind wandered to the night of her first dance. Nostalgic memories played in her mind, and she recalled the mellow songs playing on the Victrola as she and Martin drew looks of amazement at their ballroom dancing skills. Her cheeks flushed at the pleasant memory and the awkwardness of being out with a boy for the first time. Though their relationship was innocent and Edna had no romantic interest in Martin, she tried to picture how she might react in a romantic relationship. Would she be weak-willed like Pearl? Could she possibly find herself in the same situation at an early age? Edna shook her head. No. She would never let such a thing happen.

After two long, tense weeks of waiting for the news, the postman held out a letter. "I've seen a lot of these today." With a quick handoff of the legal-size white envelope, the postman winked. "Good luck."

Edna spied the return address. Washington State Board of Education. She held her breath, spun around, and raced into the house. Her pulse quickened. She didn't want to think about the disappointment if she failed. She held the envelope out for her mother to see. "It's the results of my examination." Clutching the letter, she took a deep breath and tore open the envelope. Her hand quivered as she unfolded the single sheet. After the salutation, the opening words read, "We are pleased to inform you… "Edna waved the acceptance letter around for a few seconds before finishing the letter. "I received a ninety-four percent overall. I'm going to high school."

Shortly before her graduation, a small parcel arrived in the mail addressed to Edna. She ran inside. "Mama, come see. Grandmother Mooney sent me a present. May I open it now?"

Mother wiped her hands on her apron and sat next to Edna at the table. "I don't see why not. I wrote to her with your good news. I'm sure it's a graduation gift."

Edna didn't bother to sit. She ripped the paper and lifted the lid from the small velvet-covered box. She withdrew a delicate silver ring with a stone the color of a clear blue lake.

Mother leaned in. "It's beautiful. It's aquamarine. Your birthstone."

With a broad smile, Edna slipped the ring onto the ring finger of her right hand.

Chapter Thirty

1916 – Saying Goodbye

Returning home in mid-April, Edna found a horse and buggy in front of the house. Edna recognized it, but couldn't place it. When she opened the door, her mother looked up from where she sat on the davenport across from Dr. Wilkes, her gaze pained and watery.

Dr. Wilkes reached across and patted her mother's hand. "Call me if he gets worse."

"Gets worse?" Edna stopped in the doorway as her body clenched. "What's wrong with Papa?"

"Your father has pneumonia."

"Is it serious? What's the cure?"

"Scientists have begun research; there are promising advances with antiserums, but at this time…" As his voice trailed off, Dr. Wilkes shook his head and stood. "Just make sure he gets plenty of rest."

Always strong and confident, her mother now appeared frail and defeated.

Edna glanced toward the bedroom. "May I see him?"

Her mother rubbed her forehead. "Only for a minute. He needs his sleep."

Edna rushed to her father's bedside. At the sight of his pale face and dull eyes, Edna choked back her emotions. She knelt and whispered a couple prayers from Sunday school until her mother came in and shooed her out. She went to her bedroom and pressed her ear to the closed door.

"You can't keep working there. Those crowded and unsanitary conditions, the strenuous work, and the cold wet weather, are making you sick."

Stubborn and proud, Papa fought back. "I've worked for Simpson Logging Company over twenty-five years. It's all I know."

"Doctor Wilkes told you the last time he saw you that at forty-four years old, you need to consider other options. Besides, you told me yourself logging was drying up on Vashon. It's time to consider moving."

Days passed with her father too weak to assist with chores. Her mother worked late into the night on her alterations, then woke at five every morning to feed the animals. Every few days, she took eggs to town to sell to help make up for her father's lost wages. Edna rushed home after school every day to start the evening dinner. Afterward she gathered eggs and took the scraps out to the pigs.

After weeks of long days, her mother announced she was selling the pigs. "Too much work for us right now with your father's health. It's one less chore and should fetch a handsome sum, which will come in handy. No sense fighting the inevitable."

With the sale of the pigs, Edna knew her time in Port Orchard was nearing an end.

As her father's strength improved, he moved from the bed to the living room. He spent his days in his favorite chair reading last week's copies of the *Seattle Times* Uncle Leland mailed to him.

Edna studied the lines of worry on his face. "Why are you reading the classified advertisements?"

Her father sighed. "Sit down." He pointed to the sofa. "The doctor thinks it is best if I don't go back to work at the logging camp. Since you are going to high school next year, we've decided to move to Seattle so you can live at home instead of with your aunt and uncle. The good Lord willing, you won't develop the loose morals your sister picked up."

A gush of anger erupted inside her, but Edna fought back the urge to defend Pearl. She swallowed her words and let her father continue.

"Your uncle says there's work in the city. Lots of new businesses are starting up, all looking for men who are willing to work hard. Plenty of well-paying jobs without being outside in the inclement weather of this area. And I'll be able to be home each night, like Inez's father."

Edna remembered her envy of Inez, who lived in a spacious two-story house with white pillars framing the front porch. "What does Mama think? She likes it here."

"Your mother is ready for a change. She won't have all the chores of the farm, and it will be good for her to be able to see her sister any time she wants."

"What about her work?"

"Your mother has been assured of a position with a tailor your aunt knows. She will be making alterations to men's suits and formal dresses sold by the Bon Marche downtown. In time, she hopes to design and create hats that she can sell at one of the millineries."

Edna remembered the last time they had visited Pearl. They had crossed the lake on the Leschi Ferry and met Uncle Frederick at Newport for the drive east across the newly built highway. "Can we buy an automobile so we don't have to take the train to visit Pearl?"

Papa chuckled. "Not right away. Maybe in time." He stood and patted her on the back. "We'll be okay. I promise."

Edna met her father's gaze. His squinty eyes created creases on his forehead. She didn't want to make him feel any worse than he already did, and the thought of seeing Pearl more frequently removed some of the sting from the news. "I know we will."

♩ ♩ ♩

In early August, Father received a job offer. "Fellow by the name of Bill Boeing recently bought an old boat-works company on the Duwamish River for a factory, wants to build flying machines out of wood. He appreciates I have a solid knowledge of timber. Turns out, he's a former timber man himself."

Not wasting any time. Edna's mother had posted an advertisement in the local paper by week's end and Papa had pounded a FOR SALE sign on a post at the end of the drive.

The increased hiring at the shipyard brought a boom to Port Orchard's population, and within weeks, Edna watched from the front porch as her mother removed the hanging FOR SALE sign. "Praise God for our good fortune the house sold so quickly and for the full asking price of twenty-three-hundred dollars. Papa has made an offer on a home on First Hill only two few miles from your aunt and uncle."

Edna's heart sank. "Are we going to move before school starts again?"

Her mother set the sign outside the door. "Your father needs to report to work by the end of the month. and classes start at Broadway High the first week in September."

Edna rested her head against her mother's shoulder. "I have to say goodbye to all my friends for the past seven years, especially Inez."

Her mother's taut face relaxed. "We fetched a fair enough price for this place, even though homes cost more in Seattle, your father expects we'll have a few modern conveniences including a modern bathroom, and he said I could buy a new enameled gas range like Marie has."

Over the next few days, Edna packed her things and the items Pearl left behind. From the open bedroom window, she inhaled the lingering smells of the pigs and chickens combined with the musty, dusty smell of wheat in the field. She inhaled the aroma of her father's pipe tobacco lingering on the lace curtains and the smoke from the cookstove permeating the air. Scents that soon would be her past. She drew in thirteen-years of memories. Within days, she would leave her childhood home behind as Pearl had years ago.

The weekend before her family's move, Inez's father picked up Edna in his Studebaker so the girls could go to see the new full-length fairy tale *Cinderella* showing at the Star Liberty Theater. Edna had read the tale written by the Grimm Brothers, upon which the movie was based. Papa gave Edna fifteen cents to pay for the movie ticket and purchase a bag of popped corn from a vendor outside the newly built theater. She counted her previous month's savings. "Maybe after the movie, we can walk next door to Myhre's Restaurant for ice cream."

Inside the theater, Edna bubbled with excitement seeing her first full-length film. She sat on the edge of her seat as Mary Pickford, in the starring role, made the book come to life on the big screen.

Afterward, Edna glided along the sidewalk toward Myhre's. She stared up at the menu posted over the counter. Her mouth watered. She'd never seen such a variety of ice cream treats. She reached into her pocket and recounted her coins before settling on a chocolate ice cream soda. When the afternoon was over, Mr. Wilbert dropped Edna off at home. In the back seat, the girls hugged and when Edna opened the door to climb out, Inez sobbed and stretched out her hand to grasp Edna's hand one last time. "Promise you'll write and tell me all about your new school."

Edna gripped her friend's hand and felt a tremor of uncertainty. "I will. Maybe your mom will let you visit the next time you go to Seattle."

Inez nodded. "I didn't expect to say goodbye to you so soon."

Inez's father turned the key and pushed the button to engage the starter. Inez pulled away. "I'm going to miss you. We promised we'd stay friends all the way to eighth grade."

"I know. I wish I didn't have to go."

The car door closed, and moments later, the car was out of sight.

The following morning, Edna slid into the center of the single seat in the borrowed wagon that replaced their buggy, now parked alongside the barn, and sold with the house. Mama climbed in next to Edna. She stared back at her home. Her eyes blinked rapidly, her mind replaying the lifetime of memories lived within the walls of the now-empty house. Papa cinched the ropes securing the trunks and boxes packed with family heirlooms, clothing, and household goods. After waking in the morning, Mama had removed the bed linens. Papa disassembled the bed frames, then piled them along with the mattresses on top of their remaining belongings before climbing onto the wagon.

"Is our furniture on the boat?"

Papa patted Edna's leg. "Yep. Some of the guys from work drove the larger pieces down to Tacoma last night and got them loaded onto a Foss tug. We'll claim it at the dock in Seattle in a day or two." With one last glance back, Papa cracked the whip, and Nellie trotted toward town.

When the family arrived at the dock in Port Orchard, Papa signaled the deckhands. They lugged baggage carts over, tagged the family's belongings, then handed Papa a claim ticket. The deckhands wheeled the family's belongings away to load onto a barge. Tired and sore from the ride, Edna couldn't wait to climb from the wagon. From her pocket, she withdrew a carrot. She stared into the mare's brown eyes. "I'm going to miss you." Edna swiped at the tears running down her cheeks. "Why can't we keep Nellie?"

Her mother reached over and patted Nellie's flowing mane. "In Seattle, there are fewer horses on the downtown streets as automobiles become the preferred transportation. We'll get around by trolley until we can buy an automobile."

"Is Nellie going to be okay?"

"The new owners will take good care of her."

Papa rejoined his family. "Say goodbye to Nellie. I've got to take her to the livery to be claimed by her new owners." He took the horse's reins. As if sensing the goodbye, Nellie shook her head, whinnied, and stomped her foot in protest.

Edna stroked Nellie's muzzle for the final time before her father led the mare away.

♪ ♪ ♪

Edna stood with her family on the barge's top deck, gazing back at the inlet and her hometown on the water's edge. Her emotions churned inside like the Cyclone Drink Mixer in Myhre's Restaurant where she had shared a frothy ice cream soda with Inez the previous day. A loud buzzing noise emanated from below the deck as the white and black vessel sliced through Puget Sound. By the time the barge docked in Seattle, Edna's head throbbed. She followed her parents down the ramp, eager to see their new home.

Her father pointed down the walkway to the end of the dock where a peculiar-looking black automobile sat parked along the street. "There's the car and driver Leland hired for us." He spoke with the deckhand, then reached into his vest pocket to retrieve his claim ticket for their belongings. They waited and watched as the remaining passengers disembarked and a crane hoisted crates from the boat's rear deck.

When the family's belongings were loaded into the hired vehicle, Papa handed the address to the driver, then helped Edna's mother up the small step and into the front seat, next to the driver. Edna climbed into the rumble seat in the back.

"Fine contraption." Papa looked over the odd automobile. "What's it called?"

"It's a Ford auto wagon."

They headed east up Cherry Street toward their new home. Fifteen minutes after leaving the dock, the automobile stopped.

"There it is." Papa grinned as he pointed to a washed-out white structure amid the better-kept homes.

Edna swallowed her disappointment. Unlike her aunt and uncle's home, this house was weathered and worn. The yard was small compared to their acres of farmland and meadow, and there was no swing hanging from an apple tree.

Papa looked over the seat at Edna. "It's not so appealing now, but it won't be long before I have this place shiny as a new Lincoln-head penny."

Edna flashed a smile. "I know it will be wonderful." She pictured her mother outside on warm evenings perched in a rocker on the freshly painted wraparound porch and sipping tea while Edna sat next to her, with her nose buried in her studies.

Her mother's excited voice renewed Edna's optimism. "It's a perfect neighborhood, close to your new school, near the trolley line, and only two miles from Marie and Leland. I couldn't ask for anything more. With a bit of elbow grease, the place will soon be singing."

Papa stepped down from the auto wagon. He handed his wife a small key and nodded toward the house. Papa joined the driver at the back of the wagon, and they unloaded the household furnishings and boxes.

With the door swung wide, the setting sun cast its light across the glass chandelier. Prisms of light danced across the dark oak floor, brightening Edna's outlook. She imagined bright new curtains hanging in the kitchen and living room windows and a fresh coat of finish on the wide-planked flooring.

Mother pointed to the wall where an old wood cookstove still stood. "I'm going to put my new range right there. She looked around.

My dishes will look splendid in my oak Hoosier, on this wall between the dining room and the kitchen."

Edna noticed the glint in her mother's eyes. "It's going to be a perfectly wonderful home for us."

♪ ♪ ♪

For the following week, Edna labored alongside her mother and father, refinishing floors, painting walls and windowsills, moving furniture into place, and unpacking boxes. She looked around her bedroom with only a four-drawer pine dresser and her single bed. At their old house, Pearl's empty bed remained in the bedroom, always a reassuring reminder of her sister's presence in her life, and in recent years, a place for her to sleep with her sons on their rare overnight visits, but now her room looked sparse. Days were spent hoeing the barren ground and readying a small plot for fall beans, carrots, and root vegetables. Evenings, Mama sewed curtains for the bedrooms and the kitchen while Papa laid new asphalt to patch the leaky roof.

A week after the move, her father started his new job with the Aero Products Company and for the first time in his life, he came home after work each evening. Seeing her father relaxed in his chair after dinner with his pipe and newspaper, told Edna life in this new city was going to good for all of them.

Chapter Thirty-One

1916 – Broadway High School

Days later, Edna stood at the steps to Broadway High facing her future. Her next step on the path to realizing her dream. A decade earlier, Pearl stood at these same steps. Pearl's dreams had veered off in a different direction than she planned. Edna could not let the same thing happen to her. The enormity of her goal matched the size of the immense structure of light-gray stone in front of her. She winced at the thought, then marched up the stairs. When Pearl attended Broadway High, it was the only high school for students living in the Seattle area. After Lincoln High in the Wallingford neighborhood, opened in 1907, Seattle High School was renamed Broadway, representing the avenue it faced. Since then, several other high schools had been built in the city to meet the demand of Seattle's growing population.

Though the outside of the school looked the same, the school had changed significantly. The new registration materials touted the school's reputation and the diversity of races, a much different population than a decade earlier. Inside, boys and girls darted across gleaming marble floor toward their classrooms with their book straps flung over their shoulders. Edna noticed the teachers' names posted on small signs next to the open doors. At the door posted with Miss Blake's name, Edna held her head high, and followed a few other girls inside.

"Welcome, ladies, please take a seat."

Edna stopped and glanced around at her classmates. Something didn't look right. Then she remembered the correspondence her parents received, informing them of a change in policy establishing separate classes for girls, to be taught by women, and boys, taught by men. All around her, dozens of girls chattered like a scurry of chipmunks. Edna took the first empty seat and folded her hands in her lap.

The girl next to her offered a smile. "Hi, I'm Helen Knowles. I don't think I've seen you around. What school did you go to last year?"

Edna sighed. "I recently moved here recently from Port Orchard."

"That's tough moving to a new place where you don't know anyone, but don't worry, I'll introduce you to some of the other kids during lunch."

The tension in Edna's shoulders relaxed. "Thanks. Do all the subjects have separate classes for boys and girls?"

Helen shrugged. "I guess so. I live right on the boundary for Queen Anne High and here. My parents..." Helen shook her head. "My mom was drawn to the idea of separate classes. What do you think?"

Edna shook her head. "It doesn't sound like progress to me. I thought women were fighting for equal rights. It seems like a step backwards. Are boys' and girls' interests and learning capacities so different? But my best friend from elementary school, Inez, attends an elite all-girl's school in Tacoma, and she's looking forward to it."

Helen's brow wrinkled. "I don't think I'd like an all-girl's school. At least Broadway High has boys, just not in the same classes. And Broadway High offers plenty of opportunities for women to participate in sports or other clubs. You simply must try out for basketball, or debate."

Edna made a face and bobbed her head in noncommittal agreement. "Maybe."

Miss Blake tapped the desk with her hand, drawing immediate silence and all eyes forward. Edna relaxed seeing the twinkle in Miss Blake's eyes and the absence of the wooden ruler used for discipline. During lunch, Helen led Edna around and introduced her to dozens of classmates who had attended Isaac Stevens Elementary with Helen for the past eight years.

By the end of the month, Edna no longer felt like an outsider, and with Helen's playful prodding Edna decided to try out for the basketball team.

"You'll meet lots of new girls and lots of boys come to watch the girls' games too."

"I'm not sure I'd like having boys watch me make a fool out of myself."

"First of all, you won't make a fool out of yourself, I've seen you shoot during PE class, and secondly, you met Cliff Jorgenson. I introduced you to him the other day? He told me he thinks you're cute."

Edna felt the blood rush to her cheeks. She turned away so Helen couldn't see her smile.

On the first day of practice, Edna stood in the gym and stared at the nearly six-foot-tall woman dressed in a long black skirt and a striped top. She raised a whistle to her lips and blew a few short shrill tweets. The two-dozen prospective basketball players quieted.

"If you are here to take this sport seriously, I welcome you. If not, please don't waste my time or yours." She waited to see if any of the girls left. When no one did, she continued. "My name is Coach Wilson. Many women who preceded you, perhaps your older sisters or cousins, worked hard for your right to play sports. Does anyone here have any family member who played basketball?"

Edna looked around, then thrust her hand up with pride. "My sister was on the basketball team at this school when it was still Seattle High."

Coach Wilson's head bobbed with obvious pleasure. "The Women's Basketball Committee was formed ten years ago, and Seattle High started its women's basketball program right afterward. Unfortunately, many people still consider it a fringe sport not to be played in public. Your job is to show them women have the same right as men to play this game."

Edna remembered Pearl talking about marching for women's rights when she was in high school. She hoped her participation would help further the acceptance of women pursuing athletic endeavors. Every day after school Edna joined the team in practice while the school adopted the new rules for women's basketball uniforms. Every day her confidence swelled and her skills improved.

After three long weeks, Edna stood outside the doors to the gym with the others waiting to see the roster of those selected for the team.

"I made it!" Helen and Edna shouted in unison and hugged each other as they jumped up and down. Edna planted a look of determination on her face. "Now we have to prove we can play the game."

Unlike when Pearl played basketball, Edna's parents sat in the stand during her first game, cheering her on. Wearing black bloomers that fastened above the knees and a white sailor top with bands of orange for the team colors, Edna moved with speed on her long legs, and with every score, her father's cheer rose above the other spectators. Edna's chest swelled with more pride than she'd experienced ever before. She understood Pearl's passion with the game and realized her sister had been a trailblazer. Midway into the season, Coach Wilson shifted Edna to the position of small forward. She scored numerous baskets during each game and led the Tigers to one of their most successful years.

Coach Wilson pulled her aside after another win. "You might be good enough with another year of playing to play basketball in college if you're planning on continuing your studies."

Edna had never considered pursuing any sport seriously, but her coach's praise motivated her even more. She couldn't wait to tell Pearl the news. She knew her sister would be proud not only of her achievement but also of her role in furthering the cause of women's sports. But two weeks before the end of the season, a player from the opposing team tripped over her. Edna fell, and broke her foot and sprained her ankle.

"I don't know how we can continue to win without you."

Helen's attempt to make Edna feel valued, only made her feel like she'd let the team down, but she quickly learned the team's success did not lie with her. Despite her absence, good luck followed the Tigers, and the women's basketball team ranked in the first position in the newly established Seattle League. Edna wondered if she'd ever play the sport again.

Chapter Thirty-Two

1917 – The US Enters the World War

With basketball season over and her broken foot weeks away from healing, Edna pushed aside thoughts of pursing sports for the remainder of the year. Instead, she focused on her studies. When she arrived at school on April 7, 1917, a large crowd had gathered in front of the school. Murmurs like the buzzing from a swarm of bees arose from the group. Helen rushed to Edna and grasped her shoulders. "Have you heard the news?"

Seeing the fear in her friend's eyes, Edna wondered if one of the teachers had dropped dead or another such unforeseen tragedy had occurred. "What news?" Edna noticed the grim faces of her classmates who quickly formed a circle around them.

Helen shook her head and spoke with slow solemn words. "President Woodrow Wilson has announced the United States is at war."

"What? Why?" Her mother hadn't said a word about it when Edna left for school, but her mother hardly ever glanced at the morning paper, always putting it on the bureau for Father to read when he got home from work.

"It's because of the Germans. My dad said German submarines sank several US passenger and merchant ships and President Wilson says the Germans have no interest in seeking a peaceful end to the conflict, so we're going to war."

Edna recalled when the war started in the summer of 1914. She remembered the news about the *Lusitania* and the worry and talk about their small town so close to the naval base. Her farther warned it might come to this, despite the president's promise he would not get the United States involved in the war. She couldn't imagine how three years later the world was fighting the same war, confronting the same brutality and the same enemy. Today, the reality of the war hit like a punch to the gut.

Several students with nerves on edge, jumped at the sharp tinny clang announcing the start of the school day. Edna's schoolbooks, clutched to her chest, rose and fell with the pounding of her heart. "Who is going to have to fight?"

One of the seniors shook his head. "My Dad thinks they might implement a draft like back in the Civil War if there aren't enough enlisted men."

Others piped in with cocky words, their chests thrust out. "If I were old enough, I'd love to show those German's what I think."

Edna looked around at the young boys, with their peach-fuzz faces and changing voices. She tried to picture them in military attire with weapons slung over their shoulders. Then she thought about her cousin, Gene. "My cousin is twenty-six. Do you think he'll have to go off to war?"

Several sets of eyes looked down, and a few voices mumbled, "Maybe."

Over the next many weeks, the topic of war dominated the newspaper and the talk at school. It seemed almost everyone had a father, brother, friend, or relative, involved in the war effort. Though life continued, leisure activities were less frequent, everyone was more reserved, and small talk on the streets was strained and abrupt. No one wanted to appear unpatriotic by enjoying life while young men were fearful, going off to war, and dying for their country. Every evening after dinner Papa chewed on his pipe and puffed with urgency as he read the newspaper from front to back, always reminding her that being educated meant more than being book smart. "Formal learning is worthwhile, but it doesn't mean much if you don't know what's going on around you."

Following his example, Edna joined him in the living room after she finished her schoolwork.

"My friend told me about the draft. What does that mean? Do you think Gene will have to go off to war?"

Her father ran his hand through his hair for a few seconds before stroking his chin. "Gene is of the age where he is required to register. The rest will be up to chance. The Selective Service Board will draw enough numbers to meet what they determine is the need for more men."

Mother looked up from her knitting. She blew out a breath, "Gene is twenty-six. He's a doctor. His skills are sure to be in demand." Her face tightened. "President Wilson is already calling it a war to end all wars. Marie said Gene is even thinking about enlisting and not waiting for the draft. I can only imagine how worried Marie and Leland must be." Her shoulders slumped. With a shake of her head, she returned to her knitting.

Several weeks after President Wilson's announcement, her father shared other news. "Seems Boeing is done making ships. Gonna focus entirely on airplanes. He's changing the name of the company to Boeing Airplane Company. With the war going on, the plant is adding round-the-clock manufacturing shifts, and the US Navy recently ordered fifty planes called flying boats."

Though exhaustion showed in her father's eyes, working indoors he looked healthier than during his years of working at the logging camp.

"I hope you're not thinking of working longer hours." Mama fumbled with the strings on her apron.

"Money is still tight, and we still want to buy one of Henry Ford's automobiles. Even Stanley and Pearl went and bought one. I don't have a choice but to take whatever work is offered."

♪ ♪ ♪

In early July, Edna came home to find her mother seated in the front room, her face strained.

"What is it? Is something wrong?"

"Your aunt called a while ago. Eugene registered last month in the first round of the draft. He was deemed medically fit and has been conscripted into the medical corps at the National Army camp" Her mother's voice cracked as she spoke. "He's a doctor, so he's in high demand to serve as a medic, which means he'll be right there with the fighting men on the front lines."

Edna went to her mother's side and squeezed her shoulders. "I'm so sorry. I imagine Aunt Marie is going to be worried the entire time Gene is away."

A few years earlier, her father had been optimistic the United States would avoid becoming involved in the war. Now, with the war in its third year, Gene would be one of hundreds of young men from the state and among thousands across the country who would go off to fight. Some of them would come home in pine boxes. "Where's the National Army camp?'

"About fifty miles south of Seattle, an area called American Lake."

Edna closed her eyes and imagined the grief her aunt and uncle must be facing. "Is there anything we can do to make Aunt Marie feel better?"

"We can pray Gene stays safe. But we can also help the war effort." Mama pulled her knitting bag closer to her.

Edna glanced at her mother. "What do you mean? How?"

Mama tugged a skein of yarn free from her bag. "Everyone who's able must learn to knit for our boys overseas."

"What do we knit?"

"Our soldiers need socks and scarves. Mabel, at the First United Methodist Church in town, is talking to all the women in the guild. They are going to deliver the socks to the Seattle chapter of the American Red Cross every month as long as the war continues. From there, they'll be shipped overseas."

Edna nodded and fished inside her mother's knitting bag. "Is it okay to use this?" She held up a tight ball of gray wool.

"Yes, I bought that specifically to make socks."

Edna ran her fingers over the yarn. "I can get started on a pair right now."

Six weeks after receiving word of Gene's draft, her aunt delivered the latest update. "Eugene just received word the new facility is named Camp Lewis. It's named in honor of Captain Meriwether Lewis from the Lewis and Clark expedition. The base wants the first draftees to be from King County, so they've instructed Gene to arrive on September 5. The city is planning a large patriotic send-off for the first round of draftees the evening prior. There's going to be a parade, a concert, and a dance." Her voice quivered, "I can't lie. I'm afraid for my boy. I hope you'll come and help us send him off."

Mama wiped a tear away. "We'll be there. Do you know where he'll be sent?"

Marie hesitated before nodding. "He's part of the Ninety-First Division, most likely on the western front in France."

Silence hung in the air. The newspaper reports of the war all gave updates on the fighting in France. "A lot of fighting going on there." Mama took her sister's hands and squeezed them.

"Gene's in a medical regiment. Makes sense he'll go where there's fighting. Scares me even more. Praise the Lord you have daughters, Abbey."

Chapter Thirty-Three

1917 – American Red Cross

Pearl lay in the darkness listening to owls hooting in the thick stand of evergreens on their property. With the United States now at war and her cousin Gene in France tending to wounded and dying soldiers, for the first time, she wondered if she'd made the right decision getting married and having children instead of becoming a nurse. In the stillness of the night, with so many risking their lives and giving up so much because of the war, her past desire to help others stirred like the creatures in the forest.

When Stanley came into the bedroom, Pearl sat up. "My aunt received a letter from Gene. She's more on edge with each letter she gets. I can only imagine how worried she and Uncle Leland are."

Stanley removed his shirt and trousers, climbed in next to his wife, and embraced her. "I know how close you were to Gene when you lived with them. You have every right to be afraid for him. War is an ugly thing."

Pearl looked into Stanley's tired eyes. "I wish I could do more. I keep reading in the paper about the shortage of nurses. Sometimes I wish I'd attended the university. I would have made a great nurse."

Stanley pinched his lips together as he wrapped his strong arms around her. "I know you would have been, but knowing you, you would volunteer to help any way you can. You would probably be in France, too, right now facing the same horrors. Instead, you're here safe with your family. Besides, you are doing something. You've been knitting socks for weeks, plus you've planted a Victory Garden which has helped increase the rations and helped to keep the price of food low for the war department."

Pearl drew back. "Knitting socks is my civic duty. That's not enough. Men and boys are dying while people like you and I can't begin to imagine what they are going through."

Stanley let go of her and rolled onto his back. His tone turned to frustration. "I don't understand. You're the mother of two with a third on the way. What more do you want? You don't have time to take on anything else."

Pearl ran her hand over her growing stomach. "You're right." There was no point in arguing. She turned away from Stanley, but she couldn't let go of her thoughts. The next evening, after the children were in bed and while Stanley worked in his shop, Pearl hurried through the record keeping for Rosenbaum Furniture Store. Instead of knitting for an hour, Pearl picked up the Issaquah Press. She accepted that she couldn't join the increasing ranks of women going abroad to serve in active duty with the Navy Nurse Corps or the Naval Reserve Force, but she still hoped to find a way to assist the cause. Her face brightened at the notice in the newspaper calling for young women with no medical experience, only domestic skills, to join the Voluntary Aid Detachment (VAD). After reading further, she groaned at the realization that the VAD positions required leaving home. She read about other opportunities for women who wanted to visit veterans at home or prepare meals for the wounded soldiers but dismissed the idea of performing any more household tasks. Frustrated, Pearl pushed the newspaper aside. The following morning after Victor left for school, Pearl drove to Issaquah with Henry in tow. She found the local chapter of the American Red Cross downtown off Sunset Street. Scooping up her son and a bag, she marched inside. "I have several pair of knitted socks to donate."

The mid-fifties woman behind the desk reached out to take the bag from Pearl. She peered inside. "These look beautiful. Thank you." She smiled at Henry and took note of Pearl's growing belly. "It looks like you have your hands full. You must be dedicated to the cause." She motioned to the two chairs in front of her. "Please, take a seat."

Pearl took a seat while Henry climbed onto the other chair.

211

The volunteer rested her elbows on her desk. "Do you have a loved one who is overseas?"

"My cousin is a doctor on the front lines in France."

The volunteer beamed. "Are you a nurse, or do you have any nursing training"?

Pearl slumped. "No. When I was in high school, I dreamed of becoming a nurse. That's one reason I want to help with the Red Cross." Pearl rubbed her belly. "With two children, and a third on the way, I know I'll never have the opportunity to become a nurse, but I want to feel I'm doing something to contribute besides knitting socks."

The volunteer nodded. "It's too bad you're not a nurse. With the war and thousands of nurses working abroad, there is a shortage of trained nurses to serve our rural communities." She sat in thought for a moment, then smiled. "How is your sewing?"

"My sewing?" Pearl tried not to appear disappointed. She didn't come here to volunteer for monotonous sewing jobs.

"Our chapter is helping the war effort by sewing bandages to ship to the medics in the field."

Pearl thought about Gene and what he must be facing. Bandages sewn by local women right here in Issaquah might make their way to him. "I can do that." Her words spilled out before she stopped to wonder how she would find the time. "I have several months before the baby comes. After that, I don't know."

"I understand." The woman pushed her chair back. "I'll get you a supply kit and an instruction book."

Within minutes, Pearl had enough gauze to keep her busy for the next month or more. She got up to leave.

"Hold on for a moment."

Pearl turned around and watched the woman open a desk drawer. "One way you can learn the basics of nursing is through first-aid training. I'm sure with children you'll need to know first-aid eventually." She held the book, not much larger than a pamphlet, out to Pearl. "The Red Cross is releasing a new edition of their first-aid textbook. This is the first edition. Please take it. I have lots of copies. Read it, and maybe when your children are older, you can come back, and we can find a place for you."

"Thanks." Pearl took the book and ran her hand over the cover of the light gray book. "I appreciate it. I'm sure it will come in handy." She waved goodbye.

Chapter Thirty-Four

1918 – Old Dreams Ignited

After two healthy births, Pearl's third pregnancy was beset with intense lower back pain. Barely seven months into her pregnancy, she was afflicted by cramps. At first, she tried to dismiss the symptoms as nothing more than emotional strain. After an unusually uncomfortable night, she woke to increased pressure on her pelvis. She eased her way from the bed and right away noticed the baby sat lower. She shook Stanley awake. "I think this baby might come early. Can I take you to work this morning after Victor leaves for school? I want to drive to the Red Cross office and ask if I should be concerned."

An hour later, sitting across from the volunteer, Pearl described her discomfort while Henry sat serenely on her lap.

The volunteer sat with her hands folded on the desk. "I'm not a midwife or obstetric nurse, but I have some training. You could be right. This baby might not wait too much longer. Where do you plan to deliver?"

"I was hoping to have a home delivery, the same as my last two. I have a midwife lined up. She delivered my sons." Pearl saw the woman wring her hands in thought. A sharp cramp, or maybe even a significant contraction, seized her.

"Are you having labor pains now?"

Pearl shrugged. "Maybe, but I'm not even eight months along."

A wide-eyed look of unease sent a tremble down Pearl's aching back.

"You might want to check with your midwife, see what she says, but my opinion is you should probably deliver this baby at a hospital because of the uncertainty that accompanies a premature birth." Following her advice, Pearl used their phone and called her aunt.

As soon as school was out, Pearl called Edna and asked her to stay with the boys. "I may be in early labor. I need you to stay with the boys for a few nights. Stanley's going to drive me to Seattle to Swedish Hospital."

♪ ♪ ♪

Stanley escorted Pearl to the front desk. "My wife believes she's in premature labor."

The receptionist beckoned an orderly who disappeared around the corner only briefly before he returned with a wheelchair.

"Take this woman straight to the delivery room and call Dr. Caldwell while I obtain the necessary information from her husband."

Pearl's nerves got the best of her. Her voice quivered. "I'm scared. I don't want to be alone."

The nurse spoke with reassurance. "Is this your first baby?"

"No, but I've never been in a hospital before, my other children were delivered at home with a midwife."

Stanley reached for his wife's hand. "You'll be fine. I'll be right here."

Passing the forms to Stanley, the admittance clerk reassured Pearl. "You're in good hands."

The orderly assisted Pearl into the wheelchair, then wheeled her away. Minutes later she was resting in comfort in a hospital bed, but everything was happening so quickly. She tensed through the contractions as two nurses stood by and Dr. Caldwell checked her progress. She stiffened with the uncomfortable feeling of a male doctor and pulled away. She wished she were home in her bed with her aunt by her side. She closed her eyes to shut out the humiliation. But within a half hour of her arrival, one of the nurses put her hand on Pearl's shoulder.

"You're coming along quickly. It's time for you to push."

Pearl obeyed, and soon collapsed onto the mattress.

"It's a girl." The nurse appeared beside her, almost angelic with her white nearly floor-length uniform and a white hat perched on her head like a halo. She handed the tiny infant to Pearl.

Pearl lifted her shoulders and took her baby from the nurse. Spent and sweaty, her breathing came in soft pants. A swell of satisfaction overwhelmed her. "I have a daughter." Her words came as reverent as an amen to a prayer. Though Pearl loved her two sons as much as any mother could love her children, life now felt complete.

Without any complications, Doctor Caldwell completed the final stages of her birthing and came to stand by Pearl's side. "She's tiny, which is to be expected for a baby born more than a month early. We'll weigh her in a bit, but she looks about four pounds and appears healthy. I can only let you hold her for a minute. Her low birth weight puts her at risk. Your husband mentioned you planned on a home birth. It's fortunate you recognized the signs of premature labor and made the decision to come to the hospital. Your quick thinking and your instincts to come here greatly increase your daughter's chances of good health for the long term. She will have to spend a few days in an incubator to help keep her body temperature up."

Pearl stroked the baby's fine dark hair, sharply contrasting with her almost transparent pale skin. She envisioned her daughter's entire future. She pressed her lips to her cheek and whispered. "I'll never let anything bad happen to you. I promise." The thought struck her like a slap to the face. She pulled away and gazed into her daughter's innocent blue eyes. With trembling hands, she clutched the baby tighter. In that moment, memories from years ago resurfaced. She now understood her mother feeling betrayed when she discovered Pearl's loss of innocence. Her mother had imagined a perfect life for her daughter, the same as Pearl now did. She thought about her plans to attend the university, derailed by her decision to keep Victor.

Dr. Caldwell shook his head. "We need to take your baby to the nursery now."

One of the nurses bent down, took the baby, and wrapped her in a blanket. "Don't worry. She'll be fine."

In a blink of her eyes, her precious daughter was gone.

Sensing Pearl's loss, the second nurse approached. "My name's Nancy. I'll be with you most of the day." She began removing soiled linens. "You are absolutely glowing. Is she your firstborn?"

Pearl laughed. "My third. But my first daughter, and the first baby I've delivered at a hospital."

"Well, Swedish Hospital is a fine hospital. One of the best and most up to date on all the latest procedures and the highest standards of sterilization. You and your newborn will be well cared for."

Pearl nodded, comforted by the woman who looked to be barely over twenty years old. "How long have you been a nurse?"

Nancy stopped scurrying about. "Almost two years. I went to nursing school right here at Swedish. After nursing school there's a required exam to become certified by the licensing board."

"Do you enjoy your work?"

"How could I not? I get to share in the joy of a new mother's happiest moment."

Without warning, her old desire stirred. Pearl watched Nancy as she skittered around the room. If Pearl had followed a different path, she could be helping to deliver babies. "Do you know Doctor Chapman?"

"No. Does he practice here at Swedish?"

"I don't know where he works. It doesn't matter. It was so long ago. I met him on a steamboat when I moved to Seattle. Talking with him made me think about becoming a nurse."

"Why did you change your mind?"

Not many people knew the details of Pearl's past. Today, three children later, Pearl's shame from years ago no longer mattered. She stammered. "I had to get married young. It ruined my plans to become a nurse, but I have no regrets. My life is full."

"I understand." Nancy's warmth put Pearl at ease.

Pearl had what many women envied. A husband who loved and supported her comfortably and three healthy children: two sons, and now a daughter. Was it wrong to want more despite her happiness? She thought about Dr. Chapman saying her opportunities were endless. Nothing she had accomplished was anything but ordinary. Nothing seemed meaningful. She thought about Dr. Kate Barrett, who, became a doctor, even with a husband and a family.

"I have other patients to tend to. I'll be in to check on you a little later." Short of the door, Nancy turned back. "You know, it's not too late. The Red Cross provides training. I know your hands are going to be full for the near future, but remember, women are much stronger and more capable than we've been given credit for in the past." She tossed a knowing look at Pearl as if she'd been privy to Pearl's long-suppressed dream. "I'll tell your husband he can see you now."

Minutes later, Stanley rushed in and kissed her on the forehead. He grinned as wide as she'd ever seen. "I was just at the nursery. We have a daughter."

Pearl smiled and took Stanley's hand. "She's tiny, but the doctor said she looks healthy."

The door creaked and Pearl turned, surprised to see Dr. Caldwell. She straightened her gown and drew the covers higher. "Is my daughter okay?"

Doctor Caldwell pulled an empty chair to her bedside and looked at both Pearl and Stanley. "Because your daughter was born before full term, she faces a higher risk of health issues as she gets older, particularly issues with the lungs."

Stanley moved closer to Pearl and put his hands on her shoulder. "Is it serious?"

The doctor raised his hands in a questioning gesture. "Her chances of long-term serious problems are decreased since she's in an incubator. Even a decade ago, a lot of early births resulted in death. I'm not saying your daughter will or will not face any illnesses, though there is an increased chance of illnesses such as asthma or problems with hearing and vision. I don't see anything at this time to indicate any life-threatening concern, but of course, it's too early to know for sure." He pushed the chair back and got up. "Get some rest. You've been through enough for one day. You can ask one of the nurses to take you to see your daughter in a few hours."

Her precious baby was in an incubator somewhere out of her sight, out of her arms. Pearl collapsed back onto the mattress. She remembered the premature babies in incubators at Luna Park, on display for the gawking crowd. She sighed, relieved the baby was healthy and nearby without the crowd's curious eyes upon her, grateful for modern medicine, for the doctor, and most of all, for the reassuring words from Nancy.

Stanley kissed her on the forehead. "You need your sleep; I'll deliver the news to your parents. I'll be back tomorrow. We'll stay in town with your folks until you come home." He turned to leave but looked back when Peal called out.

"Her name is Marjorie Ann. We'll call her Margie."

Chapter Thirty-Five

1918 – The Great War Ends

The spring and summer of 1918 brought the deployment of two million US soldiers to France. An atmosphere of hopefulness draped the country as British and Canadian soldiers made significant advances on the Western Front. By the time Edna returned to school the first week in September, the conversation among the boys had shifted. Instead of worrying about the threat of the draft or of enlisting upon graduating, there was a new optimism as they discussed plans for their futures. Edna came home from school at the end of her first week to find her mother and aunt reading the latest casualty report in the newspaper.

"It's been more than three years since the sinking of the *Lusitania*. Finally, there are indications the war may be coming to an end. Maybe soon I can stop reading about the casualties every day." Aunt Marie gripped a floral handkerchief as she shook her head. "So many of young men…" Her voice trailed off. "The paper reports before the war is over, one hundred thousand Americans alone will have died. I can't imagine how many of those Gene watched die while he tried to save them."

Edna pushed aside a pile of dresses and shirts, the alterations her mother was sewing for the townsfolk. She put her books down and sat down across from her aunt. "Is Gene okay?"

Her aunt looked up. "I'm afraid to read his letter." She withdrew an envelope from her pocket. "Last month when he wrote, he revealed his division was being deployed to an area in northeastern France."

219

Edna had heard talk from the kids at school about the high number of casualties in France. Sitting across from her aunt at the table, Edna saw fear in her aunt's eyes.

"I pray every day for his safe return." Mother took her older sister's hand. They bowed their heads for a few moments.

Edna sat in silence feeling insignificant. Her cousin was across the globe, selflessly risking his life to help others while she was safe at home. "I'm sure Gene will come home safely."

"I won't rest easy until he does." Aunt Marie dabbed her forehead with her handkerchief and handed the letter to Edna. "I can't bring myself to read it. Every time I read one of his letters, I cry. Will you read it to me?"

Her mother nodded to her. Edna hesitated, then slipped her finger under the flap, withdrew the single sheet, and read aloud.

"Dear Mom and Dad,
I am well, but growing weary. Every day, there are more killed and more wounded to tend to. A lot has happened, and it is horrible watching so many die, but I am proud to be here to help save some lives. Though the fighting is constant, there is hope. The Allied forces successful advances over the summer, have brought new optimism for the outcome of the war. Allied troops have taken back almost all German-occupied France and part of Belgium. Many have found new strength during this time. Some have turned to faith and prayer, though previously not religious. Though none of us expected the war to last this long, we are hopeful we will be on our way home soon."

Edna squeezed her aunt's hand. "Can you imagine? Wouldn't it be the best gift to have him home for Christmas?"

With the reports from the war front increasingly more favorable during the following weeks, the city's excitement, and involvement in support of the war ramped up. Posters for Liberty Bonds plastered windows of businesses all around town.

Her father returned from work one day wearing a broad smile. "Boeing has posters up all over. I'm too old to serve in the war, and like the posters read, 'If you can't enlist, invest.'" He showed Abbey and Edna the two fifty-dollar Liberty Bonds he'd purchased at the recruitment office. "Buying bonds is my patriotic duty and will provide a measure of financial security for our future."

♪ ♪ ♪

As the end of September approached with signs the war was nearing an end, Edna's father sat focused on the evening news. Too intent to draw a puff, he let his pipe hang from his lips.

Edna peered over his shoulder and wrinkled her nose. The odor of smoke held fast in the fibers of his sweater. She read the bold headlines. S*panish Flu Has Country in Grips.* "What's the Spanish Flu?"

Papa bit down on his pipe and chewed the tip. "They say it's a new type of influenza that's striking the military bases in the Midwest, most likely brought back home by soldiers returning from war. Read something about it a few months back. Didn't think much of it, but now Seattle's commissioner of health is warning the disease will probably reach the Pacific Northwest, including Seattle."

Edna held her breath remembering how ill her father had been in the past. Her voice quivered as she spoke. "Could we catch it?"

Papa shrugged. "Hard to say. People are dying from it, but mostly men who are already weak from being away at war. Nothing we need to fret about right now." He patted her arm.

In the coming days, the tone of the news coverage painted a more serious picture. Instead of reporting death tolls from the war, the daily paper's front page carried increasing reports of soldiers developing pneumonia. Over the dinner table, Papa shared the latest from the daily paper. "Things aren't looking good at Camp Lewis. They're reporting over one hundred cases of the new influenza, and across the sound at the Bremerton Naval Training Station as well as at the shipyard, officials are ordering men to keep away from gatherings of any kind. The sanitary officer there says these cases are not being considered the Spanish Flu that's affecting the East Coast." He stroked his chin. "Sounds like they're whitewashing it to me. Too much coincidence. Guess we'll have to wait and see. No one knows what's going to happen next."

Edna had read several articles about the soldiers in infirmaries turning blue from lack of oxygen and dying quickly. Once more, the fear she felt when Papa was sick in the past emerged. "Are we going to get the new flu too?"

Papa shook his head. "Right now, it's likely the virus will affect weary soldiers whose bodies are fragile from being away at war for so long. What's more alarming is the rate at which the virus is spreading."

Edna rubbed her forehead. After all her cousin had gone through, she couldn't fathom that now another invisible threat would confront him upon his return. "Gene's going to come back in the middle of all this."

With this new virus affecting the weak, Edna was grateful her father had a new job away from the crowded unsanitary conditions that certainly would have affected him and possibly this time even killed him. In early October the virus hit Seattle with surprising fury. Each day's headlines relayed news of the widespread infections and deaths from the unseen horror the world, and now their city, faced. First came the warnings to stay indoors, if possible, along with the mandate to wear a mask outdoors to help avoid the spread of the virus. At the same time, Aunt Marie received word Gene was coming home. His letter to his family said he would be returning to Camp Lewis for a few days before catching the train home. Aunt Marie was giddy, but only weeks later her aunt and uncle received a wire from the army base.

Aunt Marie's eyes were red when she relayed the letter's contents to Edna and her mother. "The base is now in lockdown. They're prohibiting anyone from entering or leaving the camp due to the spread of the new flu."

By now Mayor Ole Hanson had ordered the closure of schools, churches, and shows, until further notice, in an attempt to save lives. Threatened by the new fear at home as the war still raged halfway around the world, she feared for her safety. Most of all, for her father and his health. She couldn't bear the thought of him becoming ill again.

Edna imagined all her classmates whooping and hollering for joy, but the thought of disrupting her daily schedule made her uneasy, "What am I going to do for four weeks with school closed? How will I ever catch up on my studies?"

"You're smart enough to keep up with your studies from home. I don't imagine the closures will last too long." Papa huffed. "You can bet the school board will add the missed days to the end of the term."

Without school, Edna helped put up beans and peas and gathered herbs, which she tied into bundles and tacked to a rod hung next to the kitchen cupboards. She spent her days embroidering handkerchiefs and flipping through the pages of the *Ladies' Home Journal, McCall's Magazine,* or the *Seattle Times,* searching out recipes that sounded promising. One day she tried a recipe for peanut-butter fudge that turned out so badly she had to throw it out. During all her experimentation, Edna discovered she enjoyed baking and considered the path as a home economics teacher. Her stuck-inside-the-house mood was boosted by the arrival of a letter from Inez. Edna ripped it open the moment it arrived.

> My dearest friend,
> I'm sorry it has been so long since I've written. The influenza is raging badly here. The movie theater, barbershops, and churches are closed in Tacoma, as are the public schools. Since this is a private school and most of the girls here are boarders, not much has changed. The instructors have rearranged the classrooms to seat us further apart. All the girls are missing their families because of the uncertainty surrounding the disease and the quarantine we are facing. Since I plan on becoming a nurse, I've been granted permission to volunteer at Tacoma General Hospital. I expect to learn a lot during my time there. I hope you and your family are well. I look forward to hearing from you soon. I miss you and can't wait until we can see each other again.
> Your friend,
> Inez.

The letter from Inez increased Edna's longing for human interaction. She immediately sat down and responded to her friend, wishing her friend continued health and ending with a promise to visit her in Tacoma as soon as the lockdown was lifted.

By the end of October, her father's evening update included the latest mandate from the mayor. "No one will be allowed on a streetcar without a mask."

Over the next weeks, Edna dutifully covered her nose and mouth with masks she and her mother made from old scraps. Neighbors, similarly shielded behind their masks, called out to whoever passed by with the latest word as to who in the neighborhood had come down with the virus.

On Sunday, November tenth, Edna awoke in the middle of the night to whistles and bells and all sorts of other noises. She ran to her parent's room and knocked on their door. "I can't sleep. What's happening?"

Papa rubbed his forehead and looked at the clock. Nearly midnight. He peered out the window. Dozens of neighbors had filed into the middle of the street. Others stood on their porches in pajamas or robes, waving small flags and holding their hands across their chests. He pushed the window open and yelled out. "What's going on?"

Above the whoops and roars from the crowd, long-hoped-for words responded in unison. "The war is over. Praise God and Woodrow Wilson!"

For a few minutes, Edna stared at the growing multitude. She wondered how her aunt and uncle were feeling at this moment. Gene would be home safe and sound. She wished she could run the two miles to their house and hug her aunt.

Instead, Papa shooed her back to bed. "There'll be plenty of time for celebrating tomorrow."

By morning, the neighborhood had calmed, but the exhilaration still hung in the air. Edna stepped onto the front porch. Several neighbors huddled together, holding coffee cups, and chatting as cars and jam-packed buses sped along the usually quiet street headed in the direction of downtown Seattle with windows down and horns honking. People shouted, "There's going to be a big parade." Edna tipped her head to take in the clamor that rose above the hills. Absorbed in the magnitude of the historical event, Edna knew she had to be part of it. She turned and ran inside. Papa held up the early edition of the newspaper. "GREAT WAR OVER—Armistice with Germany signed." The newspaper account noted that hours after signing the treaty, at 11 am on 11 November 1918—"the eleventh hour of the eleventh day of the eleventh month"—a ceasefire came into effect. After five weeks of gloomy fall days and reading about sobering death tolls of young men and women who had died from influenza, it was time to celebrate.

"Please, Papa. Everyone is going downtown. Please. May I go?"

Mama came into the room clutching a dishtowel. Her parents exchanged glances, then shrugged.

"Why don't you see if one of your school friends is going?"

Edna's face brightened. She knew right away who would relish the adventure with her.

Less than an hour later, on a trolley that clanged its way west, Edna and Helen sat by windows, wide-eyed as crowds formed at every intersection.

Edna watched the jubilant display outside. "I've never seen anything like this." She brought her hands to her head.

In the heart of it all, the trolley stopped to let the riders off. Parades of people piled into the streets. Everyone in the city was going crazy. Despite Mayor Hansen's orders to avoid large gatherings and to wear face masks outside, the epidemic seemed to be the last thing on the minds of Seattleites. Horns honked from every automobile in the city. Revelers clanged with spoons on impromptu drums of metal lunch boxes. Downtown, singers and pipers, clogged the streets, and bands of every size played American Tin Pan Alley music. Edna and Helen chimed in as the band played Irving Berlin's song, "For Your Country and My Country." For a few hours, all the worries of the past years of war, and the weeks of restriction vanished.

The day after Armistice Day and six-weeks after restrictions were established, Mayor Hanson announced much-awaited news. The influenza epidemic was winding down. *The Seattle Times* proclaimed schools and businesses could reopen but strongly advised wearing masks in public places. Eager for school the next day, Edna thought about all her family had to be thankful for with Thanksgiving less than three weeks away. The war was over. The United States played a significant role in beating Germany. Gene was safe and coming home. And though the influenza epidemic had taken the lives of several hundred thousand people in the United States alone, Edna and her family had survived.

♪ ♪ ♪

Weeks later as the country teetered between grieving the lives of loved ones lost in the war and from the pandemic and simultaneously rejoicing as survivors returned from the battlefield, Edna received a letter from Port Orchard. She recognized the familiar return address of her grade school friend, Inez, but the unfamiliar handwriting confused her. She carried the letter from the postal box to the kitchen and sat down.

"Dear Edna." Edna felt the blood drain from her face. Something in the way the letter began sent a warning tremor over her body. Inez always began her letters, "Dearest friend." Edna's eyes raced over the words that followed. "Spanish flu... fever... died. We are deeply saddened by the death of our beloved Inez."

Edna clutched the letter, crumpling it like the crushing feeling in her chest. It couldn't be true. Edna threw the letter to the floor and sobbed. She never imagined someone so young dying so unexpectedly. Her first real friend was dead.

Chapter Thirty-Six

1919 – Seattle Strike

After the war, local headlines announced, "Soldiers and Sailors Must Be Employed Now." But as the returning heroes of war struggled to return to their prewar lives, many found it difficult to find work with less demand for products in the aftermath of the war. Metalworkers at the shipyard staged a walkout and encouraged other unions to join in as a show of solidarity. Only four months after the end of the war and the pandemic, life turned topsy-turvy for many Seattle residents.

In early February, voices from the living room roused Edna from sleep. She slipped out of bed and tiptoed to the door, cracking it open with a slow twist of the knob. She pressed her ear to the crack. Snippets of conversation drifted in.

A firm male voice dominated the conversation. "You have to understand tens of thousands of men are walking. The city will grind to a halt. I heard Mayor Hanson's called up troops from Camp Lewis to help keep the peace."

"It sounds like Mayor Hanson is expecting violence. Do you think it will come to that?" Her father's unmistakable voice had an urgency to it.

"Hard to say. I heard Hanson's calling on army veterans to assist the police in ensuring order. Be glad you took the job for Bill Boeing instead of at the shipyard. They've already been out on strike for two weeks."

Edna raised her brows as she recognized the voice. She didn't understand what happened that brought Uncle Leland to their house at eleven o'clock at night. She pressed her ear tighter to the door and fought the shaking in her hands.

"I don't imagine it will impact the Boeing Airplane Company, but there's talk of streetcar stoppage and even stores shuttering. I've been warned to expect a work stoppage at the post office. The walkout will be a coordinated effort across the city. Just be prepared for the worst."

After Uncle Leland left, her parents talked in their room for over an hour. Edna tried to make sense of the parts she heard. The next evening Papa came home from work, his eyes droopy from lack of sleep the previous night. From under his arm, he pulled out a copy of *The Seattle Star* and slammed it onto the table.

"What is that? I've never seen that newspaper before." Edna pulled out a chair and sat next to him. The headlines proclaimed, "STRIKE CALLED." Edna skimmed the front page. The entire page decried the general strike in which twenty-five thousand union workers walked off their jobs in support of the shipyard workers.

"It's another daily paper. Tends to draw the pro-labor readership."

"What does it mean? Are you going to have to strike too?"

Papa assured her his job was safe. "Tension's been building in the factories since the end of the war. Their pay has been frozen for two years. Lots of men are fed up. The government is trying to force lower wages than they've been earning."

Edna read aloud an article from the front page. "'Streetcar gongs ceased their clamor; newsboys cast their unsold papers into the street; from the doors of mill and factory, store and workshop streamed sixty-five thousand working men. School children with fear in their hearts hurried homeward. The life stream of a great city stopped.'"

"What's it like downtown? Is it as bad as this sounds?"

Papa stroked his beard. "Pretty much. Stores and businesses are shuttered and quiet. Don't know what Mayor Hanson's thinking. He went and deputized lots of regular folks and armed them all. The streets downtown are littered with propaganda flyers about how workers need to overthrow their bosses. Hear talk of some even blaming the Russians and their revolution for this strike." Her father shook his head in disbelief.

"Are you worried? Lots of kids in school say their fathers are on strike. I heard streetcar men, barbers, factory workers, even hotel maids, are striking."

Her father patted her hand. "Don't you worry. We'll be fine. I don't think it will last long."

Five days after the strike began, trolleys and streetcars rolled on the city streets as before. Papa came home from work without the worry lines of the past week. "I'm not sure how our mayor will weather this, but the strike is over without any arrests or violence, only his own threats that any man attempting to take control of the government will be shot. Can't wait to hear what all his trumped-up security cost us taxpayers."

♪ ♪ ♪

Though the strike had ended and by summer the flu pandemic that had traveled the globe for over a year had run its course, life did not improve for most workers in the city. On the first day of her senior year, September eighth, Cliff greeted Edna with the news that President Woodrow Wilson was coming to town. "Seattle is one of the cities where the president is hoping to gather support for the World War I peace treaty and for the establishment of the League of Nations."

Edna was unfamiliar with what the League of Nations was about, but following her father's example of keeping abreast of current events, she prodded Cliff for more information. Getting nothing further, they agreed to meet the following weekend and go together to see the president.

On Saturday, Edna stood at the King Street Station with Cliff and Helen and hundreds of other onlookers, all trying to catch a glimpse of President Woodrow Wilson. At one thirty sharp, the train chugged into the station.

"He's here!" Edna cheered and waved her arms in the air. News reporters lugging heavy cameras on wood tripods or clutching small notebooks rushed toward the arriving train.

Shouts erupted from near the train. "Stay back. Stay back." Uniformed officers barked orders while black-suited secret service cleared a path and stood at full attention staring at the crowd.

"I see him." Cliff, with the advantage of his height, jumped up and pointed.

"We can't see him." Edna and Helen stood on their tiptoes and peered into the distance, where the crowd grew increasingly thick.

Cliff grabbed Edna's hand. "That's okay. The newspaper article mentioned where he was going. Let's head to the parade route and get a place up front. Follow me."

Edna and Helen followed Cliff as they headed downtown along with thousands of Seattleites.

"There he is!"

President Woodrow Wilson stood in the open automobile as he and his motorcade and secret service agents proceeded north along Second Avenue, acknowledging people with a wave or a nod.

When the president's car drove past them, Edna turned to her friends. "Does anyone need to get home right away? I want to hear him speak. I want to be educated on the issues when I vote for the first time next year."

They both shook their heads, and the friends made their way to "The Arena" on Fifth Avenue to hear the twenty-eighth president of the United States. They stood and listened as the president spoke of establishing a world body to settle future conflicts among nations with its aim to establish a place where disputes between nations could be discussed and mediated.

Facing a crowd of several thousand onlookers his voice boomed. "I can predict with absolute certainty that within another generation there will be another world war if the nations of the world do not concert the method by which to prevent it."

Edna took in every word. She turned to Helen. "I can't wait until next year so I can vote."

Chapter Thirty-Seven

1920 – Looking Ahead

In late spring, Edna woke with the chills. Her heart pounded so hard it frightened her. Too fatigued to roust herself, she called for her mother with weak raspy words.

Fixing her gaze on Edna, her mother covered her mouth. Her eyes wide with fear, she placed the back of her hand on Edna's forehead. "My Lord. You're burning up." Her footsteps banged on the wood floor as she hurried from the room, returning a minute later with a thermometer. Her mother watched the clock for a full five minutes before she checked the reading. "Your fever's 102 degrees." Mother shook the thermometer down. "Stick out your tongue." Her eyebrows knitted, she stroked Edna's forehead and shook her head. "Let me see your arms and legs."

Edna flung back the blanket and sheet. The cool breeze on her skin immediately offered some reprieve. She hitched up her cotton gown and stared at the small red spots covering her arms and legs. Her breath caught. "What's wrong with me?"

Mother's chin quivered. "Does your throat hurt?"

Edna winced and nodded. Her mother's trembling lips sent a chill down Edna's back. "Is it smallpox?"

"Yes, it appears so."

Her mother's hushed voice made Edna wonder if she was afraid the intensity of her words might magnify the disease or make it more real. Unable to squelch her emotions, Edna shouted. "Small pox? I can't have smallpox." She covered her mouth to hold back the overpowering fear that seemed to engulf her. "Am I going to die?"

Her mother held up her hand. "Don't fret yet. It might only be a mild case. Didn't you say your friend, Cliff, had smallpox?"

"Yeah. We're in French class together. He came to school while he had a fever and was contagious. He didn't know until later."

"It's going to be okay. Cliff didn't die. He recovered, and you will too. It's lucky we are living in the city. I'll call the doctor and see what he suggests. In the meantime, you should try to sleep."

An hour later, her mother switched off the brass lamp by the bedside. "The doctor says there is no real treatment for smallpox, but he said it's important to lie in the dark. Light can affect your eyes." She pulled a bottle of isopropyl alcohol from a paper sack. "I had to go downtown to Bartell's. This will help prevent scarring." She gently wiped the alcohol all over Edna's body with a cotton rag.

"Scarring? Am I going to have scars?" Edna brought her hands to her cheeks and stroked her smooth complexion. "I can't have scars; how will I ever face a classroom of children as a teacher?"

Her mother took Edna's hands in hers. "Try not to scratch the sores as they heal, and we'll keep applying the rubbing alcohol. I'm sure you'll hardly notice any scars." She handed Edna a cup.

Edna raised the cup and sniffed. She drew her head back at the malty odor.

"Drink. This will help you sleep."

"What is it?"

"Whiskey. The doctor instructed me to give it to you. It's hot and mixed with water and sugar. Purely medicinal."

Turning up her nose, Edna sipped the whiskey and made a face as she handed the cup back to her mother.

"I'm afraid this means two weeks of isolation for you."

Edna moaned. She still recalled the quarantine from the pandemic a year and a half earlier. She hated the thought of being isolated from her friends for the second time in her life. "Does that mean even from Papa?"

Her mother nodded, "I'm afraid so. We can't risk your father getting ill and missing work for weeks on end."

Edna's entire body clenched. "This can't be happening. I can't fall behind in school. What about my college applications?"

"Calm down. You're getting yourself in a tizzy. I'm sure Helen or Cliff will be happy to bring you your assignments, and there's plenty of time for applications to college. You may be bedridden, but you can still read and write."

♪ ♪ ♪

While Edna missed school and her classmates, she enjoyed the attention she received in the form of get-well cards and flowers from her friends. While she recovered, Edna busily poured over her options for colleges and universities in the state. The University of Washington had high appeal with its close proximity and its reputation, but Washington also had two teaching colleges, known as normal schools, one north of Seattle, Washington State Normal School at Bellingham, and the Washington State Normal School in Ellensburg. Convinced she needed the freedom to experience life away from her parents and the city, Edna favored the normal school in Ellensburg, in eastern Washington, the first teaching college in the state of Washington. She also was comforted by the smaller campus and the enrollment of only a few hundred students, compared to more than three thousand students at the university.

"Are you sure you want to go so far from home when the University of Washington is so close? You could continue to live at home and avoid the cost of room and board. And you'll probably even run into some of the girls and boys from Broadway High."

Prepared for this, Edna reminded her mother of her desire to become more independent. "Besides, the normal schools were established for the sole purpose of educating teachers. Class sizes will be smaller, and the student body almost entirely focused on the goal of teaching. Their motto is, 'by teaching we learn.'"

Offering only a long exhale, Edna's mother shook her head. "I've heard the winters can be particularly cold in eastern Washington, and you won't know a soul. You've never lived away from home. What about your friends from high school? Are any of them going off to one of those normal schools?"

Edna clutched her forehead, wishing her mother didn't ask so many questions. "No one else I know is going to be a teacher. Pearl moved away to go to high school, remember? I'm going off to college. It's about time I get to experience new opportunities. Let's wait and see where I get accepted, okay?"

♪ ♪ ♪

In early June, after twelve years of schooling, her graduation night arrived. Edna smoothed the long gray skirt her mother made specifically for this special occasion and ran her hand over the purple sweater she'd purchased at the Bon Marche last month. She studied her reflection in the full-length mirror as she brushed rouge on her cheeks. Then dressed and with her makeup applied and her braids wrapped and pinned around her head, she stood back and beamed at the reflection of the confident young woman in the mirror.

When she strode into the front room, Father was waiting by the door dressed in his black suit. Mama wore a deep plum skirt with a high waistband that fell modestly above the ankle. The skirt looked stunning next to the light pink silk blouse with the round neckline. Taken aback, Edna gawked at the detailed embroidery her mother had splurged on at one of the department stores downtown. Her look, so much more refined than Edna had seen previously, reminded Edna of her Aunt Marie. "You look beautiful, Mama."

The glint in Mother's eyes brightened when Papa pulled a large round box from behind his back and passed it to Edna. "Here's a reward for all your hard work. Your mother told me you made the honor roll again this year."

She chewed her lips as she untied the white satin ribbon holding the surprise gift. She lifted the lid and drew a long sigh. "Oh, Papa." Placing the box on the coffee table, Edna withdrew a hat. "It matches my sweater perfectly." Edna placed the wide-brimmed black-felt hat with the fuchsia sash on her head. "It's just the flea's ankles."

♪ ♪ ♪

With high school behind her, and her acceptance at the Ellensburg Normal School secured, Edna was delighted by Uncle Leland's invitation to the Postmaster's Ball at the Masonic Hall.

"A ball?"

Her uncle's eyes carried a glint of conspiracy. "There will be plenty of opportunities to meet young men of your age and with similar educational aspirations. The Postmaster's Ball is where Charlotte met Jack. And here they've been happily married for nearly fifteen years."

Edna's heart skipped a beat at the romantic notion, straight from a fairy tale. She couldn't hold back her excitement as she hugged her uncle. "It sounds wonderful, but I won't know anyone."

Uncle Leland chuckled. "Of course, you may bring along a guest." He cocked his head. "Is there someone special I should know about? Perhaps that young man who took you to the eighth-grade dance."

Edna blushed. "Definitely not. Cliff and I are simply dear friends."

"Perhaps you have a friend you can bring."

She squeezed her eyes shut to block out the memory of Inez. She remembered watching *Cinderella* at the movie theater with Inez and how they dreamed about someday going to a ball together. If Inez were alive, she'd certainly invite Inez. She remembered her aunt telling her all her deceased loves ones were in heaven looking down on her. The thought of Inez looking down and cheering for her, comforted Edna.

Edna telephoned Helen right away and arranged to meet at Green Lake. Edna knew the trolley route to the lake and mentally prepared her plea before she arrived.

"Please, Helen, I won't know a soul." Eyes pleading, Edna took her best friend's hand. "We might meet someone."

"Are you talking about men?" With a shake of her head, Helen giggled. "Are you sure you want to do that? We're both going off to college in two months, and besides, I don't have anything to wear."

Edna brought her hands to her face and moaned. She'd never been to a ball but knew the event would be much more formal than anything she had attended in the past. "Goodness. I didn't even think about needing a dress."

Helen shook her head. "At least your mother is a good seamstress. I'm going to have to count my savings or beg my father to let me buy a new dress."

"Does that mean you'll go with me?" Edna hugged herself and sighed. Her fairy-tale imagining of years ago danced in her mind.

At home, her closet revealed no suitable options. She pleaded with her mother. "I've never been to a ball. I need a proper dress."

Her mother's delay in answering worried Edna, but finally her mother acquiesced. "Every young woman deserves a new dress for her first ball. We'll go to town tomorrow and shop for fabric." Her mother picked up one of her magazines and handed it to Edna.

Edna thumbed through the latest monthly issue of *The Delineator*. She flipped past the pages with styles for children and ran her hand over the glossy pages showing the latest in fashion for the modern woman through colored sketches and the latest sewing patterns from Butterick. Sitting next to Edna, her mother offered advice on selecting the appropriate attire for the occasion. Edna squealed at the picture of a short fringed-hem dress.

Mother studied the picture. "Is this the dress you expect me to make?"

"Isn't it the best?"

Her mother rubbed her neck above the high collar of her dated dress. "Isn't this a bit risqué? The neckline is so low; I'm sure you don't want to show too much decolletage." Her breath seemed to catch. "And I dare say, it's a tad on the short side."

"Oh, Mama." Edna brought her hand to her forehead. "These are new times. Women fought for a long time for more freedom, and even the right to vote. Someday women will hold positions of power. Women finally can have their own identities. They don't have to dress so proper and constrained any longer. Really, Mother, it's time to toss your corset for one of the new brassieres that work quite well and aren't nearly so binding."

Her mother's cheeks reddened and she quickly focused on the drawings in the magazine. "You're allowed your own identity, but I'm not making that dress." With an exaggerated move, she flipped the page. "No proper young woman wears that style."

Edna sighed and continued to turn the pages. She and Mother finally settled on a dress with an off the floor, drop waist style with a laced collar.

"This dress will look charming in either satin or silk. We'll check out the prices tomorrow. You'll need to borrow a few accessories to complete the look." Mother knitted her brow.

Edna knew she was estimating the costs of the affair. "I have a little money from selling the greeting cards I made. I'm certain I have enough for new shoes."

Her mother's shoulders relaxed. "I'm sure your aunt will have an appropriate necklace and handbag for you to borrow."

The evening of the ball, Edna's arms tingled, and her insides leaped. She looked over her dressing table strewn with several new cosmetics, ready to transform her. She glanced in the mirror at her complexion. She raised her eyes to the heavens and let her breath out. The pit marks from the smallpox were minimal. She picked up the recently purchased cake of mascara. With a steady hand, she dipped the brush in the saucer of water and brushed the thick black paste onto her lashes. Batting her newly thick and lengthy lashes, she picked up the tube of dark red lipstick even Mama didn't know she had. With her fingernail, she slid the small lever on the side of the tube to raise the wax-based color. She executed the strokes she had earlier practiced, filling in her lips to form the perfect shape. She wrapped her long, braided hair atop her head and pinned it with hairpins, finishing off her stylish hairdo with a rhinestone hair comb.

A knock at her door startled her. Her mother stepped inside and gasped. "I hope you're not going to the ball with your face painted like a floozy."

With a sigh of frustration, Edna rested her elbows on the dressing table. "Mother, this is how all the girls look when they go out in the evening." She waved her mother away with a friendly but exasperated flick of the wrist and eased on a new pair of nude silk stockings with a zig-zag pattern, slipping them high onto her thighs. She checked the seam to ensure it fell straight on her legs and fastened them to her garter belt. Mother would think it scandalous having her legs seen in public, especially with the new shorter length of her dress. But to Edna, the new fashion of the time was an indication of change for women, and for her. She slithered into her teal-blue satin dress with a wide satin ribbon belted below the slightly gathered waist. She turned in circles and marveled at how the loose-fitting dress, with its scalloped hem, swung and moved with her. The lacy scooped neckline emphasized the double strands of pearls she had borrowed from Aunt Marie. Though it was spring, she grabbed a borrowed chinchilla stole to cocoon her against the chill of the evening. To finish off the look of her evening attire, Edna grabbed a bell-shaped cloche hat and the small beaded handbag, also borrowed from her aunt. She studied herself in the large full-length mirror, cocked her head at the reflection, and smiled. She was the picture of fashion just like in the May issue of *Cosmopolitan Magazine*.

♪ ♪ ♪

Helen's father dropped her off at the Mooney house and the girls were flighty with excitement. Uncle Leland and Aunt Marie arrived to pick up Edna and Helen as promised. Edna did a double-take at the sight of her aunt. Though in her mid-forties, Aunt Marie's presence evoked confidence and elegance. Her silvery-blue dress hung barely below her knees and shimmered in the post lights lining the sidewalk.

"Are you girls excited?"

Their heads bobbed like pigeons as they clambered into the back of the Model T.

"Where is the lodge, Uncle?"

"It's not far from the University of Washington. We have time to motor by the university if you're interested."

Edna hadn't visited the university campus since the fair of 1909. Uncle Leland pulled the car near the main entrance, where the fair gates had stood eleven years earlier. The large fountain now dominated the hub of the campus. Green patches of lawn radiated outward from the fountain and walkways where temporary structures once spotted the grounds. Only a dozen students strolled between the large brick buildings housing the various college classrooms instead of the tens of thousands who bustled between exhibits in 1909. Helen, still unsettled on her choice in upper-level education opportunities, stared in awe of the size and beauty of the college grounds with

Mount Rainier visible in the distance even in the gray and pink of dusk.

"Wow. How come you're not going to school here instead of all the way in Ellensburg?"

"I want to become a teacher. It's the only thing I've dreamed of since I was a child. The state normal school is a better fit for me."

Minutes later, they rolled to a stop in front of the white neoclassical building, the location of the ball. The building reminded Edna of elaborate buildings from the world's fair. Big black letters identified the hall: Masonic Hall #141. Though Edna's father and grandfather were both members of the secret male-only organization, her father rarely participated while living in Port Orchard and hadn't shown interest in the monthly meetings since moving to Seattle. She wondered if he were active in the group if he and her mother would be attending such a formal event.

Inside the heavy double doors, an enormous brass and crystal chandelier hung from the high ceiling. Hundreds of glass prisms reflected light on the white marble floor. Each time the door swung open, drops of light danced across the floor in the wisp of wind from outside. The reflected light appeared to whirl in time with the music echoing from the hall where the ball was already in full swing.

She exchanged excited smiles with Helen at the sound of the lively, quick, rhythmic jazz filling the hall. Eager to take in the activities, Edna grabbed Helen by the hand and started toward the dance hall. Aunt Marie held up her hand. "A proper woman needs to powder her face first." She nodded to Leland to go ahead of her. Marie led the girls down the hall into the women's room. Inside, Marie used the facilities and reapplied her lipstick and rouge. Edna and Helen followed suit. Edna used her hand to comb back her hair and tuck in loose strands. Aunt Marie spoke in a hushed voice. "I'm glad it will be a dry event. Your uncle has been known to have a little too good of a time when the alcohol flowed freely at such events as this." She brought her finger to her lips.

"Don't worry." Edna cast her a knowing glance. "I won't say anything."

Marie smiled and led the way back to the large hall.

Music rocked the dance floors with horns—saxophones, trombones, and trumpets—smooth and soulful one minute and rough and raspy the next. Edna and Helen took chairs at a round table with her aunt and uncle. The ages of the guests ranged from young men and women to postal workers and spouses likely into their sixties.

Since Edna knew all the latest dance steps and she easily recalled the moves from her course in ballroom dancing from eighth grade, she was quite popular, and her dance card was full the entire evening. Between dances, the girls sipped ginger ale and ate a wide variety of tea sandwiches. During the evening, Helen had spent as much time watching the guests as dancing. Two hours into the evening, she nudged Edna. "That young man over there has been staring at us all evening."

Edna cocked her head and studied him. Seeing he'd caught their attention he strode toward them on his long legs. When he stopped in front of Edna and extended his hand, her heart skipped a beat.

"My name's Ivan. Would you like to dance?"

Chapter Thirty-Eight

1920 – Woodland Park Zoo

In late August, Pearl, Stanley, and their family filed off the Northern Pacific passenger car at the King Street Station. At the bottom of the steps, Pearl inhaled salty air and automobile exhaust, so unlike the woodsy scented air east of the city.

"Where's the zoo?" Victor hopped around like a skittery cottontail.

Stanley placed his hand on Victor's shoulder to settle his son a bit. "We have a short walk yet to meet your grandmother. Then we'll catch a trolley to the zoo."

Holding Margie, Pearl followed her husband and boys down the hill to Second Avenue. At Pioneer Square, people gathered beneath the cast-iron-and-glass pergola sheltering passengers waiting for cable cars. From the waiting crowd, an arm shot up and waved. Pearl turned to glimpse her sister calling out to her. With a skip in her steps, Pearl was soon wrapped in her sister's embrace.

Victor rushed to his grandmother. "Mama says we're all going to the Woodland Park Zoo. She says there's lots of animals, and we're going to have a picnic."

"That's right. More animals than you can count." Her mother reached out to take Margie.

"Margie, do you remember your grandmother?"

Margie buried her face in her mother's shoulder before she lifted her head with a bashful smile and with outstretched arms reached for her grandmother.

241

Her mother's eyes glinted as she cuddled and cooed. "She has your dimples and your long eyelashes."

"Do you think so?" Pearl's eyes glanced back and forth between her mother and her daughter. Three generations of women. She tipped her head and squinted, trying to imagine her mother as a young girl, striving to see a common familial trait.

Mother stroked Marjorie's silky dark hair.

Pearl continued to study her mother's face. "I think Margie resembles you, too, Mother." She turned to Edna. "I'm sorry I couldn't make it to your graduation."

"It's okay." Edna scooped Henry into her arms. "I'm glad we're able to spend a little time together before I leave for eastern Washington next month."

Pearl caught sight of the familiar totem pole a short distance away and the small kiosk across the street, still advertising ice-cold root beer. Memories from more than a decade earlier flooded her. Memories of her first day in the city. Though many of the sights and buildings were the same, the city had grown; it had changed to adapt to the times, just as she had.

Edna's voice jolted Pearl from her thoughts. "Pearl, hurry up, we have to get on."

Suddenly aware of the waiting trolley, Pearl marveled at the number of automobiles and the absence of horses and carriages from years earlier when automobiles were still a rarity. "I love the quiet of the country, but I miss the city in some ways."

Stanley gathered his sons like wayward chicks and steered them to the streetcar. "My uncle read the city built a new Fremont bridge to replace the old wooden trestle after they widened the channel for the ship canal. It's supposed to be quite the engineering marvel." Stanley ushered his sons onboard and deposited the fare for the whole family. Victor clambered onto a bench seat and pressed his nose to the window. Henry shrugged out of his sweater and leaned across to get a peek too.

Edna sat next to her sister and reached into an oversize handbag. "I have something for Margie." She held out the gift. "I was going to pass Miss Molly on to Margie, but she's so well-worn. This is Raggedy Ann. Do you think Margie will like her as much as we loved Molly?"

Pearl took the present from her sister and danced the rag doll with red yarn hair in front of her smiling two-year-old. "I'm sure she will love her. Can you say hi to Ann?" Watching Margie clutching the doll to her, Pearl's eyes stung. It didn't seem that long ago when she hugged Miss Molly in the same way her daughter was hugging her new rag doll.

Victor and Henry's wide eyes never looked away from the window as the trolley traveled from Pioneer Square along the waterfront.

Victor pointed to the water where a ferry was pulling away from the dock. "Look, Mama. A boat."

An automatic smile crossed her face. "I grew up across the water on that piece of land way far in the distance."

"Really? Can we go there someday?"

Sweet memories of her childhood flooded Pearl. "Maybe someday."

Minutes later, the trolley stopped at Fremont. Victor jumped up from his seat. "Are we there? I don't see the animals."

"Almost, we have another short ride. We'll be there soon."

By the time the private trolley provided by Woodland Park pulled up and stopped in front of the arched gate, Victor and Henry were wiggling in their seats. Pearl took in the site she'd not seen in almost a decade. Still heavily treed, this part of the city reminded her of the east side of Lake Washington. The boys scurried down the steps ahead of their father. The chirp of birds, squeals of excited children, and grunts of far-off animals filled the air. As Pearl checked to ensure all her children and belongings were accounted for, everyone startled at a sudden loud, high-pitched scream. They followed the crowd moving in the direction of the ruckus.

"What is that?" Victor covered his ears.

Henry jumped up and down at the sight of the large, luminescent, royal-blue, bird, dragging vibrant tail feathers behind. "It's so pretty."

"That's a peacock."

The bird walked freely past the visitors, stopped, screeched again a few times, then puffed his chest and fanned his tail feathers to the *oohs* and *ahhs* of the onlookers.

The show of color over, Victor tugged at his mother's dress and looked up and down the paved walkway. "Where are the bears? I want to see the bears."

Pearl followed wooden posts pointing out the various exhibits, including the direction to the bears. Along the meandering paths, they saw leopards and kangaroos. "Watch out for cars." Pearl grabbed Henry's hand as they crossed one of several public roads that divided the zoo to form a shortcut from North 59th Street to Fremont Avenue in front of the bear enclosures.

Victor took hold of his grandmother's hand and gazed at the white sign posted along the street. "What does '12 mph' mean?"

After strolling among the barred cages, over cold concrete floors housing polar bears and Jerry the brown bear, they followed the path to monkey island and watched the zookeepers feed the monkeys. Nearby, ostriches buried their heads in the sand. Pearl's mother stopped. She dabbed at her forehead with a handkerchief.

"I need a rest."

Pearl welcomed the chance to take a break. Her feet and her arms ached from carrying Margie off and on for the past hour. "I agree." She studied the guideposts and pointed the way. "The picnic area is this way. We can rest for a spell while we eat our lunch."

The boys dashed ahead beyond the grassy respite. They stopped in their tracks, then turned with eyes as big as cinnamon rolls at the sight of the large playground with swings and a wading pool. "The pool is as big as our house."

The boys jumped up and down begging and pleading to go to the wading pool. Pearl rolled her eyes at their outburst.

Stanley, too, seemed eager to frolic with his sons. "How about if they roll their pants legs up and only get their feet wet?"

Pearl held firm. "We don't have any change of clothes."

Her mother nudged her. "Don't be so strict. Come on, let the boys have their fun. We can sit here and relax and set out lunch."

Pearl recalled her resentment all the times her mother refused to let her do things the other girls were allowed. She vowed she would not do the same. "Remember, it's a wading pool. Don't splash and get yourselves all wet."

Stanley ran after the boys to the pool while Edna disappeared to take Marjorie to the swings. Pearl and her mother found a table near the playground and set out ham sandwiches and apple slices. They put two thermos bottles on the table, one filled with lemonade and the other with hot tea. Pearl spread a blanket, and the women plopped exhausted onto the cozy wool spread, sipped their tea, and breathed in the melding of grass and barnyard smells.

Pearl lay back and closed her eyes. She couldn't remember the last time she had enjoyed even a few moments of peace and quiet. A sudden shriek interrupted her tranquility. She shot upright and peered in the direction of the wading pool. Hearing Henry crying, Pearl started toward him, and within moments, Henry flung his soaking wet body into her arms.

"I fell in." Henry sobbed into Pearl's now-wet dress. "Victor shoved me."

As Stanley approached with Victor, their eyes downcast, Pearl couldn't decide whether to yell or laugh.

Pearl watched her mother fluff Henry's hair a bit to dry it, then wrap the blanket around him. "Slip out of your trousers and your shirt. I'll wring them out and set them in the sun. By the time we're done eating they should at least be partially dry."

Pearl took a deep breath and nodded as she thanked her mother.

Half an hour later, satisfied by their break and meal, Pearl shook out Henry's clothes. Though still damp, she handed him the trousers to slip into. Remembering his sweater, she pulled the sweater over him trying not to smile too much. "You look fine. Your pants will finish drying in no time."

On the return to the trolley stop, Henry tugged on his mother's skirt, "Look, Mama. Ponies. May we ride one?"

Pearl looked down the walkway. A curved fence enclosed an area where children sat on small horses and were led around the oval enclosure by an attendant. She didn't dare say no. Despite her son's shirtless outfit, he was having the time of his life. She fumbled in her coin purse, found two nickels, and handed one to each of her sons. "Don't forget to hold on to the bridle."

Once more, their father chased after them as they galloped off to the pony ring with smiles stretching the width of their round faces.

Chapter Thirty-Nine

1920 – The Normal School

Edna awoke and cast aside her bed covers, like the childhood she was about to leave behind. Her suitcase stood packed by her bedroom door. She glanced at the clock, and though there was plenty of time, her eagerness drove her to hasten her morning routine and her last-minute preparations. In less than three hours, she would wave goodbye to her parents at the Union Station and board the Chicago Milwaukee and Puget Sound Railway for Ellensburg.

A knock at the door came at the same time the door cracked open. "Are you up, dear?" Her mother lingered in the doorway.

Edna wondered if the sadness she saw in her mother's eyes was only a reflection of her own conflicting emotions. Refusing to reveal her gloom, Edna smiled. "I wouldn't oversleep on such an important day."

Her mother lingered in the doorway. Edna followed her mother's gaze to her dresser.

"It's a going away present."

Edna ran to the dresser and held up a light-blue pleated skirt, a silky white blouse, and a blue cable cardigan. "Mama, you shouldn't have. This must have cost a lot."

Mama wiped her moist eyes. "You deserve an outfit fitting of a college girl."

"Thank you, Mama." Edna felt the emotions swelling in her eyes as she hugged her mother. "I'll be down for breakfast soon."

Edna washed and dressed in her new outfit. She donned a light touch of rouge and stroked on a tad of black mascara, just enough to look more mature, but not enough to send her father into a tizzy. She pinned her hair back with a rhinestone comb placed above each ear. She looked at her outfit, far more sophisticated than the younger styles she wore only last year. Even her lace-up black leather oxfords reflected a change from the fussy high-topped boots of her childhood.

A twinge of pain tightened her neck and shoulders, reminding her of the weight she carried as the first family member to strive for a college diploma. In her parents' time, the children of most working-class families were lucky to reach the sixth grade, which was the case with both of Edna's parents. Pearl had made it through grade twelve even with her unforeseen situation. Today, Edna was ready to begin the final phase of her education. In two years, she would have her teaching certificate. Barely able to contain the mixed emotions of fear and excitement, Edna gripped her suitcase and strode out the bedroom door without looking back.

Papa pulled the car in front of the King Street Station shortly after eight thirty. Her mother tried to encourage him to park. "We need to make sure she gets on the train."

"I'll be fine, Mother. I'm going off to college, not to elementary school."

Never one for emotion, her father's voice cracked when he said goodbye from the open car window. Her mother hopped from the car and clasped Edna's shoulders with a firm grasp.

"I still need to purchase my ticket, Mama." Edna looked deep into her mother's eyes.

"I know." Mama released her grasp on her youngest child. "Be sure to write when you can."

Edna turned and trudged up the steep marble steps and into a flurry of commotion. Edna threaded her way through the throngs of passengers coming and going. Her confidence soared like the occasional bald eagle she'd seen gliding over the sound. She traipsed across the tiled floor to the ticket window. "One one-way ticket to Ellensburg, please."

The man behind the caged window studied Edna for a moment before a slight smile crossed the ticket seller's lips. "Another passenger off to become a teacher, eh?"

After nodding and handing over the fare, Edna pocketed the ticket to her future. As she walked toward the exit, light from the semicircular window facing the tracks lit the entire high-vaulted waiting chamber. She sat on a tall oak bench nearest the exit and noticed the classical columns and the series of archways which reminded her of all the support and different paths which had led her here this day.

The piercing shriek of the whistle jolted Edna back to the moment. The sleek white-steel express chugged to a stop at the station. Edna drifted along with the crowd in a haze matching the vapor from the steam engine. She boarded a Pullman passenger car near the middle of the long train. As she passed through several compartments, she glanced at the seated passengers, spying several boys and girls around her age. Or were they now men and women? Were they also on their way to Ellensburg? She found an empty seat to allow her time in solitude for the eight-hour trip. At nine o'clock promptly, the whistle blew and the train clicked and clacked on its way. Seated next to the window, she watched, entranced, as the scenery flew by. The train snaked past winding rivers, through the snowcapped mountains, up long grades, and around sharp curves. She visualized her next two years and guessed her road would also be winding and with challenging obstacles to overcome. Whatever lay ahead, her dream of becoming a teacher was now within her grasp. She wouldn't fail.

As the train crossed Snoqualmie Pass and continued east, the mountains and evergreen trees of western Washington disappeared, replaced by dry, flat land dotted with sagebrush and scrub pines. By the time the train pulled into the depot in Ellensburg, a sudden sensation of fear swept away her earlier confidence. Anxious to meet her roommate and see her accommodations for the school year, she sighed a surge of relief at the sight of a tall, pleasant-looking gentleman wearing a three-piece gray suit and sporting a Derby hat. He held a hand-lettered sign, "Welcome incoming Normal School Students." From the admittance letter she had received, Edna knew the man was the president of the college. Fellow students stood by his side with big smiles.

Edna approached and offered her hand. "How do you do?"

The president removed his hat. "Pleased to meet each of you. I am George Black, the president of Washington State Normal School. I need each of you to give me your name."

A boy with dark hair spoke first. "Craig Johansen, sir."

The fair-skinned tall chap nodded. "I'm Nelson Broderick"

Edna wondered if they, too, were upcoming teachers, or were more likely there for the reputation of the recently expanded athletic program,

Edna waited until the others gave their names and then offered hers. "I'm Edna Mooney."

One by one President Black checked them off his list. "Well, you're exactly who I expected. Follow me." He strode ahead with an air of authority before stopping in front of a large automobile. "It's a six-passenger ride, so it's going to be a bit snug. But we don't have far to go."

Edna gazed upon the yellow and red Packard, possibly the finest car she'd ever laid eyes on, and climbed in after the others.

The president pointed out a few businesses on the way. "This here's the National Bank of Ellensburg. Next to it is Perry Drug Store, for notions and such, then across the street, Burroughs Store for reasonably priced clothing items." He pointed out the First Methodist Church and the public library which Andrew Carnegie himself had funded.

When the car slowed in front of the school's main entrance, all eyes focused on the red brick building. Edna stared up at the six-story tower with "Washington State Normal School" etched in the cement over the arched doorway flanked by pillars.

"I'll be taking you to your dormitories now. I see Miss Mooney and Miss Ellsworth will be staying at the on-campus dormitory, Kamola Hall. Next, I'll deliver Mister Johansen and Mister Broderick as well as Miss Halverson, to the private homes where each of you will reside."

Edna took in all the buildings and the surrounding campus as the car wheeled past. It was nowhere near the size of the University of Washington campus; still, she marveled at its grandeur and the exquisitely manicured grounds.

Mr. Black stopped the car and, in a grand sweeping motion, heralded their arrival. "First stop, Kamola Hall."

Naomi Wark

Edna opened the door, exited, grabbed her bag, and waited while Susan Ellsworth climbed out. They waved to the rest of the passengers. "I'm sure we'll see you in some classes." The girls thanked President Black, then watched the car disappear around the bend. Eighth Street in front of the school was muddy and full of ruts from recent rain. Edna trod with caution to the main entrance. She pushed through the revolving door with Susan right behind. The steps were well-worn in the spot where people naturally stepped on their way in and out.

Once inside, Susan grinned. "I'm on this floor."

Edna continued to the second flight, flung open the heavy door, and glanced up and down the hall. She looked at the room numbers and made her way in the direction of her assigned room. At room 220, she paused. A note taped on the door with her name printed atop instructed her to see the dorm mother, Miss Kennedy, in room 315. Tired from the long day, Edna let out her breath, and tromped to the third floor.

She knocked on the door to room 315. A slender fortyish woman with bright-red hair swung the door wide. "Miss Mooney? I'm afraid your roommate, Jessica, has come down with a case of measles. I'm afraid you will not be able to stay in your room for a few more days."

At the unexpected news, Edna didn't know whether to cry or scream. "What does that mean? What am I going to do?"

Miss Kennedy raised her hands as if dismissing Edna's worries. "I've had time to think about the situation." She motioned to the end of the hall where a small pile of bedding lay atop a cot-sized mattress on the floor. "I've made up a cot for you."

Spying Edna's raised eyebrows, Miss Kennedy's voice took an apologetic turn. "I'm sorry; the hall is filled to capacity. A few other students have fallen ill, and our medical room had no available beds. I don't feel I should relocate your roommate, Jessica, or send her home. You understand, don't you, dear?"

Frustration built like the swell of a wave about to dash onto the shore. She inhaled. Her irritation deflated. "I understand. It's fine." She hoped she sounded more sincere than she felt. Edna followed Miss Kennedy to the end of the hall and plopped onto the lumpy mattress.

Songs of Spring

♪ ♪ ♪

Before dawn, an eerie high-pitched whistle sent a tremble through Edna. She woke to two unfamiliar faces staring down at her.

"Did you sleep well?'

Edna shook her head to clear the fog from her restless sleep. "No. Is it always this noisy?"

One of the girls laughed. "That was the silk train you heard. It's carrying expensive silk to customers back East. My father told me the insurance is less if they go fast, so it travels at a faster speed than other trains."

The second student cocked her head and chimed in with a hint of confusion in her voice, mingling with a touch of ribbing. "It's not loud if you sleep in the rooms and not in the hall. Why are you sleeping out here?"

Edna shared her calamitous story.

The two girls looked at each other. "Guess you found the shared restroom last night? You better get moving if you don't want to be late for orientation. You can keep your luggage in our room if you want until it's safe for you to sleep in your room."

After a much-needed shower from her day on the train and her rough night, Edna stopped by room 317 and deposited her belongings at Cheryl and Barbara's. She pulled out the assigned campus map from her skirt pocket and found her way to Walnut Street and the dining hall. After a quick bite of toast with jam and a glass of orange juice, Edna followed the crowd past a marsh of cattails and water across E Street to the administration building for new-student orientation. Not surprisingly, since the college was a teaching college, Edna discovered immediately that girls outnumbered the fellows three to one.

After three nights in the hallway, Miss Kennedy gave Edna the news that her roommate was no longer contagious and showed Edna to her assigned room.

"I took the bed by the window. I hope you don't mind?" Jessica extended her hand. "I'm so sorry you had to camp in the hall the past few nights."

251

Edna shrugged. "It's okay. It's not your fault. Besides, I've had the opportunity to check out the events the community holds to help the incoming students feel welcome." Edna couldn't wait to stroll through the town and learn about all the opportunities the small college offered.

When the autumn harvest started, Edna joined Jessica and a bunch of girls from Kamola Hall, including Cheryl and Barbara, for her first hayrack ride. Sitting atop a cart loaded with hay and pulled by a tractor driven by Barbara's father, a local farmer, Edna could not have imagined a more relaxing and fun way to spend the day. For the next several months, Edna's life felt like a set of gaily painted Russian nesting dolls, with each new experience building upon the prior and enriching her life.

Edna's first free night after her first jam-packed month of school, she wrote to Pearl. A pang of guilt wrenched her stomach as she signed the letter. She didn't want to come across as cheeky and make Pearl envious of her college experience when Pearl's life had made an unpredictable turn and robbed her of the opportunity. Everything about college life and dorm life fit Edna's dreams and expectations as if custom made by a fine tailor in downtown Seattle.

When the girls in her dormitory found out she played basketball in high school, they pressured her into trying out for the basketball team. "Lots of girls here are from smaller high schools that didn't have women's basketball teams. You simply must join the team."

Edna always considered herself athletic, so she agreed. Girls' basketball had grown in popularity and seemed more widely accepted in this college town than in high school. She loved the modern mid-length, black shorts, and the red and black cotton T-shirt with a picture of the school mascot, Wellington P Wildcat, on the back. Of course, kneepads were required to keep the girls from hurting their fragile knees. The male cheer team even attended most games to encourage the women on with the cheer known by the Wildcats as, the Normal Yell. *"Zip, Boom, Bah! Who, Gah, Hah! W.S.N.S., Rah! Rah! Rah!"*

Chapter Forty

1920 – Sister Envy

Pearl trudged up her driveway to the mailbox. Inside, she found a letter from Ellensburg. She clutched two-year old Margie tighter to her chest and ran the full length of their three-hundred-foot driveway back to the house. Her heart pounded from the exertion combined with the anticipation of Edna's letter. She sat Margie in a chair next to her and placed a soda cracker in front of her before opening the letter.

Dear Pearl,

I hope you are well. I imagine your youngsters are sprouting like pole beans. I suspect in time I will become homesick. Right now, everything is so new and exciting I don't know where to begin. I am getting on well with my roommate, Jessica. There are so many opportunities to partake in here in Ellensburg. I can't wait until winter. The girls say when the ponds and rivers freeze over there will be plenty of ice-skating. I remember wanting to go ice skating on Green Lake in Seattle, but the only year the lake froze over was the year of the snowstorm so I never had the chance. All the local girls have skates so I can easily borrow a pair. I'm excite to try ice-skating for the first time.

I attended a Chautauqua assembly. Can you imagine? I never heard of such a thing, but they are quite frequent and popular among college and university students as well as the local residents. Even President Roosevelt has been quoted as saying, that Chautauqua is "the most American thing in America." Well, in case you are not familiar, this is what happened. Several of the girls from my dormitory invited me to attend one held in a big tent in a playfield north of the administration building. The Chautauqua opened with a reading from the Bible, then a hymn was sung, and the Lord's Prayer was recited in unison. Oh, the smell of over a hundred sweaty students in the hot tent on mashed, damp grass still lingers. We listened to the music at the beginning, then slipped out under the tent and away to cooler spots before the main speakers and entertainers began. I must say, I felt a bit uneasy sneaking out like that. I've become quite a cheeky girl in my adventures here. Sometimes boys from Erwin Hall, three blocks away, sneak food over. They haul it up to the second floor at Kamola without Miss Kennedy, the dorm mistress, knowing. It's risky, and you would think we were starving to death, but it's a dare we enjoy. I will be home for Christmas and look forward to seeing you, Stanley, and the children.

Love, your sister,

Edna

Like embers sparking in a fireplace, Pearl's emotions ignited. Her eyes glistened as she absorbed her sister's words. "Good for her." Her whispered words floated in the air like leaves captured by a breeze, reminding her how with one brief flurry, her dream of attending university shifted in a different direction, from a dorm room with a college roommate to a boarding house for wayward girls. Wondering *what if* and *if only* meant nothing. Edna was experiencing the college life Pearl had only dreamed of and was within reach of grasping her dreams.

Margie banged her hand on the table. "More."

Pearl took a couple more crackers from the sleeve and placed one in each of Margie's chubby hands. For a moment Pearl envied her sister and the endless opportunities that lay ahead for her. As Doctor Lucien Chapman predicted years earlier, becoming a nurse now meant a minimum of nine months at the University of Washington to serve as a public health nurse and longer yet to work in a hospital or clinic. She recalled her admiration for Dr. Kate Barrett, both raising a family and obtaining her medical degree. But Pearl and Stanley did not possess the same financial resources as Dr. Kate Barrett, who hired a nanny to assist with her child raising. An overwhelming heaviness weighed down on her with the realization she would never attend any university and she would never become a nurse.

Her daughter's chomping drew Pearl's attention. Her despair faded as she watched Margie try to cram both crackers into her mouth at the same time. Pearl laughed until she cried.

After regaining her self-control, Pearl swept Margie up, cleaned her hands and face and went to her dresser. Inside the top drawer, underneath her nightgowns and underclothing, was a small pamphlet, which Pearl withdrew. She squatted and smiled at Margie. "Your aunt, Edna, is pursuing her dream. Now it's time for your Mama to do the same."

With Henry now in first grade and Victor in fifth grade, Pearl appreciated the relative quiet and calm of her days after years of raising two rowdy, active boys. Margie piled blocks as her older brothers had before, but, unlike them she was content to wait until the stacked pile toppled, rather than swatting it down prematurely. Pearl sat on the sofa and read the brochure she had received from the Red Cross three years earlier. She knew what she needed to do.

Early the next day, Pearl sat across from a fortyish female volunteer with the Issaquah Chapter of the American Red Cross. Margie wriggled on Pearl's lap struggling to be set down. The woman's elbows rested on the desk, and she rested her chin on her laced hands as she listened with interest to Pearl.

"Is there someplace I can volunteer with the Red Cross?

The volunteer's face brightened. She raised a hand with a nod of understanding. "You want to know how you can help others without having any medical background."

"Yes. I don't have a lot of free time. As you can see, I have a toddler, and I have two older boys in school. But my aunt was involved with the suffragettes, and my sister is getting her certificate to teach. I need to feel like I'm doing something useful."

"You don't think raising three children is useful?"

"Yes, of course it is, but I don't think it's enough for me."

"One of the main concerns the Red Cross is involved with currently, is offering public programs such as first-aid training. Our training offers you the information and skills you need to help adults and children during many emergency situations. We do have a time commitment. Are you willing to commit to three hours a week?"

Pearl rubbed her forehead. She considered her answer. She knew Stanley would question how she could possibly add one more task to her day, but she also knew it would be the closest she would come to fulfilling her dream of being a nurse. "Sure. I'll make time."

Chapter Forty-One

1920 – Jacob

Anxious for her Christmas break after three months away from home, Edna trudged through the snow at 6:00 a.m. for the one mile walk to the train station. Several friends who lived in town had volunteered to find her a ride to the station, but Edna didn't want to put anyone out on the day before Christmas, and she was used to the walk. This morning, the extreme cold of eastern Washington and the ever-present wind for which the city had a long-standing reputation proved more brutal than she had imagined. She tightened the crocheted scarf around her neck and strode with swift steps while jamming her gloved hands deeper into her pockets, missing her furry muff from childhood. The icy wind nipped her nose. Her breath huffed out in short spurts of steam through her scarf. Thoughts of seeing her family prodded her on, along with visions of hot-from-the oven snickerdoodles and fresh gingerbread that seemed to help warm the brisk air. Even with a heavy carry-on suitcase, Edna made the train station in less than twenty minutes.

She hurried to the ticket window. "One-way to Seattle."

Ten minutes later, she climbed aboard the sleek Milwaukee and St. Paul and dropped into the first empty seat. Tired from rising for the early train, she rested her head against the cold window, dusted with frost on the outside, and dozed off.

When she woke from her nap, the frosty-sagebrush, barren side of eastern Washington was behind her, replaced by the towering evergreens of the western side of the state.

Though she'd been gone only three months, when Papa met her at Union Station, he regarded her with a tip of his head. "Look at you. I can tell college life agrees with you."

♪ ♪ ♪

Several hours later, Pearl and her family arrived after their long drive around the north end of Lake Washington. All three children dashed to the tree. Edna's mother's face glowed like the shiny hand-painted balls on the tree as the children *oohed* and *ahhed* at the towering evergreen that filled the room with the scent of the forest Edna missed in the city.

"Are these presents for us?" Victor bent down and snatched a gaily wrapped gift from under the tree. Pearl rushed in and returned the gift to the floor. "You'll have to wait and see."

Stanley placed a few more gifts under the tree, drawing a hug from his mother-in-law. "You did invite your uncle for Christmas dinner tomorrow, didn't you? It's been so long since we've seen him."

Stanley assured her his uncle and parents would all be coming the following day for dinner. Edna noticed that without the daily tasks of tending to animals and an extensive garden, her mother seemed more relaxed, and her eyes more alive than she'd seen in years. Then, watching as her niece and nephews huddled under the tree and spoke in hushed tones trying to guess what was inside the assorted presents, Edna felt an emptiness in her chest. She envied her sister and suddenly ached to experience motherhood.

Christmas morning, Papa strolled in dressed in his only white dress shirt, struggling with his red bow tie. He grumbled like a pouty schoolboy. "Do I have to wear this fool thing?"

Mother scurried to help him straighten the tie. "Of course, you do. I made it especially for today. Quit your grumbling."

Everyone piled into their respective cars and drove to the First Methodist Church on Fifth and Marion. Inside the church, cedar boughs draped the brick walls, filling the house of worship with the spirit of Christmas.

Edna took in the sight of red bows affixed to each of the pews and wreaths lining both sides of the nave. "The church is decorated so splendidly."

Papa whispered. "Your mother made the decorations."

Mother frowned. "Don't exaggerate, George. The Ladies Aid Society donated funds. I did help, along with the other half-dozen women in the Women's Sunday School group."

The children looked up at the high-domed ceiling. At the sound of the first chords of music, their gaze turned to the enormous pipe organ and the dozens of robed members of the choir. Margie seemed entranced by the singing and did her best to sing along to "O Come, All Ye Faithful."

After morning worship, the children darted straight to the tree, plopped down, and crossed their legs with their hands folded in their laps. Victor looked over his shoulder and called out. "We're ready to see what Santa Claus brought."

Stanley shook his head with a smile and helped the children out of their coats while Pearl handed each a peppermint stick to keep them quiet while Mother and Edna warmed milk on the stove for mugs of hot cocoa. Soon the entire family was seated, passing out gaily wrapped packages.

Papa loosened his suspenders, settled into his chair, rubbed his graying beard, and lit up his pipe sending an aromatic vanilla scent into the air to mix with the myriad of scents already in the room.

Victor looked at his grandfather and elbowed Henry. "Granddad looks like Santa Claus."

Papa put his finger aside his nose and winked.

At four o'clock, Mama assigned tasks to her daughters, and Pearl, in turn, assigned the chore of setting the table to Victor and Henry. "The guests will be here anytime now."

When the doorbell rang. Pearl greeted Gene with a hug. "It's been years since I've seen you." She then offered a hand to his fiancée, Marta, a fair-skinned young woman who appeared to be of Nordic descent.

Edna showed them to the living room still partially strewn with bits of ribbon and unwrapped toys under the tree. Pearl called to her children. "This is your second cousin, Gene, and his friend, Marta."

Pearl took their coats. When they were seated, she asked, "Are you still setting bones?"

Gene put his hand on his fiancée's lap. "No, I'm working for Ballard Hospital. They used to handle a lot of hand injuries from the mill workers, but we're now primarily a maternity hospital."

Edna glanced at her sister and saw a sad smile. She knew Pearl still felt pangs of regret she never had the opportunity to become a nurse.

Only minutes later, Aunt Marie and Uncle Leland arrived, followed by Stanley's parents and Uncle Frederick. Aside from Uncle Frederick, every adult had a partner. Edna watched her family members exchange nudges of affection. Her thoughts turned to Ivan and the need to be close to someone. She'd written to Ivan several times during her first three months in Ellensburg, and he'd asked her to call on him when she returned home for the Christmas break. At the time, she had dismissed the idea, but now, witnessing the affection exchanged between Pearl and Stanley, Edna reconsidered. After all, he'd left a favorable impression, and she had no other plans for the remainder of her stay.

After debating her decision for two days, Edna approached her father. "May I borrow the car?"

Papa's eyes widened. "Why do you need a car?"

Her mouth went dry. She swallowed and concentrated on not biting her lip, which was a telltale sign her parents knew well now. She hated to lie, but neither Mama nor Papa would understand. "I'd like to visit Helen if it's okay."

"Queen Ann isn't far. Why don't you take the trolley?"

Before she could respond, Mama cocked her head and glanced at her daughter's maroon and black calf-length dress. "You're wearing that to see Helen? Isn't it a bit flashy?"

"Mother, this style is all the rage."

The raised eyebrows relayed doubt, but Edna knew Mama wouldn't press any further.

"Let her drive, George. It will be good for her to gain experience shifting on all these hills."

When Edna got behind the wheel, she pulled away without looking back. She sensed her mother's eyes following her, wondering if she was really off to visit Helen. Her sister's indiscretions, even so

259

many years later, was a sensitive topic, so Edna hesitated telling her mother much about her intentions involving members of the opposite sex. Her mother would surely chide her character if she discovered what she was up to. Women did not call on men in her mother's time, but these days were different. These days represented a shift from old-style life. Though prohibition had restricted the consumption of alcohol, every other aspect of society was more relaxed and progressive. The giddiness she felt the evening of the Postman's Ball returned and pushed aside any doubt of the propriety of calling on a man. Cars wheeling down the streets outnumbered horses and carriages and fashion no longer limited a woman's movement. High boots, corsets, and long skirts were out. Cardigan sweaters replaced tight-fitting jackets allowing freedom for women to partake in golfing and racket sports without the constraints of a decade earlier.

Edna looked down at her dress and realized how high it rode on her thighs when she sat. She tugged on her hem as she drove south, questioning her choice of attire. Forty minutes later she pulled the car up to the address in Renton that Ivan had indicated in his correspondence. At the realization she had used far more gasoline than the short trip to Helen's house would have required, she panicked. Having failed to look at the gauge before she left home, she had no idea how much she'd used. She'd have to stop on the way home and have the attendant fill the tank. The tank was more than half empty—maybe five or six gallons used. She checked her wallet for the dollar and a half she'd require to fill the tank. She hoped her impulsive trip to see Ivan would be worth it.

She was a bundle of nerves as she looked at the modest brick house he shared with his parents. What if his parents were home? She realized she should have notified him of her intentions before she drove nearly twenty miles. She withdrew her ivory-colored compact from her handbag and applied a quick swipe of red lipstick and another line of dark eyeliner. She gazed at herself in the small round mirror, then blotted her lips before clicking the compact closed. She glanced toward the front door as she climbed out, then smoothed her dress and straightened her sweater. Certain the front window curtains were drawn aside when she parked in the front of the house, she fretted at the sight of the now-closed window coverings. She fluffed her hair, which for a change hung in loose bouncy curls instead of pinned atop her head. Confident, Edna strutted to the door and knocked. The door opened within seconds, confirming her suspicion someone had been at the window peering out at her. Surprised by the man standing in front of her, Edna awkwardly blurted out, "You're not Ivan."

The tall lanky chap resembling Ivan, only older with a more chiseled chin, smiled. "Ivan's not here. Won't I do?"

The cockiness in his tone caught Edna off guard. Her blood surged. Confused by his brazenness, she rendered her best attempt at displeasure with hands on hips and haughtiness in her tone. "I'm Edna. I'm here to see Ivan. I wrote to him weeks ago and told him I'd drop by." She stiffened to project confidence despite her trembling legs.

The door swung open. "My name is Jacob; I'm Ivan's older brother." He reached out, took Edna's arm, and led her inside. Edna couldn't fight the emotion growing as she gazed into Jacob's large blue eyes with the longest lashes she had ever seen on a man. His hair was short but wavy. She'd never imagined what love at first sight might feel like, until now.

Jacob directed her to the sofa in the living room. "I'm sorry, Ivan didn't mention you were coming tonight."

Edna buried her chin in her chest and shifted on the cushion. "Well he didn't really know. I wrote to him to inform him I would be home for Christmas. He responded and told me to stop by sometime."

"Where did you meet Ivan?"

"We met at the Postman's Ball. We exchanged a few letters while I was away at school." As she relayed her story, she realized how little she knew about him or his family.

The house creaked. Jacob glanced at the ceiling and the upstairs, before his eyes rested on her again. "You have a beautiful face."

Edna brought her hand to her cheek, warm to the touch despite the chill that ran down her back. Jacob's smile indicated he knew his comment mattered to her. His gaze drifted from her face to her dress.

He raised his eyebrows. "I've got a car. We could go for a drive. You can tell me all about yourself."

Self-conscious but flattered, Edna felt the warmth from her cheeks radiating. She began to suspect the entire incident was a setup. She shifted with unease and tugged at the bottom of her skirt again.

She wondered if Ivan was upstairs avoiding her. Sweat formed on her brow. "Could I have a glass of water, please?"

Jacob jumped up. "We don't have to go anywhere. If you'd prefer, we can stay here." He disappeared into the kitchen.

Edna took several gulps of the cool water. She could hear her heart beating so loud it reminded her of the chug of the automobile engine. "I should probably leave. You can tell Ivan I stopped by."

She combed her fingers through her hair damp with sweat. She immediately wished she'd applied fresh deodorant before coming.

Jacob took a seat opposite her. "Please, I'd like to get to know you. I can tell you anything you want to know about me."

"Well for starters, what do you do for a living?"

"I'm a corporal in the army."

Her mother's warning to stay away from sailors and soldiers as they can't be trusted to remain faithful resounded in Edna's brain. She crossed her arms, ready to tell him she had no desire to date an enlisted man, but those blue eyes held her gaze. "Were you in the war?"

The twinkle disappeared from his eyes. "Yeah. That's something I'd rather not talk about right now. Maybe another time. What about you? What do you do?"

Edna exhaled. The entire evening was a mistake. She thought about the dances she'd shared with Ivan and the few letters. Her fingers trembled as she reached for another gulp of water. She'd been foolish coming to see Ivan. He had no interest in her. Her frustration was about to let loose. She wouldn't cry in front of this man she'd just met. "I probably should get going."

The sound of approaching footsteps, startled Edna.

"Oh. I'm sorry. I didn't realize you had company, Jacob."

Jacob tossed his head in his mother's direction. "It's okay, Mom. This is Edna. She dropped in to visit Ivan."

Rising from the sofa, Edna extended her hand. "Hello, Mrs. Pearson. I'm Edna Mooney."

"I'm pleased to meet you. Don't let me interrupt. I'm just going to heat a cup of coffee, then I'll be out of your way."

"That's okay. I was leaving anyway." Edna turned to see Jacob shake his head.

Jacob rose and followed her to the door. "I'm serious. I'd like to see you again. Can I pick you up at your place tomorrow? There's a respectable dance club in Seattle. Strictly no alcohol, nice clean fun. Will you go with me?"

Edna inched her way to the door. "I'll think about it." She reached into her handbag and withdrew a pen and slip of paper. She wrote a phone number on it and handed it to Jacob. "You may call me tomorrow morning. I'll let you know."

As she drove home, her head whirled, she felt light-headed. What would her parents think of her driving all this way to visit a man she knew little about? As she neared her house, she remembered she needed to fill the gas tank and decided to swing by Helen's house. Surely her best friend would have some sage advice about what to do, and her excuse for needing the car for the evening would at least ring partially true.

♪ ♪ ♪

Before returning to school, Edna went on a few dates with Jacob. He'd been a perfect gentleman. She was delighted to hear he attended the normal school in Bellingham for a year before he enlisted in 1917 when the United States entered the war. "I decided after a year in Bellingham, I couldn't see myself as a teacher."

Finding something in common with him, Edna relaxed in his company. "All I've ever wanted to do since I was a young girl is to be a teacher."

"I admire that. I'm sure you'll make a fine teacher. I learned I'm more proficient with mechanical things. Since the end of the war, I've been repairing radio and communications equipment."

Hearing her mother's voice in her head, Edna struggled to find the right words. "Are you going to stay in the army?"

"My enlistment contract is up in six months. I haven't decided yet if I'll reenlist. Someday, I want to own a farm. What do you think?"

Naomi Wark

Edna's hopes sagged. "I grew up in Port Orchard, we had some animals and a large garden. I had my share of chores. I don't know if I can see me farming for the rest of my life."

"That's okay. It's simply an idea. Promise you'll write when you get back to Ellensburg. Army life doesn't always leave a lot of free time, but I'll write when I can."

There was a spring in her step when she walked in the front door to her parent's house after Jacob dropped her off and kissed her on the cheek.

Still swooning from Jacob's kiss, Edna flushed seeing her father still awake, puffing in on his pipe. He stroked his chin when she walked into the living room. "Be sure to consider the commitment required being involved with a man whose life will constantly be upended by the military."

"Papa. It's only our second date. Besides, he's not sure he's going to stay in the army."

Her mother shook her head. "Well, that's good news. I told you what I thought about enlisted men. At least your sister picked a young man who wasn't a soldier."

Her father raised his brows. "You said he works with radios and such? Tell him, if decides to leave the army, Boeing is hiring skilled men."

"Sure, Papa. I'm going to write to him, but we're going to be over a hundred miles apart. I'm not going to let Jacob or any man get in the way of my goal to become a teacher."

Her father nodded. "That's smart. I don't want you to find yourself in the same position as Pearl."

♪ ♪ ♪

Edna couldn't forget about Jacob when she returned to school. She couldn't decide if he was brash or merely self-assured. Something about him both excited and scared her. Gene had shared little about his experiences in France, and Edna knew enough not to prod Jacob on sharing his experiences during the war though she wished she'd pressed further on his goals in life.

264

Unable to silence her thoughts, Edna longed for clarity so she could focus on her studies. She wished she had time to talk with Pearl. She needed someone with whom she could confide. She sat on her bed with her legs crossed and decided to ask her roommate. "I don't know what to do, Jessica."

Her roommate looked up from her studies. "About what?"

Edna hesitated, she didn't like the thought of opening up to her roommate, but Jessica always seemed so in control. "I met a fellow over Christmas break. I'm attracted to him, but I'm not sure he's good for me. I'm confused."

Jessica looked down as she answered. "I believe in the power of prayer. I ask for guidance when I'm unsure about things."

Edna thought about Jessica's words for a moment. Perhaps prayer was what she needed now. "Does it help?"

Jessica paused. She tilted her head and looked hard at Edna. "You told me you were intrigued by the Chautauqua assembly we attended in the fall. You can always enroll in an elective Bible study course, or join Christian Endeavour. It may help."

"What's that?"

"It's a nondenominational youth group. Its purpose is to encourage youth to dedicate their lives to Christ, but it's a great opportunity for faith and fellowship. You should come with me sometime."

Edna pulled out her class load for the second semester, Appreciation of Art and Design, Physical Culture, and the required Elocution class to help prepare all teachers to effectively express themselves in attitude, voice, and speech. "My course load is too heavy to take another class. Maybe I'll go with you to one of your Christian Endeavour meetings. It may help me understand what I want in life besides teaching."

The following Sunday, Edna gave in to Jessica's invitation to attend the Presbyterian Church. She didn't find it much different from her experience with the Methodist church, but she felt welcomed by the community.

"This is from the Book of James. It is a good reminder to read each day." Jessica handed Edna a small piece of paper with a verse printed on it.

Edna taped the Bible verse to her study desk. "Is anyone among you suffering? Let him pray. Is anyone cheerful? Let him sing praise." This would be her motto. Pray in times of uncertainty and rejoice in times of happiness.

Edna prayed for the wisdom to make a wise decision. A few weeks after returning to Ellensburg, she gathered her courage and wrote to Jacob. She made it clear she would not consider seeing him again if he disapproved of her desire to continue her education and, upon graduation, pursue a career as a teacher. His response would guide her next move.

Less than two weeks later, Edna held her breath before opening Jacob's letter. She couldn't hold back her smile as she read his words vowing to never hold her back from pursuing her dreams. Then her breath caught. She reread Jacob's last words. He'd decided to reenlist, this time in the Army Signal Corp. Her body tensed. How could he make such a decision without her? Perhaps she wasn't as important to him as she imagined. She refolded the letter and put it in the top drawer of her desk.

Mid-February, Edna returned from class to find a copy of the *Campus Crier* on her bed. The student newspaper was folded to show off an advertisement. Jessica jumped up from her small desk and squealed when Edna picked it up to read it. "Take a gander. I'm really jazzed about it. Aren't you?"

Edna scanned the large text surrounded by a border of hearts, advertising the first official dance of the school year, the weekend before Valentine's Day. Official dances were infrequent due to the faculty and trustees who couldn't agree on appropriate dancing positions or upon suitable music. Edna responded with a weak nod.

"What's wrong? Don't tell me you're not excited? It should be way better than the informal dances in the Nash Building."

The image of Jacob whirling her on the dance floor at the Highland Park Club, made her warm with desire. Remembering Jacob's last letter, Edna's heart fluttered. "Of course. Definitely better than the illegal barn dances we sneak off to in Selah."

The first day of spring, Edna's nineteenth birthday, brought warm dry weather to Ellensburg along with an abundance of outdoor activities including picnics on the busy Yakima River. This Sunday, it meant the thrill of Edna's first logger rodeo.

Jessica, who hailed from Yakima, was giddy. "Trust me, Edna, the Logger Rodeo is unlike anything you've ever seen."

Edna sat engrossed as the loggers with their pike poles walked on the wet, fast-moving logs, pushing them away from the bank as they struggled to maintain their balance. She chuckled when the mental image of her father as a younger logger flashed in her mind. She couldn't picture him parading around entertaining spectators. But at the sight of these men of twenty to thirty years old, their biceps bulging underneath the rolled-up sleeves of their flannel shirts, Edna could not stop thinking about Jacob. She pictured Jacob standing on the logs, his arms outstretched attempting to keep his balance. She guessed as a soldier he'd passed many tests of endurance and strength. Watching these men, Edna realized how much she missed him. A splash from an off-balance logger drew cheers and jeers from the crowd and jostled Edna's mind back to the present. Sitting on a blanket on a grassy patch by the river with Jessica, Edna lay back and closed her eyes. She pondered her life married to a soldier.

Chapter Forty-Two

1921 – Romance

A t the end of her first year at the normal school, Edna returned home for the summer, eager to resume the romance that had flourished over the past five months as she and Jacob exchanged letters.

Papa met her at Union Station, and Mother greeted her with a hug before she trudged upstairs to put her things in her room for her three-month stay. Her mother poked her head in the bedroom doorway. "Jacob called earlier in the week. He said to tell you he's sorry, but his orders came without any advance notice. He has a mandatory training class at the Presidio army base in Monterey for six weeks. There wasn't time to get a letter to you before you returned."

Edna plopped onto the mattress. Her imaginings of romantic strolls along the Seattle waterfront, long talks about their future, and, of course, the dances at the new dance halls in the city, would have to wait. Though she yearned to spend time with Jacob before looking for summer employment, his absence meant the chance to earn more for next year's tuition. With a year of higher education behind her and a portfolio of drawings from her numerous art and design classes, Edna applied for a job with Fox's, a jeweler on Third Avenue in downtown Seattle.

The jewelry store owner, Harry, peered over his round wire spectacles as he sized her up. "The position requires someone with a creative eye to assist in the design of custom pieces for the well-to-do of the city and beyond. Do you have any background in jewelry design?

"No, but I've taken several art and design classes in college, and I've done a lot of needlepoint, which requires detail work." Edna passed him the portfolio of sketches she'd prepared after reading about the position.

Harry rubbed his chin as he flipped through the pencil drawings. "You seem to have an eye for detail, but my store has a reputation for its workmanship. Why are you interested in this particular position?

"I've always enjoyed art. Someday I hope to be an art teacher."

"Jewelry design is different, but I see from your drawings you have a unique talent. Do you think you can do the job?"

She tingled inside at the opportunity to use her creativity. Many of her college acquaintances would spend their summer working in a stodgy office as secretaries or sitting behind a switchboard as telephone operators. Edna took a breath and held back her desire to whoop with joy. "Absolutely. I promise you'll be pleased with my designs."

Her summer employment secure, Edna practically skipped to the trolley. The fifteen dollars per week would cover her ten dollars quarterly tuition as well as her living expenses and books for the coming year. She welcomed the demanding and intricate work that kept her mind occupied and off Jacob. But as the weeks wore on, she struggled with seeing the minute details of the pieces. After she arrived home following a full eight-hour shift, a dull throb behind her eyes triggered a headache. She found an aspirin in the medicine cabinet and waited for the aching to subside.

"You received a letter." Her mother waved an envelope in the air.

Edna inhaled the perfumed scented envelope. "It's from Helen." She sat at the kitchen table and ripped the envelope open. Her eyes blurred. She squinted and moved the letter closer.

"What's wrong?" Mama watched her for a moment. "Are you having trouble with your vision?" She studied Edna's eyes. "Your eyes are bloodshot."

"I can't seem to see as well as I need to, especially at work."

Mother removed her glasses and held them out. "You could need glasses. Perhaps you should see an optometrist."

Edna made a face. "I guess you're right. I'll schedule an examination." She returned to the letter in hand. "Helen is getting married. She's asked me to be her maid of honor."

Her mother arched her eyebrows. "Helen? Has she set a date?"

Scanning the remainder of the letter, Edna shook her head. "No. She's thinking possibly next summer."

Her mother relaxed. "It's nice that these days young ladies don't have the same pressure to rush into marriage that I did."

"I agree. Don't worry."

Her mother raised her eyebrows. "I understand they still don't allow married women to become teachers."

Edna refolded Helen's letter. "I know, Mother. I'm not even going to think about getting married until I have a teaching position. Even then, I plan to wait several years." Edna shook her head and pocketed the letter. "There's really nothing more to talk about." She gave her mother a peck on the cheek and walked away.

Three days later, Edna kept her appointment with the optometrist. As she suspected, the optometrist wrote a prescription and placed an order for a pair of glasses. Two weeks later, she walked into to Fox's sporting her new wire-rimmed spectacles. She hated the way she looked in glasses and hoped she wouldn't have to wear them around Jacob, but she was forced to admit her headaches disappeared and the spectacles aided her with the closeup work.

Harry removed his glasses with a nod. "This detail work is what forced me into wearing spectacles. Better to get them now before your eyes get any worse. You've got a natural talent for design. You have a job with me anytime you want."

Edna straightened on her swivel stool. She appreciated the compliment but decided the work was far too intense to pursue as a career, further affirming her desire to become a teacher. Despite the store's reputation, some weeks offered her free time to examine the merchandise and find inspiration for new pieces. As she studied the various metals, settings, diamond shapes, and different stones, Edna couldn't keep from pondering what type of ring she might select if Jacob proposed. She wondered if Jacob would surprise her with a ring when she least expected it.

To avoid pining over Jacob in the evenings, Edna enrolled in an art class at the Cornish School held in the Booth Building on

Broadway and Pine, an easy streetcar ride from home. The watercolor class, *Perspective Life,* was taught by an instructor from India, Daljeet Sengupta. Never having heard an Indian accent, Edna was charmed by Daljeet's crisp, clipped, clearly enunciated words. Many of her classmates were soldiers, home from the war, and trying to fit back into society. Some of them snuffed. She didn't know for sure, but she'd heard a drug called cocaine was popular among former soldiers. Bothered by their behavior, she wondered if, during Jacob's stint in the army, he had developed a similar vice. If so, she could never accept it. She'd have to confront him before she allowed their relationship to go any further. She hadn't responded to Jacob's most recent letter, but addressing the question in a letter would only create a chasm in their relationship. Her questions and concern would have to wait until he returned home.

Her summer work schedule and painting class left Edna too busy to give a second thought to dating other men. Though she thought about Jacob in his absence, her interactions with her art school classmates who'd returned from the war left her with an almost objectionable dislike of men in uniform. By the time Jacob's letter arrived, informing her he was returning in early August and looked forward to seeing her again, she waffled between her desire to pick up where they left off and ending their relationship. But his words of affection, so sincere, almost poetic, moved her, and she ached to have someone special, someone like Helen had found in her beau, Bill. Someone like Pearl had found in Stanley.

When Jacob telephoned to say he had two days of leave and couldn't wait to see her, Edna abandoned her doubts. "I can't wait either."

Seeing Jacob for the first time in over seven months, Edna went weak in the knees when she answered the door.

Jacob wasted no time in sweeping her into his arms. "I've missed you."

A sudden rush of pleasure stirred an unfamiliar sensation that warmed her from deep inside as he pressed his lips to hers and held her in a long embrace. She tensed. Was this the same sensation Pearl experienced? The same shaky knees that drew her to surrender herself to Stanley? Edna pulled away and took a step back.

"What's wrong?"

Edna stammered an excuse. "I've never seen you in uniform before."

He stood with an air of authority in the khaki, almost drab olive-green breeches, and tunic. He removed his hat and bowed. "Your car awaits."

Soon they were in Jacob's Ford heading south toward Camp Lewis.

"I thought it was time for you to see the base."

Regaining her resolve, Edna broached the delicate subject. "I was surprised you reenlisted. The last time we spoke, you said you were thinking of sitting for a civil service job."

Jacob shook his head. "I knew you'd be upset, but the opportunity to stay in the army and be promoted was too good to pass up."

"What will you be doing? The war is over, and you said there's not much training going on at the base."

"You're right. With the lean budget, the camp is in poor condition. Right now, only about one thousand men live in the barracks, and the secretary of war promised in 1916 that a minimum troop level of fifteen thousand would be maintained. The Rotary Club has called for the government to use the camp or return the land to Pierce County."

"So why stay in the army? It seems like a dead end."

"Just because Camp Lewis is dying, doesn't mean there aren't opportunities elsewhere in the service. My new position will be, supply specialist. I will be sent to various bases around the country to review their procurement and inventory procedures. I'll direct policy and procedures updates as needed. I may be away for long assignments for the next year or two, but you still have another year in Ellensburg anyway, so it shouldn't be too hard on us."

Though Edna was prepared to be angry, she couldn't dispute his reasoning. She had asked him to wait for her and not to stand in her way. How could she stand in his way? Besides, his absence for a year or two, would allow her to focus her energy on her studies and on obtaining a teaching position without any pressure from Jacob.

"You're right. You need to do what is best for your career."

"I'm glad you understand." Jacob pointed to the north side of the road. An American flag flapped atop a pole in front of the Camp

Lewis Inn. "We're almost there. This area is called American Lake. The inn was built by the Salvation Army toward the end of the war. Besides providing a place for family members to stay, they hold a variety of social events here." He suggestively raised his brows. "Sometimes, even dances."

Jacob turned off Highway 99 and slowed. Up ahead, Edna could see the main gate to Camp Lewis. Two rock fortresses, supporting lookouts made from logs, stood like sentinels, one on each side of the road. A sign announcing Camp Lewis stretched between them.

"This is the main entrance to the camp. It's also called the Liberty Gate. Everyone entering the camp must pass through this gate."

The significance of being on base struck her. She was important enough to see where Jacob worked and perhaps meet a few of his friends.

Jacob rolled to a stop and handed his military ID to the guard at the gate. "We're going to the hostess house to hear that young violinist from Tacoma, Vivian Gough, perform."

After being in the dark regarding the evening, Edna relaxed. The romantic evening with Jacob she'd dreamed of during the past few months was about to begin.

Chapter Forty-Three

1922 – Graduation

Outside the train depot in Ellensburg, Edna paced with nervous energy, which helped warm her as the famous northwesterly gusts blew through the open waiting area. Though it was the end of May, Edna clutched her arms across herself, bundled in winter wear awaiting the arrival of the Milwaukee and St. Paul. Today, after completing her requirements for her teaching certificate, a rush of relief and accomplishment fueled her, not the uncertainty and fear of two years earlier when she boarded the same train to begin the pursuit of her higher education. She watched the clock on the depot's red-brick wall, amazed by how slowly the hand moved, yet how quickly the past two years had sped by.

The engine's chugging purr approached, accompanied by a loud, sharp whistle that pierced the chatter of students mulling around, awaiting family for the graduation ceremony the following day. Soon the clatter of the metal wheels slowed as the train neared, rattling the row of windows facing the tracks. Edna's heartbeat quickened at the sight of the black engine trailing steam, like the tail of a kite, along the tops of the passenger cars.

The train squealed and rolled to a gentle stop in front of the small depot. The conductor tugged on his long black waistcoat as he climbed down the steps. He checked his pocket watch and marched to the first car, placed the compact stairs at the bottom of the doorway, and extended a hand to assist the disembarking passengers. A porter followed behind. In quick steps, he moved between the third and fourth cars to oversee those arrivals. Edna's eyes darted back and forth among the cars until Edna spied her mother and father and rushed to greet them.

♪ ♪ ♪

The next morning, at eight thirty, Edna's parents arrived for breakfast in the dining hall. They grabbed a plastic tray and filed in line along with dozens of parents from out of town, who like them, had spent the night at the Majestic Hotel.

They ate in silence for a while before emotion swept over Edna. "Can you believe after fourteen years; my studies are at an end?"

Edna's mother took her hands. "Your father and I are so proud of you."

"Thank you. You and Papa have sacrificed so much."

"We're just happy you achieved your dream." Her father pulled out his pocket watch. "How far is the walk to the gymnasium?"

"It's on the other side of campus, about three blocks"

Mother took another bite of the scrambled eggs from the plate filled with bacon, fried potatoes, and hotcakes. "I can't remember the last time I had a breakfast I didn't have to prepare."

By ten o'clock, with her parents seated on the right side of the auditorium, Edna rushed to the women's locker room and slipped into her gown and pinned her cap to her locks with bobby pins. She took her place in line, along with the hundred-plus classmates obtaining certificates. Edna followed the group into the gym, where she filed into her seat. The school orchestra's brass section started soft and low and increased in crescendo as the last of the graduates hurried into their places. Miss Quimby, one of the counselors, nodded to the music professor and conductor. The volume of the music swelled, and the first of the graduates from Washington State Normal School class of 1922 marched down the aisle to "Pomp and Circumstance." Edna looked around one last time at the huge crowd. She stood erect and proud as the procession moved forward and spilled into rows of folding chairs. At last, the last names beginning with the letter *M* were announced. Edna stood with her row.

When the girl ahead of her took the stage, Edna held her breath.

"Edna Mooney."

She strode across the stage. Her head held high, she shook hands with Mr. Leahy, the head of the Department of Education, and accepted her two-year teacher's certificate. Marching offstage, she flipped her tassel with a wide grin while glancing around at the hundreds of spectators. Back at her assigned row, with her diploma gripped in her right hand, she scanned the sea of heads, hoping to spy her mother and father. Failing to see them, she sighed and plopped into her seat. Two hours and over two-hundred diplomas and certificates later, the president of the college, Mr. Black, offered a final congratulatory speech, followed by a loud cheer from the graduates. In unison, all the graduates reached for their graduation caps and yanked them from their heads. With whoops and cheers, black mortarboards with red tassels flew into the air. Tossing hers, Edna felt flooded by a sense of freedom and exhilaration. She not only had achieved her goals, but she'd made her family and her sister proud as well. Edna headed for the bleachers to find her parents.

♪ ♪ ♪

Without any idea where she would eventually teach come the fall, Edna moved back in with her parents for the summer. Besides finding employment for the fall, she needed to be involved in Helen's wedding, only a month away. Her obligations as maid of honor kept her busy planning the wedding banquet with Helen's mother and making the bows for the church pews. With its growing population, Seattle now had over a dozen elementary schools, all of which required teaching only a single grade as opposed to a one-room school like she first attended. Staying in the city with its access to transportation, including the train that traveled both south to Camp Lewis and east to Issaquah, seemed ideal, until she read a letter from Pearl. *"I hope you will at least consider moving east of Lake Washington to one of the new bedroom communities spurred on by the timber and coal trades. We could see each other all the time. If you get a position nearby, you can stay with us until you find your own place. We can finally have the kind of friendship we missed out on when we were younger, and you'll get to see your niece and nephews more."*

♪ ♪ ♪

The weekend after the Fourth of July, Helen arrived at Edna's house for her final dress fitting. "Can you believe my wedding is only a week away?" Helen sashayed around the living room of Edna's parents' house, her dress brushing ever so slightly along the oak floor as she ran her hand over the white silk gown. "The dress fits like a dream. You're so kind, Mrs. Mooney, to do the alterations for me."

"I'm pleased to do it for you, Helen." Edna's mother ran her hand over the seams of the puffy sleeves and checked the lace on the bodice as she spoke, "Edna's lucky to have found such a good friend after our move here. She lost a dear friend from elementary school to the pandemic a few years ago. The two girls always dreamed of being in each other's weddings."

"Edna told me about Inez. Edna's friendship means a lot to me too. I hope someday to be in Edna's wedding." She looked over her shoulder at the pastel-yellow flapper-style dress draped over the back of the davenport. "Try on your bridesmaid's dress, Edna."

Edna swooped the dress into her arms and headed for her bedroom.

Two days before the wedding, Jacob surprised Edna with an unannounced appearance at her home. "What are you doing here? I wasn't expecting you so soon." Stunned, she stood, unblinking, afraid she was imagining him.

"I wanted to surprise you and have the chance to spend a little time alone before Helen's wedding." Jacob took her hands and pulled her to him. "Don't I get a better welcome after nearly a year apart?"

Held in his firm embrace, she felt the air go out of her. She sighed and caught her breath. She hurried with her goodbyes to her parents and rushed out to Jacob's waiting car. Later, strolling casually around Green Lake hand in hand, Edna relaxed. Jacob was more laid back than last time they'd been together. She welcomed how safe she felt as he held her hand. His confidence exuded strength, further drawing her to him.

Stopping mid-stroll, Jacob turned Edna to face him. "Have you found a teaching job yet?"

"Not yet. I'm thinking of moving east of the lake, closer to Pearl. I never had much chance to really get to know her growing up."

Jacob took her in his arms. "Don't go too far. I hope to move back to Washington next year, and I want my gal nearby."

An uneasy feeling radiated throughout Edna's chest. She pulled away. "I've just graduated. I'm not ready to make a commitment yet."

Seeing the confusion on Jacob's face, she took his hands. "I'm simply saying, let me find a position that suits me, and when you move back, we'll see what happens. Okay?"

Jacob's brow creased, but he held his tongue and kissed her with as much passion as Edna had ever experienced.

The next day, Jacob arrived to escort Edna to Helen's wedding in a brown pin-striped three-piece suit over a starched white linen shirt, looking as dapper as any Hollywood leading man. Tucked inside his button vest, Jacob wore a yellow tie selected to match the yellow in Edna's bridesmaid dress. Edna's chest swelled at his impeccable attire. He removed his derby hat and stepped inside. She tried not to blush when Jacob looked her up and down with Charlie Chaplin raised brows, revealing his big blue eyes. "I love the new red lipstick. Turn around. I want to see your new hairstyle."

Edna licked her lips in a sensual tease before she complied. "It's called a chignon. It's all the rage." She smoothed her silky hair, now pinned in a knotted bun at the nape of her neck, before she turned back around to find his brow furrowed. "What's wrong? Don't you like it?"

Jacob shrugged. "A little too stern looking for my taste. You look like a schoolmarm."

"Careful." Edna coyly cocked her head. "That's what I'm going to be." She looked at the small carved-wood clock on the mantle. "I'm almost ready. Let me grab my dress and shoes. We can't be late for the wedding photos."

Chapter Forty-Four

1922 – A Teacher at Last

S oon after Helen's wedding, Edna's former roommate, Jessica, sent word she had secured a teaching position on the east side of Lake Sammamish, in the small town of Carnation, not far from where Pearl and Stanley lived. Several of her former classmates had written with news of where and what grade they were teaching in the fall. Edna realized she had to decide. Right away, she dismissed moving to DuPont, as Jacob hoped. After living with her parents, the notion of moving away from Seattle offered the autonomy she craved. The immediate future she envisioned involved living close enough to Seattle to visit her parents, but far enough away to feel independent. Jessica securing a position in Carnation, only boosted her plan. Edna wrote to Pearl to inform her of her intention to secure a position east of Lake Washington.

When Pearl wrote back with news the primary teacher in nearby Monohon was not returning in the fall, Edna packed an overnight case, and the next morning, her father took her to the station to catch the early train to Issaquah.

♪ ♪ ♪

"You are single, aren't you?" The school district superintendent, Mr. Severson, glanced at Edna's left hand as he spoke across the dark wood desk during the interview. "I trust you have been informed of the rules of the state. Married women are not allowed to teach without special dispensation."

Edna nodded. "I understand."

"You will be expected to maintain a strict curfew of eight o'clock, and you are not to keep company with men other than your father or other family members. The contract spells out the other rules that are grounds for immediate dismissal."

Edna pasted a smile of acceptance on her face. She'd reached her goal. She was certified to teach. Even her feelings for Jacob wouldn't stand in her way. If anything, taking a teaching position with such rigid pronouncements would offer a valid excuse to delay any nuptials at which Jacob had hinted.

"Stand up." The harsh words came in the tone of an order. "Let me take a look at you."

Offended at being treated like goods on display, Edna obliged. Rising from her chair, she smoothed her long black skirt as she stood. "Is something wrong?"

The superintendent peered over his spectacles and paused as he ran his hand through his hair before offering a smug nod of approval. "You appear to be a respectable woman. I expect you'll have no problem adhering to the dress code."

"No, sir. Not at all."

"I'm curious why you want to teach in such a small school. I see you attended high school in Seattle. I'm sure you realize there's a substantial difference in attempting to teach all grades simultaneously."

Edna told Mr. Severson about her early educational experience.

He shuffled the papers on his desk and pushed a form toward Edna. "This is the standard first-year teacher contract. Read it and sign at the bottom if you are accepting of its terms."

Edna gushed but maintained her composure. Was he offering her the job? Holding back her enthusiasm, Edna read every word. Most of the contract restated the rules of which she'd already been made aware, including the clause stating state law required all teachers to remain single during the duration of their contract. She would be responsible for teaching all grades from first through eighth and for cleaning her classroom. For the fulfillment of these duties for the eight-month contact, she would receive eighty-dollars per month. Her face brightened as she read a clause not discussed previously. "Am I to be provided with complimentary living accommodations?"

The superintendent nodded. "It's small, but it's convenient. Located across the road from the school." He narrowed his gaze. "It should suffice for a young single woman who isn't prone to entertaining gentlemen in her home."

Maintaining her strict school-teacher posture, Edna held back her joy,

"Would you like to see your living quarters?"

"Of course." Edna clasped her hands together, thrilled by the district's living accommodations and not having to find a boarding house.

The superintendent hesitated before his face took on a serious tone. "Don't expect too much."

She guessed his cautionary warning of the dwelling gave away enough information to curb any high expectations of grandiose housing. Edna followed the tall mid-fifties man as he stepped with quick, deliberate steps across the road to the house provided by the school. From the outside, the place looked as if it was built before the turn of the century. The white paint was cracked and peeled, and the front porch creaked underneath their weight as the key turned and the door opened.

"You're lucky." Mr. Severson walked across the black and white linoleum flooring of the kitchen, long stripped of any finish. He flipped a switch, and an overhead bulb flickered to life. "Only got electricity installed here two years ago." He tapped on the old black stove along the wall near the small window that looked across to the school. "Still gonna have to use this here stove for cooking and heat." He swept his arm in an arc around the room. "Shouldn't be a problem since there's not much space to heat."

Edna took in the small house of around four hundred square feet. The white painted cupboards weren't much, but they were adequate for the sparse cooking pots and the cast-iron pan Pearl had given her along with the few plates and bowls mother promised her when she found a place of her own. "That's fine. My sister and brother-in-law live on forty acres. I'm sure I'll have plenty of wood for heating and cooking." She frowned at the pump at the kitchen sink. A memory took her back to Port Orchard when they didn't have hot and cold running water, prompting the next logical thought. No indoor toilet. She spun around with a hint of concern. "Is there an indoor bathroom?"

Mr. Severson's forehead crinkled. He pointed to a curtained-off area behind the kitchen, which Edna had assumed was a back porch. He walked over and pulled the curtain open, revealing a small clawfoot tub, a washbasin with a wall mirror, and a commode. "It's not as modern as you'll find in the city, and flushing can be a bit temperamental, but otherwise, if there isn't a heavy rain, the pipes should do their job, and everything should be fine. I recommend using water conservatively though."

Off the kitchen, the living area held assorted well-used mismatched furnishings. Noticing Edna's downcast look, the schoolmaster jutted his chin toward the backyard. "The home comes furnished, but if you want to bring any of your own belongings, feel free. There's an old shed out back where you can store anything you don't use."

The living space sported faded mint-green wallpaper with small purple violets and cracked paint on all walls. Mr. Severson walked to the wall opposite the compact bathroom and reached up to reveal a single Murphy bed flanked by built-in shelves. He lowered the bed into the wood-planked living room. "And this is your bedroom."

"Well, at least I don't have to worry about buying a bed." Edna put on the best smile of gratitude she could muster. It wasn't much, but the rent was free, and more importantly, for the term of her teaching contract, it was hers.

As they walked back across the street, a short beep from a car horn, signaled Stanley's arrival. Mr. Severson eyed Edna and cleared his throat. She saw the look of distrust in his eyes. Stanley hopped out of the car and extended his hand. "I'm Stanley Rosenberg, Edna's brother-in-law. We live nearby, in Preston."

Mr. Severson gripped Stanley's outstretched hand and nodded his approval. "I see. You're here to pick up Miss Mooney?"

Back at Pearl's house for a few days, Edna couldn't wait to share her good news.

"Is everything okay?" Pearl guided Edna inside and put the kettle on the stove.

"I've been offered the job."

Pearl squealed and squeezed her sister. "The job in Monohon? Tell me all about it. Do you need a place to stay?"

Ena shook her head. "The district provides a small house as the teacher's quarters."

Pearl made a face. "I know the house you're talking about. It looks pretty run-down."

"I have to admit, it's seen better days. It's been around since before the turn of the century and not much work's been done to improve it since then, but there is plumbing and an indoor commode."

Don't worry. I'll ask Stanley to stop by sometime. I'm certain he'd be happy to help you fix anything that requires repair. I've got plenty of blankets you can use, and we can work together to sew curtains. You simply must let me help you fix it up."

"Are you sure you're not too busy?"

"I can bring the kids; we can find something to keep them busy, maybe cleaning up a bit outside." Pearl stopped talking and looked at Edna. Her eyes watered.

Edna hugged her sister. "What is it? Is everything okay?"

"I moved away when you were only four. Just think, after sixteen years, we finally have the chance to really get to know each other and be sisters."

Chapter Forty-Five

1922 – Doubts

With the fire stoked in the small coal stove, Edna stood, her hands on her hips, and absorbed her achievement, ready for her first day of school. Before her students arrived, she wrote her name in both cursive and large printed letters, across the five-foot-long chalkboard at the front of the room. At the sight of the first of her students skipping and shuffling up the dirt path, Edna straightened the bow on her collar and tugged on her ruffled sleeves. "Welcome." Edna greeted each boy and girl with a curt nod as they arrived. "Please take your seats."

The chattering children, age six through thirteen, paraded in and followed the same ritual she had, twenty years earlier, only most carried store-bought domed-shaped lunch boxes with decorated scenes of children playing instead of old pails. They deposited their lunches along the closet shelf before sliding into their places along the wood benches. When all the students were seated, Edna strode to the front of the room. She tapped her hand on her oak desk, and the room fell silent. Twenty-eight pairs of eyes gazed at her. She inhaled and began. "Good morning, students. I am your new teacher, Miss Mooney."

After taking roll call, Edna informed the students of her expectations for the school year. She instructed them on the appropriate behavior both inside and outside the classroom. "Misbehavior will not be tolerated. Punishment will include breaking up the chunks of coal or staying after to clean the classroom. Repeat offenders will find themselves standing in the corner."

As she handed out the school primers for each grade, Edna paused, stunned by a girl with unruly hair the color of fire. Her thoughts strayed to her first day of school when she met her friend Inez, with the same warm color in her hair. Her throat tightened with emotion as she wondered what Inez would be doing now if she hadn't died from influenza.

Edna strolled down the center aisle, counting, and distributing the textbooks for each grade. The student's eagerness resonated through the room as they thumbed through their new books. Edna reached for her ruler. A memory of Miss Finney disciplining students with a ferule stick at the slightest offense popped into her mind. Edna looked at the ruler and subconsciously rubbed her knuckles at the memory. She'd vowed even then that when she became a teacher, she would instruct with strict discipline but also kindness. Placing the ruler in a drawer, she picked up the small brass bell on her desk and rang it. "Quiet down, please, children."

Busy with lessons all day, and preparing plans and correcting papers each night, Edna's weeks raced by. At the end of October, Jacob wrote to her and explained he'd received a promotion to Petty Officer First Class with a pay increase to ninety-two dollars a month. He hoped his next promotion would bring a significant salary increase and put him in a position to support a wife and family. Stunned by his inference, Edna's skin tingled. Living near Pearl and her nephews for the past months reinforced Edna's yearning for family. Though she'd dated Jacob for nearly two years, she'd also gone out on occasion with other men, and she suspected Jacob had also enjoyed the company of other women who lived much closer to Camp Lewis.

"What do you think? What should I do?" Edna showed her sister the letter.

Pearl took Edna's hand. "Do you love him?"

Edna swallowed hard. She hung her head with a shake. "I have strong feelings about him, but I only just began teaching, and I'm not ready yet to settle down."

"Heed my advice. I had to marry earlier than I wanted."

Edna hesitated for a few moments, then looked into her sister's eyes. "Do you regret getting married?"

"No, but as much as I love my family, I must confess, seeing you with a career and freedom, I sometimes think how my life would be different if we had waited. Don't rush into anything if you don't have to."

Pearl was right. Edna knew what she had to do. As she wrote back, the words flowed like rehearsed lines from a play. The same lines she'd repeated to herself over the past years. She wrote about her desire to marry and have children; with the understanding she could not commit to marriage until she established herself as a teacher. It wasn't until the letter was folded and stuffed into an envelope Edna realized her words were impersonal. It could have been written for anyone. What did that say about her feelings for Jacob?

Chapter Forty-Six

1922 – Life Saving First Aid

Despite the warmth of the wood stove, living near the mountains in a wooded environment produced a lingering damp chill in the Rosenberg house. During the fall and winter, Pearl insisted her children wear an extra layer of clothing every morning until the house warmed.

On most school days, bedlam ruled the mornings, so Henry's ongoing hollering for his mother faded into the hustle of the morning like background noise.

Rounding the corner of the kitchen, Henry yelled louder. "Mama, didn't you hear me? Margie's breathing funny. She sounds like a whistle."

Pearl turned an ear to the whimpers from Margie's room. She dropped the knife she'd been using to slap peanut butter and jam onto slices of bread, glanced at the clock, turned off the pot of Cream of Wheat, and ran up the stairs to her daughter's bedroom.

"What's wrong, honey?" Pearl bent over her daughter and placed her hand on Margie's forehead. The subtle warmth to the touch didn't alarm Pearl, but Margie's sunken eyes and blue-tinged lips, the color of eggplant, did.

Margie panted through a few weak coughs. "I don't feel good."

Think. Pearl's heart quickened, rising and racing. Pearl took a deep breath to calm herself and to slow her breathing. "Where does it hurt?" She placed her hand on her daughter's abdomen. "Here?"

"No." Margie moved her mother's hand up to the left side of her chest. "Here."

"That's your heart. How is it hurting? Is it burning like a tummy ache?"

Margie fought to speak though labored breaths, but only faint cracked words escaped her lips.

Pearl placed her ear next to Margie's lips. Margie's raspy voice sent a shiver like a gust of wind, over Pearl. Her muscles tightened. "Do you hurt anywhere else?"

Margie shook her head, but her weak words delivered a shudder over Pearl. "Mama. I can't breathe."

At the sound of footsteps drawing near, Pearl turned to see Victor and Henry standing in the doorway.

His face pale, Victor murmured. "What's wrong with her, Mama?"

Pearl shook her head and shooed him out. "Serve yourself and your brother, Cream of Wheat, then gather your books for school."

"But Mama." Victor stood firm. "What about Margie?"

Pearl remembered the first-aid book the woman at Red Cross had given her. She grabbed Victor's shoulders. "Stay with her." Pearl rushed from the room and returned with the small book with a red cross on the front. Seated on the edge of Margie's bed, Pearl squeezed her eyes shut and tried to recall what she had learned in her first-aid classes. She stroked Margie's forehead. "Try not to worry, breathe slowly. You're going to be okay."

Pearl turned the page to the table of contents and ran her finger down the list of illnesses. She stopped when she reached asthma. The doctor's words from five years earlier echoed. He had warned Pearl that Margie faced an increased risk of lung problems, including asthma. Now, sitting next to her precious little girl struggling to breathe, the serious nature of Margie's condition sank in. She quickly scanned the chapter about asthma for what may have caused the sudden attack. The damp air and perhaps something else, something external, was irritating Margie's bronchial tubes and making it hard for her to breathe. There were any of several factors that might be responsible for her reaction: mold, pollen, grass, trees, even the smoke from the wood stove.

Pearl scanned the treatments, then turned to Margie and boosted her by the armpits to a seated position. "You need to sit up." Pearl called for Henry to fetch the pillows from their beds. She positioned them behind Margie. "Sitting will make it easier for you to breathe. Take slow, deep breaths."

Pearl forced herself to remain focused as she repeated a breathing exercise she'd learned during her Red Cross class. "Breathe with me, Margie." Pearl demonstrated a deep inhale and long exhale as she continued to read. "I'll be right back. Keep taking deep breaths." Pearl set the book on the bed.

The panic in Margie's eyes frightened Pearl as she dashed to the kitchen and returned with a cup of hot tea with a strainer filled with mustard seed.

Margie wrinkled her face as her mother held out the cup to her. "What is it?"

"Tea with mustard seeds. Please, try to drink it. The caffeine in the tea will be good for you, and the ground mustard seed should work quickly to help you breathe better."

Margie nodded her head, leaned in, and took several gulps of the tea. As her head rested back against the pillows, Pearl watched and waited, prompting Margie to drink more.

Victor and Henry once more appeared at the door.

"Your sister's going to be okay. Run along so you're not late for school."

Pearl listened for the banging of the door and then lay down next to her daughter. Her hand shook as she brushed her daughter's dark bangs from her forehead and leaned in close. Already, the color was returning to Margie's lips and her breaths came less burdened, almost normal, but Pearl suspected this would not be an isolated incident. Pearl clutched the first-aid book to her chest. The dampness from the deep woods along with the wood stove for heat, likely triggered her daughter's attack. For a moment, she wished they were back in Kirkland, with oil heat and fewer trees to cause breathing problems. Pearl stayed next to her daughter. Though Margie dozed off, Pearl was reluctant to leave her side, fearful her daughter's breathing could turn labored again. She thought about her dream to help save lives as a nurse. Her actions today, had likely done just that.

Chapter Forty-Seven

1923 – Promise of Marriage

With the school year over and at Jacob's urging, Edna left her tiny house in Monohon, and returned to Seattle for the summer. She telephoned Jacob as soon as she was home, and they arranged a date. The following evening the doorbell chimed. Edna's chest tightened. She rushed to the mirror to check her makeup one last time.

"You're acting like a silly schoolgirl." Her mother's wrinkled nose and sharp words relayed her displeasure.

"I know. I haven't seen Jacob in so long. I can't help but feel jumpy."

"Gracious. I'll answer it." Mother headed for the door.

"No. Please. I'll get it." Edna flew past her mother before the bell rang a second time.

From the front stoop, Edna was taken by the scent of Jacob's musky cologne. He had not worn cologne for her previously. Dressed more casually than he'd been on earlier dates, he wore pleated trousers with wide cuffs and a pullover brown knit vest with no jacket. She leaned in to inhale the earthy scent. "Where are we going?"

Playing coy as Jacob often did, he ignored her. He stepped inside. Jacob shook her father's hand. "I promise to have her home by midnight if that's agreeable to you?"

Papa pulled his watch out. "I appreciate your respect. Midnight is fine."

Jacob thanked him and led Edna to his car.

"You didn't tell me where we're going."

Jacob jabbed the ignition button and concentrated on the road. "You'll have to wait and see."

Edna smoothed her new red crepe dress and pondered the numerous possibilities for nightlife the city offered.

"I love your dress. It's more salacious than what I've seen you in before. Did you buy it for someone else?"

Edna narrowed her gaze. She'd never given him reason to suspect she was interested in anyone else. "My mother's a dressmaker. She has to be up to date on the modern attitudes and latest fashion trends. She made this for me." Edna wrapped her shawl tighter around her to conceal it from his leering eyes.

Jacob pulled the car into a gravel lot on the corner of Third and Pine. Her eyes immediately caught the neon sign from the new dancing academy, Dehoney's. She'd written to Jacob about the popular dance club after Helen visited it before her move. Delighted by Jacob's effort to please her, Edna checked her felt cloche atop her new shorter hair. She opened her beaded clutch, freshened her lips, and patted on an extra measure of rouge. Feeling Jacob's eyes on her, Edna licked her scarlet lips in a suggestive flirt. Perhaps he was more romantic than she had credited him with.

"A few friends from the base are going to join us here with their dates. I hope that's okay?"

Her stomach clenched. Their first date in six months and he invited his army buddies. Through a painted-on ruby-red smile, she responded, "Of course."

Though alcohol was still outlawed, Edna guessed Jacob had a hip flask underneath his jacket, and many of his buddies likewise would have a nip hidden somewhere. She took Jacob's arm as they entered through the heavy oak doors of the big brick hall. Crystal chandeliers hung from high ceilings gilded with gold. Glass prisms by the hundreds reflected tiny rainbows of light across the large dance floor, perfect for dancing. A five-piece jazz band performed from the wooden stage in the front of the massive hall. If her parents had seen the dance moves of women shimmying around the marble floor and loitering along the walls blowing airy rings into the air with fags, they would have considered Dehoney's obscene and the women loose and lewd. But Edna couldn't wait to get out on the spacious oak-planked wooden dance floor and blend into the scandalous crowd of flappers.

_ine on." She tugged at Jacob's arm, prodding him out to the center of the crowd, knowing he much preferred to sit back and listen and watch. "You didn't bring me here to sit on the sidelines."

Though Jacob sighed loudly, his eyes gave away his desire to see her shake and wiggle with the new dance moves. He led her to the dance floor to join the others in dancing to all the latest tunes, including "Barney Google," a tune taken from the comic strip in the newspaper. The horns blared and Jacob tried his best to step and tap in time to the foxtrot, two-step, and waltz. Edna laughed, watching his arms swing to the music. The fringe on her dress swayed in time to the fast-hopping Charleston. In college, Edna preferred to keep her dance card full. She didn't like the idea of dancing with only one gentleman during the dances in Ellensburg, but tonight her brain turned topsy-turvy. As other couples moved on and off the dance floor, Edna was fascinated by the passion that seemed to pass like an electrical charge between them with each nuzzle or flirty look. She turned to look at her beau once again, wondering if what she felt was truly love. As Jacob leaned in, Edna anticipated a tender kiss. Instead, Jacob pulled his flask from his pocket. "Do you want a bit of refreshment?"

The sparks of fiery emotion ceased, replaced by a spark of anger. Jacob persisted in his request even though he knew Edna didn't much favor the taste of alcohol. Her eyes darted around the room. Her ire boiled at the sight of a couple of Jacob's buddies watching, awaiting her reaction. He seemed to take pleasure in putting her on the spot in front of the group they were with. Not wanting to appease them, and not wishing to cause a scene, Edna smiled sweetly and went along with his distasteful request. She glared at Jacob and took a gulp. Inside she fumed like a newly stoked fire as her cheeks and forehead flushed, warmed by the hours of dancing. She wiped her hand across her forehead. She wished she'd shared her dance card with several other eligible men who had caught her eye and asked her to dance.

Still fuming, she excused herself to powder her nose. She removed the rhinestone slides from her hair and finger-combed her loose waves away from her head before replacing the hair accessories. A glance in the mirror revealed her flushed skin and exposed her anger. She splashed her face with water. The coolness squelched her burning cheeks, but not the fire seething inside at the disrespect she'd taken from Jacob. She patted her face dry, then pulled out her small compact and freshened her face with fresh foundation. Next, she slipped off her shoes. Even her feet burned from overuse. She massaged them, taking her time, intentionally forcing Jacob to wait on her. After a couple minutes of cool and calm, Edna returned the shoes to her feet, flung her shoulders back, and marched out with dignity.

As Edna strode back to the dance floor, she glanced around to locate Jacob. She spied him at the bar next to a bleached blonde and narrowed her eyes. At the bar, she announced her arrival with a lady-like cough and sidled next to her date. Draping her arm around his shoulder, she displayed her long elegant fingers with fiery-red polish. Her eyes glowed like hot embers; she hoped Jacob felt their burn.

The girl, a bit older than Edna, with a low scooped neckline, jiggled her bosom for Edna's benefit. With a breathy voice, she batted her thick painted lashes, tipped her chin to Edna, and pulled a drag from a cigarette she held with a long, gold-tipped cigarette holder. The tip of the cigarette glowed reddish-orange in the semi lit room. "Sorry, sweetie, I'm sure you don't object to me chatting with your handsome man, do you?"

Edna turned her gaze to Jacob. Was this why he had taken to wearing cologne? Is this why he asked about her seeing other men? Was he seeing other women or interested in pursuing other women in her absence? She turned away from the puff of smoke and coughed before refocusing her eyes on her target. Her voice dripped with sarcasm thick as honey. "Not at all; I simply adore your lipstick." Edna cocked her head and leaned in speaking loud enough for the girl and Jacob to hear. "Tell me, dear, is that the color all the women wear, who get paid to entertain lonely men?" Pleased with her calm but biting retort, Edna stared at the woman who glowered before she broke eye contact.

The woman's cheeks turned even brighter than the shocking color of carnival fairy floss. The blonde flung back her long tresses. "What? How dare you." She stomped away.

Jacob snickered. His smirk relayed his pleasure in their exchange. "Don't tell me you're jealous."

"Jealous? Over a cheap tramp who was only using you to buy her a Schlitz? I'd like to go home now."

"C'mon, Edna, don't be such a stick-in-the-mud. How about I get us each a near beer? No need to rush out. We were simply talking."

Edna pursed her lips. "You're always trying to manipulate me and make me out to be the person who doesn't enjoy having fun."

"Fine. It's not like I'm having fun anyway." Jacob relented, reached inside his jacket, and threw back a swig from his illegal flask. He tapped the bottom of the empty cannister to make a point and stomped toward the door. "Let's go then."

With the abrupt change in Jacob's attitude, the thrill of the evening drained away, leaving it as empty as Jacob's flask. The warm June night air did little to melt the frigid atmosphere of the car as they drove back home in a wintery silence.

♪ ♪ ♪

The following day Jacob pleaded for forgiveness. "I only have two more days before I have to return to the base. I don't want to leave with you angry at me. You know you're the only one I care about." Jacob cast his eyes downward, his brows knitted.

Edna sensed his mind was on something else. She feared for what it might be as she felt her breath catch. "What's wrong?"

He dropped to one knee and gazed at her. "Marry me, I beg you." His cobalt eyes caught the reflection of the porch light.

Edna recalled the strong attraction she had experienced the night they met. She recalled being swept away by his charisma. All the frigid friction of the past evening thawed. Edna opened her mouth to speak, but her tongue seized. Her emotions churned, a melding of lust and anger. How was it possible for a woman to love a man, truly love him, if she was shamed by his tendency to disparage others?

"Please, Edna. You know I love you and I know you love me. Say you'll marry me."

Seeing Jacob humbled at her feet, Edna weighed the heavy decision. She cared for him, but the uncertainty ate at her like moths on aging fabric. The uncertainty not of Jacob's love but of her own. At twenty-one years old, she at one time would have been considered a spinster, an old maid. But these were modern times; women were freer to be who and what they wanted without regard to society's impositions. Could she be certain her feelings were strong enough? She still had other suitors who cared for her. Cliff had recently written to her. He was the kind of man who would always respect her, but they were friends. Any romantic gestures had been mere flirtations. She picked her words as carefully as one might choose where to step on thin ice.

"I can't get married and still continue to teach."

His hands outstretched; Jacob softened his voice. "We don't have to get married right away. I'll wait. Just promise me—when you're ready to settle down, you'll chose me."

Without further consideration, and uncertain from where her words came, her declaration poured out. "I promise. Someday."

No longer narrow and concerned, Jacob's eyes flickered with joy. He pushed off his bent knee and leaned over Edna slowly drawing her lips to his. Prickles of excitement danced like delicate raindrops over her body. Her doubts vanished. She was safe and secure in her beau's strong arms.

Chapter Forty-Eight

1923 – An Old Beau

For days, a haze of uncertainty hung like low clouds over Edna. She wished she hadn't been so quick to share the news with her parents about the proposal, but living in their home, she couldn't keep the secret of Jacob's proclamation. While her mother couldn't wait to share the news with Marie, her father peppered her with questions.

"Your whole life, you've dreamed of becoming a teacher. You're willing to give all that up for a man who plans on staying in the army?

"Please, Papa. Jacob knows I want to teach a few more years."

"Well, that's a relief. I hope you're not going to sit around here all summer pining over him when he's not around."

"Papa, that's one of the reasons I became a teacher. I work long hours for nine months. I'm entitled to my time off, but don't worry. I'm going to find a temporary position. I need to at least earn enough money to go visit Helen and her husband before I return to school in September."

By the following week, she found a position at the Fremont Branch Library. She wrote to Helen and confirmed the last week of August for her much-needed getaway.

Dear Helen,

I am thrilled you have invited me to spend time with you and Bill, this summer. Can you believe it's been almost an entire year since your wedding and since I last saw you? I have secured a temporary position at the local library, cleaning and sorting books. The work is not challenging but I will earn $17.65 for seven days of work and have agreed to stay on if they have other tasks. It would be nice to save a few extra dollars for spending

money for next fall. I hope the end of August agrees with your
schedule. I can't wait to spend a week in your lovely home and
catch up.
Your dear friend,
Edna

At the end of August, Jacob arranged three days off to spend time
with Edna before she left for eastern Washington. They caught a
trolley downtown and strolled along the waterfront, starting at
Colman Dock on Pier 52. Invigorated by the fresh breeze, Edna gazed
across the water and pointed to the mass of land on the other side.
"When I moved from Port Orchard, I never imagined feeling so
comfortable anywhere else. But I've learned to adapt to Seattle and
now to the small town of Monohon."

"Then you wouldn't mind moving across the country if the army
transfers me again?"

Edna's mood changed. "Are you being transferred? You just
returned."

"Not right now, but it's always a possibility with being in the
service. I want to know what you would think. You know, being
married to a soldier who has no control over where he might be asked
to go."

Edna squeezed his hand and told him she would follow him
anywhere. "Let's not talk about that right now. I want to teach for a
few more years before we talk of marriage."

As they stood on the dock, Jacob seemed distracted.

She wondered where his mind was. A steamer moored and
passengers filed off. Many of them carried bags of produce or bundles
of flowers. Edna watched them head south and guessed they were
headed to the newly expanded Pike Place Market to sell their wares.

"Let's eat at the public market." Edna tugged Jacob from his
contemplation. They followed the crowd traveling south along the
waterfront. "Mama say's all the stalls have moved inside and there's
a new section called the Sanitary Market for delicatessens,
restaurants, bakeries, and butchers."

"Sounds perfect. I've been hankering for oysters for a while. I'm
ready for a real meal after eating so much rationed foods. Few of
which tasted decent."

Edna turned up her nose. "I don't care for oysters, but I can't wait to have the fresh Dungeness crab caught right here in Puget Sound."

The menu posted outside The Athenian Seafood Restaurant met with their approval, and right away they were led to their seats. The aroma inside the cozy place mirrored the smells of the sound—fishy, salty, and tangy. Edna's mouth watered at the plates of food carried past as they awaited their courses. Tasting the hint of sherry added to her Crab Newburg over toast, Edna declared she'd never eaten anything so amazing in her life. After Jacob pressured her, Edna tasted his Oysters Rockefeller. It didn't taste nearly as disagreeable as she thought it might, but she was glad to finish off her meal with the last bites of the sweet crab.

Jacob paid the tab and proceeded up Pike Street.

"Where are we going?"

Jacob's eyes smiled with mystery as he continued up the hill before turning right once they reached Third Avenue. He slowed his pace when they reached Third and Union, and Edna found herself looking in through the plate-glass window of Weisfield and Goldberg Jewelers. "I've received the official notice. I'm being transferred back to Washington. I'm going to be taking a position with the new veteran's hospital being built at American Lake. We can get married now."

She shook her head. "No. I told you before. I want to teach a few years and married women are not allowed to teach."

"We can at least look at rings so I know what you like."

Edna couldn't keep from staring at the neat rows of rings and necklaces of gold and platinum embedded with diamonds and semiprecious stones. Ever since her short stint at Fox's Jewelers, she had known exactly the type of ring she wanted. Hesitant at first, Edna acquiesced with a sparkle in her eyes equal to the diamonds on display. "Okay. We can look, but promise you won't insist on buying one today. I don't want to be seen with a ring. It will announce our engagement and I'm certain the school district will not look favorably upon my engagement. They could terminate my contract."

Two days later, Edna packed her bag for her visit to Helen's house in Alpine on the shores of Lake Cavanaugh at the base of the Cascade Mountains. Jacob drove her to Union Station. An uneasy silence existed between them after she had refused to let him buy an engagement ring.

The train whistle blew, warning its upcoming departure, but Edna stood next to Jacob as the last passengers embarked. Smoke billowed from the stack wrapping her in a shroud. The final call came. "All aboard." Jacob reached out and embraced her. They embraced, not like lovers, but more like a brother and sister might. Edna fought back the burning sensation behind her eyes. She ached for a deeper more meaningful embrace. She ached for the taste of his lips against hers but turned away and boarded the train.

Four hours later, the engine slowed and a softer whistle moaned the train's arrival into the station in Skykomish. Edna stepped off the Pullman car. A momentary fear gripped her as she looked around and didn't catch sight of Helen. She hoped her friend had understood the arrival information. Then, from across the platform, Edna heard her name called. She waved an acknowledgment and retrieved her bag from the train. Her tension eased as she maneuvered through the passengers both coming and going with a sigh of relief.

Helen's husband, Bill hugged her. "How nice to see you, Edna. Helen is so looking forward to your visit."

Bill's welcome was so warm and sincere. Edna felt a twinge of envy wishing Jacob were as friendly and outgoing as Bill. She hoped Helen realized how lucky she was to have him.

Bill took Edna's bag from her and proceeded away from the station toward his automobile. "We've made plans for dinner tonight at Luigi's; I hope you like pasta, and I hope you won't care we invited Cliff to join us. Helen thought you wouldn't mind since you've all been friends for several years."

Stunned by the prospect of seeing an old classmate, Edna didn't know what to say. She hadn't seen Cliff since high school though they exchanged letters and Christmas postcards. "Where does he live now?"

"Not too far from here, east of Mount. Vernon."

"It's fine." She thought about her old friend and couldn't hold back the tickle of joy budding inside. On the drive to Helen's home, Edna realized she should have informed her friend she was engaged. But after all, there could be no harm with an innocent dinner with an old friend.

Over dinner Cliff became quite chummy. "What have you been up to, my dear friend?" He casually stretched and draped his arm around Edna's shoulder. Flattered by his playfulness, Edna blushed and played along. She licked her lips, refreshing the shine on the bright red lipstick. The expression in Cliff's eyes told her she'd succeeded in her flirtatious game at which she was rather good. Though flirting infuriated Jacob, Edna didn't know why it should. He didn't seem to mind when beautiful women came on to him. She tingled all over and giggled as Cliff nuzzled her neck.

Edna looked at her left hand, the ring finger still bare and decided to play along. "I graduated from the normal school in Ellensburg. I'm an elementary school teacher at a small school outside of Issaquah in the town of Monohon."

"I knew you would become a teacher like you always wanted.

Seeing the genuine happiness in Cliff's eyes, Edna once again contemplated her engagement and wondered if she could adjust to being the wife to a man in the military. After dinner, Cliff said goodbye at Helen and Bill's door. A peck on the cheek, nothing really, though Edna had to admit she enjoyed the attention. Inside, she closed her eyes and inhaled the lingering woodsy scent of Cliff's cologne. She opened her eyes as the scent triggered guilt at the memory of Jacob's cologne.

Helen woke her in the morning with the news Cliff had come by earlier to see her. "He wants to take you into town for the barn dance tonight." Helen eyed Edna, waiting for a response. "So? Is the old spark of romance returning?"

"You know we've never had that kind of relationship." Edna returned the smile but failed to mention her engagement. Jacob knew she was going to go out with others. There was no harm in seeing her old friend again. Though Jacob was the jealous type, he wasn't around, and he didn't care much for dancing while Cliff always enjoyed the dance floor. Cliff possessed some skill with the latest dance moves like the jitterbug. Besides they were merely friends.

As always, Cliff was noble when he came to take her to the dance. Edna glanced over her shoulder with one final mock glower that Helen and Bill weren't joining them. As the band started its swing-style rhythm, Cliff wrapped his arm around her waist and they took to the dance floor. They stepped in time to the foxtrot, and the floral arrangements on stage stirred her memory of the sweet scent of lavender and carnations from the wrist corsage Cliff brought her the night of their eighth-grade dance. She still had the corsage in a green velvet-covered-keepsake box stashed deep in her hope chest. As Cliff drew her close, Edna wondered, though, what Jacob would think if he could see how other men appreciated her and wanted to be with her. She sensed the eyes of other men upon her. Men had always lined up to dance with her. Tonight, she'd dance only with Cliff, one last time. She knew she had to be honest with him and tell him about Jacob.

Edna returned to Helen's at two o'clock in the morning, shocked to see Helen still awake, waiting for her. "You know he cares for you?"

Edna tipped her head and studied her friend "What are you talking about?"

"Cliff. He told me he had feelings for you."

"That's ridiculous, Helen. He can't have feelings for me. We've always been just friends. Besides, I haven't told you, but I'm promised to Jacob Pearson."

Helen hands flew up in disbelief. "Engaged? To Jacob?"

Helen's loud dramatic sigh told Edna she did not approve. She shook her head and reached for Edna's left hand. "I don't see a ring."

Edna's face warmed. Helen was a dear friend, but Edna did not want to explain her situation to her friend. "You know married women aren't allowed to teach. We've decided to wait with a ring so it doesn't interfere with my position. Jacob loves me. I know you don't approve, but he's smart and dashing."

Helen's words softened. She reached out to embrace Edna. "Congratulations, I wish you well, but you had better tell Cliff of your engagement and stop leading him on before you hurt him."

"I will. I would never hurt Cliff. I didn't know he cared for me that way." Edna said good night to Helen and dragged herself to the small settee, her sleeping space during her stay. She sank onto the cushioned seat and shook her head. Poor Cliff. Regret pierced her heart. She had no idea his feelings were true. He didn't know about Jacob and straight away she wished she had shared her feelings for him and told him of her engagement.

Helen woke Edna early and handed her a letter. "This was on the front porch. It's for you."

Edna pushed her sheet and blanket aside and sat. She took the large envelope, too bulky to be a single-sheet letter. Exhaling, she slid her finger under the flap of the sealed envelope and poured the contents onto her lap. She unfolded the top piece of paper and read. "It's from Cliff. He says he knows I don't care for him in the same way he cares for me. He sensed it last evening." She flipped through the photos and cards she'd mailed to him over the years, now dumped on her lap. At the realization of the depth of Cliff's affection for her, a lump formed in her throat almost daring the words to come out. "Yes, he does love me." As she finished reading his goodbye letter, Edna wept at the thought of their friendship and affection coming to an end. He wrote with such romantic and flowery language. Edna sat on Helen's sofa and cried.

Chapter Forty-Nine

1924 – Engaged

Jacob's tolerance was waning by the end of Edna's second year of teaching. He wrote urging her to consider leaving her teaching position at Monohon and find a teaching job closer to his post at Camp Lewis where he was helping to oversee the construction of a new veteran's hospital built by the War Department at American Lake. "We've been seeing each other for three and a half years. I moved back here to be closer to you. It's time you prove you're committed to our relationship; otherwise, maybe we should go our separate ways."

Deep down, Edna knew he was right. Jacob had been patient with her desire to establish her career. If she truly cared for him, she needed to make some concessions. Edna prepared a letter detailing her tasks and teaching methods and mailed it to a half-dozen schools throughout south Seattle and Tacoma.

With reluctance, Edna shared her decision with Pearl. "I've written to Jacob. I informed him of my intention to look for an open teaching position in Seattle or Tacoma. I told him I would not give notice at Monohon unless I have a new offer before the coming school year."

Pearl shook her head. "I knew it was only a matter of time. You can't blame him. But I'm going to miss you."

Within the month, Edna received a response from McKinley Hill elementary school in Tacoma. The school was seeking a new second-grade teacher and she was advised to call and arrange an immediate interview. A sudden pang of doubt surfaced. A move to Tacoma meant Pearl and her niece and nephews would no longer be part of her daily life. For two years Pearl had been her strongest confidant and Stanley was always available to help unstick windows, mend loose stair boards, or deliver another load of firewood. A move to Tacoma meant starting over. Her parents wouldn't be far, probably less than an hour, and she guessed Jacob would visit as many chances as possible, but the uncertainty knotted her stomach.

Two weeks later, with a job secured for the coming year, Edna gave her notice at Monohon School and mentally prepared to leave her first home. Another fear gripped her. She'd need to find a place to live. Without the free housing provided by Monohon, she'd have the additional expense of rent, and she had no idea what rental units might cost. Luckily the contract with the Tacoma School District paid $935 for the term of the contract, a boost of almost $300 for the year. If she could find a place for twenty-five dollars a month, she'd break even. The calculation wasn't optimistic.

Saying goodbye to her students brought more emotion than she predicted. Many of them made farewell cards wishing her well. Stanley and Pearl made her a lunch for the train ride and drove her to the train depot in Issaquah.

At the station, a middle-aged, gray-suited porter appeared. "Help with your baggage, Miss?"

Edna looked down at the old brown leather trunk weighing around forty pounds. She nodded and reached into her handbag for a quarter. He loaded the trunk and the large suitcase onto a cart and pushed it toward the waiting train.

Edna hugged her sister goodbye. The speedy tears of her childhood returned. "I can't imagine how I could have survived these past two years without you."

Stanley kissed Edna on the cheek and said farewell. Her heart heavy, Edna kissed the children, thanked Stanley, and with drooped shoulders turned to board the Northern Pacific for Seattle for a quick overnight with her parents before she settled into her new apartment in Tacoma.

The next morning, her father loaded her belongings into the back of his Ford. Edna squeezed in next to the trunk and a box of miscellaneous kitchenware her mother scrounged together for her.

As the car zipped down Highway 1 toward Tacoma, the City of Destiny, her mother prodded Edna for information. "Do you know anything about your new apartment?"

"Jacob found the place for me. It's only four blocks from the school. An army buddy knows someone in the same apartment complex. He says it's a fairly new place and the rent is only twenty-two dollars a month and includes the water and heat."

Papa grunted. "As long as you know how to find it."

"I have the address, and I think I'll remember how to get to my new school. It shouldn't be too difficult to find from there."

"You're sure it's furnished?"

"Jacob told me it has a bed and bureau and a small kitchenette set, along with a sofa. I'm not sure what else."

Papa shook his head. "Pretty foolhardy to agree to a place you haven't seen."

Mama patted her father's leg. "I'm sure it will be fine. We have an extra end table for her to use and the chair that Uncle Leland said he'd get delivered when he can borrow a truck."

As Highway 1 became Pacific Highway, Papa followed the road southwest, past Federal Way and into Fife. He looked around. "I need you to help me out here, Edna, I'm not familiar with the roads this far south."

Edna sat forward and looked out the front window. "It's not too much farther. You should see a road sign for McKinley Avenue, turn there. I can show you my new school and from there we can look for the Park Street Apartments."

Spying the familiar route, Edna told her father to take the next turn. Within a few blocks she pointed to a three-story brick building. "There it is. That's McKinley Elementary School."

"Gracious." Her mother brought her hand to her cheek. "It's hard to imagine all that space for just the elementary grades."

"Well, it's not just for classrooms. There are offices, a science laboratory, an indoor gymnasium, and in the basement, a lunchroom, so the students don't have to eat at their desks."

"Sure is different from where you attended school."

Edna nodded "It's also going to be a lot different from where I taught for the past two years, but it's a good move. I can't wait to not only have students to talk with all day, but peers with whom I can share my experiences as well. Plus, I have a new city to explore."

Two days after the move, Jacob drove to Tacoma. With the new apartment only half an hour from Camp Lewis, Edna looked forward to more frequent visits.

"You might want to grab a cardigan; I want to show you the waterfront. It's a lot different from the waterfront in Seattle."

They motored north along Pacific Avenue, and within minutes, they were driving along a narrow arm of water.

From the car window, Jacob pointed out the various points of interest. "This is called the City Waterway. It leads out to Commencement Bay."

At the intersection of Dock Street, in the train yard of the Northern Pacific Railroad, a small shanty town marred the beauty of the scenic waterway. Shacks, built from scrap lumber and old sheet metal most likely gathered from the Port of Tacoma and the shipbuilding facilities across the inlet, sprouted like unsightly weeds in a manicured lawn. "That's the Port of Tacoma over there. One of the major shipping ports in the Pacific Northwest."

A scrawny stray dog sniffed around a pile of debris looking for scraps. Several young children hooted as they ran around and played amid the corrugated metal and broken boards. Edna shuddered, wondering if these young kids attended school and if any would be in her class. Farther down, Jacob parked the car near the Eleventh Street Bridge and they climbed out. Edna shivered inside her wool jacket as the wind blew off the water on the west side of the bay, assailing her with the odor of seaweed and fish from the nearby fishing vessels.

Jacob pointed to a boathouse. "That's the Foss Launch and Tug Company." Docks jutted out into the inlet where gulls sat atop white and green tugboats lettered with the names Foss across the bow of one, and Foss 6 on the other. Jacob turned and pointed toward the bluff west of the waterway.

Edna followed his gaze. She gaped at the grandest structure she'd ever seen, an enormous gray stone building on a high bluff overlooking Commencement Bay. "What is that?"

"The Tacoma Hotel. What would you say to spending a night there?"

Edna tipped her head and sighed at the fairy-tale-like building with cone-shaped turrets that took up an entire city block. "I bet it's expensive."

A wink and a shrug accompanied Jacob's response. "I thought maybe we could spend our wedding night there. What do you think?"

Since their unplanned visit to Weisfield's Jewelers, Edna had managed to avoid the conversation of marriage by quoting the verbiage from her teaching contract. "You know the rule. I agree the idea is archaic, and I'm sure it's only a matter of time before schools loosen the restriction."

Deep down Edna didn't believe her own words. Thus far, neither the school nor the state school superintendent gave any indication of changing their position regarding married women and teaching. On the contrary, Edna was certain the superintendent had made an extra effort to check her left hand on the two occasions he stopped by her school in Monohan. Now that Jacob's position as a supply specialist at the Veteran's Hospital was secure, and she was beginning her third year of teaching, Edna knew she could not put Jacob off for much longer.

Jacob looked away from her, but not before Edna noticed the disappointment in his eyes from her lack of enthusiasm.

He looked down and mumbled barely loud enough for her to hear. "I'm not going to wait much longer."

When school let out for Christmas break, Edna's heart fluttered in anticipation. She couldn't wait to see Jacob despite his insistence they spend Christmas Day with his brother and parents, in Renton.

"My mother keeps reminding me it's not right for us to spend the day apart since we're engaged."

"We're not engaged officially. Doesn't she know I don't even have a ring yet?"

"You know mothers. It doesn't matter to her. She just wants you to think of her as family now. I've already told her we'd both be there Christmas Day. Ivan's looking forward to seeing you again."

Edna clutched her forehead. She wished Jacob hadn't mentioned Ivan. She imagined the kidding Jacob must be facing with his younger brother married while he remained single.

"But I've never spent a Christmas Day away from my family in my life." Edna's head clouded with the realization of how much marriage would complicate her life. She was no longer a child. At nearly twenty-three years old, she couldn't expect to spend every Christmas of her entire life with her parents. After Pearl married, she and Stanley managed to spend different holidays with both sides of their families. Pearl had called to say she would be spending the day in Preston with Stanley's parents and Uncle Frederick. Maybe it was time for Edna to look ahead instead of backward.

Thursday at two o'clock, Jacob escorted Edna to his car for their evening at his parent's home.

Jacob seemed moody and she tried to ease into a conversation. "You haven't told me much about your new job."

Jacob shook his head and chuckled, immediately breaking the tension. "For a neurological psychiatric hospital, it's not bad. One of the goals is to make the facility as self-sufficient as possible. There's a large chicken coop, so we get fresh eggs daily. They've already planted an orchard with apples, pears, and peaches. I'm not sure how much land is set aside for pasture but there's a hundred sheep. In the spring they will begin planting an extensive vegetable garden. The patients who are well enough to help will get their exercise, and the hospital utilizes the food the place produces, except for some of the sheep meat which we trade for beef with Western State Hospital."

Edna relaxed. She admired Jacob's ability to take a less than favorable situation and put a positive spin on it.

"The new job is keeping me busy. So much to do ordering supplies for the new veteran's hospital. It's a tough environment, though, caring for the fifty veterans that were transferred from Western State Psychiatric Hospital."

"Do you interact with them much?"

"Not really, but sometimes I have a chance to stop and chat awhile. I can relate to the personal hell these men suffered through that put them in such a facility. I hope someday some of the men improve and are able to return to their families."

Edna empathized with Jacob's role. "I know it's not the same, but a few children in my school need extra help and understanding as they come from less well-to-do backgrounds. I admire you for trying to help them."

Jacob shook his head and grinned. "You never know what you're going to learn from these guys. Several have told me how they get a huge kick out of sitting outside and watching the crows."

Tipping her head in confusion, Edna looked at Jacob. "Crows?"

"Yeah. I guess the landscaper planted a bunch of mulberry trees. The birds like to eat the overripe berries and they get drunk. I guess one bird was so drunk it could flap only one wing at a time. When it finally got airborne it crashed into the roof and slid down, only to get caught on a gutter."

Edna laughed. "I know all about birds and fermented berries. Not just crows. I understand it can be quite a sight."

"In the spring, crow watching is now a favorite pastime for many of the patients."

Edna realized she hadn't seen Jacob so relaxed and carefree for a long time. He was clearly content with his new position, even excited. She breathed easier and looked forward to the evening with his family and seeing Ivan and getting to know Ivan's wife, Norma, a little better. Before long, Edna spied the house she'd first seen three-and-a-half years earlier. When she made the bold unplanned trip to visit Ivan, she never imagined it would lead to a relationship with his brother. After opening her car door, Jacob escorted her up the front porch. A swag of cedar boughs adorned with a red bow, welcomed them from the front door.

Inside, the brightly lit home, Edna inhaled warmth and a melding of pleasant aromas. Sprigs of holly with white ribbon wrapped the stair rail. In the background, "Silent Night" played on a Victrola.

"Welcome, dear. It's so kind of you to join us. It's been so long since we've seen you." Like a gust of wind, Jacob's mother swept into the room. She draped her arm across Edna's shoulders and steered her away from Jacob and into the kitchen. "Let me get you a cup of eggnog, and we can sit down for some lady talk." She grabbed a ladle and nodded toward a small bottle of brandy. "I know it's not legal, but Ivan is in retail beverage distribution and on occasion he nabs a bottle of rum or brandy. Should I add a tad to your drink?"

"Sure. That would be nice, thank you."

After handing Edna a china cup, Mrs. Pearson patted a kitchen chair. "Come, sit. Have a piece of divinity." She pushed a small saucer with the same floral pattern as the cup, in front of Edna.

Edna took a bite. "I appreciate you letting me join your family for Christmas, Mrs. Pearson."

"Please, we're nearly family. Call me, Yvette. I hope you don't mind, but I must ask." Yvette lowered her voice and glanced toward the living room. "Are you leading my son on?"

The abrupt shift from divinity sweetness to sour milk, caught Edna unaware of what Jacob had told her. "N-no." Edna stammered. "Not at all."

Yvette leaned across the table and took Edna's left hand in hers. "Then why aren't you wearing his ring yet?"

Pulling her hand back, Edna bit her tongue. The last thing she wanted to do was create a scene on Christmas Day at her soon-to-be in-laws' house. "I'm sure Jacob told you, I'm a teacher, and the law is very clear. Married women are forbidden to teach."

Edna's future mother-in-law looked as if she'd swallowed a sip of brandy straight up. "I know all that, but the real question is why do you even want to teach? You're of the age where you should be married and having little ones. Jacob is perfectly capable of supporting you without you having to work."

The discomfort Edna felt the first time she'd been in this house returned. Once more she wondered if this was a setup. She couldn't believe how old-fashioned Jacob's mother was. She forced a gracious smile but vowed she would not give in to outside pressure to expedite any wedding. Though she was in serious need of more eggnog and brandy, Edna excused herself to use the powder room. She had to decompress and signal Jacob to come rescue her.

♪ ♪ ♪

Pushing away the outdated opinion of a woman's place as a homemaker, Edna assisted with the dinner preparations. A knock at the door sent Yvette scurrying to greet Ivan and Norma. Ivan winked when he saw Edna. An irritated flush burned her cheeks. She wished Ivan wasn't coming toward her for a welcoming hug while at the same time Yvette gushed over Norma welcoming her new "daughter" in a less than subtle voice. One more jab within hearing range, for Edna's benefit. Edna wanted to disappear, but soldiered through and joined Norma and the brothers in the living room while Yvette disappeared, much to Edna's delight, back into her kitchen.

Despite the overbearing hostess and Ivan's cockiness, Edna warmed to the family during a dinner of traditional ham, yams, canned green beans, and baking powder biscuits as good as Edna's mothers.

"I hope you like to cook. Poor Jacob has eaten enough army rations in his life and when he's home he loves his mother's cooking. Some women are so secretive with their recipes. Not me. I'm more than happy to share any of my recipes or cooking tips with you."

Breathe, Edna recited to herself. How much more uncomfortable could the evening get?

When the table was cleared, Edna hoped Jacob would make an excuse to duck out from the rest of the evening's festivities, but instead he led her into the living room. "Time to open presents."

After maintaining her composure all night, Edna's jaw stiffened. She remembered a line from college course on literature and the study of language. She remembered the author, but not the book's title. Nietzsche had written, "If looks could kill, we would long ago have been done for."

"Why didn't you tell me?" She gritted her teeth though her whisper. "I didn't bring my gift for you and I don't have anything for your parents."

Jacob's eyes sparkled with mischief. "That's okay, but I have something for you and I want to give it to you tonight." He led her to the sofa facing the tree adorned with gold bows, strings of small gold balls and ruby cranberries. The tree was elegant but lacked the homey touches she'd grown accustomed to in her family.

Yvette rushed in to take a nearby seat as an uneasy feeling shrouded her.

"Ivan, Dad, please gather round."

Edna's chest pounded as Jacob turned to face her. He struggled to reach deep into his pocket, then withdrew a small red-leather jewelry box and held it out.

Edna read the gold lettering from the Weisfield and Goldberg across the top of the box. Her hands reflexively covered her mouth.

Jacob flipped the top open, revealing a simple band with a modest round diamond. He removed the ring and held it out. "I hope

I remembered correctly which ring you liked. It's close to a half-carat, Art-Deco style, set in white gold."

Edna giggled at Jacob's sale pitch, which almost mirrored the clerk at the store a year ago. She held her left hand out to receive the ring. "It's beautiful."

She wouldn't crush this moment. She would accept the ring, but remove it while teaching. No need to let the school know of her plans. She promised herself she had worked too hard and desired to teach another year before she married.

Jacob slipped the ring onto her ring finger. Her trepidation of the day vanished. Cheers arose from Jacob's family and his mother jumped from her chair announcing how excited she was for the summer wedding. Jacob took his cue from his bride-to-be. "Mother, it's our decision. We don't need any pressure from you."

Edna squeezed Jacob's hand. Her doubts faded. She couldn't wait to tell her parents. Mother would be giddy, especially since her firstborn daughter married in such a quick secretive ceremony under unfavorable conditions. She'd insist upon a large formal wedding, perhaps even in the Methodist church. Edna mulled over the possibility. She wasn't sure what Jacob would think of a church wedding, but it didn't matter. She would gladly marry in the church to make her parents happy. She owed them that much. After all her parent's had endured, all Edna wanted was to make them happy.

Chapter Fifty

1925 – Marriage

When school started again after the winter break, Edna tucked the satin-lined box holding her engagement ring in a bureau drawer. Marriage was against the rules, but the teaching contract didn't say anything about being engaged. Still, it was knowledge the school principal could use against her in extending her teaching contract for another year. Everything within her wanted to proclaim her news, but she couldn't trust the gossip mill. It was still early in the school year. She had worked too hard and her parents had sacrificed too much for her to risk being terminated.

The week before spring break, as the final bell rang, Edna opened the door to dismiss the class. Unannounced, Jacob stood in the hallway. He jumped out of the way as the children rushed by nearly running into him. He looked around, then took her hands and leaned in to kiss her. Edna waited for his lips to meet hers, but when she opened her eyes, Jacob's face looked pained. He dropped her hands. "Why aren't you wearing your ring?"

Edna stuffed her hands into her pockets. "No one here knows I'm engaged. I'm still the new teacher, and I don't want to give the school a reason to let me go."

Jacob took a step back. "I've never stood in the way of you having a career, but I'm beginning to think you don't really want to get married. Have you even told anyone about me?

Edna ignored the question, embarrassed by the truth. "I promise, we'll get married next summer. I just want to teach one more year after this. Even my father recognizes how important teaching is to me. Why can't you see that?"

Jacob's blue eyes dimmed. Edna held her breath fearful of an outburst in the hall as her coworkers began to leave their classrooms. Jacob took a deep breath and rubbed his day-old whiskers. "If you can keep our engagement secret, why don't we just go ahead and get married? You don't have to tell anyone at school. We can keep the marriage secret just the same."

"You can't be serious?"

"Why not? When do you sign your teaching contract for next fall?"

"Generally, it's late April or May so the school can anticipate its needs for the coming year."

"So, if you sign the contract in May and we get married the following month, your marital status at the time wouldn't be a lie."

"It's not that simple. They can terminate me at any time during the year." She didn't want to tell Jacob she had entertained the thought. But she'd always been taught to follow the rules, not break them. The idea of deceiving not only the school administration but her peers and school parents unsettled her. "I don't feel right lying to the school; besides it could jeopardize future positions within the district."

Jacob looked deflated. "I'm through putting my life on hold. I have been offered an opportunity to assist with a new hospital the army is building at Fort Snelling. Maybe I should consider it. You seem to think you can have everything you want. You can't be a teacher and be married too. You need to decide what you want more."

"You've only been back for two years. Besides, your demand is not fair." Edna's words came out louder than she intended and drew the attention of several other teachers. "Men can keep their jobs and get married. Why can't women?"

"I don't know. It's just how it is."

Jacob's words sparked a childhood snub. She remembered being told she couldn't play marbles because she was a girl. Marbles were for boys. It was just the way things were. Before Edna could find her voice, Jacob did an about-face and marched away down the hall. She wondered if she expected too much from him, too much from society. Pearl had it easy. She never tried to have a job outside the home while married. She was content to be a wife and a mother. Before she'd finished second grade, Edna had managed to beat the boys at marbles in elementary school, but now she wondered if her challenge to Jacob was too much. She was playing a game for keepsies, and she stood to lose.

♪ ♪ ♪

Threatened by Jacob's ultimatum, Edna gave in. She'd taught for three years and would resume her profession after they had a family and the children were of school age. Hopefully in time, Washington State, and other states, would grant married women the right to teach just as they had been among the first states to give women the right to vote. She eagerly called Helen and shared the news.

Three weeks later, Helen joined Edna as they strolled down the aisles of the bridal department at the Bon Marche. Helen's excitement fueled Edna. After two years of ups and downs in her relationship, and after two years of indecision, she was caressing elegant gowns, one of the final chores before her wedding, only two months away. Images and fantasies from childhood books drifted through her mind. She remembered strolling past the large windows of the store as a young girl when she dreamed of the day she would wear a gown like the princesses she read about in her childhood, like Cinderella or Princess Aurora, in "Sleeping Beauty."

"I can't believe you're finally buying a wedding dress."

"Me neither. Jacob didn't give me much choice, did he?"

Helen led the way down a row of white and ivory-colored dresses hanging on racks. "You always have a choice. You aren't doing this just for him are you?"

"No. I'd hoped to teach another year, but Jacob was right. Part of me has been procrastinating, unwilling to surrender my independence." Edna ran her hand over the silk and satin dresses with elegant embellishments of pearls and glass beads, others decorated with lace or tulle. Edna thought of all the dresses her mother made during her life. She considered the years of learning the skill and the patience required to sew such detailed dresses. As she stroked the dresses, she knew any commitment to marriage would also require insight and patience. She was not naive. Witnessing her father's long absences, Pearl's premature marriage, and Jacob's occasional irrational outbursts, she knew marriage would be rough and bumpy at times, not smooth and comforting like the touch of the fabric she now stroked.

Helen removed a hanger from one of the racks and draped the floor-length gown across her outstretched arms. "It's gorgeous. Can't you picture yourself in this dress?"

Edna examined the chiffon dress. She shrugged. "My mother would love it, but it's a bit too formal for my taste."

Helen hung the dress back on the rack. "Well, it's certainly not something I can wear in my current condition." She cupped her growing belly in her hands and chuckled. "Can you believe, within the month, I'm going to have a baby? I hope I can squeeze into my bridesmaid dress by your wedding day."

A few minutes later, Edna squealed. She withdrew a hanger and held the white gown against her body. What do you think?" She stroked a white wrap-around dress of silk and crepe.

Helen shook her head. "It doesn't look like a traditional wedding dress."

"That's the point." Edna ran her hand over the hundreds of tiny gold metallic beads hand-sewn onto the bodice and the V-neckline of the dress. "Egyptian style clothing is in vogue right now since they discovered and opened the tomb of King Tutankhamen last year." Edna carried the dress to the full-length mirror outside the dressing room and admired it for a long while. Intrigued by the culture of Egypt since her classes in art history a few years earlier, Edna immediately knew this was the perfect dress for her. Though her hair was much lighter than the jet-black hair associated with the famous queens of Egypt, and her skin was fairer, Edna pursed her lips and jutted her chin as she imagined Queen Nefertiti wearing the gown. Flipping over the small price tag, Edna grimaced. "Only real queens can afford to buy this."

Seeing Edna's face, Helen asked. "How much is it?"

"Fifteen dollars."

"Wow. Maybe you should just ask your mother to make you a dress. I'm sure she'd love to. Think of the money you'd save."

"I can't. We talked about it, but her arthritis has been flaring up. Besides, as skillful as she is, there's no way she'd be able to do all the beadwork this dress has." A broad grin stretched across her face. "I'm going to try it on." She turned to Helen. "Are you coming?"

Inside the small dressing room, Edna slipped into the dress with Helen's help. She turned to see her reflection from all angles. The wide gold trim around the waist and the buckle emblazoned with a profile of King Tut emphasized her slender figure. "It's perfect. Of course, I'll need a new pair of shoes. "Black suede baby dolls are popular, and they can be worn for general use. What do you think?"

Helen made a face. "I don't know. I think the black will be too stark against the white dress. Maybe brown would be better." She cocked her head for a moment and admired the dress. "It certainly is different from other wedding dresses. Are you going to wear a veil?"

"Mother's a milner. She showed me a fantastically stylish hat. I'll ask her to make the hat for me."

♪ ♪ ♪

The day before her wedding, Edna packed a small suitcase with everything she would need for her wedding day as well as the wedding night. Mother had the wedding gown at her house so she could design the appropriate head piece and press the dress for the big day.

As he had hinted a year earlier, Jacob had booked a room at the world-class Tacoma Hotel. Edna's heart fluttered as she imagined lying next to Jacob, her bare skin stroked by elegant sheets and surrendering herself to him. A prickling sensation ran up her arms and inner thighs, both exciting and frightening her.

A horn honking alerted her to Irene's arrival. Her fellow teacher had agreed to drive her to the Puget Sound Electric Railway station on Pacific Avenue for the trip to Seattle. Snatching her bag, Edna took one more look around at her modest abode, now near empty with boxes packed and stacked along the wall.

At the station, Irene hugged her. "It was fun working with you. I wish you and your husband all the best."

317

Within minutes, the passengers hustled and bustled as the dark-green train with the gray roof and gold lettering pulled into view and ground to a stop. A brakeman hopped off and set a stool down and began to help passengers off the train with a smile or a friendly nod. Minutes later, Edna climbed aboard Motorcar No. 514, a combination express, and passenger car. She took a seat in the lead car behind the swinging glass doors where the smokers sat and waited while the conductor collected fares, then dashed away to pick up the stools. At precisely nine fifteen, he hollered, "All Aboard." The bell clanged twice to signal the motorman to proceed. In forty minutes, she would be at the interurban station on Occidental, where her father would meet her. Outside, clouds shrouded the sky. She hoped it wasn't a premonition, and willed a slice of sun to poke through the ashen-colored gloom. She needed a sign to reassure her of a bright future.

The following morning, in her old bedroom, her mind wandered to the day she had lied to her parents and driven to Renton. The day she met Jacob and the day the dizzying merry-go-round of emotions began. Through the filtered sunlight, Edna could see her gown hanging on the door hook. She hoped the fairy-tale dress would guarantee a fairy-tale life, but she was too old to believe in fairy tales. She was barely dressed when her mother words brightened Edna's day.

"Pearl's here."

The tension in Edna's neck and shoulders loosened. She rushed to the door. Edna's niece and nephews dashed inside and into their grandmother's waiting arms. Stanley joined Papa in the living room while Mama hummed and served biscuits and milk to the youngsters.

"How are you doing?" Pearl prodded Edna to the bedroom.

"I'm nervous." Edna held out a shaky hand. "Do you have any last-minute words of advice? I've always looked up to you."

Pearl sat next to Edna on the bed. "That's funny. I always felt I let you down. I wasn't there for you as much as I should have been, and I've always admired you. Look at you. A college graduate and a teacher, and now you're to be married in a few hours. You always followed the rules, stayed focused and you achieved all your dreams.

Edna reached for her sister's hands. "You and Stanley are happy. Your children are healthy. I envy you. I hope Jacob and I can be half as happy as you."

Pearl squeezed Edna. "Marriage isn't always easy. Trust me. There will be days when you wonder if you made a mistake. That's normal, but yes, I'm content with how my life turned out." She removed a strand of pearls from her neck. "I wasn't sure if you had something old, to follow tradition, but I want you to wear these today. Mama gave them to me to wear for my wedding." Pearl leaned over and fastened the strand of creamy pearls around Edna's neck.

Edna touched the smooth iridescent beads. "They're beautiful. Are you sure?"

Placing her hand on Edna's back, Pearl teased. "You do know I'm only loaning them to you. You can consider them something borrowed as well as something old."

Only hours later, Mother carried the wedding dress out to their new blue Chevrolet. Edna hurried after her mother with a straw basket that held her stockings, shoes, hat, and makeup and climbed into the big back seat next to her dress. Victor and Henry, wearing matching navy suits, scampered after Marjorie into Pearl and Stanley's car.

The car clicked and rumbled as it headed to Fifth Avenue and Marion. Minutes later, the terra-cotta-topped dome of the First United Methodist Church came into view. As Papa parked the car along the street in front of the brick church, Edna glanced around for her beau. Spying her soon-to-be in-laws and Ivan entering the narthex, the tightness in her chest released. Jacob appeared in the doorway, wearing a double-breasted dark-gray suit with a black bow tie. His face brightened when he spied her looking at him. He started toward her.

Pearl appeared and stepped in front of Edna, blocking Jacob's way. "It's bad luck to see the bride before the ceremony." She spun Edna around and marched her toward the women's restroom to slip into her gown.

Helen rushed up the stairs behind them. "I'm sorry we're late. Bill's suit trousers were too tight. I had to let them out a bit. I guess I've been feeding him too much since our wedding." She took Edna's hands in hers. "I brought you the something blue you asked for."

Pearl cocked her head as Edna's best friend reached into her handbag. Edna lifted her leg and the women all giggled as Helen slid a royal-blue garter onto Edna's thigh high nylon.

Organ music resonated from the sanctuary, indicating guests were arriving. Edna buried her face in her hands and breathed deeply.

"Are you okay?" Pearl draped her arm around Edna's shoulders.

"I'm fine. A bit nervous is all."

Minutes later, with shaking hands, Pearl helped slip the gown over Edna's shoulders. Stepping back, she admired Edna. "You are the picture of elegance."

Edna walked to the large plate-glass mirror. Helen adjusted a few bobby pins that held her hair back in a neat chignon underneath the white felt cloche hat her mother had made, with a wide brim folded up and a long dangling white feather on the side.

Her mother kissed Edna on the cheek. "I know you and Jacob will be happy together."

Taking a deep breath, Edna strode into the narthex and took her place at the door. She watched Jacob and his best man, Ivan, enter from the side lobby and stand next to the minister in front of the altar. The love in his eyes put her fluttering heart at ease as the first notes from Mendelssohn's "Wedding March," reverberated throughout the Beaux-Arts-style sanctuary. The wedding guests stood and turned their gaze to the back of the church. Edna took in the sight of so many friends and family gathered to watch her and Jacob exchange vows. Her chest heaved from nerves. Stanley linked his arm through Edna's mother's and started down the center aisle, followed by Helen and Bill. Following the bridesmaid and groomsman, Pearl stunned the wedding guests, wearing a deep-plum colored dress. Behind their mother, Victor and Henry each held a pillow with matching gold bands. After a nudge, Margie followed the procession, wearing a lilac dress, dropping purple and white rose petals from a small white basket. The keyboard fell silent for a few beats, then with increased resonance the familiar tune of "Here Comes the Bride" rang out. Edna linked her arm through her father's and glided down the aisle.

Chapter Fifty-One

1926 – Dreams Fulfilled

Pearl knocked softly before she pushed open the door to the hospital room, carrying a large knit handbag.

Edna's eyes brightened. "You came."

"Of course, I came. How are you doing?"

Dark circles under her sister's eyes showed her exhaustion. Edna sat up and propped the pillow behind her. "You should have warned me how painful labor could be."

Pearl set down her bag "I didn't want to worry you." She peered into the bassinette next to Edna's bed. "A girl?"

Edna nodded. "Bernice Abigail, after Jacob's grandmother and our mother."

"She's beautiful. She has Jacob's dark hair. Has he seen her yet?"

"No. I called the base. I'm sure he'll come as soon as he can." She shook her head. "I wish I could have delivered at home with a midwife. I would feel a lot better than I do right now. I don't remember a thing."

"It's called twilight sleep. You were given medicine to not only stop the pain, but to keep you from remembering anything about the childbirth." She looked around the room with a tan curtain separating Edna's bed from another patients. "You are lucky to have a hospital so close by. When I delivered Margie, we had to drive well over an hour." Pearl reached into her knit bag and pulled out a pair of booties. "I brought you something. Do you remember these?"

Taking the small blue slippers from her sister, Edna ran her hand over them. Her eyes moistened. "I remember. I made these for Victor when he was born. They were my first knitting project. I can't believe you kept them all these years."

"I kept them just for this special day." Pearl pulled a chair next to her sister and reached into her bag again. "I brought you something else." She withdrew a leather-bound book and showed it to Edna.

Edna gazed at the book. "I haven't seen this Bible since I was a little girl. Mama said it's been in the family for two hundred years."

Pearl sighed with bittersweet memories as she handed the family heirloom to her sister. "I'm not planning on any more children. It's time to pass this on to you."

Edna ran her hand over the leather cover with its gold-gilded edges. She flipped several delicate parchment pages until she found what she was looking for. At the top in large font, it read, "FAMILY RECORD." Beneath the headings for births, deaths, and marriages, numerous entries inked in black and blue dated back to the year 1710.

"Today, you get to record your daughter's birth."

Edna scanned the entries from the past years. "This is amazing." She continued to flip through the pages. "Ten generations of our ancestors. Here's Mother and Father. 'Abigail Barth and George Mooney, married June 21, 1891.'" Edna's face brightened. She looked at Pearl with a wide grin. "'Pearl Anna Mooney born October 1, 1892.' And here is the entry Mama made for my birth. 'Edna Marie Mooney, born March 21, 1902.'"

Pearl leaned over and tapped a spot in the book. "Here's where I recorded my marriage to Stanley, and the births of Victor, Henry, and Marjorie."

As Edna thumbed through the sacred book, something slipped from deep in the pages and fell into Edna's lap.

Pearl rescued the fragile find. "Did Mama ever show you this?"

"No. I don't think so." Edna took the bouquet of pressed faded blossoms of pink, purple, yellow, and orange wrapped in a faded pink bow. "What is this? Why did Mama keep it?"

Pearl's eyes danced with the memory of the dried wildflowers, as fresh in her mind on this day as when she picked them. "Right after you were born, I went outside and plucked every kind of flower I could see for a gift for you." Pearl sighed. "I never knew Mother saved them until Victor was born and she gave me the Bible. I'd forgotten about them over the years."

Edna slipped the dried arrangement back between the pages. "I never knew."

"There's something else you never knew." Pearl scooted a chair next to her sister's bedside. "I'm ashamed to admit it, even after all these years. I liked being an only child, and I was mad at first when Mama said she was having another baby. I didn't want to share Mother and Father with anyone. Then I envied you when you went away to college. I see now how selfish I was."

Prickles of discomfort stung Pearl as she admitted her resentment from a lifetime ago.

A male voice from the doorway jolted Pearl, and she turned to see a doctor entering the room.

"How are you feeling, Mrs. Pearson?" The white-coated older gentleman stepped inside. "I hope I'm not interrupting; I didn't realize you had company."

Pearl pushed her chair back from the bedside. "I can step out if you like."

"You can stay. I'm just checking to make sure Mrs. Pearson is feeling okay."

Something familiar in his voice made Pearl examine the doctor's face.

Edna set the Bible and booties aside and sat up as the doctor took Edna's wrist and pressed his thumb and forefinger to it. "Dr. Kirby asked me to check in on you. He was called to an emergency caesarean. I'm Dr. Chapman."

Pearl clutched her hand to her chest. "Doctor Lucien Chapman?"

"Yes, that's right. Have we met?" He turned with curiosity in his eyes.

"Yes. We met twenty years ago, on the *Athlon*. I was moving to my aunt and uncle's house to attend high school."

Doctor Chapman rubbed his chin. "Sorry. Twenty years was a long time ago."

"I understand. You gave me some words of advice, which I've always remembered."

Dr. Chapman shrugged. "I have a way of prattling off axioms. What words of wisdom did I impart to you?"

"You told me the vastness of my opportunities was endless."

323

"Ah, yes. That's sounds like something I would say. So, I take it, then, you took my advice."

Pearl looked down at the floor. How could she tell him? "I wanted to. Unfortunately, my opportunities were limited when I became a mother at an early age."

Dr. Chapman sighed and nodded. "Life has a way of tossing in obstacles. We must face the challenges along with the smooth sailing. So, you're a wife and mother? Nothing wrong with that."

Suddenly swallowed by regret, Pearl looked at Dr. Chapman and shook her head. "I wanted to make a difference and save lives, like you do. But I never became a nurse. I'm just a housewife."

Edna interrupted. "That's not true. You're a mother to three, you've helped several women with birthing their babies, you help your husband with his business, and you teach first-aid classes for the Red Cross."

Doctor Chapman smiled. "Sounds to me like you've accomplished a lot. You don't need to become a nurse to make a difference or even save lives."

Long ago memories of Uncle Frederick bleeding and Margie struggling to breathe popped into Pearl's mind. She had made a difference. Possibly even saved their lives. "I suppose you're right. My cousin is a doctor, and my nine-year-old daughter says she wants to be a doctor someday. Do you think that is possible?"

"Of course. I've met a few female doctors in my day. I expect we'll see more in years to come."

Pearl remembered Dr. Kate Barrett. Margie becoming a doctor was within the realm of possibility.

"Things have changed in the past twenty years, and mark my words; you'll see more progress as your children get to be your age."

Pearl thought about the changes she'd witnessed in her life. Women now had the vote, and schools were introducing more sports to young girls. Women dressed in more colorful and less cumbersome garb. More women were working outside the home, and a woman had even won the Pulitzer Prize for the first time.

Dr. Chapman patted Edna on the shoulder. "Would you like to hold your daughter again?" His eyes sparkled as he placed Bernice in her mother's arms. "She's got your fair complexion." He turned and faced Pearl. "I'm so pleased to see you have succeeded in finding happiness."

Pearl shook his hand. "Thank you. I'm glad we got to meet again."

Dr. Chapman wished both sisters good luck, then turned and left the room. Pearl stood for a few seconds overcome by this twist of fate that brought Dr. Chapman into her life again. She reflected upon the kind doctor's departing words to her onboard the *Athlon* the day they met. She thought about her family and the events of the past two decades. Her mind spun like the moulded cylinders on her uncle's graphophone. She could almost hear the jaunty but scratchy tunes from her past. Dr. Chapman was right. She'd written her own unique story and despite the ups and downs, she felt complete. With each passing day the harmony and discord of her life would continue to compete for prominence in a song she was still composing. A swelling crescendo of love encircled Pearl as she gazed upon Edna with her daughter at her breast.

Bibliography

"1918 Pandemic Influenza Historic Timeline," Centers for Disease Control and Prevention., March 20, 2018. https://www.cdc.gov/flu/pandemic-resources/1918-commemoration/pandemic-timeline-1918.htm

Archambault, Alan H. *Images of America: Fort Lewis.* Charleston, SC: Arcadia Publishing.2002

Becker, Paula. "Firland Sanatorium," Historylink.org. September 2002, https://www.historylink.org/File/3928

Crowley, Walt. "Woodland Park Zoo," HistoryLink.org, July 8, 1999, www.historylink.org/File/1481

Denfeld, Duane Colt. "Fort Lewis, Part1:1917-1927," HistoryLink.org, January 16, 2008, http://historylink.org/File/8455)

"Florence Crittenton Homes: A History" VCU Libraries: Social Welfare History Project. http://socialwelfare.library.vcu.edu/programs/child-welfarechild-labor/florence-crittenton-homes-history/

Forsen, John. Podrabsky, Gayle. (2009). *Alaska Yukon Pacific Exposition:* Seattle's Forgotten World's Fair, 2002, DVD.

Hinchliff, Catherine. "Port Orchard-Thumbnail History," HistoryLink.org, October 10, 2010 http://www.historylink.org/File/9550
"History" First United Methodist Church of Seattle, http://firstchurchseattle.org/about/history/

"History of Seattle before 1900," Wikipedia,
https://en.wikipedia.org/wiki/History_of_Seattle_before_1900

Ho, Vanessa. Woodland-Park-Zoo: The-early-years, Seattle PI.
December 12, 2014, https://www.seattlepi.com/local/seattle-
history/slideshow/Woodland-Park-Zoo-The-early-years-
99479/item-85307

"Issaquah's Northern Pacific Depot." Issaquah History
Museums, December 09, 2015,
http://www.issaquahhistory.org/buildings-sites/issaquah-depot-
museum

Judd, Ron. "Setting the Record Straight on the Seattle General
Strike," *The Seattle Times: Pacific NW Magazine,* February 06,
2019, https://www.seattletimes.com/pacific-nw-
magazine/setting-the-record-straight-on-the-1919-seattle-
general-strike/

"Luna Park Seattle," PDX History.com,
http:/pdxhistory.com/html/luna park seattle.html.

Naff, Aaron J. *Images of America: Seattle's Luna Park,
Charleston SC:* Arcadia Publishing. 2011.

O'Reily, Shauna and Brennan. *Images of America: Alaska
Yukon Pacific Exposition,* Charleston, SC: Arcadia Publishing,
2009.

Stein, Alan J. "Issaquah's Thumbnail History"
HistoryLink.org. July 14, 2003,
https://www.historylink.org/File/4220
Thompson, Nile and Marr, Carolyn J. (2002) *Building for
Learning: Seattle Public School Histories, 1862-2000* Seattle:
Seattle Public Schools, January 2002, quoted on
http://www.historylink.org/File/10475

"World War 1 and the American Red Cross," American Red Cross. https://www.redcross.org/content/dam/redcross/National/history-wwi.pdf

About the Author

Naomi Wark resides on Camano Island in Washington, the location of both her novels. The inspiration for Songs of Spring and her debut novel, Wildflowers in Winter, comes from diaries and notes left behind upon the death of a grandmother with dementia.

The theme of Naomi's books focuses on family, caregiving, encouragement, and forgiveness. Naomi holds a certificate in Commercial Fiction from the University of Washington and is active in several writers' groups. Excerpts from *Songs of Spring* won second and third place finishes from EPIC Group Writers and Skagit Valley Writer's League. Besides writing, Naomi enjoys gardening, long walks along the neighborhood beaches, and volunteering with the Stanwood Camano Food Bank.

To learn more about her writing visit Naomi at naomiwarkauthor.com or follow her on facebook at naomiwarkauthor.

Please feel free to share your thoughts about *Songs of Spring* by leaving a review on your favorite book lover's platform.

Questions for Book Club Discussion

1. How did what was happening in the world affect Pearl and Edna along with their family?

2. What was the primary theme or message of the book? Did the author successfully fulfill your expectations?

3. What emotions did this book evoke?

4. In what ways were women held back during the early twentieth century? How did this impact what Pearl and Edna were able to achieve?

5. What did you think of the book's title? How does it relate to the book's content?

6. Did you learn anything new about the time period from reading this book?

7. Was the research credible? What did you find most surprising? Least believable?

8. Was the book too long? What would you cut?

9. Could you relate to any of the characters? Who?

10. Did the book seem realistic? How well do you think the author created the world in the book?

11. Did this book make you think about how some people still are facing constraints in their lives today?

Made in the USA
Columbia, SC
07 October 2023

23860876R00187